Ba~~~ out of the
Blue

ANNE
MATHER

ANNIE
WEST

MELANIE
MILBURNE

MILLS

Mills & Boon, an imprint of Harlequin (UK) Limited, Eton House, 18-24 Paradise Road, Richmond, Surrey TW9 1SR

BABY OUT OF THE BLUE
© Harlequin Enterprises II B.V./S.à.r.l 2013

The Greek Tycoon's Pregnant Wife © Anne Mather 2007
Forgotten Mistress, Secret Love-Child © Annie West 2009
The Secret Baby Bargain © Melanie Milburne 2006

ISBN: 978 0 263 90683 7

011-0813

Harlequin (UK) policy is to use papers that are natural, renewable and recyclable products and made from wood grown in sustainable forests. The logging and manufacturing processes conform to the legal environmental regulations of the country of origin.

Printed and bound in Spain
by Blackprint CPI, Barcelona

THE GREEK TYCOON'S PREGNANT WIFE

ANNE
MATHER

THE BABY COLLECTION

May 2013   **June 2013**

July 2013   **August 2013**

Anne Mather says: 'I've always wanted to write —which is not to say I've always wanted to be a professional writer. For years I wrote only for my own pleasure and it wasn't until my husband suggested I send one of my stories to a publisher that we put several publishers' names into a hat and pulled one out. The rest, as they say, is history. And now, more than one hundred and fifty books later, I'm literally—excuse the pun—staggered by what happened. I had written all through my childhood and into my teens, the stories changing from children's adventures to torrid Gypsy passions. My mother used to gather these up from time to time, when my bedroom became too untidy, and dispose of them! The trouble was, I never used to finish any of the stories and *Caroline*, my first published book, was the first book I'd actually completed. I was newly married then and my daughter was just a baby, and it was quite a job juggling my household chores and scribbling away in exercise books every chance I got. Not very professional, but that's the way it was.

I now have two grown-up children, a son and daughter, and two adorable grandchildren, Abigail and Ben. My e-mail address is mystic-am@msn. com, and I'd be happy to hear from any of my readers.'

CHAPTER ONE

JANE let herself into her apartment and headed straight for the fridge. It might be empty of anything to eat, but she knew she'd left a half-pack of colas on the shelf. Pulling out one of the chilled cans, she flipped the tab and drank. Then, savouring its coolness on her tongue, she kicked off her shoes and walked back into the living area.

It was good to be home, she thought, looking round the large space that served as both living and dining room. She was glad now she'd had the builder knock down the wall that had once separated the two rooms. Together with a small service kitchen, her bedroom and the adjoining bathroom, it had been her home for the past five years.

She'd dropped her suitcase in the small entry hall and as she went to retrieve it, she saw the message light blinking on her answering machine. Her mother, she thought resignedly. Mrs Lang would be anxious to hear that her daughter had arrived home safely. Even though she was familiar with the internet and would no doubt have checked flight arrivals at Heathrow, she still needed the confirmation of Jane's voice to assure her that all was well.

Sighing, Jane pressed the key to retrieve her messages and waited patiently for Mrs Lang's recorded voice to speak. Her friends knew she was away, and all business calls would be routed to the gallery. So she was unprepared when a disturbingly familiar male voice spoke her name.

'Jane? Jane, are you there? If you are, pick up, will you? *Ineh poli simandiko.*' It's important.

Jane sank down weakly onto the small ottoman she kept beside the phone. Despite her determination never to let Demetri Souvakis into her life again, she couldn't deny that his rich dark voice with its distinctive accent still had the power to turn her weak at the knees.

But then, it wasn't his voice that had made him a millionaire several times over before his twenty-fifth birthday. That had come from his heritage and his complete ruthlessness in business, she reminded herself, a ruthlessness that had somehow spilled over into his private life.

Jane expelled an unsteady breath now and was still trying to calm her racing pulse when a second message started. 'It's me, Jane,' he said. 'Your husband. *Theos*, I know you're there. Don't make me have to come looking for you. Can't we at least deal with one another like civilised adults?'

That helped. The arrogance in his voice, the way he just assumed she'd be available whenever he chose to contact her. And how could he call himself her husband when for the past five years he hadn't cared if she was dead or alive?

Her nails dug into her palms in her efforts to control the anger that swept through her, but that didn't stop the painful memories from tearing her hard-won objectivity to shreds. How dared he contact her now as if he had some right to do so? As far as she was concerned, she'd cut him out of her life.

Well, almost.

She sighed. She remembered when she'd first encountered his father at the gallery where she'd worked in London. Leo

Souvakis had been so charming, so polite. He'd explained that he was looking for a piece of sculpture to take back to Greece, a bronze, if possible, to match the other pieces he'd collected over the years.

Jane had only been working at the gallery for a short time, but already she'd begun to show an aptitude for recognising talent when she saw it. And the delicate sculpture of the goddess Diana by a virtually unknown artist seemed an appropriate choice to make.

Leo Souvakis had been delighted, both by the piece and by Jane, and they'd been discussing the relative merits of oriental pottery and porcelain when Demetri Souvakis had appeared…

Jane shook her head. She so much didn't want to think about this now. She'd just come back from a very successful trip to Australia and Thailand and what she really wanted to do was go to bed. She'd been travelling for the better part of fourteen hours, the unexpected layover in Dubai not part of her agenda.

She was just about to get up, determined not to be intimidated, when a third message began. 'Jane? Are you there, darling? I thought you told me you'd be home by eight o'clock. It's half-past now and I'm getting worried. Ring me as soon as you get in. I'll be waiting.'

Putting all thought of her other calls to the back of her mind, Jane reached for the receiver. Pressing the pre-set key, she waited only a couple of rings before her mother picked up. 'Hi, Mum,' she said, trying to inject a note of confidence into her voice. 'Sorry you've been worried. The plane made an unscheduled stop in Dubai.'

'Oh, I see.' Mrs Lang sounded relieved. 'I thought it might be something like that. So, are you OK? Did you have a good trip? You'll have to tell me all about it over lunch.'

Lunch? Jane only just managed to suppress a groan. There

was no way she was going to feel up to having lunch with her mother today. 'Not today,' she said apologetically, knowing Mrs Lang wouldn't take kindly to her refusal. 'I'm beat, Mum. I need at least eight hours of sleep before I do anything else.'

Her mother tutted. 'Eight hours. Really, Jane, I rarely get more than four hours a night! Didn't you sleep on the plane?'

'Not much.' Jane wished she were less honest. 'How about lunch tomorrow, Mum? That'll give me time to come round.'

There was silence for a moment, and then Mrs Lang said, 'You've been away for almost three weeks, Jane. I'd have thought you'd want to see your mother. Particularly as you know I'm stuck in this house most of the day.'

Whose fault is that? Jane was tempted to ask, but she didn't want to start an argument. 'Why don't you ask Lucy to have lunch with you?' she suggested instead. 'I'm sure she'd jump at the chance.'

'I'm sure she would, too.' But Mrs Lang was not enthusiastic. 'Besides, if your sister comes here for lunch, I'll have Paul and Jessica running all over the house.'

'They are your grandchildren, Mum.'

'Yes, and they're totally undisciplined.'

'Oh, Mum…'

'Anyway, if you can't be bothered to visit your mother, I'll have to make do with my own company.' Mrs Lang sniffed. 'What a shame! I wanted to tell you who came to see me last week.'

Demetri!

Jane expelled a calming breath. 'You had a visitor?' she asked, trying to sound only vaguely interested. 'Well, that was nice.'

'It wasn't *nice* at all,' her mother snapped angrily. Then, with a sound of impatience, 'Oh, I suppose he told you. Is he the reason I'm being put off until tomorrow?'

'No!' Jane caught her breath. 'But I assume you're talking

about Demetri. He left a couple of messages on my machine. When he couldn't get an answer, he must have guessed you'd know where I was.'

'Which, of course, I did.'

'Did you tell him?' Jane was wary.

'I said you were abroad,' declared Mrs Lang tersely. 'I hope you didn't expect me to lie for you, Jane.'

'No.' Jane sighed. 'Did he say what he wanted to speak to me about?'

'As I said earlier, if you want to hear all about it, you'll have to wait until you have time for me in your busy schedule. You know I don't like discussing family matters over the phone.' She paused. 'I'll expect you tomorrow, shall I?'

Jane gritted her teeth. She so didn't need this. She'd had a successful trip and she'd been looking forward to taking a couple of days break before having to return to the gallery. Now she felt compelled to go and see her mother, if only to find out what this was all about.

'How about supper?' she asked, knowing Mrs Lang was going to love this. Having her eldest daughter over a barrel was one of the joys of her life. It so rarely happened these days, although when Jane had been living with Demetri she'd constantly been aware that her mother was waiting for the marriage to fail. When it had, she'd been there to pick up the pieces, though Jane had known there'd been a measure of satisfaction in being proved right once again.

'Supper?' she echoed now. She considered. 'Tonight, you mean?'

It was a game, Jane knew, but she was too tired to play it. 'Whenever suits you,' she said wearily. 'Leave a message when you've made up your mind.'

'Now, is that any way to treat your mother?' But Mrs Lang

seemed to realise it was time to back off. 'Tonight will be fine, darling,' she said serenely. 'Shall we say seven o'clock? Or is that too early for you?'

'Seven's OK.' Jane's tone was flat. 'Thanks, Mum. I'll see you then.'

It was a relief to hang up the receiver and, when the phone rang again before she could move away, she snatched it up with a definite edge to her voice. But it was only a cold call, asking her if she was interested in buying a new kitchen, and she slammed it down with a definite feeling of exploitation.

Of course, she realised belatedly, it could have been Demetri, but she didn't think that was likely. Demetri was no doubt in London on business and he'd have no time to think about his estranged wife if he had meetings to attend. She would come fairly low on his agenda. As she'd always done, she thought bitterly. Judging by his tone of voice, she had no reason to think he'd changed.

Sighing, she abandoned any idea of unpacking until later and trailed into the bathroom to take a quick shower. She looked exhausted, she thought, tucking strands of honey-blonde hair back behind her ears. Gazing into the mirror, she wondered how much she'd changed in the last five years. There were tiny lines fanning out from the corners of her eyes, but her skin was still smooth in other places. Of course, she'd gained a couple of inches around her hips, which was annoying, but her breasts were firm even if they'd filled out, too.

Oh, well, who cares? she thought, too tired to even dry herself properly after her shower. Twisting her still damp hair into a loose knot on top of her head, she tumbled naked between the sheets. And not even her worries about why Demetri might want to see her could keep her eyes open.

The phone awakened her. At least, she thought it was the

phone, but when she groped for the extension beside the bed the ringing still went on. It was the doorbell, she realised. Someone wanted access to one of the apartments and was probably ringing every bell in the building until they got lucky.

Sighing, she flopped back against the pillows and looked at the clock on the bedside cabinet. It was almost noon. She'd slept for less than four hours, but that was something, she supposed. Amazingly, she didn't feel as tired as she'd done when she flew east. Coping with jet lag was always easier in this direction.

The bell rang again and, throwing back the covers, Jane slipped her arms into the sleeves of a green silk wrapper. Then, padding across the living room to the intercom, she lifted the handset. 'Yes?'

'Jane?' It was Demetri, and her stomach made a sickening dive. 'Jane, I know it's you. *Hristo*, will you open the door?'

Jane didn't move. She couldn't. She felt frozen. The faint sense of disorientation she'd felt when she'd first woken up seemed to be paralysing her ability to speak. It was too soon, she thought. She needed time to pull herself together. If she'd ever considered encountering her estranged husband again, she'd assumed it would be on her terms, not his.

'Jane!' She heard him swear in his own language. 'Jane, I know you're in there. Your mother was kind enough to tell me you'd be home today.' His voice was becoming more impatient. 'Come on, open the door. Do you want me to be arrested for soliciting or some such thing?'

Anyone less likely to allow himself to be arrested for soliciting Jane could hardly imagine. Demetri Souvakis was far too sure of himself for that. Besides which, that was just an excuse to get her to press the release button. Her fellow flatmates were evidently out at work—or shopping in the case of Mrs Dalladay—and she was his only means of access.

'I'm not even dressed yet, Demetri,' she blurted at last, aware that her voice had a breathy sound to it. It was all she could think of to say, but it wasn't enough.

'*Aghapita*, seeing you naked is nothing new to me,' he reminded her drily. 'Come. I've been trying to reach you for the better part of a week. We can't all spend half the day in bed.'

That got her juices flowing again. 'I've just flown over six thousand miles, Demetri,' she told him tartly. 'And if I remember correctly, you don't do jet lag very well yourself.'

'Ah, yes. *Signomi*. Sorry.' But he didn't sound it. 'I guess that was thoughtless. Put it down to frustration. I'm not very good at that either.'

'Tell me about it.' Jane tried to sound sardonic. 'How are you, Demetri? Still as impatient as ever, I see.'

'*Theos*, I have been patient, *ghineka*. Now, are you going to open up, or must I break down this—' there was a pause while he obviously endeavoured to control his anger '—this door?'

Jane's jaw took on a stubborn curve. She badly wanted to call his bluff. Only the embarrassment she would suffer if he made good on his threat deterred her, and without another word she jabbed a finger onto the button.

There was a low buzz as the door downstairs was released and then the sound of footsteps on the stairs. Heavy footsteps, climbing the stairs with a speed that had her retreating to the far side of the living room. She'd left the door ajar and, although she told herself she didn't care what he thought of her, it occurred to her belatedly that she hadn't even brushed her hair since she'd tumbled so unexpectedly out of bed.

She was finger-combing it behind her ears when Demetri appeared in the doorway. Tall and lean, with the thick dark hair of his ancestors, he too looked older, she reassured herself. But despite the threads of grey at his temples, his face, with its familiar trace of dark stubble, was tougher, harder than she remembered, but just as attractive.

His presence had lost none of its impact, reminding her of the day he strode into the gallery, looking for his father. When the old man had introduced them he'd been polite, but hardly flattering, treating her with a cool indifference she'd half resented then.

Now Demetri paused in the doorway, and then stepped into the apartment. So this was where she lived, he thought broodingly. He'd heard she was doing well at her job. He couldn't help admiring the huge expanse of living space that swept from the front to the back of the old Victorian building. The sun pouring in from the windows at each end filling the place with a watery light.

But for all his irritation at the way she'd kept him waiting outside, it was to Jane that his eyes were irresistibly drawn. She stood the width of the room away, her arms wrapped protectively about herself. She was wearing a silk robe that she was holding tightly around her. As if he'd threatened her, he reflected, disliking the notion. For pity's sake, what was she expecting him to do? Jump her bones?

'Jane,' he said, before that idea could take hold and destroy his detachment, and her lips, which she'd been pressing together, relaxed a little. She looked good, he thought unwillingly. Too good to a man who was planning to marry another woman as soon as he was free. But then, Jane had always had that effect on him. It was why he'd married her, for God's sake. Why he'd been so reluctant to find another woman to take her place.

Why his mother had been so opposed to him doing this himself!

'Demetri,' Jane responded stiffly, and when he leaned against the door to close it she stood a little taller, as if bracing herself for whatever was to come.

She wasn't wearing any make-up, of course, and he suspected the colour in her cheeks owed more to a mental rather than a physical source. Green eyes, which used to haunt his sleep, as clear as the mountain-fed lakes on Kalithi.

'How have you been?' he asked, straightening away from the door, and Jane's mouth went a little dry when he moved further into the room. He had an indolent grace of movement that made anything he wore look like a designer item, though she guessed the casual cargo pants and black leather jacket were the real thing.

He was still wearing his wedding ring, she noticed. The wedding ring she'd bought him when they'd exchanged their vows in the small chapel on Kalithi, the island his family owned and where he lived when he wasn't flying around the world attending to the demands of his shipping empire. His father had retired before they'd married, much against his mother's wishes. But then, she'd never wanted Demetri to marry an English girl, particularly one who had opinions of her own.

'I'm OK,' she said now, forcing a tight smile. 'Tired, of course. But then, I haven't had much sleep in the last twenty-four hours.'

'And I woke you up?' Demetri came to stand beside one of a pair of mulberry printed sofas that faced each other across a taupe rug. It was the only floor covering at this end of the room, the stripped maple floor requiring little adornment. A dark brow arched in reluctant apology. 'I'm sorry about that.'

'Are you?' Jane gave an indifferent shrug. 'So, do you want to tell me what you're doing here, Demetri? You didn't come here just to pass the time of day. You said it was important.'

Demetri averted his eyes, concentrating instead on his fingers massaging one of the sofa cushions. 'It is,' he said flatly.

Then he lifted his head again, giving her a look out of night-dark eyes, causing a shiver of apprehension to slide down her spine. 'I want a divorce, Jane. Is that straight enough for you?'

CHAPTER TWO

Now it was Jane's turn to look away from his cold stare. Despite her best efforts, she was trembling, and she hoped like hell that he couldn't see it.

It wasn't a total shock to her, of course. For years after their separation she'd lived with the very real expectation that sooner or later Demetri was going to want his freedom. She was sure his mother would persuade him, if no one else. And she'd wanted it, too, in those days. But somehow, with the passage of time, she'd actually begun to believe that it was never going to happen.

'You OK?'

Dammit, he had noticed. And he was coming across the room towards her. Jane had to get out of there, and fast, before he started feeling sorry for her. She didn't think she could bear that.

'Let me get dressed,' she said, speaking without breathing, knowing that if she sucked in a gulp of air the sobs that were rising in her throat would choke her.

'Janie…'

The name he used to call her when he was making love to her was almost her undoing. 'Just give me a minute,' she said and, opening the door into her bedroom, she closed it firmly behind her.

But once she was alone, she couldn't prevent the storm of

emotion that engulfed her. Hot tears streamed down her cheeks and, with her nose running too, she groped her way across the room to the bathroom. Grabbing a handful of tissues from the box she kept there, she endeavoured to staunch the salty flow, sinking down onto the toilet seat and burying her face in her hands.

'*Agapita—*'

She didn't know how long she'd been sitting there when he spoke. Dear God! Her head jerked up in disbelief. Demetri was standing in the bathroom doorway watching her and she knew she'd never felt so humiliated in her life.

'Get out!' she choked, struggling to get to her feet. 'How—how dare you come in here? You have no right to invade my privacy like this.'

Demetri merely sighed and propped his shoulder against the frame of the door. Then he regarded her with disturbing gentleness. 'I dare because I care about you,' he said, his accent thickening with emotion. '*Theos*, Janie, how was I to know you'd react like this? I'd have thought you'd be glad to get me out of your life.'

Jane sniffed. 'I am.'

'It looks like it.'

'Oh, don't flatter yourself, Demetri. I've just flown halfway around the world and I'm exhausted.' It was an effort but she managed a tight smile. 'It was a shock. I don't deny it. But I'm not crying because I'm—heartbroken. Far from it.'

Demetri didn't look convinced. 'So—what? You usually break down like this when you get back from a trip? Is that what you're saying?'

'Don't be even more of a jerk than you have to be,' Jane retorted, struggling to regain a little of her composure. 'OK. What do you want me to say, Demetri? That I'm—crushed? Desolated? That hearing the arrogant louse I married is going to inflict himself on some other poor female has devastated me?' She managed a harsh laugh. 'Don't hold your breath.'

Despite himself, Demetri was angered by her words. He'd come to find her with the best of intentions, he told himself, and now here she was, tearing his good will to shreds. That was so like Jane: shooting first and regretting it later. Only something told him that this time she wasn't about to back down.

He straightened. 'You're an ungrateful bitch, do you know that?' he snapped, his hands clenching into fists at his sides.

'So you've told me,' she retorted, scrubbing her cheeks with the tissues one last time before flushing them down the lavatory.

'Well, perhaps you ought to curb your tongue,' he muttered. 'My lawyer tells me that in the circumstances, I don't have to offer you anything by way of a settlement.'

Jane's lips parted. 'I don't want your money. I never did!' she exclaimed scornfully. 'Just get out of here. I want to get dressed.'

Demetri stared at her. For all her air of bravado, he was fairly sure she wasn't half as confident as she was trying to appear. Those incredible green eyes still shimmered with unshed tears, and her mouth—the mouth he'd kissed so many times— couldn't quite hide its tremor.

And, although her words had irritated him beyond all reason, he found himself saying, 'If that's what you want?'

'What else is there?'

Tilting her head up to his, Jane stared back at him and he felt an unwilling twinge of admiration for the way she was handling herself now. A twinge of admiration, yes—and something else, something he didn't even want to put a name to. Something that had him suddenly moving to close the space between them.

The bath was at her back and Jane had nowhere to go. So when he put out his hand and looped his fingers behind her neck, she could only stand there and let him look down at her with what she was sure was a mixture of amusement and derision in his eyes.

'How about this?' he suggested, his voice rougher than before, and, before she could anticipate what he was about to do, he'd bent towards her and covered her mouth with his.

Jane didn't know how she stopped her legs from buckling beneath her. It was so long since Demetri had touched her, so long since she'd felt those long fingers against her skin. Heat was coming off him in waves, enveloping her in its sensual embrace, and, although she'd determined not to close her eyes, seeing the closeness of his long lashes, the dusky shadow of his jawline, she so much wanted to do so and sink into his kiss.

But how could that be? A moment ago they'd been dumping on one another, and now—now she was letting him touch her, kiss her, push his thigh between her legs as if she wasn't throbbing there already.

It had to be because she'd been crying, she told herself, trying to rationalise something that refused to be rationalised. She was always twice as emotional when she'd been crying and Demetri knew that very well. Oh, yes, who better? He'd made her cry so many times before…

But right now that didn't seem half as important as it should, and when he said, 'Ah, *mora*,' right against her mouth, her lips parted on a breath of submission. And then his tongue was in her mouth, sweeping intimately over hers, taking possession with a hunger that was far too appealing.

Demetri trailed his lips across her cheek, savouring the lingering taste of her tears. Her skin was soft, smooth, endlessly fascinating, and he slid an arm around her waist and pulled her close against him.

Sanity seemed to have deserted him. The reasons why he'd

come here blurred by the depth of his sudden desire. His hand found the cord of her robe, loosened it, allowed the sides to fall apart. Then he was gazing at full round breasts, their peaks as hard in the flesh as they'd looked outlined beneath the silk.

With heavy-lidded eyes he watched himself cup one swollen globe in his hand, let his thumb rub over the sensitive nipple with an urgency that bordered on violence, and he swore. '*Skata*, Jane,' he groaned, suspecting even then that he was going to regret this. But, *Theos,* she was where he wanted her to be, nestled against him, causing him a hard-on that was in danger of giving him a heart attack if he didn't relieve the pressure soon.

Jane swayed, her own emotions rushing dangerously close to meltdown. She couldn't let him do this, she told herself. She had to get away from him. But when she moaned into his mouth, Demetri sensed she wanted him to go on.

Her robe was off her shoulders now, and, when he swept her up into his arms and carried her into the adjoining bedroom, she felt it slip away onto the floor. Then she was on her back on the bed that was still warm from when she'd left it. Demetri was tearing off his jacket and T-shirt, exposing the muscled strength of his hard brown flesh to her distracted gaze.

He came down beside her, straddling her body with powerful thighs, the revealing bulge of his erection tenting the suddenly tight crotch of his trousers. 'Demetri,' she breathed weakly, half in protest, and for an answer he bent and took one straining nipple into his mouth.

It was too much. Jane couldn't fight him any more. With Demetri suckling her breast, she was already throbbing with the need for him to touch her in other, wetter, places. She wanted to reach out and stroke him, to trace the line of soft hair that disappeared into his waistband. But when she reached for his zip, he stopped her.

'Soon, *agapi mou*,' he said, shifting back so he could unfasten his trousers and tug them off. 'Just not too soon, hmm?'

If he'd been wearing any underwear, it disappeared along with his trousers and Jane could see his manhood rearing proudly from its nest of dark hair. Then he parted her legs and lowered his head, laving her with his tongue until he had her twisting and turning beneath him.

'*Theos*, you taste so sweet,' he muttered thickly. 'Shall I make you come?'

'Not—not without you,' she said, her voice unsteady, yet not too wrapped up in her own needs not to know she wanted him inside her when she climaxed.

'*Iseh etimi*,' he groaned. Are you ready? And with one swift, hard lunge he thrust into her, his thick length stretching her and filling her so completely that she let out a breathless cry. Then, with his body hair brushing her thighs, he expelled a hoarse breath. 'You're so tight. Did I hurt you?'

'I'm OK,' she assured him huskily, her muscles quickening automatically about him. 'Just—just do it, Demetri. Don't—wait…'

As if he could, thought Demetri grimly. It was hard enough to control the urge he had to slam himself into her until it was done. Only the desire to savour the moment had him rocking back on his heels, looking down at the point where their bodies were joined so completely. However crazy this might be, he'd never wanted her more than he did right now.

'Demetri,' she protested weakly, and with a groan he pushed into her again. She closed about him, slick and tight, and the driving need for satisfaction blanked his mind.

'*Ineh ereos*,' he said thickly. You're beautiful. Then rocking back again, '*Theos*, I don't want this to end.'

'Me neither,' she confessed, but that didn't stop her from

lifting her legs to wind them about his hips. Then he felt the convulsion as she lost control and holding back became academic.

Her liquid heat drenched him, more than enough to send him over the edge. He moaned as the force of his release spilled from him. Shuddering with mindless pleasure, he emptied himself into her, and then slumped across her body in a total state of abandon.

Demetri opened his eyes to the sound of a shower running. For a moment he stared up at the ceiling above his head, seeing nothing familiar in its papered surface, sure he'd never seen a ceiling in that particular shade of peach before.

Then his eyes lowered to the windows, tall casement windows, shaded by ruched Roman blinds in a contrasting shade of lime green. The blinds were drawn against the daylight that was visible in a line above the sill.

Totally unfamiliar.

Yet suddenly totally recognisable.

Demetri sucked in a jagged breath, pushed himself into an upright position and looked about the room with unbelieving eyes. God, he was in Jane's apartment, Jane's bed! What in hell had he been thinking of? He'd come here to ask her for a divorce, not to have sex with her, for pity's sake.

He closed his eyes again, hoping against hope that it was all some crazy dream, that when he opened them again he'd be back in his own bedroom in Kalithi, with the sound of the Mediterranean a gentle murmur in his ears.

But it wasn't to be. When he lifted his lids for a second time, it was to find he was still occupying Jane's bed, a single sheet, which he suspected she'd thrown over him, covering him from hip to thigh.

Which was just as well, he reflected, conscious that an

awareness of his surroundings had done nothing to quell an arousal that was as vigorous as it was inappropriate. *Hristo*, he was supposed to be thinking of a way to get out of this with his dignity intact, not allowing his mind to wander into the bathroom and the delights of sharing Jane's shower.

Forcing himself to get out of bed, he groped for his boxers and pulled them on. Then, without giving himself time to think, he tugged his T-shirt over his head and stepped into his trousers, only cursing when he hurt himself fastening his zip.

The shower ceased abruptly, and, although he was tempted to wait and see what she'd be wearing when she came out of the bathroom, common sense had him snatching up his shoes and jacket and letting himself out of the bedroom before he made another mistake.

In the living room, he pushed his feet into his loafers and pulled on his jacket. Then he combed slightly unsteady fingers through his hair. *Theos,* he thought, looking about him, how had it happened? How had a simple conversation turned into a sensual assault on his senses?

Why had he been fool enough to go in there? Why hadn't he waited until she'd composed herself and then completed the interview with speed and objectivity? It was what she'd said she wanted, for heaven's sake. And when she'd first quit the room, he'd assumed she'd gone to get dressed and nothing else. It was only as the minutes had slipped by and there'd been no sound from the bedroom that he'd become suspicious.

Anxious, even, he conceded wryly. Jane had always been able to do that to him. In the three years they'd been together, he'd lost count of the number of occasions when she'd walked out on him. The fact was, he'd usually gone after her, desperate to assure himself that she was all right. Just like today.

He sighed. Even so, finding her in tears like that shouldn't have affected him as much as it had. It wasn't his fault they weren't still together, and if him asking for a divorce meant that much to her, why hadn't she tried to see him again before the situation had deteriorated as badly as it had?

None of it made any sense, not least the pleasure he'd gained from making love to her just now. He hated to admit it, but he hadn't enjoyed himself so much since the last time they'd been together.

Having sex with other women had never done it for him. And, although when Jane had left him he'd told himself it would be easy enough to replace her, he never had. He'd lost count of the number of women his mother had paraded in front of him, hoping to persuade him that remaining single wasn't an option for him. But his marriage to Jane had spoiled him for other woman, and he'd begun to believe that whatever happened he would never have that kind of sexual satisfaction again.

But now he had.

With her!

Although he'd sat down on the sofa to put on his shoes, now he got to his feet again. He couldn't sit still, not when his whole world was in turmoil. This was supposed to have been a short meeting, the courtesy of telling her himself instead of allowing her to learn the truth from his London solicitor. Instead, as his mother had feared, he'd allowed her to get under his skin, again.

He paced across to the windows, peering out at his limousine, parked at the front of the house. The chauffeur, who worked for Souvakis International, would be wondering what he was doing. But he knew better than to make any comments to his employer or anyone else.

The sound of a door opening behind him had him swinging round almost guiltily. Another sensation that was new to him. It occurred to him then that perhaps he ought to have left before she'd finished her shower. In spite of the fact that they hadn't finished their discussion, it could have waited until tomorrow or the next day. Now it was too late.

Jane came into the room rather tentatively. She'd taken the time to dry and straighten her hair and now it hung silky smooth to her shoulders. She'd put on a dark green T-shirt that clung to her breasts, and low-rise jeans exposed a delicate wedge of creamy pale skin.

She looked just as good to him now as she'd done before, thought Demetri grimly. If he hadn't known better, he'd have wondered if she'd worn the outfit deliberately to emphasise her eyes. She certainly looked tantalising, but her expression wasn't encouraging. Her eyes were guarded, cold, watching him with a wariness that bordered on contempt.

'You're still here,' she said, when he didn't speak. Then, making her way across the room, 'D'you want coffee?'

Coffee?

Demetri didn't know whether to be relieved or insulted. Only minutes before she'd been writhing beneath him, and now she was offering him coffee, as if they'd just been passing the time of day instead of having hot, sweaty sex.

'*Efkharisto, then thelo.*' Not for me, thank you. Demetri spoke tersely, following her across the room to where a small counter separated an equally small service kitchen from the rest of the room. He hesitated, and then added unwillingly, 'You are OK?'

Jane turned from filling a filter with coffee. 'Why wouldn't I be?' she countered, though this time he noticed she broke their gaze. 'Go and sit down. I won't be long.'

'I'd rather not.' Demetri took a deep breath. 'Are we going to talk about this?'

Jane concentrated on setting the jug on the hotplate. Then,

when it was placed to her satisfaction, she opened a cupboard above her head and took down a porcelain mug. Glancing fleetingly in his direction, the mug in her hand, she said, 'Are you sure you don't want anything to drink?'

'I'm sure.' Demetri could feel impatience digging away at his good nature. What the hell was she trying to do? Pretend it had never happened? 'Jane, look at me,' he said sharply. 'No, not like that. Really look at me. What are you thinking? Tell me!'

CHAPTER THREE

JANE found it impossible to do as he asked. OK, she knew that nothing had changed really. Just because they'd had sex—pretty phenomenal sex, as it happened—didn't make a scrap of difference to Demetri. Sex was what he did. Particularly when he wanted something from her. It had always been a damn good means of getting his own way in the past. And he must be thinking she was such a pushover. He'd only had to tumble her onto the bed and she'd been practically begging him to do it.

She'd been so stupid, she thought bitterly. If only he hadn't chosen to come here at a time when she was not only exhausted from her trip, but expecting her period as well. She was always overly emotional at this time of the month. And his deliberate kindness had been the last straw.

'I'm not thinking anything,' she lied now, as the water dripped through the filter. Then, turning the tables, 'What about you? What are you thinking, Demetri?'

Believe me, you don't want to know, Demetri reflected drily, aware that his thoughts ran along the lines of taking her back to bed. But he'd be crazy to admit that. It would expose a weakness and he was already feeling far too exposed as it was.

'I'm thinking—I should apologise,' he declared at last,

choosing the least provocative option. 'I—never intended this to happen.'

'Well, that makes two of us,' said Jane at once and Demetri felt a fist twisting in his gut. Did she have to sound so dismissive? Couldn't she at least have admitted that she'd been partially to blame?

But that wasn't going to happen, he realised, and, leaving the counter, he walked back to the position he'd previously occupied beside the window. His limousine still stood there and he wished he could just get into the car and drive away. He wanted to forget what had happened, forget that when he'd come here he'd been looking for closure. Closure! His lips twisted. Instead, he'd torn away a veneer and left what felt like an open wound.

'So?' He heard her voice and turned to find Jane had come to perch on the arm of one of the sofas. She was holding a mug filled with black coffee and she lifted enquiring eyes to his face. 'Do I take it there's someone else?'

It was such a ludicrous question in the circumstances. Demetri was tempted to say 'Damn you!' and walk out. He felt so foolish having to admit that that was the reason he'd come here. That he was intending to marry someone else when he was free.

But he didn't have a choice in the matter. It was what was expected of him as his father's eldest son. When Leonidas Souvakis retired, he'd handed the control of Souvakis International to him. And such power held responsibilities, not all of them to do with the company itself.

'My father's dying,' he said at last, deciding he didn't owe her any consideration. But even so, he was unprepared for the way the colour drained out of her face.

'Leo is dying?' she echoed faintly. 'My God, why didn't you tell me?' Her soft lips parted in mute denial. 'I can't believe it. He was so—so fit; so strong.'

'Cancer is no respecter of strength or otherwise,' responded Demetri flatly. 'He found a lump. He did nothing about it. He said he was too busy.' He shrugged. 'When he did go and see the doctor, it was too late to operate.'

'Oh, God!' Jane put down her cup and pressed both hands to her cheeks. Her eyes were once again filled with tears. 'Poor Leo. He's such a good man, a kind man. He was always kind to me. He made me welcome when your mother never did.'

Demetri said nothing. He knew that what she'd said was true. His mother had never wanted him to marry an English girl. Their values were so different, she'd insisted. And ultimately she'd been proved to be right.

Now Jane attempted to pull herself together. 'How long have you known?' she asked, wondering what this had to do with Demetri wanting a divorce. She paused, trying to find a connection. 'Does he want to see me?'

Demetri was taken aback. Although he had no doubt that Leo Souvakis would have liked to see his daughter-in-law again, his mother would never agree to it. For the past five years she'd persistently begged her son to go and see a priest and try to arrange an annulment of his marriage to Jane. She was sure Father Panaystakis would do everything in his power to get some special dispensation from the church.

But, ironically, Demetri had been in no hurry to sever his relationship. It had been convenient in all sorts of ways. Not least to discourage any gold-digging female from getting the wrong idea. Now remaining unattached was no longer an option and only a divorce would do.

His silence must have given Jane her answer, however, because now she said, 'Then I don't understand. What does your father's illness have to do with you asking for a divorce?'

Demetri's sigh was heavy. He pushed his balled fists into his trouser pockets and rocked back on his heels before he spoke. '*Mi pateras*—my father,' he corrected himself, 'wants a grandchild. Grand*children*. With Yanis a priest and Stefan not interested in women, the responsibility falls to me.'

'How archaic!' Jane was sardonic. Then she frowned. 'But what about—' she hesitated '—the boy?'

'Ianthe's son?' Demetri was matter-of-fact, and Jane's nails dug into her palms. 'Marc died. I thought you knew.'

Jane was incensed. 'And you thought this, why? We haven't exactly kept in touch, Demetri.'

He shrugged as if acknowledging her words. '*Poli kala*, Marc caught pneumonia when he was only a few days old.' His voice was tight. 'The doctors tried to save him, but he was too small, too premature. He didn't stand a chance.'

Jane caught her breath. 'Poor Ianthe,' she said, finding she meant it.

'*Neh*, poor Ianthe,' echoed Demetri, though there was a distinct edge of bitterness to his tone. 'She didn't deserve that.'

'No.' Jane shook her head, reaching for her coffee again. She took a gulp, grateful for the rush of caffeine. 'So now I suppose you two are planning on getting married at last.' She tried to sound casual. 'Your mother will be pleased.'

Demetri's thin—yet oh, so sensual—lips curled into a scowl. 'No,' he told her harshly. 'I was never interested in Ianthe, despite what you believed. I intend to marry Ariadne Pavlos. You may remember the Pavlos family. Ariadne and I have been friends since we were children. She has recently returned from an extended visit to the United States.'

'How nice!' Jane tried not to let her true feelings show. Ariadne's mother, Sofia Pavlos, was a friend of Demetri's mother, she remembered. Someone else who hadn't approved of their marriage. She moistened her lips. 'Does Ariadne know about Ianthe's baby, too?'

'She knows enough,' said Demetri shortly, realising he was getting into deep water. The past was the past and there was no point in raking it all up now. He shouldn't have come here. He should have taken his lawyer's advice and let him handle it. But he hadn't realised how dangerous it would be for him to get involved with Jane again.

'Look,' he said, when the silence had become unbearable, 'I've got to get going.' He sucked in a breath before adding, 'I'm sure you hate me now, but I really didn't intend to—to—'

'Seduce me?'

'No.' Demetri was angry. 'It was hardly a seduction. You met me halfway.'

Jane's colour deepened. 'All right. Perhaps that was unjustified. But it wouldn't be the first time you used—it—against me.'

Demetri swore then. 'What do you expect me to say, Jane? I came here to warn you about the divorce, that's all. I didn't expect to find you half-naked.'

Jane gasped. 'What?' she choked. 'I'm so irresistible I got under your guard?'

'Something like that,' muttered Demetri, aware that he wasn't doing himself any favours. He straightened and moved towards the door. 'I'll have my lawyer contact you with all the details. Despite—well, despite your attitude, I won't contest any settlement your lawyer asks for.'

Jane sprang up from the sofa, almost spilling her coffee in the process. 'I've told you, I don't want any of your money, Demetri!' she exclaimed angrily. 'I'm quite capable of supporting myself, thank you.'

'*Ala—*'

'Forget it!' Without giving him any further time to defend

himself, she strode towards the outer door and jerked it open. 'Get out of here, Demetri. Before I say something I'll regret.'

Demetri flew back to Kalithi that afternoon.

He had planned to stay a couple more days. He'd been invited to attend a meeting of the Association of Oil Producers the following morning, but he'd had his assistant call and offer his apologies instead. His father wouldn't be pleased. He'd been delighted that the Souvakis Corporation had garnered such respect in the oil-producing countries, and it had also proved he had been judicious in handing control of the organisation to his son.

Demetri wasn't so sure, however. He'd already realised that being head of an organisation like Souvakis International demanded a considerable amount of his time. It might even be said that the responsibilities he'd taken on eight years ago had played no small part in the breakdown of his marriage. If he and Jane had had more time to talk about what had happened, more time for him to persuade her he was innocent of the charge she'd levelled against him, she might not have walked out as she did. But she'd believed that he was to blame for Ianthe's pregnancy, and without proof he'd been unable to convince her otherwise.

It was already dark when the powerful little Cessna landed on the island. The airstrip was a private one, owned by the Souvakis family, and although the island attracted tourists, they came by ferry, landing at the small port of Kalithi in the south of the island.

Headlights scanning the runway were an indication that his father had got the message he'd sent earlier, though he guessed the old man would want to know exactly why he had avoided speaking to him personally.

His own personal assistant, Theo Vasilis, had travelled with him, and it was he who was first off the plane, organising the transport that would take them to the Souvakis estate. A sleek four-wheel-drive vehicle stood at the edge of the tarmac, waiting for the preliminaries of landing to be over. Then, when Demetri strode across the apron to get into it, he discovered it wasn't his father's chauffeur who was driving. Ariadne Pavlos was seated behind the wheel, her glossy lips parted in a smile that was both welcoming and slightly smug.

'*Eh*,' she said, when Demetri climbed into the vehicle beside her. 'A nice surprise, no?'

Demetri's jaw tightened momentarily, the knowledge that he would have preferred not to have to deal with Ariadne tonight giving him pause. But then, realising why he was feeling this way, he forced a smile and leant across the console to kiss her. 'A very nice surprise,' he said untruthfully. 'Have you been waiting long?'

'Only about six years,' she responded artfully, her tongue making contact with his before he could pull away. 'You have missed me, yes?'

Demetri turned to fasten his seat belt. 'What do you think?' he asked, avoiding a direct reply. Then, in an effort to change the subject, 'How is my father? Not too pleased that I cut the oil conference, I'll bet.'

'He is—OK.' Ariadne spoke indifferently, glancing round with some impatience when Theo Vasilis deposited their luggage rather heavily into the back of the car. '*Prosekheh*!' she exclaimed irritably. Be careful. Then her eyes widened even further when Theo swung open the rear door and climbed into the back. Her head swung round to Demetri. 'Must he come with us?'

'Why not?' Demetri's response was innocent enough, but he couldn't deny a sense of relief that Theo was coming along. He nodded towards the laptop the other man was carrying. 'My father will expect a report on the meetings we've had while we've been in London.'

'The meetings with your wife?' suggested Ariadne silkily, her dark eyes alight with malice. 'Oh, yes. I will be interested to hear about those myself.'

Demetri expelled a long breath. 'Not that meeting,' he said flatly. 'The meetings we had with business associates.'

'Ah, but those meetings are so boring, no?' said Ariadne archly. 'Tell me about your wife. Is she going to be difficult, do you think?'

Difficult! Demetri stifled the groan of frustration that rose inside him. But, 'Not difficult, no,' he told her, and then turned again to Theo in the back seat. 'Did you collect all the papers from the plane?'

His meaning couldn't have been plainer and, although Ariadne tossed her head as she reached for the ignition, she knew better than to pursue the matter now. There'd be time enough later, Demetri could almost hear her thinking. And dammit, why not? It was because of her—and his father's illness—that he'd gone to see Jane in the first place.

Leaving the airport behind, they drove along the narrow country lane that led to the Souvakis estate. There was little to see in the car's headlights but the coarse grass that grew alongside the road and the occasional stunted cypress. But Demetri knew that running parallel with the track were the sand dunes and beyond that the blue-green waters of the Aegean. It was spring in the islands and it would be good to wake up tomorrow morning and hear the murmur of the ocean instead of the hum of traffic outside his window.

But thinking of London wasn't the wisest thing to do in the circumstances. It reminded him too much of what had happened earlier in the day. And he couldn't help but compare Ariadne's dark, somewhat sultry, good looks with his wife's fair-skinned beauty. They were so different, he thought, not welcoming the comparison: Ariadne, full-figured and voluptuous, and Jane, tall, slender, hiding her sensuous nature behind a tantalising façade of cool composure.

He squashed that thought, saying tersely, 'Did you attend your cousin's wedding?'

'Julia? But, of course.' Ariadne shrugged as the tall wooden gates that marked the entrance to the estate came into view. She flashed the car's headlights, and a man appeared from the white-painted gatehouse to one side of the gates, hurriedly releasing the latch and throwing them wide. 'Naturally, I was the only woman there without an escort. Thia Thermia said I should not have allowed you to go away at such a time.'

'She would.' Demetri's mouth compressed. He wasn't unduly worried what Thermia Adonides thought of him. She was also Ianthe's mother and because of that she already disapproved of him. He'd been amazed that she hadn't attempted to thwart his and Ariadne's relationship, but evidently the advantages of his wealth far outweighed any misgivings she might retain.

Demetri raised a hand to Georgiou, the gatekeeper, as they drove past, and then the powerful vehicle was accelerating up the long, winding drive to the main house. The villa, which stood on a small plateau overlooking the ocean, was still occupied by his parents. Demetri had built his own house on the property, but since Jane's departure he tended to spend much of his time elsewhere.

His mother often complained that they saw little of him, and it was true that until his father's illness, Demetri had spent little time at home. He worked hard, and there was no denying that his work had saved his sanity. If he'd played hard, too, he'd told himself he deserved it. He'd been certain he'd never succumb to any other woman's appeal.

And he hadn't. It was only when he'd discovered his father's illness was terminal that he'd been persuaded to consider marrying again. Ariadne was the perfect candidate: she was single, she was Greek and his mother approved of her.

A paved forecourt fronted the cluster of buildings that comprised barns and garages as well as his parents' home. Ariadne brought the car to a halt and turned off the engine. But when Theo sprang out and Demetri made to open his door, her hand on his arm arrested him.

'Wait,' she said huskily. 'Talk to me, Demetri. Tell me you haven't changed your mind.'

Demetri stared at her, the lights that encircled the courtyard illuminating the anxious expression in her dark eyes. 'Changed my mind?' he echoed, suddenly feeling horribly guilty. He put out his hand and cupped her cheek. 'Sweetheart, whatever gave you that idea?'

CHAPTER FOUR

WELL, she was pregnant.

Trying to think pragmatically, Jane took a deep breath and pushed the cartridge she'd been examining back into her bag. It was the third positive reaction she'd had in the last two weeks, and, however much she tried to persuade herself that these tests could be faulty, even she didn't believe it could happen three times in a row.

Dammit!

Smudging back a tear, she sniffed ferociously. How could it have happened? She'd been so sure that when she and Demetri had made—had had sex, she amended, fiercely, her monthly cycle had been too far along for her to conceive. She'd always been so regular in the past. Though she had to admit that when they were living together, she hadn't left anything to chance.

In the beginning, they'd both agreed that having children could wait. For a year or two, at least. And because Jane wanted to go on working, Demetri had opened a small gallery for her in the town of Kalithi itself. It had meant that she'd been able to keep in contact with Olga, who'd been happy to exchange antiquities and paintings with her erstwhile student.

It had all worked very well, and because she owned the

gallery Jane had been able to accompany Demetri on his business trips whenever she chose. It had seemed an idyllic existence, and she'd never been happier.

But then Ianthe had revealed she was pregnant, and her whole house of cards had come tumbling down about her ears. Jane hadn't been able to forgive Demetri for betraying her, her only relief in the knowledge that they had no children to suffer the break-up of their parents' marriage.

She sighed. If she was honest, she'd have to admit that taking precautions hadn't figured too highly in her thoughts when Demetri had kissed her. The sensual brush of his tongue had banished all other thoughts from her head. She'd wanted him, she acknowledged, just as much as he'd wanted her. It had been far too easy to convince herself that he wasn't just using her for his own ends.

It wasn't until two weeks later, when she still hadn't had her period, that she'd even considered the alternative. And even then it had been hard to believe that that reckless consummation had had such a result. It was five weeks now since Demetri had come to her apartment. She'd already received notification that he'd contacted his solicitors about the divorce. Dear God, what was she going to do?

The appearance of her employer forced her to shelve the problem for the moment. Although Olga Ivanovitch was almost seventy, she strode into Jane's office at the gallery with all the vitality of a much younger woman. A Russian Jew, whose parents had been living in Germany just before the last war, she and her family had fled to England. It was her father who'd founded the gallery, but Olga who had made it a success, moving the premises from Croyden to their present enviable position in the West End.

In long skirts and with a cloak floating freely about her tall generous figure, she looked a little like an ageing flower-child, Jane thought. But Olga had been her mentor, taking her on when all Jane had to commend her was a degree in fine arts from a redbrick university and an enthusiasm Olga had recognised that matched her own.

Now Olga brushed back her mane of incongruously red hair and said impatiently, 'Did he come?' And, although she'd lived in England long enough to have mastered the language completely, her accent still remained for artistic effect.

'He came,' agreed Jane, knowing at once who Olga was talking about. A famous collector of antiquities had expressed an interest in the set of bronzes Jane had brought back from Bangkok. He'd promised to call at the gallery that morning to examine them again and make his decision.

'And?' Olga couldn't hide her excitement.

'He bought them,' Jane responded drily. 'He wants them packed and delivered by courier to his home in Suffolk.'

'Wonderful!' Olga was delighted. 'And a healthy commission for you, too, *leibchen*. You have done well. I must send you away again. You have the knack for finding treasure in the most unexpected places.'

Jane managed a small smile, but inside she felt chewed-up, unable to think of anything but the cartridge she'd hidden in her bag. Her hand stole disbelievingly over her flat stomach. Was it possible that Demetri's baby was already growing inside her? How soon would it be before it became noticeable? How soon before Olga suspected that something was wrong?

And, as if she'd already sensed her employee's abstraction, Olga rested a hip on Jane's desk. 'You are looking pale,' she said, dark brows drawing together above her long nose. 'Are you getting enough sleep? Or is that young man of yours keeping you up half the night, hmm?'

Jane shuffled the papers on her desk. 'I don't have a young man, Olga. I've told you so a dozen times. Alex Hunter and I are just friends.'

'Does he know that?'

Predictably, now that the news of the bronzes was out of the way, Olga was directing all her attention towards her assistant. How would she react when she found out Jane was having a baby? How would Alex react when she'd already assured him that her relationship with Demetri was over?

Playing for time, she said weakly, 'I beg your pardon—'

'Mr Hunter,' said Olga testily. 'I was asking if he was aware that you have nothing more than friendship in mind?'

'Oh…' Jane made a helpless gesture. 'Our relationship isn't that serious. I like Alex. He's good company. But we've only known one another for a comparatively short time.'

'Long enough.' Olga was persistent. 'I worry about you, Jane, I really do. When are you going to put the past behind you and get on with your life?'

'Oh, I—'

Jane was still trying to think of an answer when Olga spoke again. 'Isn't it time you thought about getting a divorce?'

Sometimes Olga's perception was truly startling, Jane thought incredulously. At any other time, she might have admired her ability to sense what she was thinking. But not today. This was one occasion when Jane would prefer to keep her thoughts to herself.

While she waited for Jane to answer, Olga rummaged in her pocket and drew out a pack of her favourite Gauloise cigarettes. Placing one between her lips, she flicked her lighter, inhaling deeply before blowing a stream of blue smoke into the air above their heads. Jane had never liked the smell of cigarettes and this morning she found it nauseating. Feeling the bile rising in her throat, she made an incoherent little sound and then rushed wildly out of the room.

In the small bathroom that adjoined the gallery, she was violently sick. Leaning against the tiled wall afterwards, a tissue pressed to her mouth, she thought it was a long time since she'd felt so ill. What had she eaten, for God's sake? She'd only had toast for breakfast, so it couldn't be that. Mind you, she hadn't really wanted any breakfast. She'd been feeling distinctly out-of-sorts since she'd got out of bed.

And then, feeling immensely stupid, she realised what was happening. It wasn't food-poisoning. It wasn't even the smell of Olga's cigarette, although heaven knew they were an acquired taste. No, this had to be the start of morning sickness, and if she needed any further confirmation of her condition, this was it.

A tentative tapping at the door roused her. 'Jane? Jane, are you all right?' Naturally, it was Olga. 'Is something wrong?'

Everything, thought Jane heavily, struggling to pull herself together. But she managed to say, 'No, I'm OK, Olga. I think I must have eaten something that disagreed with me and when I smelled your cigarette—'

'*Mein Gott!*' Olga sounded horrified. 'My cigarette has made you ill?'

'No. No, not really.' Jane felt ashamed. She couldn't let Olga take the blame for something that was her own fault. She opened the door to find the old woman waiting outside, wringing her hands anxiously. 'Sorry about that.'

Olga said something Jane couldn't understand and then wrapped her arm about the younger woman's shoulders. Thankfully, she'd ditched the cigarette but Jane could still smell the scent of tobacco on her clothes.

'*Leibchen,*' she murmured with evident concern. 'Are you sure you and Mr Hunter are just good friends?'

'What do you mean?' Jane tried to sound confused but it didn't quite come off.

Olga sighed, looking down at her with considering eyes. 'Because…well, because I am wondering if there might be another reason for you feeling—unwell, no?'

'Another reason?' Jane swallowed.

'Do I have to draw you a picture, *leibling*?' Olga turned to take her by the shoulders, making it impossible for Jane to avoid her calculating stare. 'Is it possible that you might—be fooling yourself?'

'Fooling myself?' Jane blew out a breath, wondering if it was worth pretending she didn't understand. Giving in, she said, 'Are you suggesting I might be pregnant? Is that what you think?'

Olga shook her head. 'I'm simply saying it's a possibility you should consider, no? You wouldn't be the first young woman to fall for the charms of a handsome young man like Mr Hunter.'

Jane pulled away from her. 'I've told you!' she exclaimed fiercely. 'Alex and I—Alex and I have never—'

'Never?' Olga was sceptical.

'Never,' retorted Jane crossly. 'Now, can we talk about something else?' She scrubbed at her mouth one last time and then started back towards her office. 'Have you given any thought as to where we might find the other pieces Sir George is looking for?'

Olga shrugged, following her more slowly, and Jane knew the old woman still wasn't convinced of her answer. However, until she'd decided what she was going to do, Jane didn't feel capable of discussing her situation with anyone. For heaven's sake, she still hadn't come to terms with the fact that she was pregnant herself.

But, throughout the rest of the day, Jane found her thoughts constantly drifting to the dilemma she was facing. What was she going to do? How soon would she have to decide whether she was going to keep the baby or not? For, although her salary was generous, there was no way she could afford the cost of child-care in London on her own.

The alternative was to tell Demetri about the baby. But how could she tell her husband she was expecting a baby when he was already preparing to get a divorce? And there were other people involved, not least the woman he hoped to marry. As well as his mother. Jane could well imagine Maria Souvakis's reaction when she discovered her son had fathered another child. With the despised English girl.

Jane packed up early and left for home, telling Olga she was feeling shivery. She hoped mentioning another ailment would divert her employer's mind from the suspicions she'd voiced earlier. But feeling the woman's eyes upon her as she ran down the steps from the gallery, Jane wasn't confident she'd succeeded.

It was raining and she took the bus home, afraid that if she took the underground the smell of cigarette smoke would make her sick again. And it was such a relief to walk into the quiet, airy spaciousness of her apartment, so good to sink down onto the sofa with a freshly-made cup of tea.

However, she hadn't been sitting there for very long before the phone rang. Her mother, Jane guessed, assuming that she'd phoned the gallery and Olga had directed her here. It was to be hoped her employer hadn't decided to confide her fears to Mrs Lang. It might account for the timeliness—or untimeliness— of her call.

She contemplated not answering for all of ten seconds. But the possibility that it might be someone else had her reaching for the receiver. 'Yes,' she said, aware that her tone was less than cordial, and then she nearly dropped the instrument when Demetri's rich, dark voice came on the line.

'I see your temper hasn't improved,' he remarked drily, the slight echo indicating he was calling long-distance. 'Who has upset you this time?'

Jane caught her breath. Then, gathering her scattered senses, she said, 'Nobody's upset me, Demetri. I haven't spoken to you in weeks.'

Demetri snorted. 'Always ready with the acid comment,' he said wryly. 'I suppose you were expecting me to call.'

Jane frowned. 'Why would I expect to hear from you?' she retorted, wondering if there was a letter in today's mail she'd overlooked. This had to be something to do with the divorce. There was no other reason for Demetri to contact her. That *he* knew of, at least.

'I spoke to your mother earlier,' Demetri explained with more patience than she'd have expected. 'I didn't have the gallery's number so I was forced to contact her. She gave me the number—not without some reluctance, I have to admit—but, as you know, the effort was wasted. You're an elusive woman, Jane.' He paused. 'I trust you're feeling better.'

Jane moistened her lips. Despite the fact that her mind was buzzing with the reasons why Demetri had rung, she wondered rather apprehensively what Olga might have said. Nothing indiscreet, she assured herself, although Olga wasn't known for her discretion.

'Um—I suppose Olga told you I'd gone home because I wasn't feeling well,' she ventured cautiously.

'Something like that,' Demetri agreed obliquely. 'I hope it's nothing serious.'

Serious enough, thought Jane tensely, but Demetri hadn't rung to discuss her health. 'Just a cold,' she said, realising she had to move the conversation along. 'What did you want, Demetri?' A thought occurred to her. 'Your father's not worse, is he?'

'No.' Demetri was upbeat. 'As a matter of fact, he seems a little better. The drugs his doctors have prescribed seem to be keeping the tumour in check.'

'Oh, I'm so glad.' Jane was fervent. 'Give him my best wishes when you see him, won't you? I've thought about him a lot.'

'Really?'

'Yes, really.' Jane was stung by the trace of disbelief in his voice. 'Just because a man takes what he wants without care of the consequences doesn't mean his father deserves my contempt.'

She heard his angry intake of breath. 'You're still talking about Ianthe, I presume,' he said harshly.

Jane swallowed. 'What else?'

'Oh, I don't know.' Demetri's tone was sardonic now. 'I thought it might have been your less-than-subtle way of reminding me of what happened when I came to your apartment.'

Jane's fingers tightened round the receiver. 'Do you need reminding?'

Demetri swore. 'It was good, Jane, but it wasn't that good. If you think that's what I want to talk to you about, you're wasting your time provoking me.'

Jane gasped. 'You—you—'

'Bastard? Son of a bitch?' supplied Demetri coldly. 'Yes, I know what you think of me, Jane. You don't have to spell it out.'

'Then why are you ringing me?' she demanded. 'If it's not to apologise, I don't think I want to hear anything you have to say.'

She would have rung off then, but his hoarse 'Wait!' caused her to hesitate in the act. 'My father—my father wants to see you,' he went on grimly. 'Don't ask me why, but he does.' He sucked in a breath. 'Will you come?'

Jane was stunned. 'To Greece?'

'To Kalithi, of course.'

Jane couldn't believe it. 'You're not serious!'

'Why not?' Demetri had himself in control again. 'He would deem it a great personal favour if you would accept his invitation.'

'But…' There were so many 'buts' Jane couldn't even begin to think of them all. 'Your mother would never agree to it—'

'She has no choice.'

'—and you don't want me there—'

'That's immaterial.'

'Besides, I can't just leave my job. Olga depends on me.'

'Take a leave of absence,' said Demetri tersely. 'If it's the money you're concerned about—'

'It's not.' Jane resented his immediate supposition that money could solve everything.

'Then I don't see the problem.' He paused. 'Unless you think your boyfriend won't approve of it. You didn't tell me you had a boyfriend, Jane. How long has this been going on?'

Jane caught her breath. She was tempted to say 'It's none of your business', but in this case it was wiser not to lie. 'Alex Hunter is a friend, that's all. Not a *boy*friend. I assume Olga told you about him.' That was like her. 'Well, she's very keen for me to find someone to care about me.'

'And does he?' enquired Demetri, startling her into confusion.

'Does he what?'

'Care about you,' Demetri declared smoothly. 'Your employer tells me he's an accountant, with a very good job in the City. I have to say, I can't see you with an accountant, *aghapita*. Grey men in grey suits—isn't that what they say, *okhi*?'

'Whom I choose to see is nothing to do with you.' Jane was forced to defend Alex, regardless. She took a breath. 'You really expect me to accept your father's invitation?' she continued incredulously. She shook her head. 'Why does he want to see me? Do you know?'

'Perhaps he wants to say goodbye.' Demetri's tone was

sombre. 'I hope you will put our differences aside for the few days you will be staying at the villa. It's not as if it was ever your home. The house I built for us is some distance from the main building, as you know. If you'd prefer it, I'll keep out of your way.'

CHAPTER FIVE

IT WAS late afternoon when the ferry docked at Kalithi. It had been a three-hour journey from Andros, where Jane's flight from England had landed, and by the time she stepped ashore she was feeling decidedly weary.

It was already a week since Demetri's call and five days since a doctor had confirmed her condition. She still hadn't told anyone she was pregnant, despite the fact that the morning sickness hadn't abated, and she knew Olga wasn't deceived when Jane insisted it was just a bug.

Mrs Lang, whom she'd had to tell where she was going, had assumed her daughter's anxious appearance was apprehension about seeing the Souvakis family again. In her opinion, Jane should have refused the invitation, despite its poignant cause. It was ridiculous, she said, as Jane and Demetri were in the process of getting divorced.

Olga had been of a like mind. Knowing nothing of Demetri's visit to Jane's apartment, she naturally believed that, if Jane was pregnant, Alex Hunter was to blame. The young accountant, who worked for the firm who audited Olga's books, thankfully knew nothing of her suspicions, and like Olga he'd been totally against this trip.

'It seems funny to me that just weeks after informing you

that he wants a divorce, he suggests you go out there to see his father!' he'd exclaimed when Jane phoned to explain why she wouldn't be able to see him for a few days. 'Do you trust him? Are you sure this isn't just a ploy to get you back?'

'Oh, please!' At the end of an exhausting day Jane had found it hard to keep her patience. She'd already had a similar discussion with Olga, who wasn't at all pleased that her assistant was taking a week's unplanned-for leave. 'Demetri wants a divorce. I've told you that. But—well, his father is very ill. He says he wants to see me.'

'He *says*.' Alex had pounced on the word. 'So you've only his say-so that Leonides Souvakis is ill?'

'Demetri wouldn't lie about something like that,' Jane had replied firmly, wondering why she felt so sure about it when Demetri had lied to her before. 'Besides which, he's already got a girlfriend. A Greek girl. He intends to marry her as soon as he's free.'

'I see.'

Alex had been somewhat mollified by her answer, but Jane had wondered if Olga might not be right in thinking he had more than a platonic friendship in mind. A friend wouldn't have interrogated her, wouldn't have behaved as if he had some right to question her movements. And when he'd asked how long she planned to stay in Greece, she'd been deliberately vague.

Now, stepping onto Greek soil again, she wondered if she had been wise in coming here. How was she going to feel, seeing Demetri again and knowing she was carrying his baby? For whatever he'd said, she was fairly sure she would see him. It would be totally out of character for him to neglect his parents just because he thought she'd prefer him to stay away.

Jane only had one bag, a bulky haversack that she could loop over her shoulder, but she was still one of the last to step ashore.

There was no sign of Demetri, but she couldn't help feeling wary. She knew it was twenty minutes' drive from the small port to the Souvakis estate and she didn't remember ever seeing a taxi. Or needing one, she reflected, remembering the sleek little sports car Demetri had given her to get about the island.

She was hovering beside the pile of produce that was being unloaded from the ferry when she saw a woman watching her. She didn't think she'd seen her before, yet there was something vaguely familiar about her. Of medium height, with strong, exotic features, she was typical of many Greek women Jane had seen in the past. But her clothes and the way she held herself set her apart and Jane felt her heartbeat quicken when she started towards her.

'Are you Jane?' she asked, her accent making the words difficult to understand. Or perhaps it was the almost scornful way she spoke Jane's name that made the difference. And the fact that, although they were strangers, she hadn't used her surname.

And, because Jane was feeling tired and not altogether friendly, she replied, 'That's right. Have you been sent to meet me?'

The woman surveyed her thoroughly before responding and Jane was instantly conscious that the short-sleeved T-shirt, cropped linen trousers and canvas boots she'd worn to travel in suffered by comparison to a silk vest, a flaring peasant-style skirt and high heels. 'I have *come* to meet you,' the woman corrected her. 'Kiria Souvakis thought it would be a good idea for us to get to know one another, *neh?* I am Ariadne Pavlos. Demetri and I are to be married when he is free of his marriage to you.'

Jane was taken aback, although she had to admit it was typical of Demetri's mother to pull a stunt like this. Sending Demetri's—what?—his new girlfriend…his future fiancée? His *lover* to meet her was a little brutal even for Maria. She wondered if Demetri knew of it. She supposed he had to. Little went on here without his being aware of it.

'How nice,' she said now, refusing to let Ariadne see that she'd disturbed her. She glanced about her. 'Do you have a car?'

'*Veveha.*' Of course. Ariadne had clearly not expected Jane to take it so calmly. 'It is over here. If you'll come?'

The car was painfully familiar. Ariadne was driving the dark red sports car Demetri had bought for her. Maria's doing again, Jane guessed, though Ariadne had to have gone along with it. She couldn't decide whether Demetri's mother was calculating or merely apprehensive.

Thankfully, the heat of the day was abating. It was late afternoon, and the island was bathed in a warm golden light. Summer came early to the Aegean, and, although much of the island was composed of rock and scrubland, here on the coastal plain flowers bloomed in ripe profusion.

Dumping her haversack into the back of the small car, Jane slid into the passenger seat beside Ariadne. '*Endaxi,*' the other woman declared tersely. OK. '*Pameh!*' Let's go.

If she thought Jane might not understand her, she was mistaken. Despite the fact that she'd only lived on Kalithi for a little over two years, Jane had managed to acquire a reasonable grasp of the language. She'd had to, to run her small gallery. And Demetri had liked her to speak to him in his own language, particularly when they were making love...

The memory was disturbing, particularly as she was sitting beside the girl who would soon be Demetri's wife. Unable to prevent herself, she ran a nervous hand over the slight swell of her stomach. Common sense told her she would have to tell Demetri about the baby. But the last thing she needed was for him to think she wanted him back.

'You are staying how long?'

Ariadne's question interrupted the uneasy direction of her thoughts, which was probably just as well, she told herself severely. She wasn't here because Demetri had invited her. It was his father who wanted to see her.

'I don't know,' she answered now, although she'd already booked her return flight for the end of the week. Her eyes drifted over the headland and the rugged cliffs that descended to the blue-green waters that lapped the shoreline. It was all so beautiful. She'd forgotten exactly how beautiful it was. 'How is Leo? Demetri said he was feeling a little better.'

Ariadne took her eyes off the winding road to glance at her. 'Kirieh Souvakis is —well,' she replied after a moment, 'a little—confused, *isos*. We have been very worried about him.'

'I'm sure.' Jane tried to feel sympathetic towards her. But she had the feeling Ariadne was more concerned about her being here than she was about Demetri's father. There was a certain lack of emotion in her words.

'*Veveha,* he is most anxious to see Demetri happy at last,' Ariadne continued, apparently unaware of speaking out of turn. Or, more likely, she didn't care what Jane thought of her. 'It is not good for a man to be without a wife and family.'

Jane's lips compressed. 'Demetri has a wife,' she couldn't resist saying, and Ariadne gave her another knowing look.

'Not for much longer, *sostos?*' she murmured silkily. 'Demetri tells me you are not going to make any trouble about the divorce.'

'Does he?' Jane was tempted to say he should have thought of that before he'd gone to bed with her, but it wasn't in her nature to be deliberately cruel. 'No, well, he's probably right.'

'Probably?' Ariadne latched on to the word.

Jane turned her head towards the ocean again. 'Where is Demetri? Back at the house?'

There was a petulant silence and then Ariadne said, with

evident reluctance, 'He's away. On business. He won't be back until the end of the week.'

Jane felt a pain twist inside her. But it wasn't a physical thing, merely an acknowledgement that, despite the fact that Demetri was doing as he'd said, she was devastated by the news. So, it looked as if she wasn't going to see him, after all. That should make her decision easier.

Or not.

'You were expecting to see him, were you not?'

Ariadne couldn't leave it alone, and Jane had to bite her tongue on the bitter response she could have given. 'You couldn't be more wrong,' she said, silencing the voice inside her that told quite a different story. 'Oh, we're almost there.'

It was all too painfully familiar. The wooden gates at the foot of the drive, the winding track, edged with trees that provided a perfect screen for the house. And then the villa itself, white-painted and expansive, black shutters open, orange tiles reflecting the late-afternoon sun.

Jane caught her breath. She couldn't help it, but she quickly disguised it beneath a sudden clearing of her throat. Just because she was assailed by memories was no reason to feel nostalgic. She'd left the island of her own accord, almost destroyed by her husband's deceit.

Ariadne brought the car to a halt and Jane thrust open her door and got out before the girl could say anything else. She hadn't asked to come here and she had no intention of mitigating Ariadne's fears. If she had doubts about Demetri, let her deal with them. Jane just wanted to do what was necessary and leave. Whatever 'necessary' was.

A manservant appeared as Jane was reaching for her haversack, and she was quite willing to hand over the task to him. All the same, now that she was here, she was uncomfortably aware of the absurdity of her position, and she hoped she would be shown to her room and given time to compose herself before meeting Demetri's parents again.

'*Apo etho ineh, kiria,*' the man said after he had hefted her bag onto his shoulder. '*Parakalo, akolootha meh.*'

Jane glanced round at Ariadne, who was now standing beside the car, and the girl arched an aristocratic brow. 'He's waiting to show you to your room,' she said, and Jane nodded rather irritably.

'I do understand a little Greek,' she said. Then, curbing her frustration, 'Thank you for meeting me, Ariadne. I expect I'll see you later.'

Ariadne's lips tightened. '*Sigoora, thespinis,*' she responded shortly. Certainly. 'Kiria Souvakis has invited me to stay for a few days. She thought it might be—easier—that way.'

Easier for whom? wondered Jane ruefully as she followed the man across the paved courtyard and up shallow steps to a dappled terrace. Scarlet fuchsias and blue and white lobelia spilled from stone planters set at intervals along the shaded terrace, the roofline concealed by a tumbling mass of flowering vines.

Doors stood wide to a marble-floored entrance hall which in turn opened into a magnificent reception area. The airy feel of the place was accentuated by huge ceiling fans that wafted cool air into all the adjoining apartments, the concept of closing doors not much in evidence here.

The man indicated that Jane should follow him across the shining tiles, past a shimmering fountain whose rim was adorned with frolicking sculptures of the gods that had once ruled these islands. A wide open-tread staircase wound to the upper floor and as she climbed Jane admired the many delicate bowls of lilies that occupied every vacant surface, their vivid colours more exotic than she'd ever seen at home.

Jane knew, from when she had used to live on the island, that the villa consisted of this two-storied central building with single-storied wings stretching out at either side. When she and Demetri had stayed here, they'd occupied a suite of rooms at the end of one of the ground-floor wings, but evidently she was to be accommodated elsewhere now.

Looking down on the scene below her, Jane was struck by the feeling of isolation she felt. Only the household staff were about, and, although she'd been hoping to escape to her room without seeing Demetri's mother, now she felt oddly insulted that none of the family was there to welcome her.

But that was probably Maria's intention, she reflected, refusing to let the other woman's attitude affect her own. Perhaps it was an attempt to show her how out-of-place she had always been here among people to whom luxury was a way of life.

Even so, the stunning beauty of high-ceilinged rooms opening one from another, of silk-clad walls and sumptuous leathers, of the staff going about on silent feet, was impressive. The Souvakis family was fabulously wealthy, after all. Which had made her relationship with Demetri so unlikely and ultimately so destructive.

A galleried landing gave access to her apartments. The room the manservant gestured for her to enter was both luxurious and comfortable. An elegant sitting room opened into a large bedroom, with glass doors giving access to a balcony from both apartments.

While the man carried her haversack inside, Jane moved across to the windows. One of the long windows was slightly ajar and she could hear the faint murmur of the sea. Below, the glassy waters of the swimming pool gleamed in the afternoon sun. But beyond the gardens, tumbling dunes gave way to a white sand shoreline, the blue-green waters of the Aegean sparkling with dazzling light.

'*Soo aresi afto, thespinis?*'

The man was asking if she liked the room and Jane turned to smile at him.

'Very much,' she said, in his own language. 'Thank you.'

'*Efkharistisi mou.*' My pleasure. He smiled warmly, and then wished her a pleasant stay before letting himself out of the room.

Jane followed him to the outer door and, when it was closed behind him, she rested back against it. She felt so tired suddenly, but she knew it was a psychological weariness as much as a physical one. She ran an exploring hand across her stomach again. Dear God, it was going to be harder than she'd imagined. She hadn't been looking forward to dealing with Demetri's mother, but she'd never dreamt she might have to contend with his future fiancée as well.

She knew she ought to unpack her few belongings, but it was too much trouble right now. Leaving the door, she kicked off her boots and, walking into the bedroom, dropped down on the bed. It was a huge bed, at least six feet across and half that again in length. But it was soft and springy and very comfortable and, flopping back against the silk coverlet, she closed her eyes.

CHAPTER SIX

THE sound of someone tapping at the door awakened her.

Jane opened her eyes and for a few moments she hadn't the first idea where she was. But then the sight of billowing sheers at the windows reminded her of her arrival. The windows had been slightly ajar, she remembered, and the sultry murmur of the sea was in her ears.

She sat up abruptly, and then grabbed the edge of the mattress as the room spun around her. Nausea gripped her, but happily it was short-lived. She'd just got up too quickly, that was all, she assured herself. She'd obviously been deeply asleep.

'*Thespinis*! *Boro na bo?*'

Whoever it was was calling her now, and Jane slid reluctantly off the bed and went to the door. She hoped it wasn't Maria. She didn't feel up to coping with her mother-in-law in crumpled trousers and a damp T-shirt. She must have been sweating while she slept and now she felt hot and sticky and totally unprepared for company.

To her relief, when she opened the door, she found one of the maids waiting outside. She was carrying a tray containing a jug of iced fruit juice and a glass, and Jane realised she was very thirsty indeed.

'Thank you,' she said, taking the tray, but, although she expected the girl to go, she evidently had something more to add.

'Kirieh Souvakis asks if you will join the family for an aperitif before supper, *thespinis?*' she requested in her own language. 'Would seven-thirty be all right?'

Jane, who had already placed the tray on the nearby table and was presently pouring herself a glass of the chilled juice, turned to blink rapidly. Then, after taking a gulp of the delicious liquid, she glanced at her watch. It was almost seven o'clock and she stared at the watch disbelievingly. She must have slept for over two hours. How rude they must think her. She hadn't even bothered to pay her respects to Demetri's father.

'Um—yes. That's fine,' she said, and then, realising the girl couldn't understand her, she amended it to, '*Neh. Ineh mia khara. Efkharisto.*'

'I will tell Kirieh Souvakis, *thespinis,*' she said, once more speaking in her own language, and Jane gave her a grateful smile before closing the door.

But once the door was closed, Jane didn't waste any more time savouring the fruit juice. Carrying the glass into the bathroom with her—which wasn't a recommended option, but she was still thirsty—she turned on the shower. Then, despite the urge to explore all the many bottles and jars that occupied the glass shelf above the basin, she stripped off her shirt, trousers and underwear and stepped beneath the cooling spray.

Half an hour later, she viewed her appearance in the long mirrors of the *armoire.* The emerald-green slip dress had thankfully taken little harm from being packed in the haversack and her high-heeled strappy sandals were a gift she'd brought herself back from her trip to Thailand.

Her legs were bare, as, too, was her complexion. Her skin was still lightly tinged with colour from her previous trip to the sun. Just mascara and eyeliner and a smear of amber lipstick was necessary, she decided. It wasn't as if anyone was going to care what she looked like. Except, perhaps, Demetri's father.

Her hair was still damp, but, combed and looped behind her ears, it didn't look out of place. The dampness gave it an unexpected streak of darker colour.

Well, she was ready, she thought, deciding against carrying a bag. Opening the outer door, she stepped out onto the landing, taking a determined gulp of air before walking towards the stairs.

It was nearly dark and the area below was lit with dozens of bulbs in ceiling sconces. Shining uplighters, standing in alcoves, shadowed delicate sculptures in gold. Even the fountain fell into a floodlit basin, bathing the hall in a magical light. Still, this was what you could do when money was no object, she mused, admiring it all with her connoisseur's eye, but not with any feeling of envy.

A maid was standing at the foot of the stairs, waiting to escort her to her hosts. She was young and her eyes moved surreptitiously over Jane's appearance, making her wonder, not for the first time, whether it was possible for anyone to suspect her secret. But no. The girl was just curious. And who could blame her?

They left the hall and followed an arching passage that led to the back of the villa. The passage was open on one side and Jane could again hear the gentle soughing of the sea. It made her wonder if Leo Souvakis was entertaining his guests outside. But before they reached the terrace the maid turned aside into an enormous glass pavilion.

The orangery, for that was what Jane remembered it was, was a veritable jungle of tropical plants and trees, with fairy lights threaded among the greenery. It was cooled during the day by a very efficient air-conditioning system, but at night only a couple of fans kept the velvety warmth at bay.

The maid announced her and then Leo Souvakis was coming towards her, leaning heavily on a cane, but with a real smile of welcome on his face. Jane registered the lines of strain on his ageing features, features which were still so remarkably like his son's. 'Jane,' he said warmly, grasping both her hands with his free one and leaning towards her to bestow a kiss on both cheeks. 'How good it is to see you. But—' He surveyed her thoroughly 'you seem positively glowing. I thought Ariadne said you looked tired when you arrived.'

'I did.' Jane returned his welcome, stifling any resentment at the thought that Ariadne had been talking about her. She allowed Demetri's father to draw her forward to meet the other people in the room. 'I'm sorry. I'm afraid I fell asleep or I'd have come to thank you for your invitation sooner. It's good to see you again, too, Leo. I won't ask how you are right now. I'm sure you must get tired of answering that question.'

'How right you are, my dear.' Leo patted her hand again and released her. 'And there's no need to apologise. Evidently that sleep has effected a cure. Now, I think you know everyone, don't you? Maria, of course.' He waited while Jane exchanged a chilly kiss with her mother-in-law and then went on, 'Ariadne, whom you met earlier. And Stefan. I'm sure you remember him. And Yanis—or should I say Father Josef?' His lips tightened unexpectedly. 'He has come especially to see you.'

Jane greeted them all in turn, grateful that, apart from Ariadne, she did indeed know everyone. Until five years ago, she had considered these people her family as well as Demetri's. Even his mother, despite the fact that she had never made her welcome.

For the next few minutes, she was busy telling them all about what she'd been doing recently. Apparently Demetri had told them about the success of the gallery, how with her help it had gone from strength to strength.

She tried not to feel warmed that he'd been impressed with the responsibilities Olga had given her, and wondered if he was trying to salve his conscience. But then, he hadn't known his father was going to invite her here when he'd returned to the island, had he?

Conversation became general and during the meal, which was taken in the adjoining dining room, Jane found herself speaking to each of them in turn. The gleaming table was wide, its orchid-entwined centrepiece lit only by flickering candles in silver sconces, and the subdued light made expressions harder to read.

Demetri's mother was still chilly and Ariadne was obviously resentful to have her here, taking centre stage in what she evidently already regarded as her domain. But Leo and his two younger sons made an effort to put her at her ease. Stefan had always been sympathetic and his malicious good humour was infectious.

The biggest change was in Yanis. When Jane left the island, he'd just been beginning his training to become a priest. Now, in black robes, and with a heavy moustache and beard, he seemed a stranger. Less approachable in some ways, though he was still as gentle as he had always been.

Jane ate little and drank less. She'd accepted a very weak *ouzo* before supper, but she refused all wine with the food. If they thought it was strange when once she'd enjoyed the wine produced on Souvakis land in the Pelopponese, it wasn't commented upon. Instead, her glass was kept filled with the iced water she'd requested.

Demetri's mother had just suggested that they might adjourn to the main salon for coffee when they all heard the throbbing beat of an aircraft overhead. Though it wasn't an aeroplane, Jane realised at once. The sound they could hear was a helicopter flying low as it came in to land.

Immediately, her mouth went dry and her palms dampened unpleasantly. She set down the glass she was holding, half afraid it was going to slip out of her hand. With all of the family—except Demetri—here, there seemed only one explanation. And as if she shared her suspicions, Ariadne's eyes widened with a mixture of surprise and anticipation.

'Demetri?' she asked, looking towards Leo Souvakis, her tongue lingering sensually at the corner of her mouth. 'But I understood he wasn't expected home until the end of the week.'

'He can't wait to see you, Ari,' declared Maria Souvakis warmly. 'Why don't you go to meet him? I'm sure Leo will excuse you.'

Before Ariadne could get out of her chair, however, Demetri's father intervened. 'It could be Vasilis, Maria. Theo Vasilis,' he added, for Jane's benefit. 'Demetri's assistant. I asked him to send me some figures earlier in the day. Perhaps he has decided to deliver them himself.'

'I think not.'

As Maria attempted to assure her husband that Demetri's assistant would never use one of the company's helicopters for his own use, Jane swallowed convulsively. Dear God, Demetri couldn't be here, could he? He'd promised…

But what had he promised? she asked herself. Only that he'd keep out of her way. He'd said nothing about staying away from the island. It was his home, after all, and Ariadne was here.

'Hardly his own use, my dear,' Leo was saying now, reaching for his cane and getting up from his seat at the head of the table. He tilted his head and Jane realised the noise had ceased. 'It seems he has landed. I will go and wait for him on the terrace.'

'I can go—' began Ariadne, but Demetri's father merely waved her offer away.

'You go into the salon with the others, my dear,' he said

charmingly. 'Enjoy your coffee. If it is Demetri, I would prefer
a few moments with him alone.' He paused. 'Company matters,
katalavenis? You understand?'

Looking from Ariadne to her mother-in-law, Jane couldn't
tell which of them was the most put out by his words. 'You're
supposed to take things easy!' exclaimed Maria sharply, but Leo
only raised a finger to his lips.

'And I will,' he promised, making for the door. 'After I have
spoken with my son.'

'And why can't Demetri speak to you in your study?'
demanded Maria, going after him. 'Just because *she* is here
does not mean that Demetri cannot enter his own home.'

'Jane. Her name is Jane,' said Leo tersely, his dark eyes, so
like his eldest son's, flashing his displeasure. 'See to the coffee,
vineka. I will not be long.'

He left the room without another word and for a moment
there was silence in the room. Then, seizing her chance, Jane
pushed back her chair and got to her feet. 'If you'll excuse me,
Maria, I'd like to go to my room now. It's been a long day and
I still have unpacking to attend to.'

Yeah, right. One haversack containing a couple of dresses,
some shorts and tank-tops and underwear would take all of five
minutes to unpack. But Demetri's mother wasn't to know that,
even if Ariadne knew what she'd brought with her from the ferry.

'*Kala*—well, if you are sure?'

Jane was sure Maria—and Ariadne for that matter—couldn't
believe their luck. 'I'm sure,' she said, managing a smile for
Demetri's brothers. 'It's been nice to see you again, Stefan;
Yanis.' *Nice!* She cringed at the word. 'If I don't see you again,
thank you for making me feel so welcome.'

Leo had just reached the outer door when she entered the
hall. Taking off her sandals so as not to attract his attention, she

hurried across to the stairs and climbed swiftly to the upper floor. She was breathing rather unevenly, as much from nerves as exertion, when she reached the landing, and she paused for a moment to look down into the hall.

But when she heard the unmistakable sound of men's voices, she panicked. Hurrying across the landing, she hastily let herself into her room. The last thing she wanted was for Demetri to think she was eager to see him again. If she did decide to tell him about the baby, he mustn't think she expected him to change his mind about the divorce. Nothing had changed. He was still a lying bastard. After the way he'd behaved in London, she owed him nothing.

Moving across to the windows, drawn by a faint illumination, she saw the underwater lights gleaming in the pool below. She and Demetri used to swim there after dark when the rest of the household was sleeping, she remembered unwillingly. How horrified Maria would have been if she'd seen her precious son and his wife playing there in the nude.

Making love…

The images wouldn't go away, and leaving the window, she walked into the bedroom. She found someone had closed the window and switched on lamps at either side of the huge bed. The bed had been turned down, too, Egyptian sheets very white in the lamplight. And someone had also unpacked her haversack, hanging her other dress in the *armoire* and folding everything else into the drawers of the chest nearby.

Of course, Maria would have known this, Jane reflected, but her mother-in-law had made no attempt to dissuade her from leaving. And why should she? Maria hadn't wanted her here. Ariadne was the favourite in residence. Jane was just an annoying encumbrance that her husband had insisted on bringing back into their lives.

Jane tipped the straps of her dress off her shoulders and allowed it to fall about her ankles. She wasn't wearing a bra and her breasts seemed heavier than before. Stepping over the dress, she walked into the bathroom and stared at her reflection. Yes, there were definitely changes. She could see them. When she weighed her breasts in her hands, they felt different somehow.

Turning sideways, she laid both hands over her stomach. The lacy thong, which was all she was wearing now, exposed the slight swell she'd noticed before. Or perhaps she was only imagining it. She was barely six weeks, after all. How soon was a pregnancy visible? She should have asked her sister.

Or perhaps not. Lucy wouldn't have been able to resist telling their mother. And Mrs Lang would have been offended, and all hell would have broken loose. She sighed. No, it was probably best if she kept the news to herself, at least for the moment. Until she'd decided definitely what she was going to do.

'Admiring yourself, Jane?'

The voice was painfully familiar. What wasn't so familiar was the thickening emotion in his words. If she hadn't known better, she'd have said that Demetri had been aroused by watching her touch her body. How long had he been standing in the bathroom doorway? Had he seen her examining her breasts, perhaps? He must have done, she decided, her pulse quickening. That was why he was looking at her with such raw passion in his eyes.

CHAPTER SEVEN

SHE MADE herself turn her head and look away from him and for a long moment the silence stretched between them. She knew she ought to grab a towel to cover herself, but something—some perverse desire to taunt him, maybe—kept her from doing so. She wondered what he expected her to say to him. He must know his coming here like this, uninvited and unannounced, was breaking every rule in the book. They were getting a divorce, for heaven's sake. His fiancée-to-be was waiting for him downstairs. There was no way he could justify his actions. And she was a fool for not ordering him out of her suite immediately.

But all she said was, '*Déjà vu,* Demetri?' And knew he'd know exactly what she meant.

Glancing over her shoulder, she saw his hard face darken with frustration. 'Hardly,' he retorted, after a taut moment. 'Put some clothes on. I want to talk to you. I'll wait in the room next door.'

'The bedroom?'

'No, the sitting room,' he amended tersely. '*Viasoo!*' Hurry up!

Jane looked back at her reflection. 'Perhaps I don't want to put my clothes on,' she said softly. 'I came upstairs to go to bed. I'm tired. I think you should go now. I'll talk to you in the morning.'

'I won't be here in the morning,' replied Demetri through

clenched teeth. 'I have to attend a conference in Athens. It's due to last two days. I hope to be back by the end of the week.'

'And this concerns me—how?' Jane didn't know how she did it, but she put a note of sarcasm into her voice.

'Just get dressed,' he said shortly, unhooking a velvet-soft bathrobe from behind the bathroom door. He tossed it towards her. 'This will do.'

Jane made no attempt to catch the robe and it fell, unheeded, to the floor. Demetri swore in his own language and then he came towards her, his reflection joining hers in the mirror, picking up the robe and thrusting it onto her shoulders. 'Wear it.' he said roughly. 'Or I won't be responsible for my actions.'

'Ooh, I'm scared!'

Jane was beginning to enjoy this, although she realised she was playing with fire. Demetri was not a man to take her provocations lightly, and his expression made her breath catch in her throat.

'Jane,' he said, the hint of a threat in his voice, but, when he would have wrapped the folds of the robe about her, she deliberately moved away. The robe fell away once more, and Demetri's hands brushed against her breasts.

The feeling was excruciating, a mixture of throbbing sensitivity and burning desire. She wanted him to touch them, to rub the palms of his hands over their tender flesh, to bend his head and take one aching nipple into his mouth.

His eyes met hers in the mirror and she sensed he knew exactly what she was thinking. Which was a complete turn-off. She didn't want him to think she'd come here in the hope of rekindling their relationship, and, turning away, she bent and snatched up the robe, sliding her arms swiftly into the sleeves and drawing it tight across her trembling form.

'OK,' she said tersely. 'Let's go into the sitting room. I can't imagine what we have to say to one another but I'm sure you're going to tell me.'

Demetri stepped aside to allow her to precede him out of the bathroom and she was forced to brush past his still, forbidding frame. He was wearing a dark grey suit which he must have worn to whatever meeting he'd been attending that day, raw silk trousers and jacket, pearl-grey shirt, his tie pulled away from his collar. He looked disturbingly different from when he'd come to her apartment in London, but Jane knew he could look equally intimidating in turtleneck and jeans.

The living area seemed dark and Jane hastily switched on more lamps, anything to banish the sense of vulnerability she was feeling. Why had Demetri come to her rooms? Couldn't whatever he had to say wait until tomorrow morning? And then she remembered. He'd said he was leaving for Athens in the morning, so at least she would be spared the possible humiliation of him walking into the bathroom to find her throwing up.

Nevertheless, he still disturbed her. Tall, dark and dangerous, she thought, a subtle play on the familiar words. The room was suddenly smaller, closer, more intimate. And she had to get the idea that he'd somehow found out about the baby out of her head.

She wanted to sit down, but Demetri was making no attempt to do so and she was damned if she'd give him the satisfaction of inviting him to make himself at home. So, she held up her head and regarded him as coolly as she was able, while her stomach quivered and threatened to embarrass her all over again.

Demetri paused just beyond the archway that led from the bedroom. He was tired and he knew this wasn't the most sensible time to have a conversation with his soon-to-be-ex-wife. The very fact that she'd scuttled away as soon as she'd heard the helicopter proved that she'd had no wish to see him. Why hadn't he heeded his mother's words and waited until the following day before phoning her from Athens to assure himself that she'd received the divorce papers? Because the truth was he'd wanted to find out what Olga Ivanovitch had meant by calling him.

'I had a phone call,' he said now, and he could tell by the sudden tightening of her features that she was apprehensive of what was coming next.

'A call?' she echoed, her voice faintly squeaky. And then, gathering herself, 'How does this concern me?'

'The call was from Olga Ivanovitch,' said Demetri flatly, and saw the look of consternation come into her eyes. What was she afraid of?

'Olga?' She spoke lightly. 'But how—?'

'*Neh,* you are wondering how she was able to reach me?' And when she didn't say anything, he went on, 'I phoned her, you may remember? I was looking for you, to tell you my father had requested to see you, and evidently her phone recorded my number. Whatever, she made a point of taking note of it for possible future use.'

Jane swallowed. 'But why would Olga want to get in touch with you?'

Demetri shrugged. 'She did once sell my father a bronze statuette, did she not?'

The statuette that she had found, Jane remembered. Her introduction to Leonides Souvakis and ultimately his son...

Her hand moved almost protectively to the neckline of the robe. 'And was that what she wanted? To tell your father of some new item of interest she'd found?' It was unlikely, but the alternative was even less acceptable.

Demetri's mouth compressed. 'You think that is likely, bearing in mind she assumedly knows about his illness?'

Jane shivered, in spite of the heat of the room. 'I don't know what to think, do I?' she exclaimed, deciding that after all she had nothing to lose by speaking out. 'Why don't you tell me what she said instead of playing your little games of cat-and-mouse?'

'It is no game, *glika mou*.' Demetri unfastened another button at the neck of his shirt, allowing a tantalising glimpse of brown flesh lightly covered with dark hair. His eyes narrowed, thick lashes veiling his expression. 'Your employer is concerned about your health, Jane, not my father's. She told me you are *zerbrechlich*—which I believe means fragile—at the moment, *neh*? She said I should not do anything to upset you. Now, what do you think she meant by that? What have you been telling her?'

'Well, not the truth, obviously,' retorted Jane quickly, inwardly cursing Olga for making a difficult situation worse. 'You—you knew I wasn't well when you phoned me. Olga worries about me, that's all.'

'*Simfono*. With that, I agree.' He paused, and she knew he was registering the colour that had entered her pale cheeks as she spoke. 'But you told me it was just a cold. Colds do not usually elicit such concern.'

'No, well, Olga is a very—sympathetic person.' Jane made a helpless gesture. 'And—perhaps she doesn't trust you not to—not to—'

'Not to what, Jane?' The steps he took forward narrowed the space between them and she had to steel herself not to move away.

'To—to make a fool of me,' she said hurriedly, not prepared to admit that he could still hurt her. She shifted her weight from one foot to the other. And then, trying to make her tone light, 'Won't Ariadne be wondering where you are?'

'Ariadne trusts me,' he declared harshly, stung by the way she could put him on the defensive. 'What? You think I didn't tell her where I was going? That I had—how do you say—

sneaked up here to see the woman I can't wait to be free of without letting Ariadne know of my intentions?'

Jane pursed her lips. 'No.' She was defensive now.

'Good. Because you couldn't be more wrong.' Demetri didn't know where this anger had come from, but he was suddenly furious. Jane was here, in his parents' house, looking more beautiful than he'd ever seen her, and he resented it. He didn't want her here, he told himself. He didn't want to be reminded of what they'd once had. 'Ariadne and I understand one another.'

'Well, goody for you.' Now Jane felt a stirring of indignation, which was infinitely better than the embarrassment she'd felt before. 'So, if that's all you came to tell me, what are you waiting for? I'd really like to get to bed.'

Demetri's nostrils flared. And, just when he was sure he had himself under control, he asked the unforgivable, 'Why did you come here, Jane?'

Her eyes widened then. She was shocked. He could see it. And why not? It was a stupid question.

'Why did I come here?' she echoed, shaking her head. 'You know why I came, Demetri. Your father asked me to!'

'You could have refused.'

'Refused a dying man!' Jane was astounded. 'What do you think I am?'

'I don't know, do I?' Demetri's teeth ground together. 'What are you, Jane? Saint or sinner? I can't quite make up my mind.'

Her lips parted, and then, a note of contempt entering her voice, 'Well, at least I don't have that dilemma, Demetri. You're totally selfish through and through.'

'And you're not?' Demetri's lips curled, not sure why he felt this pressing need to pursue this, but unable to let it go. 'I suppose this means you've justified your reasons for walking out on me? Or do you have to keep reminding yourself why you made such a colossal mistake?'

'It wasn't a mistake!'

'*Okhi?* Why do I find that hard to believe? Isn't there something hypocritical about holding the moral high ground, when a few weeks ago you were flat on your back, letting me screw your brains out?'

The words sounded so much worse, laced as they were with his accent, and Jane gasped. Before she could prevent herself, her hand connected with his cheek.

Demetri made no attempt to deflect the blow and she watched, with a feeling of disbelief, as the clear marks of her fingers appeared on the left side of his face.

She regretted it instantly. She didn't do things like this. But it was too late to have second thoughts. Her hand had barely moved in a gesture of subjugation when Demetri's uncertain control snapped. With a savage exclamation in his own language she didn't understand, he locked hard fingers about her wrist and dragged her relentlessly towards him. 'If that's the way you want to play it, who am I to complain?'

'Demetri,' she cried, but it was no use.

'*Skaseh,*' he said harshly. Shut up!

'But you can't—'

'*Ipa skaseh,*' he repeated, grasping a handful of her hair and tipping her head backward. And then his hot mouth fastened itself to hers and she knew she was lost.

Anger, and the frustration he was feeling, made it impossible for him to be gentle with her. As he backed her up against the wall behind her, his tongue forced its way between her teeth. He pushed into her mouth, tasting her blood when his savage possession ground her lips against her teeth, but he had no mercy. He wanted to tear the bathrobe from her and bury himself inside her, and her fragile vulnerability was no deterrent, he found.

The moan she gave should have shamed him, but it didn't. The sounds she was making only served to drive him completely over the edge. Tearing the sides of the robe apart, he feasted his eyes on dusky-tipped nipples, already swollen and painfully erect, and on the slight swell of her stomach and the tight curls that hid her sex.

'*Isteh oreos,*' he muttered thickly. 'You are beautiful! *Keh ti thelo!*' And I want you!

Jane's hands had been trapped between them but now she dragged them free to rake frantic fingers across his cheek. Thankfully, she didn't draw blood, but when her nails scraped across his scalp he uttered a groan of protest.

'Do not pretend you do not want me, too,' he said unsteadily, and, although her hands had fastened in his hair with the intention of jerking his head away from hers, the shaken timbre of his voice tore her resolution to shreds.

'I—I don't,' she got out fiercely, but her lips told a different story when he kissed her again. Passion built between them with every sensual thrust of his tongue, and when he sucked her lower lip between his teeth, she could only clutch his neck and hang on.

'This is why you really came here, isn't it?' he demanded, his hands sliding possessively up her arms to tip the robe off her shoulders. 'You are determined to destroy me.'

'No,' she protested, as the robe fell to the floor, but Demetri wasn't listening to her. His fingers slid over her shoulders and down her back, caressing her hipbones briefly, before moving on to her bottom. Filling his hands with the rounded globes, he brought her deliberately against him, rotating his hips so she was made unmistakably aware of the pressure of his erection.

'Do you feel that?' he asked, his voice thick with emotion.
'Yes, of course you do. But do you have any idea what it's like
to be this close to you and not be a part of you?'

'Demetri—'

'You drive me crazy,' he went on, as if she hadn't spoken,
thrusting his thigh between her legs. 'Stark, staring crazy, and
I still want you even closer to me, under me, spreading your
legs for me, to give me some relief from this torment you're
putting me through.'

'Demetri—'

'Do not try to tell me I don't know what I'm saying,' he
snarled. 'I know. I know, Jane. Believe me.'

'Demetri, please—'

The husky tone of her voice vibrated through him, but he
was too far gone to listen to reason. Tucking a hand beneath
the tumbled silk of her hair, he tipped her head up to his, his
mouth silencing any further protest.

The kiss was deep and erotic, an affirmation of everything
he'd been saying, seducing her to a place where nothing
mattered but that he should go on kissing her and caressing her,
drenching her body in the mindless heat of her own arousal.

She wondered afterwards if he would have taken her there,
against the wall of her sitting room, if they hadn't been interrupted. Demetri was already using his free hand to tear his shirt
open, dragging off his tie to send it spiralling across the room.
And she—God help her!—was encouraging him, cupping his
warm neck between her palms, digging her nails into taut flesh
that smelled hot and sweaty and deliciously male.

She was rubbing herself against him, delighting in the
sensual brush of his body hair against her breasts, when there
was a tentative knock on the door.

For a moment, neither of them moved. It was as if they

were suddenly frozen, blood cooling to weld them to the spot. Demetri, his face buried in the scented curve of her shoulder, breathed a word that could more politely be described as 'Damn!' and slumped against her. And Jane tipped her head back against heavy silk damask, grateful for the wall's support.

'Jane!'

Her mouth went dry. The momentary fear that it was Demetri who'd spoken, alerting whoever was on the other side of the door to his presence, making her feel weak. But almost immediately she realised that Demetri was too enraged to say anything civil. It was another voice that was disconcertingly like Demetri's who had spoken her name.

With a strength she hadn't known she possessed, Jane managed to push Demetri's head back so he could see her lips. 'It's your father,' she mouthed, the consternation evident in her face, and with a resigned gesture he muttered, 'I know.'

'So what are you going to do about it?' she continued as he dragged himself upright and raked back his hair. She bent to snatch the bathrobe from the floor and quickly put it on. 'He can't find you here. Not like this. You've got to go.'

'Go where?' He was sardonic. 'Do you expect me to hide in the bathroom until he's gone?'

'That's one idea, certainly.' Jane swallowed and nodded her head, but Demetri only gave her a scornful look.

'*Apoklieteh!*' he whispered harshly. 'No way!'

'Jane!' There was a pregnant pause and then Leo Souvakis spoke again. 'Is someone with you, *kiria?* I can come back later, if you would rather?'

'No, I—'

Jane struggled for an answer, gazing beseechingly at Demetri, begging him to get out of sight.

But all he did was finish fastening the buttons on his shirt
and stuff it back into his trousers. Then, to her horror, he walked
across to the door and swung it open.

CHAPTER EIGHT

To HER surprise, Jane slept amazingly well.

She hadn't expected to. After the day—and evening—she'd had, she'd anticipated lying awake for hours, mulling over everything that had happened. But instead, she'd lost consciousness the moment her head hit the pillow.

A clear conscience? She didn't think so. What she'd done—what she'd allowed Demetri to do—had been unforgivable. She'd deserved to spend the night berating herself for her foolishness.

No doubt the fact that she was pregnant had had something to do with the ease with which she'd fallen asleep, she reflected ruefully. Now, rolling onto her back, she found the sun streaming through the crack in the curtains she'd drawn the night before. While she'd been in London, fretting over the alternatives she was faced with, such sleep as she'd had had been restless and plagued with tortuous dreams. But last night she'd been so exhausted, she hadn't been able to keep her eyes open.

In consequence she felt rested, more rested than she'd done in a long time. Not since Demetri had come back into her life, in fact.

However, it was time to get up and face the day and it wasn't just the familiar nausea that was causing her stomach to quiver in protest. Dear God, what had Demetri's father really thought when his son had thrown open her door and stormed out of her apartments without a word of explanation the night before? Just a terse 'Papa' in passing, and then he strode away towards the stairs as if he at least had no intention of answering any questions about his reasons for being there.

What Leo Souvakis must have thought, finding his son with the woman he was supposed to be divorcing was anyone's guess. And not 'supposed to be divorcing', Jane amended. *Was* divorcing. Hadn't she received the initial papers the day before she'd left for Kalithi? Just because she hadn't signed them yet didn't make them any the less real.

Pushing back the covers, she discovered she'd slept without the man-size T-shirt she invariably wore. But being left to face Leo's obvious confusion when his son had passed him with barely an acknowledgement had been humiliating, so it was no wonder she'd been bewildered after he'd gone. At the time, however, Demetri's father had gazed after his son as if he didn't understand the situation. And then he'd looked at Jane and found she was wearing only a bathrobe and an expression of understanding had crossed his lined face.

Jane's own face had been burning. She'd been all too aware that her lips were bruised and she had stubble burns on her cheeks. Leo wasn't a fool. He must have guessed exactly what he'd interrupted. Which was why he'd refused when she'd invited him in.

'Ah, not tonight, Jane,' he'd said, glancing once again along the landing, almost as if he'd expected his son to reappear. 'If you have everything you need, I'll wish you goodnight. Sleep well, my dear. *Kalinikhta.*'

He'd obviously decided now was not the time to indulge in casual conversation. But as Jane had said goodnight, she'd wished she'd had the nerve to say *It's not what you think!* Yet it *was* what he'd probably thought, she admitted unhappily.

How could she pretend otherwise? And what he'd thought of her behaviour, let alone his son's, was not something she was looking forward to finding out.

A maid brought her breakfast while Jane was taking her shower. She found the tray containing fruit juice, sweet rolls and coffee on her bedside table when she came out of the bathroom. She hoped the girl hadn't heard anything she shouldn't, but if she had, what of it? People were sick for various reasons, not all of them suspicious.

The smell of coffee was offputting, but, breaking off a corner of one of the rolls, she popped it into her mouth. It was good. It even made her feel a little better, and she remembered that she'd read somewhere that food could help morning sickness.

She ate two of the rolls and drank the fruit juice, her spirits improving all the time. She even swallowed half a cup of coffee and by the end she was feeling pretty good.

The maid who'd unpacked her clothes had folded all the casual items into a drawer. Jane pulled out a sleeveless tanktop, in pink with matching shorts. The colour suited her and she secured her hair with a long-toothed comb. Then, feeling a little apprehensive, she left her room. It was after nine, so perhaps someone would be about.

She wasn't thinking about Demetri, she told herself as she descended the stairs, though she couldn't help wondering if he'd left. But it was Stefan she saw first, picking out a tune on a magnificent baby grand piano in the music room, where long arched windows opened to the terrace beyond.

Crossing the hall, she paused in the entrance, and, although he couldn't have heard her silent approach, he lifted his head. 'Jane!' he exclaimed, getting up from the stool to reveal that like her he was wearing shorts and a casual shirt. He came towards her, smiling warmly. 'Did you sleep well? You were not too tired after—after your journey?'

His hesitation was telling, but Jane chose not to notice it. 'Very well,' she said, wondering if his mother would approve of the air kisses he bestowed on each of her cheeks. 'I gather you're not working today.'

When she'd left the island, Stefan had been acting as his father's secretary. But, knowing Leo as she did, Jane couldn't believe he'd approve of Stefan's attire if he was working with him.

'Not today,' he agreed, without offering any further explanation. 'Have you had breakfast? I can ask Angelena—'

'I've eaten, thanks.' Jane glanced about the sunlit salon. 'This is a lovely room. And so quiet. I'd forgotten how quiet Kalithi could be.'

'How dull, you mean,' said Stefan drily, and Jane wondered if she'd only imagined the bitterness in his voice. The night before, he'd seemed reasonably happy. But now there was a distinct air of melancholy about his plump features.

'I suppose that depends what you're looking for,' she murmured, not really wanting to get into any in-depth discussion about his life.

'So what are you looking for, Jane?' Stefan's brows arched and his tone was faintly malicious. 'Is being a success in business really all you want from life?'

'I don't know what I want,' said Jane bluntly, and it was nothing but the truth. 'Um—where is everyone? Having breakfast?'

'My father rarely comes down before lunch,' replied Stefan carelessly. 'My mother usually spends the morning with him, though, with Ariadne being here, she may decide to change her routine. Yanis has returned to the seminary, and—my other brother left over an hour ago.'

'Demetri?' Jane was amazed. She hadn't even heard the helicopter. But also relieved, she told herself. It had to be easier now he was gone.

'Demetri,' Stefan agreed. 'He expects to be back tomorrow evening.'

'Tomorrow evening!'

'Yes, tomorrow evening.' Stefan regarded her with some amusement. 'So, how do you propose to entertain yourself until then?'

Jane's colour deepened. 'I don't know what you mean. I didn't come here to see Demetri.'

'No?' He didn't sound convinced and she wondered if that was what his father and mother thought, too. Not to mention Demetri himself. But she didn't want to think about him.

'Your father asked to see me,' she said now. She linked her hands together. 'I couldn't—I didn't *want* to refuse.'

'Humph.' Stefan shrugged his shoulders. He was of a shorter build than Demetri and there was something essentially feminine about his mocking smile. 'If you say so, who am I to disagree with you? Perhaps I'm allowing Mama's influence to colour my judgement.'

Jane shook her head and would have retreated into the hall in search of friendlier company, when he spread his arms disarmingly. 'I'm sorry,' he said. 'I'm a bitch, I know. You mustn't take any notice of me, Jane. Come: let me take you for a walk. We can go down through the garden and onto the beach.'

Jane hesitated. 'Oh, I don't know whether—'

'Please.' Stefan could be charming when he chose. 'Or we could sit by the pool. I know how you like to swim.'

She might have taken that as another sly comment but at present putting on a swimsuit might be unwise. In consequence, she decided to accept Stefan's former offer. 'A walk sounds—appealing,' she said, crossing her arms and cupping her elbows in her palms. It had to be better than hanging about here waiting for her mother-in-law or Ariadne to appear.

They left the house through sliding doors that opened from the morning room. This part of the villa looked much the same as Jane remembered, with duck-egg-blue walls, yellow and white pottery on glass-topped tables and a cool marble floor. Half-drawn Roman blinds in shades of green and brown and orange should have clashed with the vivid décor, but they didn't. It was a cheerful room, spoilt only by the memory of the argument she and Demetri had had here the morning before she left the island for good.

Or what she'd thought was for good, she reflected, preceding Stefan through the sliding doors. Now there was so much confusion inside her, she didn't know what she thought.

Thankfully the terrace held no such horrors. Italian tiles, vine-hung trellises, marble steps leading down to a huge circular pool. They bypassed the steps and the cedar-wood cabins that housed both showers and a sauna, following a path that led between lawns that were presently being watered by an efficient sprinkler system. The lawns were edged with bushes of flowering cactus, the path paved and immaculately free of any weeds.

It was all very lush, very beautiful, but also incredibly hot. Jane, who hadn't thought about buying sunscreen when she'd packed her bag, hoped she wouldn't get burned. But nothing about this trip was turning out as she'd anticipated and she had to seriously revise her expectations.

There was a welcome breeze blowing when they stepped onto the sand and Jane kicked off her sandals and carried them by their straps. The sand wasn't yet hot enough to burn her feet and she walked purposefully towards the water.

'*Eh! Pio arga!* Slow down,' exclaimed Stefan, hurrying after her. 'We have all morning.'

You may have, thought Jane drily, but she didn't say it. Nevertheless, she had to wonder why Stefan was content to laze his days away here on the island when it seemed obvious his father was doing very little work at the moment.

The waves curled about her bare feet, their initial coldness giving way to a delicious warmth. This was the best time of the day to swim, she remembered ruefully. Before the sun could burn you even through the water.

'You have to learn to relax, Jane,' Stefan said, puffing a little as he came up beside her. 'You are not in England now.'

'Do you think I don't know that?' Jane kept her eyes on her feet, watching as the sand slid away beneath them. Then she shrugged and looked up at him. 'What are you doing here, Stefan? Have you been sent to keep an eye on me?'

Stefan gave her a wounded look. 'Do you think I would agree to that?'

Jane arched a mocking brow. 'I'll take that as a yes, shall I?'

'No!' He was indignant. 'I thought you might be glad of some company, is all.'

Jane regarded him intently for a few seconds and then she turned away. 'OK.' She started to walk along the sand, her feet in the shallows. 'So tell me what you've been doing. Don't you work for your father any more?'

Stefan's mouth compressed. 'I'm sure you're not interested in my problems, Jane. But I am intrigued by your relationship with Demetri. Are you aware he's going to marry Ariadne as soon as his divorce is absolute?'

'Yes, he told me.'

'And did he tell you why?'

Jane sighed. 'Is this relevant, Stefan? Demetri wants a divorce. End of story.'

'No, it's not the end of the story,' retorted Stefan shortly.

'There was no need for Demetri to get a divorce, not unless he chose to do so, of course.'

Jane frowned. 'What do you mean?'

'I mean I was perfectly willing to give our father the grand-child he so desperately craves. But I was not good enough. My relationship with Phillippe is not good enough, despite the fact that we have been together for over six years.'

Jane halted to stare at him in disbelief. 'You mean, you and Phillippe Martin are—are—'

'A couple? Yes.' Stefan raised dark brows. 'Of course, you met him, did you not? Didn't Demetri tell you we lived together?'

'He said you were—friends,' said Jane, feeling enormously stupid. Even when Demetri had told her Stefan wasn't inter-ested in women, she still hadn't put two and two together.

'Of course, I shouldn't be surprised.' Stefan was walking on now, kicking the water into a spray ahead of him. 'Demetri is our father's heir. The eldest son. The golden boy! No one else's child is good enough.'

Jane shook her head. Did Demetri know this? Had he any idea how Stefan felt? Or course, he must do. The situation was too raw not to have been discussed between Demetri and his father at some point.

'I'm sorry,' she said, knowing that was inadequate but not knowing what else to say, and Stefan gave her a reluctant smile.

'*Then pirazi,*' he said philosophically. It doesn't matter. 'Shall we go a little further?'

They walked about a quarter of a mile along the beach and then turned back. To Jane's relief, their conversation had shifted to less personal things and she was so busy trying to avoid any controversial topics that she completely forgot how hot it was.

But by the time they left the beach and threaded their way back to the terrace, she could feel her shoulders prickling. A hasty glance informed her that her arms were very red, too, and she could only guess that her face looked like a beetroot.

Which was so galling when she saw both her mother-in-law and Ariadne sitting on the terrace, securely shaded by a fringed striped canopy.

It took a great deal of courage to continue walking towards them, particularly as she was feeling a little faint now and distinctly dizzy. A situation that wasn't helped when Stefan excused himself and continued on into the villa, leaving Jane to face the two women on her own.

'Ah, Jane,' said Maria at once, her shrewd eyes quickly assessing how her daughter-in-law must be feeling. 'Why don't you come and join us? We were just having coffee.'

Jane knew Maria had no real desire for her company. It was just her way of making an embarrassing situation worse. She obviously knew that Jane would have preferred to go to her room to put some salve on her arms and shoulders, but she couldn't resist any opportunity to torment her.

And Jane, desperate not to do anything to worsen the situation, forced a tight smile, and said, 'Thank you,' before sinking weakly into the cushioned chair beside Ariadne.

But even the smell of the coffee was sickening, and, when Maria summoned the maid to get another cup, Jane licked her dry lips and said, 'Would you mind if I just had water?'

'Water?' Maria gazed at her impatiently. 'What's wrong? Aren't you well?'

'I'm hot,' said Jane quickly, desperate not to arouse suspicion. 'And very thirsty. If you don't mind?'

'She's not used to our climate,' remarked Ariadne scornfully. 'She looks like a cooked lobster, Maria. Perhaps she would prefer to go to her room.'

Jane objected to being spoken about as if she wasn't there,

but she was so grateful to the other girl for saying what she had, she didn't complain.

'I think I would prefer to do that, Maria, if you don't mind,' she murmured, getting to her feet again on legs that felt distinctly unsteady. 'Perhaps you could ask the maid to bring the water upstairs?'

Maria's mouth tightened. 'Surely you can stay for a few minutes, Jane? We haven't had an opportunity to talk together yet. Don't you want to know how my husband is feeling this morning?'

'Of course I want to know how Leo is,' protested Jane, sinking obediently back into her chair. 'I just thought—'

'I can imagine what you thought. You would prefer not to have this conversation, I have no doubt,' Maria interrupted her sharply. 'But let us be clear about something, Jane. I did not approve of Leo inviting you here. No matter what he says, you are not welcome in my home. Now that you've seen him, I hope you'll make your excuses and leave as soon as decently possible, *neh?*'

Jane expelled a shaken breath. 'Why did you allow Demetri to contact me?' she exclaimed. 'Why didn't you just pretend that you'd spoken to me and that I'd refused to come?'

'Because Leo would never have accepted that. And I care too much about Demetri to deliberately lie to him.'

Jane shook her head and then wished she hadn't. The dizziness she'd felt coming up from the beach had come back and she clutched desperately at the arms of her chair in an effort to steady herself.

Unfortunately, both Ariadne and Maria noticed and her mother-in-law gave an impatient snort. 'Oh, go to your room, then,' she said irritably. 'If you can't control yourself for five minutes, then you'd better do as Ariadne says. But don't forget what I've told you, will you? Next time I might not be half so understanding.'

Whatever that meant.

CHAPTER NINE

DEMETRI FLEW back to the island late the following afternoon. He hadn't stayed to hear the final conclusions of the delegates to the conference, making the excuse that, as his father was so ill, he'd prefer to get home.

And, without exception, everyone had understood, but he couldn't help wondering if they'd have been as understanding if they'd known that checking up on his father encompassed only half the concerns he had. He was equally anxious to see Jane again, to assure himself that she hadn't been intimidated in his absence.

He didn't know why he felt this desperate need to defend his estranged wife, but he did. It wasn't as if she'd be glad to see him. Because, despite the fact that he didn't seem able to keep his hands off her, he was fairly sure she regretted it just as much as he did.

Nevertheless, when his pilot landed the helicopter on the pad a couple of hundred yards from the villa, he breathed a sigh of relief. Without waiting for Vasilis to swing open the door and let down the steps, he accomplished the task himself and dropped down gratefully onto the tarmac.

'I won't need you tonight, Theo,' he said when the other man joined him. 'You can go home, if you wish.' Theo's parents lived on one of the other islands in the group. 'Costas will take you.'

'If it's all the same to you, I'd like to stay at the cottage,' said Theo, mentioning one of a cluster of stone dwellings where many of the staff who worked on the estate lived. He set down the two briefcases he was carrying and stowed the steps back inside the aircraft. 'I'm hoping to see Ianthe, if you have no objections?'

'Why would I object?' Demetri raised a hand to the pilot as Costas prepared to take off again. 'She's a free woman.'

'I know that, but—'

'But what?'

'Well…' Theo looked embarrassed now. 'It's common knowledge that you and she were once—were once—'

'Friends,' said Demetri harshly. 'We were friends, Theo. Friends! Not lovers, as I'm sure you've heard.'

'But your wife—'

'She didn't believe me either,' said Demetri, his pleasant mood evaporating. 'Forget it. It's all in the past now. Perhaps one day Ianthe will tell you who Marc's father really was. Until then, take my word for it, I wish you—both of you—nothing but good luck. OK?'

'Thanks.'

Demetri picked up his own briefcase and the two men separated as they reached the house, Theo to circle the villa to where the cottages were situated and Demetri to run lightly up the steps and into the reception hall.

The place seemed deserted, but almost immediately his mother appeared from the direction of the terrace. 'Demetri!' she exclaimed, evidently surprised to see him. 'Is something wrong?'

'Why should anything be wrong, Mama?' Demetri felt a sense of impatience that was out of all proportion to the perceived offence. 'I went to the conference as I promised and now I'm back.' He paused. 'Where's my father?' It was better than asking whether Jane was still here.

Maria Souvakis clicked her tongue. 'You may well ask,' she said, and it was obvious she wasn't pleased with the answer she had to give him. 'He's gone for a drive with that woman, hasn't he? I warned him that it was unwise to overtax himself, but he won't listen to me.'

Demetri knew exactly who his mother meant, and his relief was so great he didn't consider his words before saying, 'I doubt if taking a drive with Jane will overtax him greatly, Mama.'

But then a frown formed between his brows. What was he saying? He wanted Jane out of his life, didn't he? Encouraging his father to make her visit a pleasant one was hardly the action of a sensible man.

'I might have known you'd disagree with me,' declared Maria tersely. 'After all, you're the one who brought her here.'

Demetri let that go, but his mother wasn't finished. 'Thank goodness, Ariadne has gone with them,' she continued. 'She'll make sure your father doesn't do anything stupid.'

Demetri blew out a breath. 'Anything stupid?'

'Like inviting her to stay indefinitely,' she explained irritably. Then, as if realising this was hardly the way to greet her son after he'd been away, she tucked her arm through his. 'Come along. Thermia's here. We're having iced tea on the terrace. She'll be pleased to see you.'

Demetri doubted that. And the last person he wanted to see right now was Ianthe's mother. Was Ianthe with her? Could he really be that unlucky?

Remaining rooted to the spot when his mother would have drawn him across the hall, he said wearily, 'Give me a break, Ma. I'm hot and tired. What I really need is a shower and something a little stronger than iced tea!'

'Nonsense.' His mother was having none of that. 'What would Thermia think if you didn't come and say hello?'

Demetri's jaw tightened. 'Is she alone?'

'Of course not. Ianthe's with her. And I know she'll be glad of some younger company.'

Iperokha! Great! Demetri suppressed a groan. Who had invited the Adonides women here? But he didn't really need to ask. Nevertheless, Theo was going to be so disappointed when he drove into town to find Ianthe wasn't home.

Contrary to what his mother had said, Ianthe looked less than happy to see him. 'Demetri,' she murmured politely after he had greeted her mother. 'Aunt Maria said you wouldn't be back before tomorrow.' Ianthe had always called his mother 'aunt' but it was only an honorary title. The two women were actually distant cousins, even if they behaved more like sisters.

Now Demetri cast his mother a sardonic look, but she busied herself taking another glass from the chilled cabinet the maid had placed beside her. 'You'll have some iced tea, won't you, Demetri?'

'Not for me,' he said, aware that Ianthe was exchanging a furtive look with her mother. 'I can't stay. Now that I know my father's OK, I'd like to get home.'

Maria straightened, the glass in her hand. 'But Demetri, you can't mean to leave without seeing your father?'

'I'll see him later,' insisted Demetri through his teeth. 'Right now, I'd like to catch Theo before he leaves for town.'

'Theo is here?'

It was Ianthe who'd spoken, and Demetri saw a look of unguarded anticipation in her eyes.

'Yeah,' he said. 'He's staying the night in the cottage. D'you want to see him?'

'Oh, well—'

'I don't think so, Demetri.'

Ianthe and her mother spoke in unison but it was Maria

Souvakis who had the final word. 'Why would Ianthe want to see Theo Vasilis, Demetri?' she demanded. 'For heaven's sake, Thermia was just telling me that Ianthe's had more than a dozen text messages from that young man while you've been away. He's becoming a positive nuisance!'

Demetri arched a brow at Ianthe. 'Is that true?'

'That he's texted me, yes.'

'I meant the bit about him being a nuisance,' said Demetri patiently. 'He seems to think you like his company.'

Ianthe glanced awkwardly from her mother to her aunt and back again. 'Well—I do—like him,' she mumbled uncertainly and the older women exchanged an impatient look.

'So?' Demetri was getting impatient himself. 'Do you want to see him or not?' And when she kept her eyes averted, he added irritably, 'You're twenty-three, Ianthe. If you want to be friends with him, no one can stop you.'

'Demetri!'

His mother, who had seated herself beside Thermia, now looked up at him with horrified eyes, but Demetri had had enough. 'Well?' he said, pointedly, and with another anxious look in her mother's direction, Ianthe got to her feet.

'Yes, I'd like to see him,' she muttered humbly, and with a muffled oath Demetri bid a terse farewell to his mother and Thermia, and stepped back into the house with Ianthe at his heels.

They were crossing the reception hall when Demetri heard the unmistakable sound of a car coming up the drive to the house and his stomach clenched instinctively. Oh, right, he thought tiredly, wasn't this just par for the course? He'd thought things couldn't get any worse, but they just had.

'That must be your father and Ariadne and—and your wife,' offered Ianthe uneasily, and Demetri gave her a wry look.

'Yes,' he said flatly. 'I think you're right. How wonderful!'

Ianthe's eyes held an expression of reproach. 'You don't mean that.'

'Don't I?' Despite his reluctance, Demetri continued doggedly towards the outer doors. 'Well, we'll see, shall we?'

They paused in the open doorway as his father's vintage Bentley halted at the foot of the steps that led up to the terrace where they were standing. Unaware of being observed, Jane was first out of the car. She'd apparently been acting as his father's chauffeur with him beside her in the front seat. Now, she hurried round the bonnet to pull open his door, offering him a hand to alight. He did so gratefully, leaning heavily on her arm before rescuing his cane and transferring his weight to it.

'Thank you, my dear,' he said with evident warmth. And then he saw his son.

'Demetri!' he exclaimed, and Ariadne, who had been getting rather ill-temperedly out of the back of the car, lifted her head disbelievingly.

'Darling,' she cried, ignoring Jane and his father. Darting ahead of them, she reached Demetri and, grasping his free arm, she stood on tiptoe to brush her mouth against his. 'You're back!'

'You noticed.' Demetri's tone was even, but he was watching his wife and his father making their careful ascent of the steps. Then, with an inward curse, he put down his briefcase and went to help them, leaving Ariadne and Ianthe to exchange an unfriendly look.

'I can manage,' said his father irritably, and Jane permitted her husband a contemptuous stare.

'Hoping to impress your girlfriends?' she asked but the smile she'd adopted for his father's benefit turned malicious when she looked at him.

'Well, obviously I'm not impressing you,' he retorted,

ignoring his father's protests and taking his full weight on his shoulder. 'And believe it or not, I didn't know Ianthe was coming here today.'

'It's of no interest to me whether you did or not,' declared Jane, not altogether truthfully. She directed her whole attention to the old man. 'Not much further, Leo.'

'I see that.' Demetri's father shook his head. 'But I'm not an invalid, you know.'

'You're not used to climbing steps,' pointed out Demetri drily as they reached the level surface of the terrace. 'OK.' He released his father's arm. 'You're on your own now.'

'Thank you.' Leo's tone was clipped, but then, noticing Ianthe's anxious expression, his voice softened. 'Hello, little one. Where are you and Demetri off to?'

'*We're* not going anywhere,' Demetri answered him, his irritation increasing with every word his father spoke.

'I'm going to see Theo,' Ianthe explained nervously. 'Demetri says he's staying at the cottage.'

'Ah.' The old man nodded. 'And does your mother approve?'

'Whether her mother approves or not isn't relevant,' said Demetri angrily, and his father gave him a warning look.

'Just because you do exactly as you like, don't expect the same behaviour from everyone else,' he said coldly. He glanced round for Jane. 'Come, my dear, will you give me your arm?'

Jane looked uncomfortable now, and well she should, thought Demetri furiously. This was not why he'd brought her here, to drive a wedge between him and his father. Dammit, he'd had just about enough of this.

'I'd like to speak to my wife, if you can spare her for five minutes,' he said, ignoring Ariadne's disapproval. They weren't engaged yet, he told himself grimly, even if it was only a matter of time.

His father sucked in an impatient breath. 'Can't it wait, boy?' he demanded, and that word was the last straw.

'No, it can't,' said Demetri flatly. 'Jane: will you come into the library? We can talk there.'

Jane glanced about her a little desperately, but she knew she'd get no help from either Ariadne or Ianthe. Leo, after a resigned shrug of his shoulders, had already begun to make his way across the smooth marble floor, proving he didn't need her help.

'I—suppose so,' she conceded finally, with ill grace. She met Ianthe's anxious gaze. 'Don't worry. I won't keep him long.'

'Oh, for pity's sake!' Demetri gripped her arm just above her elbow and guided her decisively towards the arched corridor that led into the west wing of the villa. Then, as if feeling some remorse for the way he was treating Ariadne, he looked back and added, 'I'll see you at dinner, Ari. We'll have the whole evening to ourselves. I promise.'

Ariadne's face softened. '*Endaxi.*' OK. Her tongue circled her pink lips. '*Saghapo.*' I love you.

Demetri made no response to this, but he could tell that Jane knew exactly what Ariadne had said. Her arm stiffened and, if she could have wrenched herself free of him, she would have done so. As it was, he had to virtually frogmarch her into the book-lined apartment and slam the heavy door behind them.

Only then did he release her, and she quickly put some space between them. She went to stare out of the windows, windows that overlooked a cascade of flowering plants and shrubs falling away below them. From here, the sea looked distant, with acres of woodland marking the boundary of the Souvakis' property. But the backdrop was spectacular, the sea darkening from aquamarine to deepest sapphire.

The silence stretched, and Jane, who had determined not to be the first to speak, found her nerves growing as taut as violin strings. As always on occasions like these, she worried that he'd somehow found out about the baby. But surely if he had, she'd have heard about it before now.

Hearing the rustle of papers, she felt compelled to turn, half expecting him to be holding a private letter from her doctor. But that was so ludicrous, she couldn't believe she'd even considered it, and she was a little put out to discover he was riffling through some papers on his father's desk.

Almost trembling with indignation, she exclaimed, 'What do you think you're doing, Demetri? You invited me in here and now you're apparently reading your father's mail. If this is some kind of power play, forget it.'

Demetri remained bent over the desk, but he looked up at her through his lashes. 'It's no power play,' he told her, his eyes dropping once again to his task. Then, almost against his will, he added, 'You seem to have my father under your spell.'

Jane gasped. 'And that's what you wanted to tell me?'

'No.' At last, Demetri straightened, tossing the letter he had been examining aside. 'I wanted to ask if you'd received the divorce papers from Carl Gerrard. They should have been with you a week ago, before you left for the island.'

Jane's nostrils flared. 'Well, they weren't,' she retorted, excusing her answer on the grounds that the papers only arrived four days ago.

Demetri's brows drew together. 'You're sure about that?'

'That they didn't arrive a week ago?' she asked innocently. 'Oh, yes, I'm very sure.'

Demetri came round the desk to prop his hips against the huge slab of granite that formed its surface and folded his arms. 'Well, that's very strange,' he said, regarding her with disturbing intent. 'When I spoke to him this morning, he assured me the papers had been sent.'

'Blame the post office,' she said, casually edging towards the door. 'And now, if you'll excuse me, I'd like to go and freshen up.'

'*Akomi*. Not yet.' He didn't move but she knew as surely as if he had that she wouldn't be leaving until he was finished with her. 'Tell me,' he continued mildly. 'When are you planning to return to England?'

Jane wrapped her arms about her midriff. 'Are you wanting rid of me?'

Demetri's lips thinned. 'I simply want to know what you've told my father.'

'And not just about when I'm leaving, I'll bet,' she said provocatively. 'Don't worry, Demetri. I haven't told anyone what happened at my apartment.'

Demetri's nostrils flared. 'You say that as if it was a threat.'

'No.' Jane backed off from a full confrontation. 'I'm just re-assuring you that you have nothing to fear from me.'

'To fear?' He seemed determined to have an argument. 'Why should I fear you, Jane? I'm sure Ariadne wouldn't be inter-ested in anything you had to say.'

'You mean, she wouldn't believe me? More fool her.'

Demetri's face darkened. 'Are you saying you regret what happened?'

Jane's jaw dropped. 'Are you joking? Of course I regret it.'

'Why?' There was an edge of scorn to his tone now. 'It's not as if it was anything new for you. According to that witch you call an employer, you and your boyfriend spend a lot of time at your apartment.'

'That's not true!' Jane couldn't let him get away with that and she wished, not for the first time, that Olga would keep her nose out of her affairs.

'Why should I believe you?'

'Because Alex hasn't even been in my apartment. Don't

judge everybody by your own standards, Demetri. Whatever you may think, I don't sleep around.'

Demetri's eyes narrowed. 'So what do you do together?'

'It's none of your business.'

'Humour me.'

'No.' Jane had had enough of this. 'I don't ask what you and Ariadne do together. I don't care so long as it doesn't concern me. I don't believe I even asked what you and Ianthe did together.' Her lips curled. 'I didn't have to. I knew.'

CHAPTER TEN

'YOU knew nothing!'

Demetri came up off the desk in one swift, menacing lunge and Jane felt the hairs on the back of her neck prickle alarmingly. He was so big, so dark, so powerful. So *angry!* She couldn't help herself. She automatically backed away from him.

And found her way blocked by the leather armchair in the window embrasure behind her. It smacked into her calves and, with a little gasp of surprise, she subsided onto the seat. Demetri loomed over her and for a moment she thought he was going to strike her. But he didn't. What he did was bend towards her, gripping the arms of the chair, effectively imprisoning her in place.

'OK,' he said harshly, his breath hot against skin that was still slightly tender from the sun. She was wearing a cropped tank-top and a cream denim skirt and her sudden descent had driven the skirt halfway up her thighs. 'Here it is for the last time, *aghapi*. I have slept with Ariadne, I don't deny it. I have never slept with Ianthe.'

Jane couldn't deny the twist of pain she felt at hearing him admit that he and Ariadne were lovers, but she managed to say bitterly, 'Someone did.'

'But not me.'

'Then why did she say it was?' Jane demanded raggedly.

'Same answer as before: you'd have to ask her,' replied Demetri tersely. 'Maybe this time she'll tell you the truth.'

Jane swallowed, permitting herself a look up into his dark face. 'What I find hard to understand is how you can even associate with her if she was lying.'

'To begin with, I couldn't. But my mother—'

'Oh, right.' Jane shook her head. 'I might have known your mother would have some part in this.'

'She is fond of Ianthe,' said Demetri through his teeth. 'She regards her as family.'

'The way she never regarded me.'

Demetri sighed. 'OK. I know it was hard for you. But it would have got easier.'

'Before or after you'd slept with Ianthe?'

'I've told you—'

'All right, all right.' Jane shrugged. 'I still don't understand why it should matter to you what I think now.'

Demetri's breath sharpened. 'Because it does.'

'Why?'

'Why do you think?'

Jane's lips twisted. 'Because no one is allowed to contradict the great Demetri Souvakis?' she suggested scornfully. 'Or do you just like tormenting me?'

'Do I do that?'

His voice had thickened and this time, when Jane chanced a glance through her lashes, she surprised an odd humility in his expression.

She shivered. 'You know you do.'

'How?'

She spread her hands, indicating his arms and her confinement. 'Need I say more?'

Demetri's eyes darkened, but he had to acknowledge that she was right. 'OK,' he said. 'Point taken.' But he didn't move. 'Perhaps you ought to ask yourself why.'

'Why you like tormenting me?'

'I didn't say I liked it,' he corrected her, and now his voice was harsh with emotion. He lifted a hand, which he noticed wasn't quite steady, and took hold of her chin, turning her face up to his. 'You still drive me crazy and you know it.'

Jane trembled. He could feel it. Goosepimples appeared on her shoulders, ran down her arms to the hands that were clenched in her lap. A wave of colour swept up from her throat and into her face, warming the flesh beneath his fingers. And Demetri—God help him, he thought grimly—couldn't stop himself from dropping down onto his haunches in front of her and covering her mouth with his.

A soft moan escaped her lips, her breath filling his lungs with the taste and the smell of her. Demetri came down on one knee then and, cupping her face in his hands, he deepened the kiss until her lips parted on a gasp and he was able to plunge his tongue into her open mouth.

The sensation was exquisite: taut muscle against soft wet flesh, and it was all too easy to remember how hot and tight she'd been when he'd pushed his sex inside her. His senses swam at the memory. A mindless kind of self-destruction was driving him on. And the throbbing pulse of his erection was like a drum beating in his head.

'Demetri,' she protested, but it was barely audible. Did she really expect him to stop? When he released her mouth to seek the scented hollow of her throat her breathing quickened. And she didn't try to pull away.

His mouth and teeth were seducing her, she realised, drawing her inexorably into the web she'd known before.

Murmuring to her in his own language, he caressed her arms and the delicate curve of her shoulders, slipping down to probe beneath the hem of her tank-top.

His fingers lingered in the sensitive hollow of her spine, causing another shiver of awareness. Her flesh was filmed with dampness, her scent rising to his nostrils when he bent his head and licked her skin. But the waistband of her skirt was a barrier, and his hands slid along her thighs instead to where her legs were bared and accessible.

'*Aghapita,*' he breathed, bending his head to kiss the inner curve of her thigh. 'You are so beautiful!'

'Dear God, Demetri—don't!'

'I want to.'

He wouldn't listen to her protests, and Jane was finding it increasingly hard to hold on to her sanity. Besides, there was something enormously satisfying in hearing the break in his voice when he spoke to her, the raw emotion that no amount of arrogance could hide.

He spread her legs, his lips moving sensuously along her thigh, bestowing a trail of hot wet kisses that made her gulp and come half up out of the chair. 'Relax,' he said, pushing her down again. 'Just let me do this.'

It was insane, she thought. Didn't he care where he was, what might happen if his mother or Ariadne took it into their heads to come and see what was happening?

Evidently not. His mouth had reached the delta of her thighs and she felt his hands slip beneath her bottom and find the elasticated tape of her thong. Then, with a determination that no amount of resistance on her part could defeat, he pulled the scrap of silk away.

'That is much better,' he said thickly, lifting his head to

press a hungry kiss to her parted lips. She felt his finger probe the moist curls at the top of her legs. 'Isn't it?'

Jane couldn't speak. She could only move her head in a helpless gesture of admission. And, as if her flushed face and agitated reaction pleased him, Demetri gripped the back of her neck and brought her mouth to his again in a hard, passionate possession.

'*Se thelo,*' he groaned, and she thought it was an indication of how aroused he was that he continued to speak in his own language. 'I want you,' he repeated hoarsely. '*Angikse me!*' Touch me!

Her hands had been twisted together in her lap but now they moved almost of their own accord. With a feeling of inevitability, she clutched his shoulders, pushing his suit jacket to the floor.

Beneath his shirt, his skin was hot. His heat surged up into her fingers, almost burning her, and when he bore her back against the cushions she found he was sweating, too.

He pushed her tank-top up above her breasts, using his tongue and his teeth to bring them to tingling, sensual life. He drew the swollen nubs into his mouth, sucking hungrily, and, because her nipples were already tender, she couldn't deny the moan of anguish that escaped her.

But he wasn't hurting her. Indeed, she thought, she had never felt more excited. Her belief that a pregnant woman couldn't possibly respond in the same way as before simply wasn't true. Demetri had always been able to drive her crazy with longing and today was no exception.

She was aware of him unbuckling his belt and loosening the button at his waist and she couldn't resist. Pushing his fingers aside, she pressed his zip down and then caught her breath when his arousal pushed a handful of his silk boxer shorts into her hand. The boxers were made of the finest fabric but, when she peeled them over his erection, she had to admit that his skin was smoother and more satinlike than the richest velvet.

'*Theos,*' he said on a choked breath, and she realised how close to release he was.

'You like that?' she asked unsteadily, and he made a sound of pained submission.

'I like it,' he told her unevenly, and that was when she acknowledged that she wanted him just as much as he wanted her. Feeling his naked sex against hers, she knew the decision was no longer open to discussion. Even if she might regret it later—and she was fairly sure she would—there was nothing she wanted more.

'But we—we can't do it here,' she protested, aware that they were in full view of anybody walking past the window outside.

Demetri uttered a strangled groan. 'Don't you dare move,' he muttered, pushing her skirt up around her waist. 'This is good enough for me.'

And when Demetri pushed into her hot, slick sheath, she discovered she wasn't much interested in objecting again. He lifted her legs and encouraged her to wind them about his waist and then entered her in one smooth, satisfying lunge. He pressed in so deeply that Jane's body had to expand and stretch to accommodate him, but dear God, she thought, he made her feel whole again.

'*Aghapi mou,*' he whispered and, when she gasped, 'Am I hurting you?'

'You asked me that before,' she reminded him huskily, and he arched an anxious brow.

'Well?'

'No! God, no,' she assured him unsteadily, and, with a groan of satisfaction, Demetri looked down at where their bodies were joined.

'*Telios,*' he breathed. 'You are perfect. We are perfect together, *neh?*'

'*Neh.* I mean, yes, yes,' she got out with an effort. Then, half closing her eyes, 'Please: don't stop now.'

'I do not believe I could, *pethi mou,*' he confessed, and she was so wet, when he drew back she could hear the audible suction of his flesh against hers. 'There are limits to even my control, sweet one, and we passed them some minutes ago.' He pushed into her again and now he began to quicken his pace. '*Theos,* we belong together.'

Jane couldn't deny it. Not at that moment, not when her body convulsed around his only seconds before his release. She felt him spurting inside her, felt his heat melting all coherent thought, and clamped her thighs around him in a final act of possession.

She wasn't sure how long she lay there with Demetri cradled between her thighs. In the beginning, she couldn't have moved, and then she found she didn't want to. Their bodies were still joined and she knew it would take very little to arouse him again. His sex lay, still semi-aroused, in her, and she knew she had only to put down her hand and touch him to have him harden into desire.

But, eventually, she forced herself to raise her arm and look at her watch and saw to her horror that they'd been in the library for over an hour. Someone—probably his mother—was going to start wondering what was taking so long, and Jane could just imagine how she would react if she opened the door and found her precious son half-naked in his soon-to-be-ex-wife's arms.

It was that awareness as much as anything that made her struggle to get free. She couldn't bear the thought that Maria Souvakis might witness her humiliation. For, however she tried

to interpret it, the fact remained that once again she'd allowed
Demetri to take advantage of her. Heavens, hadn't she learned
her lesson the first time? She was pregnant, for goodness' sake.
And she hadn't got that way by any immaculate conception.

'*Komatia,* what are you doing?'

Demetri's lazy protest caused her to quicken her actions.
And because he was still semi-comatose, she was able to push
him aside and scramble off the chair.

'I'm leaving,' she said unsteadily, tugging her tank down
over her breasts and snatching up her underwear, which she
stuffed into the pocket of her skirt. She averted her eyes from
his shameless nakedness. 'If I were you, I'd put your clothes
on. I doubt if Ariadne would appreciate seeing you in your
present state of undress.'

Demetri swore, but she noticed he did as she suggested,
tugging up his trousers and fastening his zip. But when she
thought it was safe to leave, he pushed himself up from the chair
and regarded her through narrowed eyes.

'We're not through, you know,' he said harshly, and,
although she only glanced in his direction, she knew she would
never forget the sight of him with his shirt unfastened and his
zip in definite danger of slipping open again.

'I think we are,' she retorted, and this time when she headed
for the door he didn't try to stop her.

'I'll see you at dinner,' he said, and, although Jane badly
wanted to deny this, she was a guest in his father's house and
the decision wasn't hers to make.

Shaking her head, she let herself out of the door, praying that
she'd be allowed to go to her room without meeting either
Ariadne or Ianthe or some member of Demetri's family. She
wanted to be alone, she wanted time to think, and most of all she
wanted to escape this awful predicament she'd created for herself.

But that wasn't going to happen. And the idea of not having the baby was as painful to her as leaving the island was going to be. But she had to leave. And soon. Before she did something totally outrageous like telling Demetri she was going to have his baby. Ironically enough, it would have been easier to tell him she still loved him than that.

She caught her breath. Was that true? Could she have been foolish enough to fall in love with him all over again? Because whatever happened, Demetri was never going to believe she hadn't got pregnant deliberately, and did she really want a relationship based on that suspicion?

No, she had to leave here. Even if Demetri was prepared to believe her, there would always be the spectre of Ianthe's baby in the background. And he had a new relationship now, with Ariadne. She didn't have the right to disrupt his life again.

Even if he had disrupted hers...

She had reached the stairs when someone called her name. At first she thought it might be Demetri and she continued on her way. But then she realised that once again the voice had been too mild to be her husband's and, glancing back, she saw Leo leaning heavily on the banister below.

She halted immediately, supremely conscious that she was flushed and out of breath. But then, with a gesture of defeat, she came down the stairs again, hoping that the lowering sun would cast her face in shadow.

'I was just going to change,' she said when he didn't speak again, and Leo inclined his head.

'Ariadne told me that Demetri was with you,' he said at last. 'I hope he hasn't upset you again.'

Upset!

Jane felt a sob of hysteria rise in her throat and quickly fought it down. 'It—he just wanted to ask me if I'd received the divorce papers,' she said, which was true. Then, moistening her lips, she added, 'I'm glad I've got this opportunity to speak to you, actually, Leo. I think it's time I went back to England.'

Demetri's father frowned. 'You do?'

'Yes.' Jane swallowed. 'Now that Demetri's back—'

'So he has been intimidating you—'

'No.' Jane couldn't allow him to think that. 'It's just—well, I'm in the way here.'

'You're not in my way, Jane.'

'No, but you know what I'm saying.' Jane sighed. 'It's been wonderful seeing you again, Leo, but I don't belong here any more.'

Leo sighed. 'Well, if that's your decision…'

'It is.' And then, seeing his disappointment, Jane came right down the stairs to give him an impulsive hug. 'You know I don't want to leave you—'

'Then why do so?'

'I just have to,' she insisted, drawing back. 'Please say you understand.'

Leo shook his head. 'I assume you've told Demetri.'

'Um—not yet, no.'

'Don't you think he'll have something to say about it?'

'Perhaps.' Jane sighed. And then, because telling Demetri was something she couldn't face right now, she added, 'Would you do that, Leo? Tell him, I mean? But not—not before dinner, if you don't mind.'

Leo looked troubled. 'Are you afraid of him, Jane?'

'No.' Jane stifled a groan. 'I just—don't want any fuss,' she murmured awkwardly. 'And now, if you don't mind, I'd like to go and have a shower before we eat.'

CHAPTER ELEVEN

TO DEMETRI'S relief, Thermia wasn't joining them for dinner. Only his parents, Stefan and Ariadne were waiting in the orangery when he arrived, and, although he wanted to ask where Jane was, in the circumstances he decided discretion was the better part of valour.

To begin with, his father detained him in conversation about the conference he'd been attending, but as soon as the old man paused to speak to Demetri's mother, Ariadne took his place.

'What on earth took you so long this afternoon?' she exclaimed. 'You and that woman were in the library for ages. I was forced to entertain your mother and your aunt, and believe me that wasn't easy.'

'Thermia's not my aunt,' said Demetri evenly. 'Did Ianthe come back?'

'No.' Ariadne showed her displeasure. 'Did you expect she would?'

'I hoped she wouldn't,' retorted Demetri tersely. 'Ianthe and I have nothing to say to one another.'

Ariadne looked pleased at this. 'I notice your wife didn't take kindly to seeing the two of you together,' she commented. 'I suppose it brings back too many unhappy memories, hmm?'

Demetri found it difficult to conceal his resentment now. 'What unhappy memories?' he demanded. 'Jane hardly knows Ianthe.'

'No.' Ariadne shrugged. 'But seeing Ianthe must remind her of how close the two of you used to be.'

'Jane and me?'

'No.' Ariadne clicked her tongue. 'You and Ianthe. Come on, Demetri. I know the child she had was yours.'

'You don't know anything of the kind.' Demetri spoke through his teeth. 'In any case, I'd prefer not to talk about it. To you or anyone else.'

'Oh, I see.' Ariadne's dark brows lifted in amusement. 'That's what you and Jane were arguing about, was it?' She gave a snort of satisfaction. 'I can imagine how pleasant that would be.'

Demetri was tempted to say she didn't know what she was talking about, but it was easier to let her believe that he and Jane had been arguing rather than have her speculate on what else they might have been doing. *Theos,* he thought incredulously. Had he really made love to Jane in full view of the library windows? What did she do to him to make him care so little about who might see them? And when was this mad infatuation going to end?

'Your mother will be glad to see the back of her,' Ariadne was continuing, unaware that she no longer had his undivided attention. 'And I think even Leo is beginning to wish he'd never invited her here.'

Demetri doubted that. Remembering the way his father had treated Jane that afternoon, he'd been left in no doubt that the old man was very fond of her. Too fond, perhaps, if he expected his son to divorce her and marry someone else.

A twinge of awareness made him turn towards the door just in time to see his father going to greet the woman in question. This evening Jane was wearing narrow-legged silk trousers and a wide-necked silk sweater, both in black, that accentuated the intense fairness of her skin.

The sweater had been designed to slip off one or both shoulders, revealing that its owner wasn't wearing a bra. And Demetri found himself remembering the paleness of her breasts against his hands, the rosy peaks that had tasted so sweet just a couple of hours ago...

The memory caused him to harden immediately and he wished he were wearing a jacket to hide the sudden constriction of his trousers. He consoled himself with the assurance that it was fairly dark in the orangery with only scattered lanterns to provide illumination. Besides, by the time his father was willing to relinquish her undivided attention and brought Jane to join the rest of the family he had himself in control again.

'Why don't you get your wife a drink, Demetri?' his father suggested half maliciously and, although Demetri resented the familiarity, at least it gave him a reason to tear his eyes away from her.

'*Ouzo?*' he offered with what he considered was admirable tolerance, but Jane shook her head.

'Just orange juice, please,' she said, and he noticed she was avoiding his eyes, too. Then she turned to smile at his younger brother, who was lounging near by. 'Hey, Stefan, I forgot to thank you for taking me into Kalithi this morning. I do appreciate it.'

Stefan made some easy deprecatory comment, but Demetri could feel his hackles rising at the thought of Jane and his younger brother together. *Chesta,* Stefan wasn't supposed to care for the company of women. What the hell was he doing taking Jane into town? She could drive, couldn't she? Why didn't she just take herself?

In consequence, he made the mistake of looking at her when

he brought the glass of orange juice she'd requested and was rewarded by a decidedly provocative stare in return. 'Thanks,' she said. Then, as if she cared, 'Aren't you drinking this evening?'

Demetri's jaw tightened. 'I'm not in the mood,' he said, thinking privately that getting drunk might be precisely the right thing to do in his present state of mind. He arched a sardonic brow. 'So what did you buy in Kalithi? If I'd known you needed something, I could have arranged to bring it back from Athens.'

'Don't you know that a woman doesn't have to *need* anything to enjoy shopping?' Stefan interposed lightly. 'And you a married man and all.'

'Not for much longer,' put in Ariadne swiftly, not to be outdone. 'Isn't that right, darling?' She tucked her arm through Demetri's. 'You can't wait to be free.'

Demetri saw Jane press her lips together at this blatant piece of propaganda, but it was Stefan who answered for her. 'Then it's just as well I'm here to act as Jane's protector,' he remarked, slipping an arm about her waist and drawing her closer. 'We get along famously, don't we, darling?'

Jane's smile appeared again. 'Well, I must admit you've looked after me very well,' she agreed, and Demetri found himself wanting to push his fist into his brother's smug face.

'So why didn't you drive into town yourself?' he asked tersely, releasing himself from Ariadne's clinging hold. 'Your car's still in the garage, isn't it?'

'Oh, your mother's given the little Porsche to me, Demetri.' Ariadne tried to capture his arm again, but he shook her off. 'And Jane doesn't live here any more—'

'My mother had no right to give that car to anyone,' retorted Demetri furiously, and even Stefan looked surprised at his vehemence.

'It's not as if it was a new car,' he ventured, but one look at his brother's face made him bite his tongue.

'The car belongs to Jane,' insisted Demetri harshly, and now even Ariadne looked put out. '*Hristo,* why wasn't I consulted about this?'

Maria Souvakis had heard the raised voices and now she turned to look disapprovingly at her eldest son. 'For heaven's sake, Demetri, it's just a car, you know. Not the crown jewels!'

'And you couldn't wait to humiliate Jane, could you?' he snapped angrily. He turned to look at Ariadne. 'Don't tell me you went to pick her up from the ferry in the Porsche!'

'Of course I did.' It was obvious Ariadne didn't understand what all the fuss was about. 'As your mother says, it is only a car, Demetri.'

'It's Jane's car, not yours,' he returned bleakly, and now Jane knew she had to intervene before he said or did something he would definitely regret after she'd gone.

'I don't want it,' she said, meeting his incensed gaze with cool deliberation. 'Ariadne's welcome to it.' Her lips twisted. 'It goes with the territory.'

'If you think—'

Jane had no idea what Demetri might have said then had not his father called a halt to the argument. 'Dinner is served,' he told them all severely. 'Angelena has been trying to attract our attention for the past five minutes.' He gave Demetri a warning look. 'Shall we go in?'

The meal itself was something of an anticlimax. Grilled aubergines were followed by a Greek salad with *psaria* as the main course. The latter was a whole fish, baked with vegetables and served in a tomato, fennel and olive-oil sauce. It was very spicy, and probably delicious, but Jane, whose uncertain constitution hadn't been improved by the earlier altercation, found it all rather rich for her taste. She was grateful when the plates were removed and the dessert was served. The sweet flaky pastries were much more to her liking.

She didn't think anyone had noticed her lack of appetite, but when they left the table to go into the adjoining salon for coffee, she found Demetri at her side.

'Not hungry?' he asked in an undertone, and she permitted herself an impatient look in his direction.

'Are you surprised?'

'You're blaming me?'

'Well, I have to wonder what all that excessive outrage was about. You're going to marry Ariadne. Why shouldn't she have use of the car?'

Demetri's nostrils flared. 'It means that little to you?'

'Demetri, it's probably been standing idle for the last five years. Why not?'

'I've had it serviced regularly.'

'Good for you.'

Jane tried to sound indifferent, but his persistence was telling on her nerves. It was devastating to be this close to him physically, yet be aware of the gulf between them. Her mind was filled with what had happened that afternoon and she hated it that he seemed so totally removed now from that flagrant intimacy.

Demetri scowled. 'I suppose that's why you asked Stefan to take you into town,' he said harshly. 'I didn't know you and my brother were such good friends.'

'There's a lot of things you don't know about your brother,' retorted Jane shortly, and then wished she could control her impulsive tongue. She glanced quickly about the room and saw that the rest of the family were waiting for them to join them. 'We ought to sit down.'

'In a second.'

Fortunately the maid chose that moment to appear with the coffee-pot. And, although Jane was sure that both Maria and Ariadne were cursing the screen she created between them, it did allow Demetri the time to demand that she explain what she meant.

'It's not important,' she insisted, wishing she could retract her words. 'Look, your mother and Ariadne are watching us.'

'I want to know what you meant.' Demetri was insistent. 'What don't I know about Stefan? Don't tell me he's had a sudden epiphany; that he's decided he prefers women to men, after all?'

'Don't be so patronising.' Jane bitterly resented his attitude. 'Apparently Stefan and his partner have been together over six years.'

'I did know that.' Demetri lifted his shoulders. 'They have a house in Kalithi. Stefan's only spending so much time at the villa because of our father's illness.'

'That's right.' Jane was aware that all eyes were on them now. 'So there you are, then.'

Demetri's scowl deepened. 'You still haven't explained what you meant about Stefan. What don't I know that I should?'

'Oh, Demetri…' Jane sighed. 'We can't discuss it now.'

'Very well.' He inclined his head. 'I'll come to your room later. You can tell me then.'

Jane couldn't resist it. 'Won't you be with Ariadne?' she asked innocently, and was glad his family's presence prevented him from making the kind of response she deserved.

'After this afternoon?' he countered. 'I don't think so.'

'Oh, Demetri.' A sob of hysteria rose inside her and, to disguise her real feelings, she said recklessly, 'You must be getting old. When we were together, you used to have much more stamina.'

A phone rang somewhere in the house, but Demetri ignored it. He was staring at Jane with undisguised fury in his eyes, and she hastily moved around a sofa to seat herself beside his father. She knew it wasn't fair to provoke him when he couldn't answer back, but this time it seemed she'd gone too far, even for him.

'What the hell is that supposed to mean?' he demanded, coming to grip the back of the sofa behind her with white-knuckled fingers. 'Jane, I'm warning you—'

But whatever he'd been about to reveal was arrested by the sudden appearance of his father's housekeeper. Angelena halted in the doorway, and it was obvious from her flushed face and agitated hands that she had something momentous to report.

'My apologies, *kirie*,' she said, looking at Demetri, 'but you have a call from Athens.' She spoke in their own language but Jane could understand most of what she said. 'I explained that the family was at dinner, but Kirie Avensis insists on speaking to you personally. He says it is a matter of life and death!'

Demetri hesitated only a moment before turning and following the woman out of the room. His departure left an uncomfortable vacuum, which Leo filled with his usual aptitude.

'Avensis wouldn't ring unless it was something serious,' he averred half rising out of his seat and then sinking weakly back again. 'Maria, would you go and see what has happened? I would myself, but…'

He spread his hands, his meaning clear, and for once Maria didn't demur. '*Veveha*,' she said, putting down her coffee and getting to her feet. Of course. 'If you will all excuse me…'

Jane didn't know what to say, but Stefan had no such reservations. 'You could have asked me, Papa,' he said tersely. 'I am capable of carrying a message, you know.'

Leo shook his head, for once looking less than self-pos-
sessed. 'I didn't think, Stefan. I'm sorry. And of course you may
go and see if there is anything you can do.'

Stefan shook his head. 'Is there any point?'

'There may be.' His father's face had resumed its normal
composure. 'If you wouldn't mind.'

Stefan hesitated, but after a moment, he, too, got to his feet
and left the room, leaving Demetri's father with only Jane and
Ariadne for company.

'What do you think has happened?'

Ariadne voiced what they were all thinking, and Leo shook
his head again. 'Heaven knows,' he said, his fingers massaging
the head of his cane his only sign of agitation. 'One of the
tankers has had a collision, perhaps.'

Ariadne's lips parted. 'Is that serious?'

'It can be.' Leo forced a smile for their benefit. 'Let us
hope not, hmm?'

Jane wet her dry lips. 'Will—will Demetri be expected to
take charge?'

'Not necessarily,' replied the old man, before Ariadne could
tell her it was none of her business. He stared thoughtfully into
the middle distance. 'We have technical staff for that sort of
thing.' He paused. 'Of course, he may want to.'

'As you would,' said Jane understandingly, and Leo smiled
a little wistfully.

'You know me so well, my dear,' he said, patting her hand.
'Yes. I would love to be involved.'

Jane smiled and Ariadne huffed her annoyance, but just then
Maria came back into the room, adjusting her grave expression
when she saw her husband.

'Well?' Leo was impatient, and Maria sighed.

'There's been an accident,' she said, sinking down onto her

chair again and lifting her cooling cup of coffee. 'Ugh, where's Angelena? This is barely palatable—'

'What kind of accident?'

Leo wasn't about to be put off, and Maria put her cup down again. 'Demetri will handle it,' she said soothingly. 'Now, does anyone else—?'

'Maria!' Leo was glaring at her now, and, with a groan, she gave in.

'All right, all right. There's been an explosion. It's not clear yet how it happened, but the *Artemis* is holed just above the waterline.'

Leo swore then. 'Holed?' he echoed. 'Has anyone been hurt?'

'Avensis says one man has been reported injured, but other than that there are no casualties.'

'Thank God!' Leo was relieved. 'But the *Artemis*: is she in danger of sinking?'

'Possibly.' Maria leant towards him and rubbed his knee. 'It's nothing for you to worry about, Leo. As I said before, Demetri will handle it.'

Leo's frustration was evident. 'I assume he's flying back to Athens tonight?'

'He's arranging to have Costas pick him up as we speak,' agreed Maria reassuringly.

'Yes.' Leo nodded. 'The helicopter will allow him to fly straight out to the stricken vessel.'

'Oh, I shouldn't think so.' Now his wife looked dismayed and Jane felt a stab of anxiety deep inside her.

'Oh, yes.' Leo sounded definite. 'I know Demetri. He'll want to see for himself what is going on.'

'But—isn't that dangerous?'

It was Ariadne who spoke now, and Demetri's father gave her an impatient look. 'Life is dangerous,' he muttered.

'Haven't you discovered that yet?' His lips twisted. 'Jane has, haven't you, my dear?'

Jane didn't know what to say to this, but, as luck would have it, Stefan's return prevented any need for a reply.

'Has Mama told you what's happened, Papa?' he asked, leaning over the sofa where they were sitting. And at Leo's nod, 'I'm going with Demetri.' He arched mocking brows at Jane. 'Ain't that somethin'?'

Jane could only stare at him, and it was left to Maria to say anxiously, 'You can't both be going, Stefan. What about—what about your father? What about us? We may need you—'

'Let him go, Maria,' Leo interrupted her. 'Perhaps it's time I remembered I had three sons and not just two, eh, Stefan?' He paused. 'Just be careful, hmm?'

'I will, Papa.' Stefan gripped the old man's shoulder for a moment, and then, after bidding goodbye to the three women, he left the room again.

Maria looked near to tears and Jane herself felt decidedly shaken. The idea of the two men flying out to some oil tanker that had already experienced one explosion was terrifying. She wanted to go and find Demetri and tell him to take care, but she didn't have that right, and it was Ariadne who, after a moment, sprang to her feet and followed Stefan.

'Well!' Maria regarded Jane coldly. 'I hope you won't let this interfere with your plans for leaving.' She paused and ignoring her husband's obvious dismay, she continued, 'Leo tells me you want to leave as soon as possible. In the circumstances, I think that's entirely the right thing to do. Don't you?'

CHAPTER TWELVE

JANE parked her car outside her mother's house and then sat for a few moments wondering how she was going to handle this. She had to tell her mother she was going to have a baby. She couldn't take the risk that Olga might decide to make her suspicions public. Besides, she hadn't seen Mrs Lang for over a week and her mother deserved to know the truth.

Nevertheless, she wasn't looking forward to telling her who the baby's father was. After everything that had happened, the words *'I told you so'* were bound to make an appearance, and she had had enough of feeling like a pariah.

She'd left Kalithi the previous afternoon. Despite his reluctance to see her leave, Demetri's father had arranged for a helicopter to take her to Athens instead of Andros, where a first-class air ticket back to London had been waiting for her.

Jane had been very grateful, even if Demetri's mother hadn't approved. She'd slept badly the night before she left, not knowing where Demetri was or what he was doing. She couldn't deny the fears she had for both his and Stefan's safety, and if Maria hadn't made her position so impossible she might have stayed for a couple of days longer, just to assure herself that all was well.

In the event, Leo had assured her that he'd had word from

Demetri and that the news was good, but that wasn't the same as hearing it for herself. And Leo was going to be here, at the epicentre of all information, while back home in London, Jane would have to rely on the news channels for any word about the *Artemis*. And her husband.

Leo had accompanied her to the helicopter pad and said his goodbyes there, far from his wife's disapproving gaze. He'd thanked her again for coming, had expressed the wish that perhaps they'd meet again, and Jane had told him that, any time he wanted to see her, he had only to let her know.

Which had perhaps not been the wisest thing to say, in the circumstances, she acknowledged. How could she return to Kalithi when in a matter of weeks, possibly less, her condition was going to be obvious?

Still, it was unlikely to happen, she thought, feeling a twinge of despair at the thought of never seeing Demetri's father again. While they'd waited for the pilot to load her luggage, she'd got the feeling that there'd been so much more he'd wanted to say to her. She guessed he'd wanted to defend his son, but he hadn't been able to find the words.

Now, however, she had to put those days on Kalithi behind her. Her life was here, in London, and in a matter of days she would have to re-immerse herself in the business of buying and selling art and antiques. She owed it to Olga. She owed it to herself.

Mrs Lang opened the door as Jane walked up the garden path. 'Well, well!' she exclaimed, accepting her daughter's kiss before stepping back to allow her to enter the narrow hall of the townhouse. 'You didn't let me know you were back.'

'I got home last night,' said Jane, gesturing towards the kitchen at the back of the house. 'Shall we just sit in here?'

'No, we'll go upstairs.' Apart from the kitchen and a

second bathroom, all the living quarters were on the first and second floors. 'I've just made a pot of tea. You go ahead. I'll get the tray.'

Jane hesitated. 'Do you need any help?'

'I'm quite capable of carrying a tray upstairs,' retorted Mrs Lang tartly. 'I'll just be a minute.'

'OK.'

With a shrug, Jane climbed the stairs and entered her mother's living room, which overlooked the front of the house. Polished cabinets, occasional tables covered with an assortment of knick-knacks, and a neat three-piece suite. There was patterned broadloom on the floor, and lace curtains at the windows, and Jane couldn't help comparing it to the almost spartan appearance of her own apartment.

No wonder Mrs Lang didn't encourage Lucy and her brood to visit, she thought drily, trying to distract herself. Paul and Jessica couldn't help but create havoc here.

'Sit down, for goodness' sake!'

Her mother had appeared in the doorway and now she came bustling into the room to set the tray she was carrying on the low table in front of the hearth. It was warm enough outside not to need the gas fire today, but Jane could tell from the heat of the room that her mother had had the radiators on.

She seated herself in one of the armchairs, accepting the cup of tea her mother handed her. 'Thanks,' she said, grateful it wasn't coffee. She still couldn't face that on an empty stomach.

'So, there we are.' Mrs Lang perched on the sofa close by. 'This is cosy, isn't it?' Then she gave her daughter an appraising stare. 'But you're still looking peaky. Do I take it, it didn't go well?'

'It—went OK.' Jane was vague. 'Leo made me very welcome.'

'What about Demetri? Was he there?' Then she frowned. 'That reminds me: there was something about a tanker of his

catching fire. It was on the TV this morning. In the Mediterranean, I think. I don't suppose you know anything about that?'

Jane caught her breath. 'What did they say? Has—has
anyone been hurt?'

Her mother's frown deepened. 'If you mean was Demetri
mentioned, then no. Obviously, he wouldn't be. Men like him
don't get involved in minor incidents like explosions!'

'That's not true.' Jane couldn't let her get away with such a
statement. 'As a matter of fact, I did know about the accident.
It happened the night before I came home. Both Demetri and
his brother left for Athens immediately.'

'So is that why you came home?'

'No!' Jane was defensive. 'I'd already told Leo I was leaving
before it happened.'

'Oh, well…' Her mother sniffed and took a sip of her tea
before continuing, 'From what I heard, it wasn't much of a fire.
I suppose it made news because of the danger it could have
posed to other vessels.'

Jane nodded, not trusting herself to speak about it. It wasn't
the danger the tanker had posed to other vessels that had
alarmed her. Simply knowing her husband was involved had
been enough.

There was silence for a few moments and then Mrs Lang
said, 'And how was Mr Souvakis?'

'Oh—not too bad. Very thin, of course, and he doesn't have
a lot of strength. But his mind's still as active as ever.'

'Do you really think so?' Her mother sounded sceptical.

'What do you mean?'

'Well, he knows you and Demetri are getting a divorce,
doesn't he? So he must have known it wasn't the wisest thing,
inviting you out there. Surely he didn't think that bringing you
two together might cause a change of heart?'

'No.' Jane's hand trembled and she quickly replaced her cup and saucer on the tray. 'No, of course not.'

Her mother studied her thoughtfully. 'Did you?' she asked shrewdly and Jane felt the hot colour flood her cheeks.

'Did I what?'

'Hope that Demetri might change his mind?'

'No!' And it was true. When she'd left England, she hadn't hoped for any such thing. 'I—I left Demetri, Mum. Not the other way about.'

'Hmm.' Mrs Lang didn't look convinced, and Jane thought how impossible it was going to be to tell her about the baby now. 'So when are you going back to work?'

Jane expelled a weary breath. 'I don't know. Tomorrow. The day after. I'll speak to Olga.'

Her mother huffed. 'How nice to be so blasé about it.'

Jane moistened her lips. 'Well—I haven't been feeling all that good, actually.'

'Ah, I thought so.' Mrs Lang looked triumphant. 'I told you, you looked ill before you went away.'

'So you did.' Jane felt a sense of resignation.

'What is it, then? Have you been to see a doctor?'

'I went before I went away.'

'And you never said a word.' Her mother looked offended. 'I suppose you told that Ivanovitch woman what you were doing. You tell her everything. But I'm just your mother. You don't think I deserve to know what's going on—'

'I'm pregnant!'

Jane hadn't known what she was going to say until the words were spoken. She just knew she had to stop her mother making claims that simply weren't true. But afterwards, she just sat and stared at her with horrified eyes.

This time the silence was longer. Her mother put down her

own cup almost unthinkingly, swallowing several times as if her throat was suddenly very dry.

Then she said quietly, 'It's Demetri's, I suppose.'

Jane's shoulders sagged. 'Yes.'

'Oh, Jane!' She'd expected many things from her mother, but not sympathy. 'How long have you known? Is this why you really went out to Greece?'

'No!' Jane shook her head. 'Demetri doesn't know. He mustn't know. He's going to marry someone else.'

Her mother stared at her in disbelief. 'You're not serious!'

'I am.'

'But Jane, how can you let him marry someone else when you're expecting his child? You're not making any sense.'

Jane sighed. 'Mum, my being pregnant makes no difference to—to our feelings for one another.'

'I can't believe that.'

Jane bit her lip. 'What happened between Demetri and me was—a mistake. It should never have happened.'

'So why did it?'

'Oh, I don't know.' Jane was glad now she hadn't told her mother why Demetri wanted a divorce. 'I was—upset, and he—he—'

'Took advantage of you.'

'No, it wasn't like that.'

'So what was it like?'

Jane felt the colour enter her cheeks at the question. 'Mum, please. It happened. Can't you just accept that?'

Her mother looked at her closely. 'Don't you usually take precautions on—on occasions like this?'

'I don't usually have occasions like this,' replied Jane honestly. 'It was reckless, I know. But my period was due and—'

'And you thought you'd be OK?'

'Yes.'

'Dear lord!'

'I know. It was stupid. I realise that now.'

'I wonder how many young women have said that.' Mrs Lang got up from the sofa to pace restlessly about the room. 'And let's face it, he's just as much to blame.'

'He probably thought the same as you: that I'd take care of it.' She shrugged. 'It wasn't something we discussed at the time.'

'Even so—'

'Mum, this isn't Demetri's problem. It's mine. And I want to keep it that way.'

'Humph.' Her mother snorted. 'That man seems to make a habit of fathering children with women he shouldn't.' She hesitated. 'I assume you saw—what was her name?—Ianthe, while you were there.'

Jane bent her head. 'I saw her, yes.'

'And is that who he's going to marry?'

'No.' Jane hesitated. Then she said, 'Ianthe's baby died.'

Her mother's brows ascended. 'Really? How convenient!'

'It wasn't like that.' Jane had to defend the other girl. 'I believe she was very upset.'

'And was Demetri upset, too?'

'I think so.' She paused and then added, 'He still maintains the baby wasn't his.'

Mrs Lang stared at her. 'You don't believe him, do you?'

Jane made a helpless gesture. 'N...o.'

'That's something, anyway.' Her mother's face mirrored her relief. 'So what do you plan to do? Bring up the child yourself?'

'That's one option, obviously.'

'One option?' Mrs Lang frowned. 'What other options have you got? If you're not going to involve Demetri...' The words trailed away and, when she spoke again, there was real concern in her voice. 'You wouldn't consider not—not having the baby, would you? I mean,' she rushed on, 'there's no need for any hasty decisions. I'd be happy to do what I can and I know Lucy would help out.'

'Oh, Mum!' Jane felt her eyes fill with tears. 'The last thing you need is a baby here.'

'If it makes the difference between you having the baby and not, there's no argument,' retorted her mother firmly. She glanced about the cluttered room with impatient eyes. 'It's time I had a clear-out. Lucy's always telling me that. And don't forget, that baby's my grandchild, just as much as Paul and Jessica.'

'Oh, Mum,' said Jane chokily, getting up and enfolding the older woman in her arms. 'I do love you, you know.'

'I should hope you do.' Mrs Lang tried to sound indignant and didn't quite make it. 'Now drink your tea. Pregnant young women need to keep their strength up.'

CHAPTER THIRTEEN

DEMETRI was standing at the bedroom window of his house in Kalithi, staring out at the darkening ocean, when there was a tentative knock at his door.

Cursing, because he hadn't yet started to dress for dinner at the villa, he went to open it, hoping against hope that it wasn't Ariadne. He could do without another argument with her, he thought heavily. She couldn't understand why he hadn't been to her bed since seeing his estranged wife again. And God knew, he didn't have an answer for her.

But to his relief, it wasn't Ariadne. A manservant stood outside with the news that his father was waiting to see him. *His father?* Demetri didn't hesitate before following the man downstairs.

'Papa,' he said with some concern, entering the salon where the old man was reclining with evident relief on an ivory velvet sofa. 'Don't tell me you've driven here by yourself.'

'No, no.' Leo Souvakis regarded his eldest son with a mixture of affection and impatience. 'Micah brought me.' He paused. 'Though I have to say, I'm still capable of handling a motor vehicle.'

'If you say so.' Demetri slipped his hands into the pockets of his khaki shorts. But, although he adopted a conciliatory tone, he was well aware that his father's face showed the strain of walking unaided from the car into the house. 'Can I offer you a drink? Some wine, perhaps?'

Leo grimaced. 'Wine,' he muttered irritably.

'*Ouzo,* then.' Demetri walked across to the wet bar and returned a few moments later with an *ouzo* and water, the ice clinking pleasantly in the glass. 'Does that suit you better?'

'Much.' Leo took the glass and looked up at his son with a rueful expression on his face. 'You know your mother forbids me to drink this.' He took a taste, savouring the flavour of aniseed on his tongue. 'But I say, if I'm dying, why prolong the exercise?'

'You don't mean that.' Demetri dropped into the chair opposite his father, legs spread, clasped hands hanging between his knees. 'But I doubt if one rather weak drink is going to do you any harm.'

'Weak, eh?' Leo raised the glass to look into it, and then, seeing his son's face, he smiled. 'OK, I know I should be grateful. And I am. But every now and then…'

Demetri nodded. And then, because he knew the old man wouldn't have come here if he didn't have something on his mind, he said, 'So—what brings you here? Is something wrong?'

'You tell me.' Leo took another sip of the *ouzo,* regarding his son over the rim of the glass. 'Hmm, this is delicious, weak or otherwise.'

Demetri frowned, not diverted by the compliment. 'What is it you want me to tell you?'

'Oh, come on.' His father waited and, when his son didn't speak, he went on, 'Ariadne thinks you've changed your mind about getting married again. Or so she's informed your mother.'

Demetri felt the hot colour invade his face. 'Ariadne should keep her opinions to herself.'

'So it's not true?'

'That I've changed my mind about marrying her?' Demetri was defensive. 'I haven't said anything like that.'

'Or *done* anything?' suggested his father drily. 'How shall I put it? Ariadne is feeling—neglected, no?'

Demetri pushed himself to his feet. 'For pity's sake, what has she been saying?'

'I think I do not need to answer that, Demetri.'

His son groaned. 'God!'

'And if you're about to say it's got nothing to do with me, don't!' Leo looked up at him with shrewd eyes. 'Just answer me this: have you seen Jane since she went back to England?'

Demetri's jaw dropped. 'You know I haven't.'

'Do I?'

'You should. I've spent the last three weeks in Athens, dealing with the fallout from the explosion on the *Artemis*, if you'll excuse the pun. When have I had time to go to England?'

'And she hasn't visited you in Athens?'

'Who? Jane?' Demetri snorted. 'Of course not.'

'Well, if you tell me you haven't seen her, I have to believe you.' Leo took another mouthful of the *ouzo*. 'But tell me something else: have you wanted to?'

'Wanted to what?'

'See her, Demetri? See Jane? It's a simple enough question.'

Demetri swore then, pushing the chair he'd been occupying aside and striding across to the bar. Snatching up a bottle of single malt, he poured himself a stiff whisky, swallowing half of it in a gulp before turning to look at his father again.

'OK,' he said at last, raking an impatient hand over his scalp. 'Let's cut to the chase, shall we? What do you want me to say, Pa? Just tell me what you want to hear and I'll say it. That way I think we'll save a hell of a lot of time.'

Leo's mouth tightened. 'There's no need for this, Demetri. I asked you a simple question.'

'Yeah, right.'

'And I must assume from your reluctance to give me a simple answer that my concerns are justified.'

'No. No, they're not.' Demetri spoke heatedly. 'I admit, I haven't given Ariadne the attention she deserves in recent weeks, but as soon as the divorce is finalised, I'll be free to make up for it. You'll see.'

His father didn't look convinced. 'So seeing Jane again didn't make any difference to your feelings for Ariadne?'

'No!'

Leo sighed. 'Why don't I believe you?'

'Pa, how ever I feel—and I'm not saying I feel anything—Jane isn't interested in me. You know that.' He hesitated and, when his father's expression didn't change, he said doggedly, 'OK. There's a physical attraction between us. There always has been. But she's never going to forgive me for what she thinks I did to Ianthe. And nothing's going to alter that, so—'

'You could tell her the truth.'

'You think she'd believe me? She never has before.'

'That's because you've always kept something back.'

'Yes, and if she'd loved me she'd have believed me, whatever I said.'

'Oh, Demetri, don't be such a prig! How would you have felt if you'd discovered Jane was expecting a child and another man maintained he was the father?'

Demetri looked down into his glass. 'I hope I'd have given her the benefit of the doubt.'

'How gallant!' Leo was scornful. 'Demetri, I know you. You'd have kicked her out and then you'd have torn the other man apart.'

Demetri grunted. 'That's some opinion you have of me, Pa.' He paused. 'So what are you saying? That I shouldn't divorce Jane, after all?' He frowned. 'I thought you were fond of Ariadne.'

'I am fond of Ariadne.' His father was impatient. 'And when you were younger, I used to think she'd make you a good wife.' He shrugged. 'But it never happened. 'You met Jane, and I knew from the moment I saw you two together that she was the one love of your life.'

Demetri's jaw hardened. 'That was pretty fanciful, wasn't it? We didn't even like one another when we first met.'

'You may not have liked one another, but you certainly struck sparks off one another,' remarked Leo reflectively. 'You were so sure when you walked into the gallery that she was only stringing me a line.'

'Mmm.'

Demetri didn't want to remember how it had been, but he couldn't help the memories from flooding back. Finding his father discussing art with a girl who didn't look old enough to have left school, let alone be the possessor of an arts degree, had infuriated him.

Though he'd soon realised that his fury was directed towards his father as much as anyone else. Had he been jealous? He supposed he had. He'd certainly resented the fact that the old man had apparently found himself such a young and sexy companion. And when Leo had suggested that she deliver the delicate bronze he'd chosen to his hotel herself, Demetri had swiftly intervened.

He'd offered to collect the sculpture instead. There was no need for Ms Lang to put herself out, he'd said. He'd be passing the gallery again before he left England and he'd be happy to attend to the delivery personally.

Of course, she'd protested that it was no trouble, no trouble at all, and Demetri had been sure that that old harridan, Olga Ivanovitch, had been listening to their conversation and had had her own opinion of why he should want to cut his father out.

But, in the event, it was his father who'd made the decision. Smiling a little smugly, he'd agreed that that was probably the best solution, and consequently, a few days later, Demetri had called at the gallery to collect the purchase…

The gallery had appeared to be on the point of closing, he remembered. Long canvas shades had been drawn down and, when he'd opened the door, he'd half suspected the place was deserted. But then Jane had appeared from the office at the back of the showroom, and his pheromones had kicked into overdrive.

'I'm afraid we're closed—' she was beginning, when she recognised him. 'Oh, it's you!'

'*Neh,* me,' he agreed a little tersely. 'You were expecting me, I think. Did not my assistant warn you I was coming?'

'Warn me?' Green eyes sparkled and a look of amusement crossed her face. 'Are you a dangerous man, Mr Souvakis?'

'No, just an impatient one.' Demetri scowled, annoyed that she'd already put him on the defensive. 'The sculpture—it is ready?'

Her sigh was telling and he felt like an oaf for being so ill-mannered. 'It's ready,' she conceded, gesturing towards the office behind her. 'It's through here. If you'd like to come with me, I'll get your receipt.'

'*Efkaristo.*'

He was unnecessarily brusque and he didn't know why. It wasn't as if she'd been particularly flippant. He knew she'd only been trying to be friendly, and he couldn't understand what it was about her that was causing him to behave so badly.

The office was small, just a couple of filing cabinets against the far wall, a computer and a printer, and a desk that was presently covered with black plastic bags.

'Sorry about this,' she said, indicating the bags. 'I've been having a clear-out and I haven't had time to dump these out the back yet.' She shoved some papers off a chair. 'Why don't you sit down? While I try and locate that receipt.'

Demetri paused in the doorway. She was obviously run off her feet and he wasn't making life any easier for her by treating her like an inferior.

Coming to an impulsive decision, he came into the room and hefted half a dozen of the plastic bags. 'Why don't you show me where you want these putting and then you'll have room to move around, *neh?*'

Her eyes widened in surprise and, when she smiled, he was struck by her sudden beauty. He'd already acknowledged that she was an attractive young woman, but, with faint colour giving her cheeks a dusky glow and her mouth with its fuller lower lip parted to reveal the pink tip of her tongue, she was stunning.

'Oh—that's very kind of you,' she began. 'But those bags are dusty. You might stain your suit.'

'Don't worry about it, *thespinis,*' he said, oblivious to the fact that his suit was pale grey and an Armani. 'Out the back, you said?'

'Yes.'

She stared at him for a moment longer, and then, apparently deciding he meant what he said, she came round the desk again and brushed past him on her way to the door.

It was just the briefest of contacts, but he was aware of her in a way he'd never been aware of a woman before. The slenderness of her body enchanted him and, in the somewhat humid confines of the office, her womanly scent caused a sharp rush of heat to his groin.

But then she was past him and out in the narrow passageway that led to the back of the building. She opened the door and he saw other bags already stacked outside.

'Just leave them here,' she said, stepping out of the way so he could drop his burden. 'They'll be collected later.' She smiled again. 'Thanks. I do appreciate it.'

'*Efkaristisi mou,*' he said. And when she looked blank, he translated, 'My pleasure.'

Jane waited until he'd passed through the door again, before shutting and locking it. 'Well, you must be very strong,' she murmured, and for the first time she made him smile.

'*Ineh poli evyeniko,*' he told her drily. 'You're very kind. I don't often get compliments like that.'

He could have added that he couldn't remember the last time he'd done any manual labour, but that would have sounded like boasting. Instead, he contented himself with brushing a hand down the front of his suit, pulling a wry face at the smear of dirt that resisted all his efforts to remove it.

'I'm sure you get plenty of compliments,' she retorted, apparently not convinced by his denial, going ahead of him along the hall, giving him an uninterrupted view of her back.

Firm shoulders, a narrow waist, a slim yet shapely rear. And long legs, shown to advantage in the short-skirted mini-dress she was wearing. Her hair, which she'd had secured in a ponytail the first time he'd seen her, now hung in honey-streaked waves to her shoulder blades, and he knew a sudden urge to grab a handful and bury his face in its silky mass.

Forcing such thoughts aside, he found himself wondering if she had a date with some man this evening. Was that why she was wearing a dress that was so obviously unsuitable for the job she was doing? The last time he'd seen her, she'd been severely attired in a white blouse and a tailored skirt, and, although he'd noticed her legs, he couldn't remember seeing so much of them...

Dammit!

Dragging his thoughts out of the gutter, he saw they were back at the office and Jane was already opening drawers in the desk. 'It has to be here somewhere,' she was muttering to herself, and, pausing in the doorway, Demetri treated himself to the pleasure of just watching her. She was so lovely, so feminine, and it was many weeks since he'd had a woman in his bed.

Once again, he forced his eyes away from her. For heaven's sake, he chided himself, what was wrong with him? His father wasn't here now, so he couldn't excuse his behaviour on the grounds of provoking the old man. And it wasn't as if there was any shortage of women in his life. Being a wealthy man in his own right, and Leonides Souvakis' heir, opened many bedroom doors.

Of course, Jane was totally unaware of what he was thinking. She had no idea that images of her, spread-eagled beneath him, were occupying his thoughts. Thankfully, she couldn't read his mind or she wouldn't be bending over her desk like that, giving him a tantalising glimpse of her small, but very provocative, breasts.

'Where on earth can it be?' she was asking, but she was talking to herself, not to him. She pulled open the drawers again, one after the other, riffling through their contents with unflattering haste. It was obvious she wanted rid of him and that was a novelty in itself. 'It's got to be here somewhere. Olga gave it to me before she left. Just after—just after that person from your office phoned. I was sure I'd put it—ouch!'

Her cry of pain interrupted her and Demetri, who was still standing in the doorway, now came swiftly round the desk to her side. 'What have you done?'

There was blood on her finger and, without even thinking about it, he brought her hand to his mouth. He'd licked the wound clean before he realised she was gazing up at him with startled eyes, and he knew it was far too late to pretend ignorance of how his action might be interpreted.

'*Signomi,*' he said at once. 'I'm sorry. I shouldn't have done that.'

'No, you shouldn't.' She was indignant and it was painfully apparent that she didn't welcome the intimacy. 'It was stupid of me to make a fuss. It's only a paper cut.' She drew her fingers away and examined the injury for herself. 'I'll put a plaster on it and it'll be fine.'

Demetri inclined his head, stepping back to allow her to take what was apparently her handbag from a drawer of the filing cabinet and search it for plasters. A film of moisture appeared on her upper lip as she did so and he wondered if she was quite as indifferent to him as she'd have him believe.

Whatever, he chided himself, he hadn't come here to start an affair with the woman. He'd only been trying to protect his father's interests, that was all.

But that was such a lie! He had wanted to see her again. He might as well admit it. And that was when he'd thought she was a buttoned-up art student. Now, in feminine clothes and with an attitude he could cut with a knife, she was absolutely fascinating.

She'd found a plaster and, after discovering he was still watching her, she offered him a tight smile. 'I'm always getting paper cuts,' she said, peeling off the protective covering and attempting to apply the plaster to her finger. 'I sometimes think I should wear rubber gloves.'

'And hide those pretty hands?' Demetri shook his head and then, risking another rebuke, he took the plaster from her. '*Etho,* let me,' he said softly, using both hands to accomplish his task. He smoothed the plaster around her finger and smiled in satisfaction. '*Poli kalitera.* Much better, no?'

Jane looked down at their joined hands and then gave a

helpless little shrug. 'Yes. Thank you.' She blew out a nervous breath. 'Now, if you'll let me go, I'll get your package.'

Demetri's eyes held hers for a long, loaded moment before his hand fell to his side. 'If that's what you want, of course.'

Her lips parted. 'It's what you want, isn't it?'

Demetri's lips twisted. 'Oh, you have no idea what I want, Ms Lang.'

She sucked in a breath. Then, as if waking from a dream, she whirled away, shoving her bag into the filing cabinet and turning quickly back to the desk.

CHAPTER FOURTEEN

BUT almost against her will it seemed, her eyes were drawn back to his. 'What do you want, Mr Souvakis?' she asked a faint tremor evident in her voice. 'If you're looking for a one-night stand, I should tell you: I don't sleep around.'

Demetri couldn't help but admire her candour even if an involuntary exclamation spilled from his lips at her words. 'Nor do I, *thespinis,*' he said with mild indignation. 'And have I asked you to sleep with me? Forgive me, I do not recall making any such request.'

Her face flamed with hot colour now and he regretted being so blunt. Besides, if he was honest he'd admit that he had played with the idea of seducing her. More than played with the idea, dammit. He'd actually been anticipating it. That was really why he resented her perception.

'So—so long as we understand one another, Mr Souvakis,' she murmured primly, returning her gaze to her task, and Demetri knew an almost uncontrollable urge to prove to her how wrong she was.

But he made no response and after a few moments she apparently located the missing receipt. 'I knew I had it!' she exclaimed triumphantly, and Demetri, who wasn't at all interested in documentation that his assistant could collect just as easily, gave a mocking smile.

'I'll try and contain my excitement,' he remarked drily, and when she looked at him he saw her flush had deepened.

'It may not be important to you, Mr Souvakis,' she declared stiffly. 'But it's my job to see that each transaction is satisfactorily concluded. I'm sure your father wouldn't be happy without the necessary certificate of provenance for the sculpture.'

Demetri shrugged. 'I'm sure you're correct, Ms Lang. My father cares about such things, as you say.' He paused. 'Regrettably, I do not.'

'Then why did you offer to come and collect it?' she asked helplessly, and Demetri could no longer resist the urge to touch her.

'Because I wanted to see you again,' he admitted, acknowledging something that up till then he would have denied, vigorously. He ran his knuckles over the downy heat of her cheek. '*Apalos*. So soft.'

'But you said—' She jerked her face aside but she didn't move away. 'You said you didn't want to sleep with me.'

Demetri arched a lazy brow. 'Men and women do many other things besides sleep together, *thespinis*. Haven't you ever had a boyfriend?'

Her lips pursed. 'Of course I've had boyfriends.' She gave him a scornful look. 'I hope you're not going to pretend you want to be my boyfriend!'

'No.' He conceded the point. Then he grimaced. 'I do not consider myself a *boy* any longer.'

'So what are you saying?'

'Must I spell it out for you? I'd like to get to know you better. And then, if we find we are compatible, perhaps we will sleep together. Who knows?'

'I knew it!' She put some space between them and then

turned to face him with scornful eyes. 'That's all you're really interested in, isn't it? Why don't you admit it?'

'Because it's not true,' he retorted, his own anger sparking, and was amazed to find he meant it. 'Hell, do I seem like such a womaniser to you?'

'I don't know. I don't know you, Mr Souvakis.'

'Precisely. So before you start throwing insults around, perhaps you should give yourself a chance to find out.'

'I don't want to find out!' she exclaimed childishly, and Demetri felt his control slipping dangerously low.

'Are you sure about that?' he demanded, and, giving in to his baser instincts, he caught her wrist and hauled her against him. His arm wrapped around her waist and he looked down into her startled face with an unfathomable gaze. 'Are you really sure?'

For a moment she couldn't look away, but then, with a struggle, she managed to get a hand between them. Her fingers pressed insistently against his chest. 'Let go of me!'

'And if I don't?' Her slim bare legs duelling with his were a constant distraction. 'What will you do? You're alone here. You've virtually admitted as much.'

Her eyes darkened. 'Are you threatening me, Mr Souvakis?'

'No!' He was disgusted with himself for creating this situation. '*Poli kala.*' He released her. 'I suggest you give me the sculpture and I'll leave. As that seems to be what you want.'

'Yes.'

She agreed, though he thought there was a faint lack of conviction in her tone. Or perhaps that was just wishful thinking. She'd certainly not given him any reason to believe she was having second thoughts.

The parcel containing the sculpture proved to be bigger than he'd expected. 'It's all the packing,' she said ruefully, seeing his surprise. 'Can you manage?'

Demetri's lips twisted. 'Why? Are you offering to help me?'

Jane hesitated. 'If you wanted me to. I'm used to handling awkward packages.'

'And awkward customers, too,' he commented drily, and she linked her hands together at her waist and gazed at him with troubled eyes.

'I've offended you, haven't I?'

'*Hristo!*' Demetri swore. 'Why should it matter to you if I'm offended? You'll probably never see me again.'

'But I wouldn't like your father to think I'd been rude to his son.'

'Oh, right.' Demetri gave a short laugh. 'That's what all this is about, is it? You're afraid my father will take his custom elsewhere.'

Her shoulders lifted. 'I'm just an employee here, Mr Souvakis.'

'Well, don't worry.' Demetri grunted. 'My father would probably applaud your success in putting me in my place. He thinks I'm far too—what would you say?—arrogant as it is.'

Her lips twitched. 'You are.'

Demetri grimaced. 'Your humility didn't last long.'

She smiled. 'Perhaps that's because I like you better this way.'

'Making a fool of myself, you mean?'

She caught her breath. 'You couldn't make a fool of yourself if you tried.'

'No?'

'No.'

'Not even if I told you I wanted to kiss you right this minute?'

She stepped back from him. 'You wouldn't.'

Demetri shook his head and bent to pick up the box containing the sculpture. 'No, I guess this is where we go our separate ways.' He straightened, pulling a face at the weight of the package. 'D'you want to open the door for me? My car's just outside.'

'Oh—sure.' She hurried ahead of him through the darkened gallery and pulled open the glass door. 'You'll probably find a parking ticket on your windscreen. The attendants are pretty sharp around here.'

'I'll survive,' he remarked drily, turning sideways to negotiate the door and going down the steps to where a huge four-wheel-drive vehicle was parked at the kerb. 'Yeah, you're right.'

'Oh…' Jane followed him down the steps, going round the car to pull the pink slip from under the wipers. She looked at it impatiently. 'I'll ask Olga to handle this.'

Demetri had the boot open now and was pushing the heavy box inside, but he turned to say, 'Forget it. I will.'

'But you can't—'

'Want to bet?'

Jane bit her lip. 'This might not have happened if you hadn't helped me to carry those bags out and then—and then me cutting my finger…' She shook her head as he slammed the boot closed and came round the car to where she was standing. 'It's really my fault.'

'*Eh, then pirazi.* It doesn't matter.' He snatched the slip of paper out of her hand, screwed it up and tossed it into the nearest refuse bin. '*Oristeh.* I've dealt with it.'

She looked amazed. 'Is that what you do with all your parking tickets?'

'No. Only those I get by helping beautiful women,' he said mockingly, making her laugh. 'Don't worry about it.'

'You're—so—so—'

'Bad?' he suggested, checking the boot was locked and coming back to her. 'Yes, I know.'

'I wasn't going to say that,' she protested. 'I don't think you're bad!'

'But you don't like me.'

A look of confusion crossed her face and he realised she wasn't half as confident as she'd like to appear. And it would be so easy to take advantage of her here. The tree-lined avenue where the gallery was situated was quiet and shady, the sun rapidly sinking behind the buildings across the street.

But that wasn't going to happen. He wasn't about to destroy the fragile understanding that seemed to be developing between them and he was totally stunned when she suddenly put her hands on his shoulders and reached up to brush her mouth against his. 'I didn't say I didn't like you,' she said huskily, and Demetri could only slump back against the side of the car, too astonished to do anything else.

The kiss was brief, almost impersonal, but he knew she'd shocked herself, too. A look of consternation crossed her face and, although she hadn't yet turned to seek refuge in the gallery, he knew it was only a matter of time before she did so. Her eyes sought his in mute denial of what had just happened and Demetri arched an enquiring brow.

'I guess I did something right at last,' he remarked lazily, and she took a shuddering breath.

'I don't know what came over me,' she murmured and Demetri knew a kinder man might allow her to get away with that.

But he'd spent the last hour in a state of semi-arousal and her innocent appeal was the last straw. What did she think he was made of? Ice? Leaning towards her, he put his hands on her hips and pulled her against him. 'I do,' he told her, his voice thickening. 'Let me show you.'

He didn't give her time to protest. He kissed her as he'd been wanting to kiss her ever since he'd entered the gallery and seen her again. With one hand behind her head, he took possession of her lips, rubbing his mouth back and forward until the sweet scent of her breath showed her mouth was open and vulnerable.

To begin with, she tried to retain some control by bracing herself with a hand on the car at either side of him. But when he deepened the kiss, pushing his tongue deep into her mouth, she couldn't hold out any longer. With a little moan of acquiescence, she gave in. She sank against him, and he was sure she must be able to feel his erection pressing against her belly.

It was heaven and it was hell: heaven, because he wanted her so badly; hell, because, however eager she might be, he couldn't take her here in the street. Yet the urge to push her skirt up to her hips and bury himself in her soft heat was compelling, and, when she put a hand between them to stroke his throbbing arousal, he uttered an anguished groan.

'*Theos,*' he choked, aware that, despite the fairly explicit images he'd entertained himself with earlier, nothing had prepared him for this reality. It was just as well she was leaning against him, he thought. Her fingers were driving him insane.

But that was just part of it. The feel of her, the taste of her, the sensual delight in feeling her nipples peaking against his chest. She was so fiery, so responsive. All he could think about was getting naked with her, flesh against flesh, skin against skin.

That wasn't going to happen. No matter how adventurous she was out here, there was always the knowledge of the occasional passer-by to rescue her should it be necessary. Inviting her to accompany him back to an hotel room, however, was another matter entirely.

Yet once again it was Jane who amazed him. 'Let's go back inside,' she invited breathlessly. 'It's time I closed the gallery and Olga's got a half-decent sofa in her office…'

That had been the start of their affair, recalled Demetri grimly. And, despite her impulsive behaviour, he'd soon discovered that Jane had only slept with one other man. She was still hopelessly naïve, but hopelessly eager, deliciously inexperienced. She'd never had a true orgasm before, she'd confessed. Until then she'd believed that having sex was vastly overrated.

He'd soon corrected that error, he remembered a little smugly. The first time they'd made love—the first time he'd thrust into her hot, tight sheath—he'd had to silence her cries with his mouth. It had been one hell of an experience for both of them and he hadn't been able to wait before seeing her again.

Of course, there'd been obstacles. Both her mother and his hadn't approved. His own mother had been appalled when he'd told her he was falling in love with an English girl, and Jane's mother had never trusted him from the start.

But they'd overcome all objections, and, although he'd known Jane had been bewildered at the speed with which he'd made her his wife, she'd been too much in love with him to care. They'd honeymooned in the Caribbean, he reminisced painfully; long days and even longer nights on their own island, where all they'd done was eat, swim and make love. There hadn't been a lot of sleeping, he recalled, the memory as sharp and raw as ever. Dear God, how he'd loved her. He caught a breath. How he loved her still.

'Are you all right, Demetri?'

It was his father who spoke and Demetri realised he'd been staring out into the darkness beyond his windows for heaven knew how long. He'd been so lost in thought he'd forgotten that his father was waiting for him to make some response.

'I'm sorry,' he said, turning from the windows and pouring himself another drink. He needed the fortification, he thought, if he was going to get through this. 'I was just thinking, that's all.'

'About Jane?'

Demetri gazed at the older man with exasperated eyes. 'Can't I think about anything else?'

'I don't know. Can you?'

Demetri scowled. 'Leave it, Pa. If we go on with this, we're going to have words, and I don't want that.'

'Why? Because you think I can't be told the truth?' His father stared at him. 'Be honest, Demetri, why did you agree to divorce Jane and marry Ariadne? Was it only because you thought I was so desperate for a grandchild?'

Demetri sighed. 'Pa—'

'Answer me, dammit!'

'All right.' Demetri blew out a weary breath. 'All right. Maybe that was—a factor.'

'Your mother told you that, I suppose. Just as she told me that you and Ariadne had fallen in love, and Stefan that I would never recognise any child he and Phillippe might have as my own flesh and blood.'

'Stefan and Phillippe?'

'Yes.' Leo shook his head and held out his empty glass. 'Get me another drink, Demetri. You and I have things to say to one another, whether your mother likes it or not.'

CHAPTER FIFTEEN

JANE was alone in the gallery when Alex Hunter walked through the door.

For a moment she thought it was Demetri, and her heart leapt. She'd heard nothing from him since her return from Greece six weeks ago, and, although she'd told herself that was to be expected, she couldn't help wishing it wasn't so. She'd even tried to ring the villa on Kalithi, to assure herself he hadn't been hurt, but she'd never been able to get past Angelena.

She was sure Demetri's mother must have ordered the housekeeper to block her calls and, after a couple of knockbacks, Jane had given up. Besides, there'd been no further coverage in the Press, so she could only assume that both Demetri and his brother had returned from the fire unscathed.

She hadn't seen Alex since her return either, and that had been her decision. But, although she'd told him she didn't want to see him again, he wouldn't take no for an answer.

Lately, he'd accused her of making a fool of him, for letting him think they had a future together, when all she'd really wanted was to make her husband jealous. Which was patently untrue. But Jane had decided that, if that was what he wanted to believe, it might be for the best anyway.

If she'd expected he'd stop calling her, she'd been disappointed, however. Her hopes that their relationship might go back to the way it had been when he'd first come to the gallery to audit Olga's books seemed doomed to failure. Now he was here. He had no appointment with Olga today, so he couldn't make that his excuse. In fact, her employer had left over an hour ago, complaining of a headache and saying she was going home to go to bed.

She wished she'd taken Olga's advice and closed the gallery early. 'You work too hard for a woman in your condition,' Olga had said, regarding the distinct swell of Jane's stomach with a reproving eye. Ever since she'd learned her assistant was pregnant, she'd been wonderfully supportive. Even if, like Jane's mother, she didn't approve of her keeping the news of the baby from the father.

Jane had intended to close the gallery, as Olga had suggested. But then the crates that had arrived that morning had caught her eye. The carrier had opened the crates and left them to be catalogued, and Jane had decided to spend another hour with the canvases before closing up.

Now she wished she hadn't. She wasn't afraid of Alex, but she would have preferred to meet him in a more public place. If only Olga were still here, she thought, glad she was carrying a clipboard. It enabled her to use it as a shield to hide her condition from him.

The knowledge that she was letting him intimidate her in this way angered her. Which was why, when she spoke, there was a slight edge to her voice. 'Hello, Alex,' she said, mentally squaring her shoulders. 'If you've come to see Olga, she's—' she crossed her fingers '—she's gone out for a few minutes.'

Alex gave a careless shrug of his shoulders. He was a fairly tall man, but lean, his angular build not doing justice to his navy linen jacket. 'It doesn't matter,' he said. 'It wasn't Olga that I wanted to see.'

Jane suppressed a groan. 'Oh, Alex—'

'I know. You've told me that you don't want to see me again—'

'I didn't say that, exactly,' murmured Jane, thinking of the gallery. 'I just don't think we should go out together any more. I thought we were friends, but obviously you wanted something else.'

'You did, too, before you went to see your ex-husband,' said Alex at once and Jane sighed.

'He's not my ex-husband yet,' she corrected him, not really knowing why she bothered. Just because she'd heard no more from Demetri's solicitors didn't mean the divorce wasn't going ahead. 'And that's not true, Alex. My relationship with Demetri hasn't changed.'

Alex regarded her disbelievingly. 'So why can't we continue seeing one another? I thought you liked me. I thought we had some good times together.'

'We did.' Jane could so do without this. She wrapped her arms about herself over the clipboard. 'It's just—well, I don't think it's fair to you to go on pretending that we'll ever be more than friends.'

Alex scowled. 'It apparently didn't matter to you before.'

'That was before you told me how you felt,' Jane reminded him unhappily. The clipboard was digging into her stomach and she adjusted it before continuing, 'I never intended to hurt you, Alex. Honestly.'

'But you have.' Alex shifted restlessly, and then, totally without warning, he snatched the clipboard out of her grasp. 'For goodness' sake,' he exclaimed, 'can't you put that damn thing down while we're talking?'

He flung the offending item onto the floor and it skittered away across the polished boards. He watched it go and so did Jane, though for different reasons. Alex looked as if he was trying to control his temper, whereas Jane just felt totally exposed now.

She was wearing linen trousers and a rose-patterned smock top that fastened beneath her breasts and flared over her waistband. It was the kind of outfit lots of young women wore. It didn't necessarily spell pregnancy. But the swell of her stomach did. She'd always been so slender before and the distinct bulge was unmistakable.

It apparently was to Alex. His eyes seemed riveted to it. Jane was embarrassed. This was the last thing she needed. She wished he would just go and leave her alone.

'Are you pregnant?' he asked at last, in a dazed voice. Then, with some bitterness, 'I bet Demetri knows about this!'

'He doesn't.' Anger came to Jane's rescue. Walking swiftly across the floor, she bent and picked up the clipboard. 'In any case, it's nothing to do with you, Alex. I think you'd better go.'

Alex's brow furrowed. 'You haven't told Demetri he's going to be a father?'

'Did I say this baby was Demetri's?'

'No. But I just assumed—'

'You assume a lot of things,' said Jane tersely. 'Why don't you do as I asked you and leave?'

He didn't move. 'What are you going to do?'

'Excuse me?' Jane couldn't believe his audacity. 'I think that's my business, don't you?'

'Well, are you going to marry the baby's father? Whatever you say, it is Demetri's, isn't it?'

Jane gasped. 'You have no right to say that.'

'I assume that means you're not. Getting married again, I mean.'

'I am married and, as I said before, you assume too many things. Now, please, I want to close the gallery. I'd like you to go.'

Alex moved a little nearer. 'Don't be like that, Jane. I only want to help you.' He paused. 'I care about you. I still do, even if you have betrayed me with someone else.'

'I did not betray you.' Jane wished desperately that someone would come and interrupt them. 'Alex, this is silly. I'm sorry if you think I've misled you. But talking about it isn't going to change anything.'

'It could.' He was just a few feet away now. 'You could marry me instead. I think I'd make a good father. And a child needs a father, don't you agree?'

Jane was horrified. 'But I don't love you, Alex.'

'I know that.'

'Then—'

'I love you.'

'No—'

'I always have. Right from the first time I came here to do Mrs Ivanovitch's accounts. She knew how I felt. She was the one who told me what a pig your husband had been to you. She said I should just be patient. That sooner or later you'd realise I was nothing like him.'

Oh, Olga!

Jane closed her eyes for a moment, wishing her employer were there. Obviously the conversation Alex was talking about had taken place some time ago. If only Olga had been here, she could have explained that to him.

'I'm sorry,' she said again. 'I—I appreciate the compliment, Alex, I really do, but I can't marry you.'

'Why not?'

'You know why not.'

'No.' He shook his head. 'I don't think you've given the

matter enough thought. I know you don't love me now, but give it time. We'll have years to—'

'No, Alex.'

She spoke firmly, but all he did was move even closer and put his bony hands on her shoulders. 'Come on, Jane. Give me a chance. Let me show you how good it could be…'

'No, Alex.'

She was getting scared now. It was obvious she wasn't getting through to him and, whatever she said, he simply refused to listen to her.

'I don't think you appreciate the position you're in,' he went on, smoothing her arms in a way that made her skin crawl. 'A divorcee. A single mother. There aren't that many men who are prepared to take on another man's child.' He bent his head and, although she fought him, he succeeded in nuzzling her shoulder. 'Let me care for you, Jane. You know you want to.'

'I don't. Alex, please!' She pressed her hands against his chest, the clipboard falling between them. 'You have to let me go!'

'I don't *have* to do anything,' he retorted, moving in closer and pinning her back against an oil painting of the last tsar of Russia. It was one of Olga's favourites, and wasn't for sale, and the heavy gilt-edged frame dug painfully into Jane's spine. 'I can do what I like. Who's going to stop me?'

'Alex, for God's sake…'

Jane was losing hope. With the frame digging into her back and the clipboard digging into her ankle, she had never felt more helpless. And then she had an idea. She lifted her foot and kicked the clipboard hard into Alex's leg.

He swore, but for a moment his hold slackened and Jane took the opportunity it gave her. Shoving him away from her, she ran half sobbing towards the door.

The distinctive sound of the door opening halted her

headlong flight. It was late afternoon and the sun filtering through the blinds threw the visitor's face into shadow. All Jane could tell for certain was that it was a woman and her initial thought was that Olga had come back.

'Thank God you're here,' she got out unsteadily hurrying, towards her. 'Please—you must get Alex to leave me alone.'

'Alex?'

The voice was unfamiliar at first and Jane closed her eyes for a moment, praying she hadn't made a complete fool of herself in front of one of Olga's more influential clients. Then she opened her eyes again, realising she knew that accent. Ianthe Adonides of all people was standing staring at her, slim and elegant in a cream Chanel suit and pearls.

The house owned by the Souvakis family was in Bloomsbury. An elegant Georgian townhouse, overlooking Russell Square, it had three floors, a basement and an attic. It had once belonged to some minor member of the aristocracy, Jane remembered Demetri telling her. It had amused him to keep the area 'below stairs' for his own use.

Of course, that had been in the days when his mother and father had been frequent visitors to London. He'd first furnished the basement rooms when he was a teenager and that was where he'd taken Jane when they'd first become lovers. It was where he'd asked her to marry him, she remembered, her heart quickening instinctively. They'd been so happy in those days. How could she have let her own jealousy destroy what they'd had?

Why hadn't she believed him?

She asked the taxi driver to drop her at the corner of Bedford Place and walked the last few yards to the house she remembered so well. There were steps up to the glossy green door and a fanlight glowing with the light from inside. So someone was at home, she comforted herself. Of course, it could be just the housekeeper. Or even Theo Vasilis. Ianthe had told her she'd flown to England with both men, her growing relationship with Demetri's assistant the reason why she'd been invited along on what was primarily a business trip.

It was getting dark and, not wanting to be taken for a would-be intruder, Jane climbed the steps and rang the bell. Then, to give herself something to do while she waited, she checked that the belt of the loose-fitting woollen jacket she was wearing was securely tied about her waist. Until she was absolutely sure that Demetri wanted to see her again, her pride wouldn't let her use her condition to influence the outcome of this visit.

She seemed to wait for ages and only a grim determination forced her to stay the distance. Imagining Demetri checking some security monitor, and discovering it was her, tormented her. What if he refused to speak to her? What if what Ianthe had told her—that he and Ariadne were no longer seeing one another—simply wasn't true? Would she lie?

She'd certainly lied before.

The sound of a key turning put all these anxieties on hold. The deadlock was released and the door swung open on oiled hinges to reveal a rather plump, attractive woman in her late thirties. Jane's first devastating thought was that this was why Demetri and Ariadne had split up. He'd found someone else. But then the woman spoke and Jane realised that once again she was jumping to conclusions. Besides, Demetri would never allow a girlfriend of his to answer the door.

'May I help you?'

The woman's voice was polite, deferential, and Jane drew a breath. 'Um—is Mr Souvakis at home?'

The woman frowned now. 'Is he expecting you, Ms—Ms—'

'Souvakis,' said Jane at once and saw the way the woman's eyes widened with a mixture of surprise and disbelief. 'I'm— Mrs Souvakis. Demetri's wife.'

The woman blinked. Then, glancing nervously behind her, she murmured, 'I'm sorry. Mr Souvakis didn't tell me you were joining him.'

Jane wished she had the nerve to just walk into the house. But it was five years since she and Demetri had lived together and this woman didn't know her from Adam. Or should she say *Eve?*

'He's not expecting me,' she admitted uncomfortably. Then, in an effort to establish her identity, she added, 'Where is Mrs Grey?'

'Mrs Grey?' The woman looked a little less doubtful now. 'You know Mrs Grey?'

'Mr Souvakis' housekeeper, yes.' Jane nodded. 'Is she still here?'

'Mrs Grey retired three years ago,' the woman answered. 'I'm Mrs Sawyer. I took her place.'

'I see.'

Jane was feeling slightly reassured when a man's voice interrupted them. 'Who is it, Freda?' he called; from upstairs, Jane surmised. '*Ineh,* Theo? Tell him to come in.'

'It's not Mr Vasilis, Mr Souvakis,' Mrs Sawyer replied, raising her voice so he could hear, and Jane's heart almost stopped beating when she heard someone coming down the stairs.

'Well, you know I'm going out,' Demetri was saying as he reached the bottom of the stairs and strode along the hall towards the door. And then he saw Jane, and the silence that ensued was almost deafening.

'Hello, Demetri.' Jane knew it was up to her to say something. 'May I come in?'

Demetri exchanged a look with Mrs Sawyer. 'This is my

wife, Freda,' he said, unaware that they had already introduced themselves. Then, without meeting Jane's eyes, he stepped back and gestured her inside. '*Neh,* come in. I am going out, but I can spare you a few minutes. If it's urgent.'

'It is,' said Jane, giving the housekeeper an apologetic smile. The door closed and she nervously moistened her lips. 'How are you, Demetri? You look well.'

In actual fact, he looked anything but, she thought. The strain of his father's illness was obviously taking its toll on him. Ianthe had told her that Leo Souvakis was still alive, but very frail. Jane imagined he was very disappointed that Demetri's relationship with Ariadne had come to nothing.

Demetri didn't answer her and she wasn't really surprised. He must know she hadn't come here to enquire about his health. He was probably wondering why she was here, for, despite what Ianthe had said, he had made no attempt to see her during his visit.

'We'll be in the upstairs sitting room,' he told the house-keeper now. And then, after a moment's hesitation, 'Would you like coffee? Or something stronger?'

'Um—tea would be nice,' murmured Jane, still unable to face the former. 'If it's not too much trouble—'

'Tea. For one, Freda.' Demetri gave the order. Then, indicating the staircase, '*Parakalo:* you know where the sitting room is.'

Jane glanced behind her as she climbed the stairs. 'You—er—you don't live in the basement these days?' she asked, trying to lighten the mood.

'Freda and her husband have their apartment in the basement,' Demetri replied flatly. 'I haven't used it for years.'

'Oh.'

Jane couldn't think of an answer to that and instead tried to distract herself by familiarising herself with her surroundings.

Silk-lined walls, hung with priceless paintings, cushion-soft carpets, a crystal chandelier. And that was before she entered the family sitting room, with its Bokhara rugs and curved leather sofas, its elegant marble fireplace and exquisite works of art.

She paused in the doorway, where pocket doors could be slid aside to create a larger space for entertaining. When Demetri's father had been in London, the Souvakises had enjoyed a busy social life. Jane remembered parties where finding a guest without a famous name had been quite a feat.

She turned to remind Demetri of this, but he was already easing past her, crossing the room with the evident intention of getting himself a drink. And not tea, she speculated, aware that he looked much leaner than she remembered. Although his black pleated trousers and white silk shirt fitted him with glove-like precision, he had definitely lost some weight. There was more grey in the sleek beauty of his hair now and surprisingly he needed a haircut.

'So,' he said, at last, turning to rest his hips against the cabinet behind him. He was holding a glass with what she suspected was whisky in it. 'To what do I owe this unexpected appearance?'

Jane came slowly into the room. 'I notice you don't say "un-expected pleasure",' she said lightly, resisting the urge to wrap her arms about her waist. Then, because it was easier than getting to the real point of her visit, 'How is your father?'

'He's—as well as can be expected, isn't that what they say? Thank you for asking.' He paused. 'But you could have rung the villa and found that out for yourself.'

Jane didn't think so, but she didn't want to get into that now. Instead, she let a little of her emotions show. 'Oh, Demetri—'

'Please.' The look he directed towards her would have chilled an ice cube. 'You can't turn up out of the blue and expect a welcoming committee. Not after leaving Kalithi as soon as my back was turned.'

Jane's jaw dropped. 'It wasn't like that.'

'No? You knew Stefan and I were flying out to the *Artemis*. Didn't it occur to you that it might be dangerous?' He gave a short laugh. 'Or didn't you care?'

'Of course I cared.'

'*Psemata?*'

'Yes, really!' she exclaimed. 'But you knew I couldn't stay there indefinitely.' She was reluctant to mention his mother's part in her departure, but there was something she could say. 'I did ring the villa after I got back to England, but—well, I couldn't get through.'

Demetri's lips twisted. 'Do you expect me to believe that?'

'It's the truth!'

'So why couldn't you get through? Had you forgotten the number?'

'Of course not.' Jane sighed. 'Perhaps Angelena didn't understand what I wanted.'

Demetri's scepticism was evident and, in another attempt to explain her behaviour, she said unhappily, 'Ariadne resented me, you know she did.'

Demetri's brows drew together. 'Did Ariadne say something to make you leave?'

'N...o.'

'I thought not.'

'Demetri, please—'

'Please what?' He swallowed the remaining liquid in his glass in one gulp and turned to refill it. Then, with his back to her, he said, 'What do you want, Jane? Are you worried because I've let the divorce stall these last few weeks?' His shoulders rounded. 'You have to understand, I've had other things on my mind.'

'I know that.' Jane drew her lower lip between her teeth.

Then, because she had to know if Ianthe had been telling the truth, 'Are you still seeing Ariadne?'

He swung round then, his expression violent. 'What's it to you?' he demanded harshly. 'You don't care what happens to me.'

'I do!' Jane couldn't let him think that, even if his response was no answer. 'I've never stopped caring about you.'

Demetri was bitter. 'Then you have a bloody funny way of showing it.' He shook his head. 'Why don't you tell me what this is all about and get it over with?' He glanced at the slim gold watch circling his narrow wrist. 'I've got a dinner engagement in exactly forty minutes.'

'Ianthe came to see me.'

Jane hadn't intended to be so direct, but it was too late now. He was staring at her with hard, disbelieving eyes and she wondered painfully if the Greek girl's confession had come too late, also.

'*Apokliete!*' he muttered at last. No way!

'It's true.' Jane gazed at him despairingly. 'She—she came to the gallery. She told me that you and Ariadne were no longer together.'

'Ariadne and I have not been *together,* as you put it, since I came to your apartment over three months ago,' he told her coldly. 'That should hardly be news to you.'

Jane was confused. 'I don't know what you mean.' She frowned. 'When I arrived in Kalithi, Ariadne let me think—'

'That she and I were sleeping together?' Demetri was bitter. 'And you, of course, believed her.' He spread his arm dramatically. 'My wife,' he said contemptuously, 'who still thinks I'll sleep with any woman who'll have me.' He downed another mouthful of his whisky. 'And you say you care about me. Forgive me if I say that's bloody pathetic!'

CHAPTER SIXTEEN

THE arrival of Mrs Sawyer with Jane's tea gave Demetri a few minutes to compose himself. He was tempted to pour himself another drink, but the knowledge that getting drunk—again—wouldn't do him any favours made him set down his empty glass with a heavy thunk.

Jane, meanwhile, had accepted the housekeeper's suggestion and seated herself near the table where Freda had put the tray. But he noticed she made no attempt to drink the tea the woman had poured for her and Freda, after assuring herself that they had everything they needed, took it upon herself to close the doors as she left the room.

Realising he had to make some attempt to rescue the situation, Demetri forced himself to take the chair opposite his wife. Then, balled fists digging into his spread thighs, he said tersely, 'I suppose Ianthe told you she'd flown to England with Theo Vasilis and myself?'

Jane nodded. 'Yes.'

And that would be another strike against him, Demetri reflected malevolently. Had she really come here to challenge him again about something that had never happened?

He scowled. It didn't help that she was looking particularly lovely this evening. There was a glow about her, somehow, an inner warmth that made him curse the mess he'd made of both their lives. He'd never stopped wanting her, never stopped loving her. Even when he'd told himself he hated her, he'd known it was just his own pitiable need that was driving him on.

Her hair was longer, he noticed, his eyes devouring every item of her appearance. One strand curled invitingly over the shoulder of her woollen jacket; he wished she'd take the jacket off. He was a fool, he knew, but he wanted to see her breasts. They'd always been such a giveaway of the way she was really feeling.

Jane was aware that Demetri's eyes had slipped down her body and she felt the heat of his dark gaze like a fire against her skin. He'd always had this effect on her and never more so than tonight. Knowing what she did about him, knowing he had never lied to her, knowing what a stupid fool she'd been.

'You say Ianthe came to the gallery,' he prompted at last and she nodded again.

'That's right.' Then, rather than get to the point of her visit, she launched into an explanation of what had happened. 'It was just as well she did,' she said fervently. 'Alex was there—Alex Hunter, that is—and he was being a nuisance.'

Demetri's eyes narrowed. 'A nuisance? How?'

She should have been warned by the comparative mildness of his tone, but Jane was so relieved that he was talking civilly to her that she went on. 'Oh—in the usual way,' she said ruefully. 'He—well, he wouldn't accept the fact that I didn't want to see him again. Socially, I mean. If—if Ianthe hadn't come into the gallery as she did—'

'You are saying this man—this *cur*—molested you?' Demetri swore, springing to his feet with a violent oath of frustration. 'I will find him and I will kill him! How dare he lay a hand on my wife? I will make him wish he had never been born!'

Jane couldn't sit still with him towering over her. 'Am I still your wife, Demetri?' she whispered, rising to face him, and he looked at her with dark, avenging eyes.

'For the present,' he muttered harshly, subduing the urge he had to touch her. 'In any case, that is not important. This man, Hunter, will learn that no one assaults a member of my family and gets away with it.'

'He didn't—assault me, Demetri.' She sighed. 'He frightened me, that's all.'

'*Aliti!*' Bastard! Demetri swore again, raking restless fingers through his hair. 'So this time I must be grateful to Ianthe for her intervention, no?'

'Yes.'

'Ironic, is it not?'

'Perhaps.' Jane swallowed and gestured towards the sofa. 'Could we sit down again? I've got something to tell you.'

'And you think perhaps it will rob me of the strength to stand on my own two feet?'

'No…'

'Because I warn you, Jane, if you've come here to spread more of Ianthe's poison—'

'I haven't!' She put a nervous hand on his arm, feeling the muscles clench beneath her fingers. 'Please, Demetri, you have to listen to me.'

Demetri looked down at the hand resting on his arm and wondered how that tentative touch could spread an electric charge throughout his body. The desire to touch her in return, to touch her and taste her and feel that slim, lissom body yielding to the pressure of his caused an actual constriction in his chest. His pulse was racing, his heartbeat quickening in concert with his rising blood pressure. *Theos,* how the hell was he going to compose himself sufficiently to attend a business dinner in the Souvakis boardroom in less than half an hour, when all he could think about was taking her to bed?

'All right,' he said at last through clenched teeth, and she withdrew her hand and subsided onto the sofa again.

He lowered himself into the seat beside her, resisting the urge to crowd her. Even so, when she moved, her thigh was disturbingly close to his, and once again he was tempted to remind her of all they had once been to one another.

For her part, Jane was intensely aware of him watching her. His gaze fairly burned her skin and she permitted herself to run a reassuring hand over her stomach before going on.

She'd had her first scan a few days ago and seeing the baby's image on the monitor had brought a tight lump to her throat. Her mother had been with her and she'd been a great support, but Jane had wished Demetri could have been there. It was his baby, just as much as it was hers, and didn't he deserve to know he was going to be a father? But at that time, she'd believed he and Ariadne were planning their own future and how could she ruin his life for a second time?

'Well?'

Demetri was getting impatient and Jane leaned forward and took a nervous gulp of the cooling cup of tea. Then, composing herself, she said, 'I expect you're wondering what I could possibly have to say that would interest you?'

Demetri's mouth turned down. 'You think?' he queried sardonically. 'I thought you might be going to commiserate with me for not being able to sustain a lasting relationship, but I suppose that would be—how do you say?—pushing it, no?'

Jane sighed. 'Don't be sarcastic!'

Demetri's expression darkened. 'Then tell me how I'm supposed to be,' he snapped. 'Or is this just another game of provocation?'

'It's not a game.' Jane played with the belt of her jacket. 'I—still haven't told you why Ianthe came to see me.'

Demetri stiffened. 'I thought she wanted to tell you that Ariadne and I were no longer sleeping together.'

Jane's lips tightened. 'Must you be so crude?'

'*Theos,* you sound just like my mother.' He scowled. 'But she did give you reason to doubt what Ariadne had told you?'

Jane shook her head. 'Yes—'

'That's something, I suppose.'

'But in all fairness, you told me you'd slept with Ariadne,' said Jane defensively.

Demetri groaned. 'I'm not a monk, Jane.'

'I know that.'

'Oh, right. You know this because I made Ianthe my mistress just months after we got married?'

He would have got up from the sofa then but, with more courage than she'd given herself credit for, she reached out and gripped his wrist. His arm was lightly covered with dark hair but she could feel the heat emanating from him, the racing pulse beneath the skin.

'Don't go,' she said, her voice husky. 'Ianthe's told me what happened. About her baby, I mean. That—that Yanis was the father, not you.'

For a moment he just stared at her and she had no idea what he was thinking. There was such a wealth of bitterness in his gaze that she felt herself shrink from the accusations she felt sure he was going to make.

'Ianthe told you?' he said hoarsely. '*Theos,* why would she do that?'

Jane moistened her dry lips. 'I'm not entirely sure,' she admitted huskily. 'Perhaps it had something to do with the fact that you and Ariadne had split up.'

'What did my relationship with Ariadne have to do with Ianthe?'

He was bewildered and showed it and Jane desperately wanted to comfort him. But she had the feeling he wouldn't welcome her sympathy right now. 'I think,' she said, choosing her words with care, 'that she'd realised you weren't going to be happy with—with anyone else—'

'But you, you mean?' he demanded savagely, and this time she had no chance of stopping him when he wrenched his wrist out of her grasp and got to his feet. 'My God!' He strode across to the long windows that overlooked the square below. 'And I'm supposed to be grateful for this?' He turned to look at her, contempt in his eyes. 'Damn you, Jane, I don't want your pity!'

'I don't pity you, Demetri.' Herself, maybe. She got to her feet and started towards him, but his gaze speared her like a knife and she halted uncertainly. 'Please, you've got to listen to me. I know I've been a fool—'

'You got that right.'

'—but what was I supposed to do?'

Demetri's lips twisted. 'You could have believed me.'

'Yes, yes, I could.' Jane shook her head. 'That sounds so simple, doesn't it? I should have believed you, when the only other person involved insisted you were to blame.'

'Ianthe lied.'

'I know that now.' Jane held up her head. 'But you have to admit, no one—not even your father—told me who the baby's father really was.'

Demetri hunched his shoulders, running his hands up to grip the back of his neck. 'It was difficult for them, too,' he muttered.

Jane felt indignant now. 'I'll bet.'

'Yanis was just starting his training to become a priest.'

Demetri spoke heavily. 'There was no way he could have continued with his studies in those circumstances.'

'He should have thought of that before he slept with Ianthe!'

'I agree.' Demetri cast her a look out of the corners of his eyes. 'Believe me, he was left in no doubt that his behaviour had shamed him, shamed the family.'

'Not to mention your part in it,' said Jane forcefully. 'And, by extension, mine.'

'It wasn't meant to be that way.' Demetri was vehement. 'No one expected Ianthe to tell everyone that I was to blame.'

Jane's brows drew together. 'But I thought…' She tried to regroup. 'No one but you ever denied it.'

Demetri nodded. 'That was my mother's doing, I'm afraid.'

'What do you mean?'

'Oh…' His hands fell to his sides. 'It all happened a long time ago now.'

'That's no answer.'

'*Endaxi.*' All right. He turned to face her, spreading his arms in a gesture of defeat. 'You know my mother was always opposed to our marriage. When Ianthe said what she did, my mother persuaded my father and Stefan that denying it would only turn the spotlight on Yanis. Ianthe had spent a lot of time at the villa that summer. You know that.'

'Don't I just?' Jane found it hard to hide her resentment.

'*Oristeh.*' There you are. Demetri's tone was flat. 'It seemed it was the only way to save Yanis's future.' He sighed. 'And I, poor fool that I was, thought you'd believe me when I told you it wasn't my child. That our marriage was strong enough to withstand anyone's lies.'

'You could have told me the truth,' Jane insisted. 'Not just that you weren't to blame, but that Yanis was really the baby's father.'

'*Neh,* you're right. I could have done that.' Demetri regarded her sombrely. 'But, you know what? I had some pride in those days. And I was so sick that you could even think that of me after everything we'd been to one another that I thought, what the hell! Let her believe what she likes for now. In time, she'll see she was wrong.'

Jane stared at him. 'You expected me to stay, knowing how I felt?'

'*Veveso!*' Sure. 'That's what people do when they love one another. They try to work things out. It never even crossed my mind that you might leave me!' He groaned. '*Theos,* I thought we loved one another.'

'We did. I did. I did love you.' Jane was near to tears. 'And I'm not saying I didn't regret it afterwards. But you have to understand what it was like for me, too. I asked Ianthe—I begged her to tell me the truth—and she said you'd only married me on the rebound. That you and she had always cared about one another, and that that was why your mother had always opposed our marriage—'

'But that's—rubbish!' Demetri swore then. 'I was never interested in Ianthe and she knows it. She was in love with Yanis. She used to follow him around like a pet sheep. When she found out he was going to be a priest, I think she was desperate. She'd have done anything to stop him. Including throwing herself at him, I assume. And let's face it, Yanis was young, and flattered, *pithanon.* I dare say he had no idea what she had in mind.'

Jane's knees felt weak. 'If only you'd told me.'

'If only you'd told me you were leaving,' he countered savagely. 'Do you have any idea what it was like for me, coming home from a business trip to find my wife had gone to London and, according to my mother, she wasn't coming back?'

Jane pressed her lips together. 'I might have known your mother would play a part in it.'

'Yeah, well, I was devastated. If it hadn't been for my work, I think I'd have gone out of my mind.'

Jane swallowed. 'You could have come to see me. You could have told me about Yanis.'

'Oh, Jane!' Demetri sank down onto the wide window seat and leaned forward, his forearms braced on his thighs. 'Do you really think I didn't try?'

Jane was confused. 'I don't understand…'

'When it became obvious that you weren't coming back, I did try to see you, Jane. Several times. But both your mother and the Ivanovitch woman insisted you didn't want to see me.'

'No—'

'*Neh.*' He was adamant. 'I left messages on your mother's answering machine asking you to meet me. I even hung about outside the gallery, hoping I might be able to intercept you when you left. But you either slipped out the back or you avoided me in some other way.'

'I didn't know.' Jane was pale. She tried to think. 'I did stay with my mother when I first got back, and I did go to work at the gallery, as you say. I don't know how we could possibly not have seen one another.'

And then, she did. 'Oh, God,' she breathed. 'I think I know what happened.'

She remembered how, at that time, she'd been less than enthusiastic when Olga had suggested a trip to New York. She'd only been back in England for a few days and all she'd really wanted to do was hide away and lick her wounds. Getting on a plane to New York, being expected to talk business with the gallery Olga dealt with, had seemed totally beyond her.

But Olga had been so disappointed at her reaction that she'd eventually given in. She'd decided it was just Olga's way of trying to help her, of giving her something to do that would take her out of herself and give her time to deal with her pain in an environment that held no unhappy memories.

Now she recognised Olga's actions for what they'd really been. An attempt on her part, and probably on Jane's mother's, as well, to get her out of London and away from Demetri.

Demetri had been watching the play of emotions that had crossed her face as the truth dawned. But when she quickly explained what had happened, his reaction was not what she'd expected.

'So,' he spoke with resignation, 'Ianthe and my mother weren't the only ones who wanted to keep us apart.'

'No.' She gazed at him. 'I'm sorry.'

'*Neh,* so am I.' He slumped then, burying his face in his hands. '*Theos,* this is too much for me to handle.' His nails raked over his scalp. 'All this time I thought you were happy with the situation.'

Jane caught her breath. 'I thought you were.'

He looked up then. 'How could you think that?'

'How could I not?'

Demetri stared at her for a long time, then he gave a weary sigh. 'So, now we know the truth at last. That's something, I suppose.'

Jane felt sick. 'Is that all you have to say?'

'What do you expect me to say, Jane?' he demanded, bitterly. 'Do you think I am happy that I had to find out like this? All these years, all the lies people told—' He made a helpless gesture. 'I don't even know what you want from me now. Understanding? Absolution? Exoneration? You've got them. But I have to tell you honestly, I'll never forgive myself.'

'Oh, Demetri…' Jane couldn't stand the suspense a moment longer. Covering the space between them, she gazed down at his bent head with burning eyes. Then, she laid her hand on the back of his neck and discovered his hair was damp with the sweat that was pouring out of him. It was all the encouragement she needed to say softly, 'Will you ever forgive me for doubting you? For allowing other people to make such a mess of our lives?'

Demetri didn't immediately answer her, but he groped for her blindly, pulling her between his legs and burying his face against her stomach. Then, in a strangled voice, he said, 'I'm the one who needs your forgiveness, *aghapi*. If I hadn't been such a—pigheaded fool, you wouldn't have run away.'

Jane's hands came up to cradle his head against her. 'I wish I hadn't,' she whispered unsteadily. 'I wish I'd stayed. I wish I'd made Ianthe tell me the truth.' She broke off, her voice thick with emotion. 'I never stopped loving you, you know. Even when I thought I hated you, I knew it was because you could still hurt me so much.'

Demetri tipped his head back and gazed up at her. 'Do you mean that?' he asked hoarsely, but he could tell from the tears in her eyes that she did. '*Theos!*' He pressed his face against her again to hide his own ragged feelings. 'I can't believe it.'

'I wouldn't lie to you,' she said, taking his face between her palms and tilting it up to hers. She bent and bestowed a lingering kiss on his parted lips. 'Does that convince you?'

Demetri's eyes searched her face. 'So you'll stay with me? You'll come back to Kalithi with me and be my wife?'

'If that's what you want.' Jane was trembling, as much from the knowledge that his head was pressed against their baby as from her relief at knowing that he cared about her still. 'If you love me, that is. If you believe we have a future together.'

'If I love you!'

Demetri came to his feet in an instant, grasping her shoulders and pulling her roughly into his arms. He gazed down at her, his eyes dark and intimate. Then he kissed her and even the air was suddenly hot and thick with emotion.

'If I love you,' he muttered again, taking the lobe of her ear between his teeth and biting it painfully. 'Of course I love you. Why do you think I didn't let Gerrard handle the divorce for me? He wanted to. He said it wasn't a good idea for me to spend time with you again. And why do you think I wanted to see you, to have you come out to Kalithi, if it wasn't that I couldn't get you out of my head?'

'But your father—'

'Oh, yes. My father was eager to see you again. I'm not denying that. But he knew what I was doing. That was why he was so angry with me at times. Because he knew I still cared for you and I wasn't being honest with either Ariadne or myself.'

Jane touched his cheek. 'I was so jealous of Ariadne,' she admitted.

'You didn't have to be. Once I'd seen you again, I realised what a poor substitute Ariadne was.' He paused. 'But I have to admit, when I came back to the island a couple of days after the explosion on the *Artemis* and found you'd gone again, I was shattered. I couldn't believe you'd walked out on me again.'

'But your father must have told you what happened.'

Demetri shook his head. 'Or course, you don't know. My father was ill when I got back to Kalithi—' And when Jane made an anxious interjection, he raised a reassuring hand to cup her cheek. 'I think it was the shock of the explosion, minor though it was, that kept him in his bed for a few days. By the time he was up and about again, I'd gone back to Athens.'

'To Athens?'

'Yes.' Demetri pulled a wry face. 'I didn't have to, but I had to get away from the island. Once again, I think it was only my work that kept me sane. I couldn't eat; I barely slept; I was consumed with guilt and misery. Stefan was worried about me. I think he thought I was going to drink myself into an early grave.'

Jane stroked his cheek. 'I've been such a fool.'

'You don't have the monopoly on that, believe me,' Demetri assured her fiercely. His hands slid beneath the collar of her jacket, caressing the soft skin at her nape. 'I should have told you the truth about Ianthe as soon as I realised I still cared about you. But you seemed so—distant; so—in control; so—happy with your life.'

'Oh, Demetri.' Jane shivered as his hands moved over her shoulders and then tugged at the tie that kept her belt in place. 'You only had to touch me and I was on fire. Don't pretend you didn't realise it, that day you came to the apartment.'

He smiled. 'Whether you believe it or not, I didn't come to your apartment expecting to tumble you into bed.' He brushed his lips over hers and she quivered. 'I was sure you wouldn't want to see me and I was fully prepared for you to hear what I had to say and then throw me out.'

'Me, throw you out?' Jane was incredulous.

'Well, not physically, maybe, but you know what I mean. I really thought you'd be glad to be free of me at last.'

Jane's eyes widened. 'Did you really think that?'

Demetri grimaced. 'If you want the truth, I don't think I thought any of it through until I saw you. Then I realised why my mother had been so against me having any part in the divorce. She must have known how I'd feel when I saw you again.'

'And how I'd feel, too,' murmured Jane huskily. 'Oh, God, when you came into the bathroom, I just wanted to die!'

'And I just wanted to hold you,' said Demetri, tipping the woollen jacket off her shoulders and letting it fall to the floor. 'As I want to hold you now,' he continued, gazing down at her.

'Come—let me show you how much I want you. How much I'll want you for the rest of our lives.'

'But—your dinner engagement—'

'Theo can handle my dinner engagement.' His eyes darkened. 'Do you honestly think I'm going to leave you now?'

Jane hardly remembered the main bedroom suite at the townhouse. She and Demetri had only used it a couple of times in the past when Mrs Lang had been away. Jane's mother would have been offended if they hadn't accepted her hospitality, even if she'd lost no opportunity in those days to criticise Demetri's privileged way of life.

Now Jane looked about her, noticing the décor had all changed, cream and gold giving way to much more masculine tones. 'Ariadne never stayed here,' Demetri said softly, coming into the room behind her and sliding his arms about her midriff. 'I know what you're thinking, but our relationship never extended beyond the island.'

'I expect she stayed at your house there,' said Jane tensely, expecting him to notice her thickening waistline any moment.

'No.' Demetri was distracted, his lips finding the racing pulse below her earlobe. 'On those occasions when I sought Ariadne's bed, it was always at the villa.'

'I—I don't know if I want to know that.' Jane's voice was unsteady. 'I don't want to think of you making love to someone else.'

'Having sex with someone else,' Demetri corrected her gently. 'The only woman I've ever made love with is you.'

'I—well, there's been no one else in my life,' she confessed and Demetri blew softly into her ear.

'You have no idea how much pleasure that gives me, *aghapi mou*,' he told her thickly. 'I am a selfish man, I know, but I would have found it very hard to be complacent about something like that.'

Jane tilted her head back against his shoulder. 'Chauvinist!'

'I am. I admit it.' He turned her to face him. 'Can you forgive me?'

'I'll think about it.' She gazed up at him with adoring eyes. 'Oh, Demetri, do you realise that if Ianthe hadn't got a conscience at last, we might never have seen one another again?'

Demetri lifted his hands to her breasts. 'I don't believe that.'

'Why not? You're here in London and you've made no attempt to see me, have you?'

'I've seen Gerrard,' he admitted huskily. 'I've told him I don't want to continue with the divorce.'

Jane's eyes widened. 'You have?'

'Yes.' He looked rueful. 'I know what I said earlier, but I'd already decided that, if you wanted the divorce, you would have to come and see me.'

Jane knew an overwhelming sense of satisfaction, but then another thought occurred to her. 'What about your father?'

'My father knows how I feel about you,' he said simply, his fingers going to the ribbons that secured her smock. 'We had a long conversation, he and I, and he told me that my mother had led him to believe that Ariadne and I were in love.' He sighed. 'She'd also told Stefan other stuff about my father but that needn't concern us now.'

'About the fact that your father would never recognise any child of Stefan's as his grandchild?'

Demetri's brows descended. 'How do you know that?'

'Stefan told me.' She lifted her shoulders appealingly. 'We got quite close while you were away in Athens. He told me he was very hurt that his father seemed to have so little faith in him.'

'Really?' Demetri absorbed what she'd said. Then, 'Well, things are going to change. And they'll change even more when he learns I'm making him my deputy.'

Jane's eyes widened. 'Is that your father's idea?'

'No, it's mine.' Demetri was smug. 'I have no intention of risking our relationship as I did before. In the past weeks, I've realised that work is good if you've got nothing else in your life. But I do now. I have you. And your happiness is going to be my number-one priority from now on.'

'And does Stefan agree?'

'He will, when I tell him. He'll understand how ticked-off I feel knowing that while you were on the island my brother spent more time with my wife than I did.'

Jane's lips parted. 'You're jealous!'

'Yes. Yes, I am. Bloody jealous, as it goes,' he agreed thickly. He bent to brush her cheek with his tongue, kissing the soft flesh on the underside of her jaw before trailing his mouth to the scented hollow between her breasts. He loosened the ribbons. 'I want you all to myself.'

The sides of the smock fell apart and Demetri's lips sought the swollen peaks of her breasts pressing against the cream lace of her half-bra. '*Oreos,*' he whispered. Beautiful. '*Saghapo.*' I love you. He took one nipple into his mouth, suckling her through the cloth, causing a wave of longing that spread from her breasts to her stomach and from there to the place between her legs that was already wet and throbbing with need. '*Se thelo,*' he added huskily. 'I want you.'

'Oh, God, Demetri,' she choked, clinging to him urgently, and he tore one hand away to take off his tie and rip open the buttons of his shirt.

His chest, with its dark triangle of hair, brushed against

skin that was already sensitised to an unbearable pitch, and Jane decided that telling him about the baby could wait just a little longer…

Their lovemaking was wild and uncontrolled. Demetri had intended to take it slowly and deliberately, to enjoy every moment of it, but as soon as he felt her tighten around him, her muscles squeezing him and demanding his release, all his good intentions flew away. He wanted her. He needed her. And they would have plenty of time in the months and years to come to perfect something that was already as near perfect as it could get.

Tearing the coverlet aside, he pulled her to the bed, peeling off his own clothes as he did so. Jane seemed to share his urgency, for she shimmied out of her trousers and it was his pleasure to remove the rest of her clothes as he caressed her.

Then he was inside her and she was so ready for him. Feeling the slickness as he filled her with his thick shaft almost achieved his objective, but he wanted her with him every step of the way.

Jane drew up her knees and pressed the soles of her feet into the mattress, giving her the leverage she needed to push up against him. But when he would have drawn away to taste her, she dug her nails into his shoulders and urged him on. She wanted him, all of him, and the ripples of her own orgasm demanded his total possession.

And it was good, so good. Better than ever because this time there was no possibility that anyone would interrupt them. They had all evening and all night to explore the delights of their reunion, and, when Jane's climax swept her away, she heard Demetri's groan of satisfaction echoing her own.

It was dark when Jane opened her eyes again. It took a moment to adjust to the shadowy light that filtered in from the street-lights outside. But she had barely done so before a lamp was illuminated and she realised Demetri had been lying, propped on his elbow, watching her as she slept.

'Hi,' he murmured, regarding her with undisguised satisfaction. He bent to brush his lips across the soft curve of her jawline. 'I thought you were going to sleep forever.'

The dark stubble on his chin grazed hers and she blinked up at him in some surprise. 'What time is it?'

'About half-past-twelve,' he told her softly. 'Why? Are you hungry?'

'Hungry?' Jane's hand sought her stomach and then, remembering, she licked her dry lips. 'I—no. Not particularly.'

'Sure?' Demetri turned and when he came back he was holding a glass of wine in his hand. 'How about thirsty? I'm sorry I don't have any champagne, but the Chardonnay is fairly good.'

'Um…' Jane shuffled up against the pillows, realised she was completely naked and reached automatically for the sheet. 'Not for me, thanks.'

Demetri frowned, instantly aware of her uncertainty. *'Ti simveni?'* He shook his head and spoke in her language. 'What's wrong?'

'Nothing's wrong, exactly.'

Demetri was really worried now. Putting the wine aside, he turned to sit cross-legged beside her, and, although Jane knew this wasn't the time to be provocative with him, she couldn't prevent herself from putting her hand between his legs.

He hardened instantly, and her tongue circled her lips in helpless anticipation. Oh, God, she thought, she loved him so much. How could she have wasted so many years because of her foolish pride?

'What is it?' he demanded, but she noticed his hand held hers against him. 'Tell me, Jane, before I go completely out of my head.'

Jane hesitated. 'You know what you said about—about wanting me all to yourself?'

'Yes.' He was wary now.

'Well, how would you feel if I told you that six months from now that was going to change?'

Demetri frowned. 'I don't—' He broke off shaking his head. 'What are you saying? That you want—who—your mother, maybe, to come live with us?'

Jane had to smile then. 'No, not my mother, silly!' she exclaimed fiercely. She looked down at herself and then, with some hesitation, drew the sheet away. 'Haven't you noticed anything different about me? Don't you think I've put on a little weight since—since the last time we made love?'

Demetri stared into her eyes for a moment, then his gaze dropped to her stomach before lifting to her face again. '*Theos,*' he said in a shaken voice. 'You're pregnant!'

'Mmm.' Jane was nervous. 'How do you feel about it?'

'How do I feel?' Demetri rolled onto his knees and leant towards her, his hands cradling her stomach. 'How do I feel?' he echoed unsteadily. 'I'm...' His voice shook. 'I'm—staggered!' He tried to gather his thoughts. 'When were you going to tell me about this?'

Jane trembled. 'How could I tell you? I thought you were going to marry Ariadne.'

'*Hristo,* Jane, you knew why I was marrying Ariadne!'

Jane shook her head. 'I know. But—so much had happened. I couldn't bear the thought that you might think I had only got pregnant to ruin your life for a second time.'

'Not telling me about this baby would have ruined my life,' Demetri assured her forcefully. '*Theos,* a baby! I'm going to be a father! I can't believe it.'

'But—you're—happy about it?'

Demetri cupped her face in his hands and pressed a hungry kiss to her open mouth. 'I'm not just happy,' he told her thickly. 'I'm freakin' ecstatic! My wife! My baby! *Theos,* it doesn't get any better than this…'

EPILOGUE

NIKOLAS DEMETRI LEONIDES SOUVAKIS was born on Valentine's Day. He weighed in at a massive ten pounds five ounces, and Jane was pale but triumphant when her in-laws came to view the new arrival.

Demetri had been with her throughout the twenty-four hours of her labour. And, although at times he would have opted for a Caesarean, Jane had wanted to have their son naturally, wanted Demetri's hands to be the first the baby felt on his arrival into the world.

It was wonderful that Leo could be there to hold his grandson, too. Actually, in recent months, since he'd welcomed Jane back to Kalithi again and learned of her pregnancy, he seemed to have acquired a second lease of life. And despite her opposition to their reunion, even Demetri's mother had been unable to hide her pride that she was going to be a grandmother at last.

Stefan, too, had been to see his nephew, but now he'd flown to England to bring Jane's mother and sister back for a visit. Even Mrs Lang had been persuaded that her daughter had never been happier, and, because there was going to be a new baby visiting her house, she was much more tolerant of her other grandchildren's antics than she had used to be.

Olga, meanwhile, had sent a message expressing her delight

at the news. She would come out to see the baby on one of her frequent buying trips to Greece. Jane knew Olga was hoping that one day she'd reopen the gallery in Kalithi, but that would be a long time in the future, if at all.

Jane's mother and Lucy had arrived and welcomed the new baby, but now they'd returned to the villa and the suite of rooms Angelena had prepared for them. It had been agreed that all guests should stay at the villa and not with Jane and Demetri. Her daughter-in-law needed rest, Maria Souvakis had insisted, for the first time considering Jane's feelings before her own.

It was much later that night before Jane and Demetri were alone together. Jane had slept for a while and then taken a shower, and when her husband came into their bedroom she was looking deliciously relaxed and rested in an ivory satin nightgown with tiny pearl buttons down the front. Demetri thought she'd bloomed in the last six months, and their happiness was palpable.

'Tired?' Demetri asked now, coming to sit on the side of the bed nearest his wife, and Jane stroked his cheek.

'A little,' she conceded. 'But I'll get over it. How about you? You haven't even been to bed.'

Demetri shrugged. 'I don't like sleeping alone,' he confessed softly, playing with the buttons on the front of her gown.

'You don't have to,' she said at once, moving across the huge bed to give him room. 'Come on. You know you want to.'

Demetri hesitated. 'You need your sleep,' he said, glancing at the clock.

'You need yours,' she countered. 'I want you to stay, Demetri. I don't like sleeping alone either.'

Demetri regarded her for a long moment and then he stood and unfastened his shirt. Tossing it onto a chair, he followed it with his trousers, and then drew back the covers to get into bed.

'You don't sleep in boxers,' Jane pointed out huskily, and, with a rueful grimace, Demetri kicked them off as well.

'Goodness knows what Nurse Seledha will say when she brings Nikolas for his feed,' Jane added, teasingly. And when Demetri would have protested, she reached over him and turned off the lamp. 'Don't fret, my darling. She'll just be envious of me.'

FORGOTTEN MISTRESS, SECRET LOVE-CHILD

ANNIE
WEST

Annie West spent her childhood with her nose between the covers of a book—a habit she retains. After years preparing government reports and official correspondence, she decided to write something she *really* enjoys. And there's nothing she loves more than a great romance. Despite her office-bound past, she has managed a few interesting moments—including a marriage offer with the promise of a herd of camels to sweeten the contract. She is happily married to her ever-patient husband (who has never owned a dromedary). They live with their two children amongst the tall eucalypts at beautiful Lake Macquarie, on Australia's east coast. You can e-mail Annie at www.annie-west.com, or write to her at PO Box 1041, Warners Bay, NSW 2282, Australia.

This one's for Judy!

Hope it brings you joy.
Warm hugs and huge thanks to
Anna, Josie, Marilyn, Monique and Serena,
whose expertise made this book possible.

CHAPTER ONE

ALESSANDRO spared barely a glance for the promotional material he tossed into his out tray. His newest PA still hadn't learnt what he should see and what he had no time for. The textile manufacturing arm of the company would be represented at the upcoming trade fair. But one of his managers could handle that. It hardly needed the CEO to…

Oddio mio!

His gaze caught on a photo as a brochure landed askew, half covered by discarded papers.

Alessandro's eyes narrowed on the curve of a woman's smile, a tiny mole like a beauty spot drawing attention to a mouth that would catch any man's interest. Wide, lush, inviting.

Every muscle froze even as his pulse revved and blood roared in his ears.

That smile.

That mouth.

Yet it wasn't sexual awareness that arrested him. A tantalising wisp of almost-memory wafted behind his conscious thoughts. A taste, sweet as ripe summer cherries, rich and addictive.

Heat filled him, despite the climate-controlled air in his spacious office. A zap of something that might have been emotion stifled the breath in his lungs. Alessandro froze, telling himself not to analyse but to relax and let the sensations surface. *Willing* the recollections to come.

Like a lacy curtain in a breeze, the blankness cloaking his memory of those missing months two years ago rippled. It shifted, parted, and then dropped back into place.

His hands clenched, white-knuckled on the edge of his glass and black marble desk. But Alessandro didn't register pain, just the infuriating, familiar sense of nothingness.

Only to himself would he acknowledge how helpless that void made him feel. How vulnerable. It didn't matter that he'd been assured those lost months contained nothing out of the ordinary. Other people remembered that time: what he'd done and said. But he, Alessandro Mattani, had no recall.

Swift as thought, he tugged the brochure from the papers. It was an advertisement for a luxury hotel. He turned it over. A luxury hotel in Melbourne.

Alessandro waited, but no spark of recognition came. He hadn't travelled to Melbourne.

Not that he could remember.

Impatience flared and he forced it down, breathing deeply. An emotional response wouldn't help. Even if the sense of loss, of missing something vital, sometimes threatened to drive him to the edge.

He flipped over the flyer again. A woman, a receptionist, smiled at a handsome couple as they checked in. The photo was professionally styled, yet despite its air-brushed gloss, there was something riveting about the receptionist's smile.

The setting was opulent, but Alessandro had grown up with luxury and barely bothered to notice. The woman, on the other hand…she intrigued him.

The more he stared, the more he felt an atavistic premonition that made his blood pump faster and prickled the skin at his nape. She was so familiar.

Had she smiled at him like that?

A tickle of awareness started low in his belly.

A tickle of…certainty.

Carefully he catalogued her features. Dark hair pulled back sleekly from a pleasant but unremarkable face. Her nose was pert, a trifle short. Her eyes were surprisingly light for her brunette colouring. Her mouth was wide.

She wasn't beautiful. She wasn't exotic enough to turn heads. And yet she had…something. A charisma the photographer had seen and capitalised on.

Alessandro traced the angle of her cheekbone, the gentle curve of her jaw, to pause on the lush promise of her lips.

There it was again. That tingle of presentiment. The intuition that she was no stranger. It drew every muscle and sinew in his body tight, as if in readiness for action.

Behind the opaque gauze of his faulty memory something shifted.

Sensation, soft as the tentative brush of those lips against his. That taste again, of sun-ripened cherries. Irresistible. The phantom caress of delicate fingers along his jaw, over his rapidly pulsing heart. The sound of feminine sighs, the aftermath of ecstasy.

Alessandro's chest heaved as if from intense physical exertion. Sweat prickled his nape and brow as his body stirred with arousal.

Impossible!

Yet instinct clamoured with a truth he couldn't ignore.

He knew her. Had met her. Held her. Made love to her.

His nostrils flared on a surge of wholly masculine possessiveness. The primitive sense of ownership, of a male scenting his mate, was unmistakeable.

He stared at the image of a stranger from the other side of the world. If he hadn't visited Melbourne, had she travelled here to Lombardia?

Frustration at those missing months simmered.

For long minutes Alessandro considered the photograph, his thumb absently caressing the curve of her cheek.

Impossible as it seemed, the certainty grew that this woman held the key to his locked memories. Could she open them? Restore what he'd lost and obliterate the sense that he was somehow less than he'd been. The gnawing hint of dissatisfaction with his world.

Alessandro reached for the phone. He intended to have answers, no matter what it took.

'Thanks, Sarah, you're a lifesaver.' Relief flooded Carys. Today everything that could go wrong had. At least this one thing, the most important, was sorted.

'No worries,' her neighbour and babysitter responded. 'Leo will be fine staying over.'

Carys knew Sarah was right, but that didn't stop the twinge of regret, sharp in her chest. When she'd taken this job at the Landford Hotel it was with the expectation she'd be home most days at a reasonable hour. Early enough to look after her son.

She didn't want Leo growing used to an absentee parent too busy with her career to spend time with him. The sort of home life Carys had taken for granted as a child.

Especially since Leo only had her.

The twinge beneath her breast intensified, catching her breath as pain ripped through her. Even after all this time she couldn't suppress the shaft of regret and longing that pierced her whenever she remembered.

She needed to toughen up. Once upon a time she'd chased her dream, but she wasn't fool enough to believe in it any more. Not after she'd learned so cruelly how futile that dream was.

'Carys? What's wrong?'

'Nothing.' Hastily she forced a smile, knowing Sarah could read her tone even over the phone. 'I owe you one.'

'You sure do. You can babysit for us next weekend. We've got plans for a night on the town, if you can mind Ashleigh.'

'Done.' She looked at her watch. She had to get back before the next crisis hit. 'Don't forget to give Leo a goodnight kiss from me.' Stupid to feel that catch in her throat because tonight she wouldn't feed him his evening meal or kiss his plump pink cheek at bedtime.

Her son was in good hands and, she told herself sternly, she was lucky to have landed a job that usually gave her regular time with him. She was grateful the management had been impressed enough to allow her reasonably family-friendly hours.

Today was the exception. The flu that ravaged the Landford's staff had hit at the worst possible time. More than a third of the staff was off sick just when there was a series of major functions.

It didn't matter that Carys had already spent more than a full day on the job. The collapse just an hour ago of David, the senior functions manager, with a soaring temperature, meant Carys had to step into that role too.

Nerves fluttered in her stomach. This was her chance to prove herself and justify David's faith in her, having taken her on despite her incomplete qualifications. He'd been a good friend and a terrific mentor. She owed him not only her position, but the hard-won self-confidence she'd slowly built since coming to Melbourne.

'I don't know what time I'll be back, Sarah. Probably in the early hours.' Steadfastly Carys refused to worry about how she'd manage the trip home. She couldn't rely on public transport at that time, and the cost of a cab was prohibitive. 'I'll see you around breakfast time, if that's OK?'

'That's fine, Carys. Don't fret. We'll see you when we see you.'

Slowly Carys replaced the phone and stretched her hunched shoulders. She'd been working at the computer and on the phone without a break for so long her body ached all over.

She glanced at the monitor before her and saw the lines of the spreadsheet she'd opened dance and jumble before her eyes. She pinched the bridge of her nose, knowing that no matter how hard she concentrated, working on the document would be a test of endurance and determination.

Sighing, she reached for her tinted reading glasses and leaned forward.

She had to finish this. Only then could she make last minute checks on the arrangements for tonight's masked ball.

Carys stood in the corner of the ballroom near the door to the kitchens, listening to the head waiter's whispered update. It was mayhem in the kitchen with more staff struck down by this virulent flu. Only a couple of the extra waitstaff had arrived to replace those who'd phoned in ill, and the chefs were barely able to cope.

Fortunately, the guests hadn't noticed anything wrong. The

Landford prided itself on superb service, and the staff were doing everything to live up to that reputation.

The ballroom, all black and gold, was gracious and formally elegant. Antique chandeliers sparkled, casting a glow that set jewels scintillating among the A-list crowd. The guests looked impossibly chic as befitted one of Fashion Week's major events.

The room smelled of exclusive fragrances, hothouse flowers and money. Serious money. Celebrities, designers, buyers, the *crème de la crème* of Australian society, were here tonight and plenty of international high-flyers too.

And they were all her responsibility.

Carys' pulse thundered and she struggled to focus on her companion's words. She must concentrate if she wanted to ensure tonight was a success. Too much was at stake.

'All right. I'll see if we can get someone else from the restaurant to help out.' She nodded, dismissing him and turning to the house phone on the wall. She reached out to hit the speed dial number for the restaurant, then froze.

A tingling sensation began at the base of her spine. It burned its way up her back like the slide of hot ice on bare skin. Except her skin wasn't bare. She wore a regulation jacket and straight skirt, dark stockings and high heels.

Yet through the layers of clothing her skin sizzled, the hairs on her neck prickling.

Carys replaced the phone with stiff, unsteady fingers. She pivoted, turning to face the shifting, colourful crowd. Staff circulated with gourmet canapés and vintage champagne; groups broke and reformed.

The guests, most of them wearing exquisite handmade masks, were busy enjoying themselves or networking or showing off their finery. They wouldn't notice anyone who didn't belong in their rarefied circle.

That suited Carys. She didn't hanker for a place at a fairy-tale ball. Not since she'd given up on the whole Prince Charming fantasy.

Yet heat washed her cheeks. Her breath snagged in her throat and her pulse accelerated as instinct told her she was being watched.

Her heart was in her mouth as frantically she searched the throng for something, someone, familiar. Someone who could make her skin tingle and her heart race as it had before, long ago.

Briefly she shut her eyes. Madness! That was in the past. A past best forgotten.

Tiredness and nerves had simply made her imagine things.

Her path and his would never cross again. He'd made certain of that. Carys' lips twisted in a grimace as familiar pain stabbed her chest.

No! Not now. She refused to let her wayward imagination distract her. People depended on her. She had a job to do.

From across the packed room he watched her.

His fingers curled, white-knuckled, around the back of a nearby chair. Blood roared in his ears as his heart thundered out of control. The shock of recognition was so strong he shut his eyes for an instant and lightning flickered across the darkness of his closed lids.

Opening them, he saw her turn to the wall phone, her movements jerky.

It was her. Not just the woman from the brochure, but more, the woman he remembered. Correction—almost remembered.

An image teased his mind. An image of her walking away from him. Her back rigid, her steps staccato bites that ate up the ground as if she couldn't get away fast enough. Bites that echoed the rapid pulse of his drumming heart as he stood rooted to the spot. She carried a case, the taxi driver ahead of her stowing another bag in his vehicle.

Finally she paused. Alessandro's heart stopped and rose in his throat. But she didn't turn around. A moment later she was in the car as it accelerated in a spurt of gravel and swooped away down the private road from his Lake Como home.

Still he stood, prey to an alien mix of sensations. Fury, relief, disappointment, disbelief.

And hurt! Pain filled the yawning chasm inside him.

Only once before in his entire life had Alessandro felt so intensely. At five, when his mother had deserted him for a life of pampered luxury with her lover.

He stirred and shook his head, banishing the misty image, be-latedly aware again of the crowded ballroom.

Yet the powerful brew of emotions still stirred in his breast. *Maddona mia!* No wonder he felt vulnerable. Such feelings… Who was this woman to awake such responses in him?

Anger mingled with impatience. That mere chance had led him here. That he could so easily have missed this opportunity to learn more.

Deliberately he flexed his fingers and let go of the chair back, feeling at last the deep imprint of curved wood score his palm.

The wait was over.

He would have his answers now. Tonight.

Surreptitiously Carys slid a foot from her shoe and wriggled her toes. Soon the ball would be over. Then she could oversee the clearing away and setting up for the next day's fashion show.

She suppressed a rising yawn. Every bone in her body ached, and she wanted nothing more than to flop into bed.

She skirted the dance floor. She'd just check on—

A hand, large, warm and insistent took hers, pulling her to a halt. Quickly she summoned a serene expression, ready to deal with the guest who'd overstepped the boundaries by touching her. She hoped he wasn't intoxicated.

Carys had just pinned a small professional smile on her face when a tug of her hand made her turn.

The carefully crafted smile slid away.

For an instant Carys' heart stopped beating as she looked up at the man before her.

Unlike most of the revellers, he still wore his mask. His dark hair was cut brutally short, sculpting a beautifully shaped head. The mask shadowed his eyes, but she caught a gleam of dark fire. His mouth was a grim slash above a strong, firm chin.

Her eyes widened, staring at that chin. It couldn't be…

Then he moved and she caught the faint tang of an unfamil-iar cologne. Her heart dived.

Of course it wasn't him!

A scar snaked up his brow from the edge of the mask. The

man she'd known had been as devastatingly handsome as a young god. No scars. His complexion had been golden too, olive, gilded by hours in the sun, not as pale as this stranger's.

And yet…

And yet she stupidly wished in that moment it was him. Against all logic and the need to protect herself, how badly she wanted it to be so.

Carys drew herself up straighter, fumbling for poise while her nerves screamed with disappointment.

He was tall, far taller than she, even though she wore heels. Surely as tall as… No! She wasn't going there. Wasn't playing that pathetic game any more.

'Can I help you?' The words emerged huskily, more like an intimate invitation than a cool query.

Silently she cursed the way he'd thrown her off balance just by reminding her of a time, and a man, best forgotten.

'I think you've mistaken me for someone else.' She rushed into speech again, needing to rein in wayward thoughts. Her words were clipped, though she was careful not to reveal her annoyance. If she could extricate herself without a fuss, she would.

Carys tugged her hand but his grip firmed and he drew her forward. She stumbled, surprised by his implacable hold.

Tilting her head up, she looked him in the eye. She expected him to comment on the food or the music, or demand assistance in some way.

Instead his silence unnerved her.

Her skin grew tight as the illusion grew that they stood alone, cut off from the others.

Around them conversation buzzed, music swirled, and a tinkle of feminine laughter sounded. But the man in the perfectly cut dinner jacket, with the perfectly cut jaw, said nothing. Just held her.

Heat flared under her skin as again instinct shouted a warning to beware.

His hold shifted and his thumb slid over the sensitive place between her thumb and forefinger. A spike of heat transfixed her. Her eyes widened as a tremor echoed through the secret recesses of her body.

'You need to let me go.' She lifted her chin higher, wishing she could see his eyes properly.

He inclined his head, and the breath she hadn't known she held whooshed out. See? He probably just wanted something mundane like another bottle of wine for his table.

She opened her mouth to enquire when someone bumped her, propelling her towards the hard male torso before her.

Carys heard a muffled apology but barely noticed.

Large hands grasped her upper arms. In front of her stretched an expanse of exquisitely tailored elegance, that ultra-masculine chin with just the hint of a cleft and a pair of shoulders to make any woman sit up and take notice.

Shoulders just like…

Carys bit her lip. This had to end.

This was a *stranger.* So he had shoulders to die for and a jaw that seemed achingly familiar. The gold signet ring on his finger was one she'd never seen. And, despite the similar height, he was leaner than the man she'd known.

Another couple buffeted her, talking volubly as they passed. Suddenly she found herself plastered against a hard body that seemed all heat and raw strength. Her senses whirled in a giddy riot.

She imagined she could feel each muscle of his body against hers. Beneath the expensive cologne an elusive undertone of warm male skin tickled her nostrils and she inhaled sharply. He was too familiar, like a phantom from one of the endless dreams that haunted her.

His odd silence intensified her sense of unreality.

Then his hold shifted. A hand slid down her back, poised almost possessively just above her bottom, long fingers spread. Heat roared in the pit of her belly. The heat of desire. A sensation she hadn't felt, it seemed, in a lifetime.

Her body responded to the ultra-masculine allure of his, softening, trembling—

'I need to go.' Carys jerked her head back from the muscled chest that drew her like a magnet. 'Please!'

Her mouth trembled in a wobbly grimace, and to her dismay

hot tears prickled her eyes. Part of her yearned crazily to succumb to his potent maleness.

Because he reminded her of the one man who had taught her the dangers of instant physical attraction.

She had to get out of here.

With a strength born of desperation, she wrenched herself free and stumbled back, off balance when he released her instantly.

Carys took a shaky step away, then another.

The man in the dark mask watched her, eyes unreadable, his body as still as a predator about to pounce.

Her throat squeezed tight in inexplicable panic. She opened her mouth but no sound came. Then she spun and blindly forced her way through the crowd.

Wearily Carys tucked a strand of hair behind her ear. The last of the guests had finally gone and the vast ballroom was empty but for the staff tidying up and moving furniture.

The chirrup of a house phone snagged her attention. She found herself crossing her fingers that there were no more problems. Not tonight, correction, this morning. She was running on empty.

She was still unsettled by the memory of the stranger. The man who'd seemed so familiar yet couldn't be.

'Hello?'

'Carys? Glad I caught you.' She recognised the new guy on night duty at reception. 'You've got an urgent call. I'll connect you.'

Instantly all weariness vanished at the sound of those dreaded words 'urgent call'. Carys' stomach dropped and fear filled the void. Was it Leo? An illness? An accident?

She twisted a button on her jacket, waiting breathlessly for bad news as her nerves stretched taut.

It would be tonight of all nights that something went wrong. She should have found a way to get home earlier.

The click of the new connection was loud in her ears. As was the silence that followed, a waiting silence.

'Sarah? What's wrong? What's happened?'

There was a pause in which she heard the echo of her own breathing.

Then a voice like black velvet emerged.

'Carys.'

Just one word and every hair on her body rose. It was the voice that haunted her dreams. A voice that, despite everything, still had the power to thicken her blood, turning it to warm treacle.

Her knees buckled and she found herself sitting on the edge of a table that had been moved up against the wall.

Her fingers splayed over her throat in a desperate gesture of vulnerability.

It couldn't be!

Her mouth opened and her throat worked, but no sound emerged.

'We need to meet,' said the voice of her past. 'Now.'

CHAPTER TWO

'WHO is this?' Carys' voice emerged as a raw croak.

It couldn't be.

Not here. Not now.

Not after she'd finally convinced herself she never wanted to see him again. Fate couldn't be so cruel.

Yet some wayward self-destructive impulse sent a buzz of excitement skimming along her nerves. Once she'd longed for him to make contact, to come after her, tell her he'd been wrong. Tell her…no, she wasn't so credulous as to believe in such fantasies any more.

What did he want? Her hand tightened like a claw at her throat. A premonition of danger filled her, icing her blood.

'You know who it is, Carys.' Just the way he pronounced her name with that sexy Italian accent turned the word into a caress that melted her insides.

He'd always threatened her self-control. Carys remembered murmured enticements in that dark coffee voice and how he'd persuaded her to give up everything she'd worked for just for the privilege of being with him.

Fool!

She shivered and sat up straighter, berating herself.

'Please identify yourself,' she said tersely.

It couldn't be him. He'd never follow her to Australia. He'd made that clear when she'd left with her tail between her legs.

But the memory of the stranger tonight at the ball, the masked man who'd made her think of *him,* battered at her disbelief. Wildly she shook her head, trying to clear a brain overloaded by exhaustion and stress.

Was she going mad? Seeing him, even hearing him, when she knew perfectly well he was ensconced in his oh-so-exclusive world of rich, elegant, aristocratic friends. Of high-flying business deals and blue blood and glamour.

Where people like her only provided brief amusement.

'Don't pretend not to know me, Carys. I have no time for puerile games.' He paused as if waiting for her to rush into speech. 'It's Alessandro Mattani.'

Silence throbbed as she clutched the receiver. Her heart crashed against her ribs. She would have slid to the floor if she hadn't already been sitting.

'Alessandro…'

'Mattani. I'm sure you recognise the name.' His voice was sharp as a razor.

Recognise the name! Once she'd even hoped to share it with him.

A bubble of hysterical laughter threatened to explode from her stiff lips. Carys slapped her palm across her mouth, concentrating on deep breaths. She needed oxygen.

The room spun crazily and dark spots whirled in her vision.

A clatter jerked her back to full awareness, and she looked down as if from an enormous distance to see the phone had slipped from her nerveless fingers onto the table.

Alessandro Mattani.

The man she'd loved.

The man who'd broken her heart.

A sound caught her attention and Carys looked up, suddenly aware again of her surroundings. The last of the staff were leaving and waving goodnight.

Belatedly she lifted a hand in acknowledgement.

Dazedly she looked around. The stage was set for tomorrow's fashion show. Enormous jardinières with arrangements of exotic orchids and jungle greenery had been strategically positioned as she'd instructed. The lights were dimmed and she was alone.

But for the voice on the other end of the line. The voice of her dreams.

Tentatively, as if reaching out to touch an untamed animal, Carys stretched her fingers to the phone. She lifted it, and a deep voice barked in her ear.

'Carys?'

'I'm here.'

Silence, but for the impatient hiss of indrawn breath.

'No more games. I want to see you.'

Well, bully for him. She was past the stage of worrying what Alessandro Mattani wanted.

Besides, she wasn't foolish enough to go near him again. Even now she didn't trust her hard-won defences against the man who'd only had to smile and crook his finger to get what he wanted from her. She'd surrendered her job, all her plans, even her self-respect to be with him.

Carys stiffened her spine and braced her palm on the table beside her.

'That's not possible.'

'Of course it's possible,' he bit out. 'I'm just twelve floors away.'

Twelve floors? Her heart galloped faster. Here, in Melbourne? At the Landford?

Her gaze swerved to the edge of the dance floor, instinct and disbelief warring.

'That *was* you tonight? At the ball?' If she'd been less stunned, she might have cared about how much her strained voice revealed. But she was battling shock. She had no thought to spare for pride.

He didn't answer.

Heat sparked low in her abdomen and washed through her like a flood tide. It *had* been him. He'd held her in his arms.

How often had she yearned for his embrace? Despite what she'd told herself about forgetting the past.

He'd held her and she hadn't known him?

But she had, hadn't she? Despite the new cologne, the paleness of his once-golden skin, the scar.

Fear jolted through her, stealing her breath.

He'd been hurt! How badly? Urgent questions clamoured on her tongue.

Shakily Carys gathered the tattered remnants of control. She ignored the unspoken questions, opting for the most important one.

'What do you want?' Her voice sounded stretched too thin, like beaten metal about to snap under pressure.

'I've already told you.' Impatience threaded his words. 'To see you.'

She couldn't prevent a snort of disbelief at his words. How times had changed.

Finally pride came to her rescue.

'It's late. I've had a long day and I'm going home. There's nothing more to say between us.' Tentatively she slipped her feet to the floor, waiting to see if her legs would collapse under her.

'Are you sure?' His words, soft and deep like the alpine eiderdowns they'd once shared, brushed across her senses. His voice was alive with erotic undercurrents.

She jerked upright.

Flame licked that secret needy place deep inside her, the place that had been cold and empty ever since she'd left him. The realisation drew her anger.

No, she wasn't sure. That was the hell of it.

'I'm in the presidential suite,' he said after a moment. 'I'll expect you in ten minutes.'

'You have no right to give me orders.' Belatedly she found her voice.

'You don't wish to meet me?' Incredulity coloured his tone.

Had he never had a knock-back from a woman?

Certainly not from her. She'd been putty in his elegant, powerful hands from the instant she'd fallen head over heels for him.

'The past is the past.' At the last moment she prevented herself saying his name. She didn't want the sound of it on her lips. It was too intimate, evoked too many memories.

'Perhaps so. But *I* wish to meet *you*.' His tone made it clear that he wasn't about to go down on bended knee and beg her forgiveness.

Carys rubbed her forehead. The very thought of Alessandro, darling of the jet set, commercial power-broker and hundred percent red-hot macho Italian male on his knees before any woman was ludicrous.

'You have ten minutes,' he reiterated.

'And if I don't come?'

He took his time responding. 'That's your choice, Ms Wells.' His formality in that silky smooth voice held more threat than any bluster. Or was that her imagination?

'I have personal matters to discuss. I thought you'd prefer to do that in the privacy of my suite. Of course, I can see you instead during business hours tomorrow.' He paused. 'I understand you share an office with colleagues? Presumably they won't be inconvenienced by our conversation.'

He left the sentence dangling and Carys bit her lip, imagining how her workmates would react to Alessandro and his *personal matters*.

'No doubt your manager won't mind you taking time off to deal with a private matter,' he purred in that outrageously delicious accent. 'Even though I understand you're only here on an extended probation?'

Carys' jaw dropped. He'd had her records investigated! How else could he know about her long probation period since she'd been employed without completing her qualifications?

Those employment details were supposed to be confidential.

Her defensive hackles rose as the old sense of inadequacy surfaced. Of not being good enough. Not making the grade. And more, of being cornered, facing an implacable, unstoppable force that threatened to overpower her.

Defeat tasted bitter on her tongue.

Or was that fear? Fear that, despite his initial rejection, Alessandro had come to take Leo from her.

Her shoulders tightened.

'Ten minutes,' she confirmed.

Alessandro stood at the full-length window, staring across the Yarra River to the lights of Melbourne's cityscape.

He didn't see them. Instead his brain conjured an image of blue-grey eyes, wide and apparently guileless.

He shifted as heat shot through his body straight from his groin at the memory of her soft body nestled against him.

From the moment he'd sighted her across the ballroom, he'd known. The awareness he'd experienced looking at her photo was nothing compared with tonight's instant gut-deep certainty.

This woman was his.

Alessandro tossed back the espresso his butler had brewed, feeling the shot of caffeine in his blood.

His earlier flash of memory told him they hadn't parted amicably. Hell, she'd walked out on him! No other lover had ever done that.

Yet he knew with absolute certainty there was still something between them. Something that accounted for the nagging dissatisfaction that had plagued him since the accident.

Why had they separated?

He intended to discover everything about the yawning blankness that was his memory of the months preceding his accident.

He refused to let her escape till he had answers.

From the moment he'd held her, the sense of unfinished business between them had been overwhelming. Even now he felt the low-grade hum of awareness, waiting for her.

There was more too. Not just the immediate sense of connection and possessiveness. There was an inner turmoil that surely must be long-dormant emotions.

He'd watched her, listened to her, and been dumbstruck by the intensity of his conflicting feelings.

Alessandro had harnessed all his willpower to drive himself to recover from his injuries and turn around the faltering family business. He'd blocked out everything but the need to haul the company from the brink of disaster. Everything else had been a pallid blur.

Until now no one had come close to breaking through his guarded self-possession. Not his step-mother, not the many women angling for his attention. Not his friends.

Despite his wide social circle, he was a loner like his father.

The old man had isolated himself, focusing only on business after his first wife's betrayal and desertion.

As a result Alessandro had learned the Mattani way early, concealing his boyish grief and bewilderment behind a façade. Over the years that façade of calm had become reality. He'd developed the knack of repressing strong emotions, distancing himself from personal vulnerability.

Until tonight. When he'd come face to face with Carys Wells. And he'd...*felt* things. A stirring of discontent, desire, loss.

He frowned. He had no time for emotions.

Lust, yes. He was no stranger to physical desire. That was easily assuaged. But the disturbing sensations churning in his belly were unfamiliar, caused by something more complex.

A knock sounded on the door. Grateful for the interruption to his unpalatable thoughts, Alessandro put down his cup and turned as the butler crossed the foyer.

Alessandro was surprised to register his shoulders stiffening, locking as tension hardened his stance.

Since when had he, Alessandro Mattani, experienced nerves? Even when the specialists had shaken their heads over his injuries, referring to complications and a long convalescence, all he'd felt was impatience to get out of hospital. Especially when he'd learned the impact his accident, so soon after his father's death, had caused.

The commercial vultures had begun circling, ready to take advantage of the mistakes his father had made in those last months and of Alessandro's incapacity.

'Ms Wells, sir.' The butler ushered her into the sitting room.

She stood as if poised for flight, just inside the door. Once more that shock of connection smacked him square in the chest. He rocked back on his feet.

Jerkily she lifted a hand to smooth her hair, then dropped it as she caught his scrutiny.

Tension, palpable and vibrating, strung out between their locked gazes.

Carys Wells looked out of place in the opulence of Melbourne's most exclusive hotel suite. Unless, of course, she was here to provide a personal service to the occupant. Delivering a message or bringing room service.

Alessandro's thoughts jagged on the sort of *personal* service he'd like her to provide.

It didn't matter that he knew any number of more beautiful women. Clever, high achievers who combined chic style, business savvy and an eagerness to share his bed.

Something about Carys set her apart.

Her curves would horrify the perpetually dieting women he knew in Milano. Her dark hair was severely styled, if you could call scraping it back into a bun a style. Her make-up was discreet, and she wore a sensible navy suit that no woman of his acquaintance would be seen dead in.

Yet the way her face had lit with emotion earlier hinted at a more subtle attractiveness. And those legs… The sight of her shapely calves and trim ankles in high heels and dark stockings tugged at his long-dormant libido.

Alessandro's hands flexed. He wanted to explore further, to discover if her legs were as sexy all the way up.

Instinct—or was it memory?—told him her legs were superb. Just as he knew he'd found pleasure in her neatly curved figure and her deliciously full lips.

Belatedly he dragged his gaze from the woman who'd lured him halfway around the world.

The way she sidetracked him was unprecedented. One way or another he had to get her out of his system.

'*Grazie,* Robson. That's all for tonight.'

The butler inclined his head. 'There are refreshments on the sideboard should you require them, sir, madam.' Not by so much as a flicker did he indicate he knew the woman before him to be a co-worker. Then he moved silently away towards the kitchen and the staff entrance.

'Please—' Alessandro gestured to the nearby lounge '—take a seat.'

For a moment he thought she wasn't going to accept. Finally she walked across the antique carpet to sit in a cavernous wing chair. The glow of lamps lit her face, revealing a tension around her pursed lips he hadn't noticed before. She looked tired.

Alessandro flicked a look at his watch. It was very late. He'd become accustomed to working long into the night, fuelled by caffeine and his own formidable drive.

Conscience niggled. He should have left this till tomorrow. But he'd been unable to ignore the edgy frustration that drove him relentlessly. He was so close he couldn't rest till he had answers from her.

He'd already been stymied once. Alessandro had confronted her at the ball only to find he'd been robbed of composure and even the power of speech by a shocking blast of recognition. He'd frozen, the one thought in his atrophying mind to hold her and not let her go.

The completeness of that instant of vulnerability had stunned and shamed him. *Never* had he felt at such a loss. Not in business. Definitely not in his dealings with women.

Now he was himself once more. It would not happen again. *Alessandro Mattani did not do vulnerable.*

He thrust aside the momentary doubt at his tactics and strode across to the sideboard.

'Tea, coffee?' he offered. 'Wine?'

'I don't want anything.' She sat straighter, her chin hitched high in unspoken defiance. That spark of rebellion brought colour to her cheeks and made her eyes sparkle.

Alessandro paused, watching fascinated as she transformed from drab to intriguing in an instant. Then he turned, poured himself a small measure of cognac, and took a seat opposite her.

All the while she watched him with those luminous eyes that had captivated him the moment he saw her.

What did she see? Was she cataloguing the differences in him? It surprised him to discover how much he wanted to read her thoughts. Know what she felt. Did she too experience this gnawing tension, like an ache between the ribs?

'I see you've noticed my scar.'

The wash of colour along her cheekbones intensified, but she didn't look away. Nor did she respond.

Alessandro wasn't vain enough to worry about his marred face. Besides, it was his wealth and position as much as his looks to which women responded. They might say they wanted a man of charm or kindness, but he knew how fickle they were. Neither marriage vows nor ties of blood between mother and child could hold them when they found someone who offered more wealth and prestige.

That didn't bother Alessandro. He had both in abundance. If ever he wanted a woman permanently he'd have his pick. Some time in the future. Not now.

He swirled the fine brandy in its glass, inhaling its mellow scent.

'Am I so repulsive, then?' He shot her a look that dared her to prevaricate.

Repulsive? Carys wished he were. Then maybe she could tear her gaze away. Her heart hammered. She struggled to hide her shortened breathing as she felt the tug of his potent masculine aura.

It had always been the same. But she'd prayed time and common sense would cure her of the fatal weakness.

She met his intense moss-green gaze, recognised the way his thick dark lashes shadowed his eyes. His eyelids dropped as if to hide his thoughts. The familiarity of that expression, as much as its banked heat, made her insides squirm in mixed delight and distress.

'You got me here to talk about your looks?' Carys had more sense than to answer his question.

To her horror she found him more attractive than ever. Even the scar leading from just beneath one straight black eyebrow up to his temple failed to detract from the beautiful spare lines of his leanly sculpted face.

She gripped her hands tight in her lap, alarmed to discover that, when it came to pure animal attraction, Alessandro still exerted a power she couldn't deny.

Just as well she had more sense than to succumb to it. She was cured. Surely she was.

'You keep staring at it.' He lifted the brandy to his lips. Carys watched the movement of his throat as he swallowed and her pulse tripped crazily. She'd rarely seen him in formal clothes, but they only enhanced his magnetism.

Alessandro had been an enigma, suave and sophisticated, impossibly elegant even in the most casual clothes, even *without* clothes. But at the same time there'd been something earthy and all-male about him. Something innately stronger than the varnish of wealth and centuries of good breeding.

'What are you thinking?' he asked.

Heat flared in her cheeks as Carys realised she was imagining him naked, long-limbed and strong. She tore her gaze away.

She might despise him, but she was still woman enough to respond to his sheer sex appeal.

'Nothing. I was just thinking about how you've changed.' It was only half a lie.

'Have I altered so much?' She sensed movement and turned her head to find him leaning forward, elbows on his knees.

She shrugged. 'It's been…' Just in time she stopped herself. He didn't need to know she recalled to the day how long it had been. 'A while. People change.'

'How have I changed?'

Carys wondered at the intensity of his stare. She felt it like the caress of a jade blade across her skin, smooth but potentially lethal.

'Well, there's the scar for a start.'

She closed her lips before she could blurt out questions about his health. Had he been in an accident? Or, her thudding heartbeat faltered, had it been surgery?

Sternly she told herself she didn't care.

'I'm in excellent health now.' The murmured words surprised her. How had he read her mind?

'Of course you are,' she said too quickly. 'Otherwise you wouldn't be here.' If he was ill he'd be in Italy, under the care of the country's top doctors, not summoning her to his room in the early hours to talk about…what *did* he want?

Carys' nerves spasmed in denial. There could only be one reason for his presence. Only one thing he wanted.

Her son.

Surely Alessandro's presence here meant he'd decided belatedly that he wanted Leo after all.

Alessandro didn't do things by halves. If he wanted something he'd take it all. And surely any normal Italian male would want his own son?

Fear wrapped icy fingers around her heart. If she was right, what chance did she have of stopping him?

'How else have I changed?'

Carys frowned at this fixation with his looks. The man she'd known had been careless about that, though he'd dressed with the instinctive panache of one who'd grown up amongst a chic, fashion-conscious set.

'You're paler than before. And thinner.'

When they'd met, he'd been on a skiing holiday, his olive skin burnished dark golden-brown by the alpine sun. His body was all hard-packed muscle and rangy height. Carys had looked into his dancing green eyes and sensuous smile that made her feel she was the only other person on the planet. Without a second thought she'd fallen for him like a ton of bricks.

Now he seemed pared down, but that only emphasised his spectacular bone structure. The way he moved made it clear he hadn't lost his whipcord strength and abundant energy.

He lifted the brandy to his lips again, but not before she read a wry grimace. 'I've been working long hours.'

Such long hours he'd stopped eating?

Carys looked away, silently berating herself for caring.

'Some things don't change, then.'

Those last weeks, Alessandro had used work as an excuse not to be with her. At first she'd thought there was a problem with the business, or with Alessandro assuming its control after his father's death, but her tentative questions, her attempts to understand and offer support, had been firmly rebuffed.

The company was fine. He was fine. She worried too much. He just had responsibilities to fulfil. She remembered the litany.

Methodically Alessandro had shut her out of his life, day by day and hour by hour. Till their only communication was during the brief pre-dawn hours when he'd take her with a blistering-hot passion that had threatened to consume them both.

Until she'd discovered it wasn't just business taking him away. That he'd had time for other things, other…people. How gullible she'd been, believing he'd be content with the naïve, unsophisticated woman who shared his bed...

'Being the CEO of a multi-national enterprise requires commitment.'

'I know that.' She'd given up worrying about the ridiculous hours he'd begun working. Given up trying to understand what had happened to the charming, attentive man with whom she'd fallen in love. That man had worked hard too, but he'd known how to switch off. How to enjoy being with her.

Her stomach churned. Whatever they'd once shared was over. He'd left her in no doubt she'd never live up to his exacting standards.

What was she doing here?

Her throat closed as the futility of their conversation swamped her. This could lead nowhere, achieve nothing but the reopening of painful wounds.

Carys shot to her feet. 'It's been...interesting seeing you again. But I have to go. It's late.'

The words were barely out of her mouth when he was before her, looming so close she had to tilt her head to meet his eyes. His gaze licked like flame across her skin.

Instinctively she stepped back, only to find her way blocked. Heat engulfed her as her brain processed frantic messages. Of surprise. Of anger. Of excitement.

'You can't leave yet.'

'I can and will.' She refused to play the fool for him again. 'We're finished.'

'Finished?' One straight brow quirked up, and his mouth curved in a tight, unamused smile. 'Then what about this?'

He snagged her close with one long arm so she landed hard against him. Then he lowered his head.

CHAPTER THREE

'ALESSANDRO!'

Her voice was scratchy with surprise as she said his name for the first time, making him pause. Yet the sound was familiar. He felt it deep in his bones.

She was familiar, the way her body melded to his, all feminine enticement as he pinioned her to him.

He'd tried to hold back. Go slow. Behave sensibly.

But from the moment she'd walked in everything had changed. His caution, his adherence to the niceties of social behaviour had melted away. Now he operated on raw, primal instinct that overrode logic and convention.

He held her satisfyingly close. With her breasts cushioned against his torso, her hips pressed against him. He felt anticipation surge.

When she'd arrived, looking weary yet defiant, he'd questioned his need to confront her tonight. But those doubts disintegrated as her body softened against his and he heard the tell-tale hitch in her breathing.

There might be fire in her eyes, but the way she fitted against him belied her indignation.

This was mutual.

He had no conscious recollection of her but his body remembered her. The stirring in his loins told its own tale of familiarity and desire.

He looked down into grey-blue eyes, darkening with sparks

of azure and indigo, and felt he was falling through mist, towards a bright sunny place.

He inhaled her spicy soft cinnamon fragrance and his brain cried *Yes! This is the one!*

'Alessandro!' Her voice was more determined now, like her hands pushing at his chest. Yet that underpinning note of hesitancy betrayed her.

He lifted one hand to palm her face. Her cheek was soft and pale as milk. Her eyelids fluttered and drooped then snapped wide open.

'You have no right to do this. Let me go.' Yet she'd stopped struggling, merely stood straighter and unyielding in his embrace.

'No right?' He swiped his thumb across her mouth, tugging at her lower lip, feeling its luscious pad and the moist heat of her breath against his skin.

Her mouth opened and those eyelids flickered betrayingly.

Tendrils of fire twisted and coiled through his body, unfurling and spreading as he watched her response to that simple caress.

He widened his stance, surrounding her with his thighs and pulling her closer to his pelvis.

The promise of bliss was a primitive tattoo in his blood, pounding heavier, faster, demanding action. Yet Alessandro reined in the impulse to demand more. He had to know, to understand, as well as feel.

'You give me the right when you respond to me that way.' Again he slid his thumb along her mouth, this time pressing deeper till he felt her tongue slick against his finger.

He stiffened, every muscle clamped tight at the roiling surge of need that engulfed him.

Madonna mia! How potent was this woman, that the mere touch of her tongue could splinter his control?

Surprise darkened her eyes. She felt it too.

'I'm not…doing anything,' she protested in a hoarse voice that told its own story. Suddenly she was pushing at him again, trying to lever herself away.

'Carys.' He loved the sound of her name on his tongue. Just as he anticipated, he was addicted to the taste of her lips. 'Would you deny me? Deny this?'

Deftly he slid his hand round to cup her head, feeling the silky weight of her hair against his palm. Then he drew her close, bending to meet her lips.

She turned her head, refusing access to her mouth. His senses filled with the velvet softness of her skin, the sweet temptation of her body's perfume, as he brushed his lips below her ear.

Her restless movements stopped instantly. Arrested by the same sensations that bombarded him? Desire and heady bliss?

He slid his mouth over her neck, then up to her ear, circling the delicate lobe with his tongue.

She started in his arms as if zapped by the same jolt of energy that skewered him to the spot. Through the pounding in his ears he half heard, half felt her sigh.

'You can't deny this,' he murmured.

Her skin tasted clean and sweet, like spring flowers made of flesh. Hungrily he nuzzled the corner of her jaw, the edge of her chin, the beauty spot beside her mouth.

Bracing to pull back just a fraction, he looked down into her face.

His lips curved in a tight, satisfied smile when he saw closed eyes, lips parted invitingly, as if urging him to claim her.

Her hair had started to come down as she tried to avoid his grip. Now, looking at the long strands of wavy silk falling across his wrist, he realised it wasn't black as he'd thought in the ballroom. It was darkest brown, tinged with sparks of russet fire.

An image filled his brain, of rich dark hair spread over plump white pillows. Of his hands threading through its satiny splendour, splaying it out like a radiant sunburst.

Not just an image.

A memory!

Of Carys, lying sleepily in bed with him. Of her lazy smile, so dazzling it rivalled the brilliance of the snow-lit scene visible through the window above the bed.

The impact of that sudden recollection rocked him off balance, his arms tightening automatically around her.

For the second time in one night he'd remembered!

He'd known coming here was right.

With this woman he could unlock the closed door to the past.

Restore all that was lost. Once he remembered he'd be free of this lurking awareness of something missing, of something incomplete in his life.

Then he could move on, content with his life again.

'Alessandro.' Her eyes were open now and aware. He read shock there and chagrin in the way she gnawed at her lip. 'Let me go. Please.'

He'd been taught to respect a woman's wishes. The Mattani code of honour was deeply ingrained, and he would never force himself on a woman. But it was too late to dissemble. Carys wanted this as much as he, despite her words.

Surely one kiss couldn't hurt.

'After this,' he murmured. 'I promise you'll enjoy it.' Almost as much as he intended to.

He captured her head, turned her face up to his, and slanted his mouth over hers.

Carys strained to shove him away. Desperation lent power to her tired limbs, yet she made no impact on him. If anything his wide shoulders loomed closer. He was stronger than her by far.

The knowledge should have frightened her. Yet part of her exulted. The unreformed hedonist inside her that she'd only discovered when she'd met Alessandro. The lover who'd been enraptured by his masculinity and athletic power. The heartbroken woman who'd loved and lost and secretly hoped to have her love returned.

Her struggle was as much within herself as against him.

Warm lips covered her mouth, and a judder of shocking need raked her from head to toe. It was instant, all-consuming and undeniable.

But she refused to give in to it. She pressed her palms against his shoulders and leant back as far as his encompassing arm allowed. Frantic to escape, she remembered too well how she'd always responded to him.

His kiss was unexpectedly tender, a gentle caress of firm lips along the closed line of her mouth.

His unfamiliar cologne, subtle yet masculine, tinged the air.

The heat of his body warmed hers. His arms held her as if he'd never let her go.

Another illusion.

Carys tried to whip up her resolve, her scorn. But her mind fought a losing battle when her body was already capitulating.

'No!' She had to get away. Had to stand firm against him. 'I don't—'

It was too late. With the unerring instinct of a born predator, Alessandro took advantage of her momentary lapse and plunged his tongue into her open mouth.

Her breath stopped as reality splintered into fragments around her. He caressed her tongue, the inside of her cheeks. The dark world behind her closed eyelids came alive with flashes of fire. He grasped the back of her head, then tilted his own so he could delve deeper with a slow thoroughness that made her shudder in response.

Her hands on his shoulders curved, holding tight. Her panic faded. Tentatively her mouth moved with his, following the dance of desire they'd created together time and again. Carys mimicked his movements and slowly, like a sleeper waking from hibernation, felt the life force surge in her blood. Hunger gnawed her belly.

Soon she answered his demands with her own.

This felt so *right*.

His arms curved close, tugging her intimately against him. His kiss lured, delighted and provoked her into a response that escalated from tentative to eager and unashamed.

Now Carys' hands slipped from his shoulders to his neck, then up to furrow through his short, crisp hair and mould his head with desperate fingers. He was real, solid and wonderful, not the ephemeral phantom of her dreams. She needed him close, closer, to satisfy the burgeoning craving for more.

Heady, half-formed memories bombarded her. Of Alessandro pleasuring her. Of him holding her tight in his arms as if he'd never let her go. Of the instant spark of recognition and understanding that had passed between them the moment they'd met.

But these were tiny flickers, mere shadows of thought. She was absorbed in relearning the feel of Alessandro. His hair, his lips and tongue, the hot steel of his arms around her, the muscle and bone strength of his long body. His taste and scent.

Carys leaned in, glorying in the slide of achingly full breasts against his hard torso. She rose on tiptoe, seeking more, trying to get closer, to absorb herself into the wonderful luxury, the effervescent excitement of his kiss.

With a muffled groan, Alessandro lashed his other arm around her, lower, wrapping round her buttocks and lifting her off the ground.

Yes! Carys gave herself up to each exquisite sensation: of their mouths meshing, of his formidable strength enveloping her, of burning hot skin beneath her fingers as she moulded his jaw and cheeks.

Alessandro moved. She felt his thighs shift around her as he walked, and then there was something solid behind her while Alessandro pressed close. A wall? A couch? She'd lost all sense of perspective.

He tilted his hips in a slow grinding movement and desire blasted through her. His pelvis and hers were in perfect alignment, the heavy bulge in his trousers a portent of pleasure to come.

Instinctively she curved her body up to meet him. A throb began deep between her legs, an edgy neediness that strung her tight with anticipation.

'Temptress. Siren.' His muttered words were hoarse, as if squeezed out under duress.

Carys let her head loll against a hard surface and gulped oxygen into her air-starved lungs. Alessandro ravished her face and throat with burning kisses that ignited tiny explosions of pleasure through her taut body. And all the while he pushed close as if he could melt the barrier of their clothes and bring them both the bliss they craved.

One large hand slid down her hip and over her thigh, igniting tremors of fresh awareness. When his palm climbed back, her skirt bunched beneath it, riding higher and higher.

Carys opened her mouth, vaguely aware of the need to protest, but his mouth slammed into hers again, robbing her of breath and the beginnings of thought.

Once more Alessandro pleasured her, this time with a kiss so sweet yet so demanding it devoured the last of her resistance. She lolled back as he drew forth every last shred of hidden longing.

Willingly Carys complied as he lifted her leg up around his hip, and then the other. The bittersweet ache between her legs, and deeper, inside her womb, became a steady throb. Encircling him with her legs, she squeezed tight.

As if he understood, Alessandro pressed close again, pushing his erection just…there.

Yes! That was what she wanted. To have him warm the empty places in her body and her soul that had been chilled for so long.

Large hands slid under the tight, rumpled fabric of her skirt, up her thighs till they reached bare, quivering flesh.

'Stockings,' he breathed against her mouth. 'You dress to drive a man insane.'

She wasn't listening. Carys heard the low burr of his voice, felt his breath against her lips, but the words made no sense. Only the approval in his tone was real.

Haphazardly she ripped at his bow tie, desperate for his hot skin bare beneath her palms.

Long fingers slid around her thighs, stroking and teasing her sensitive skin. She jerked and squirmed, tugging at his shirt till, with a rip, it tore open.

A torrent of slurred Italian signalled his approval. But she barely noticed for heaven was in the touch of wiry hair and steamy satiny flesh under her hands. In the rapid pulse of his heart pounding against her touch.

His hands moved, and a knuckle brushed against the damp cotton of her panties.

'*Cara,*' he growled deep in his throat. 'I *knew* you wanted this as much as I do.' He insinuated probing fingers beneath the elastic of her underwear while, with his other hand, he fumbled at his belt.

Reality, hard and relentless, broke upon her in an instant of icy clarity. The heady, exquisite arousal faded as her mind kicked into gear.

Was it the greedy touch of his fingers in that most intimate of places? The practised way he undid his belt and ripped open the fastening of his trousers? The smug satisfaction in his voice?

He didn't even want *her,* an outraged voice cried in her head. He wanted 'this'. Sex. Physical satisfaction.

Presumably any woman would do. Carys was just conveniently available.

More than available. Willing. Desperate for him.

Aghast, Carys stiffened.

What had she done? She'd let her loneliness, memories of the bliss they'd once shared, lead her into self-destructive temptation.

'No! Stop.' Mortified, she shoved with all her might, wriggling to dislodge his questing fingers and unwrap her legs. 'Let me go!'

She moved so unexpectedly he didn't prevent her and even moved back a precious few centimetres, allowing her to slide her legs free. That was when she registered it was a wall behind her, as her stockinged feet hit the floor. She had to brace herself against the weakness in her knees so she didn't collapse.

He'd almost had her, up against the wall of his suite! Fully clothed!

The glorious heat they'd shared bled away as mortification and disbelief welled. After all that had happened how *could* she have been so weak?

'Carys…'

She batted his hands away, stumbling to escape and tripping over a discarded shoe.

Her self respect was in shreds. Her chest heaved with distress as she fumbled with shaky fingers to push her straight skirt down her hips. Her eyes blurred.

'Let me.'

'No!' Carys whirled to face him, arms outstretched to keep him at bay.

Even with lipstick on his jaw, and his jacket and dress shirt torn open to reveal a dusky, hair-dusted chest, he looked in command, powerful and controlled.

Sexier than any man had a right to be.

Then she saw the way his chest rose and fell, as if from exertion. The tendons in his neck stood out and his facial muscles were drawn too tight. A flush of colour slanted across his cheeks and his nostrils flared as if he fought for oxygen.

The evidence of simple animal lust. That was all Alessandro had ever felt for her.

When would she learn? Self-disgust filled her.

Her poor tortured heart compressed as a weight as big as Flinders Street Station pushed down on her chest. Breathing was agony.

But the realisation of what she'd almost done was worse. One kiss…one kiss and she'd been scrabbling at his shirt, desperate to feel his body against hers, urging him on to take her.

Her chin crumpled and she bit her lip. She'd invited her own degradation.

Once again Alessandro had proved himself a consummate seducer. But that was no excuse. She should be able to resist him. She had to. Where was her self-respect?

'Don't touch me,' she whispered as she wriggled her hips, tugging the skirt down. She kept her eyes above his waist, not wanting to see what she'd felt pressing intimately against her, inviting her to mindless pleasure.

Involuntarily her internal muscles clenched. Her betraying body was still ready for his possession. The knowledge flattened the last remnant of her pride.

'*Va bene*. As you wish.' The feral gleam in Alessandro's eyes warned her he wouldn't be thwarted for long. 'Instead we will talk. For now.'

Fire scorched her throat and she looked away, unable to meet his dark scrutiny any longer.

Slowly Carys backed across the floor, feet sinking into the plush depth of carpet. He didn't follow her but stood, arms akimbo, as if waiting for her to come to her senses.

'We have to talk, Carys.'

Like hell they did. They'd done enough *talking* for one night. The brush of cool air on her heated skin made her frown and reach for her throat, only to discover her blouse hung open to reveal her white cotton bra.

How had that happened? Carys clutched the edges of her

blouse together with numb fingers. She shot an accusing glare across the room, but Alessandro said nothing, merely raised an eyebrow and crossed his arms over his chest as if waiting for her to come to her senses.

For all his immobility she couldn't rid herself of the notion he merely waited to pounce.

Would she have the resolve to stop him next time?

'I'm not staying here to be attacked again.'

'Attacked!' He drew himself up to his full height and stared down his long aristocratic nose at her. 'Hardly that. You were panting for my touch.'

His arrogant claim was the final straw because it was true. Her resolution had failed. She was weak and nothing could protect her from him. Nothing but bluff.

She shrugged, the movement more stiff than insouciant.

'I was curious, that's all. And,' she hurried on as he opened his mouth to reject her explanation, 'and besides, it's been a while since I…'

'You've been saving yourself, *cara?* Is that it?' His smoky voice urged her to assent and blurt out that there'd been no one since him. Wouldn't he just love that!

Fury sizzled along her veins. Glorious wrath at the man who'd taken her innocence, her love and her trust and thought he could have her again at the click of his fingers.

'No,' Carys lied. It would just feed his ego to know there'd been no one since him. She shifted her gaze.

He held her in thrall. What would it take to make him relinquish his pursuit? Desperation drove her to blurt out the first thing she could think of to stop him.

'My boyfriend and I had a disagreement and—'

'Boyfriend?' His voice thundered through the suite. 'You were missing your *boyfriend?* You can't tell me you were thinking of him just now?'

'Can't I?' Carys swung her head round and felt his dark green stare like frozen shards of crystal grazing her skin.

'I don't believe you.' But she'd sown the seed of doubt. That was obvious from his sudden pallor.

A tiny fillip of triumph rose. Maybe she could make herself safe from him after all.

'Believe what you like, Conte Mattani.'

'Don't use that title with me,' he snapped. 'I'm not some stranger.'

She said nothing, merely backed a few more steps towards the foyer.

'You don't intend to leave looking like that,' he announced in a cold, disapproving tone.

Carys felt the weight of her hair tumbling round her shoulders and knew she looked as if she'd been ravaged to within an inch of her life. She was barefoot, half undressed, her lips bruised and swollen from the intensity of their passion, and her nipples thrust shamelessly against the cotton of her bra. Anyone looking at her would know precisely what she'd been doing.

She had a choice: an ignominious flight from the presidential suite looking like a complete wanton or a cosy *tête a tête* with Alessandro Mattani.

She was across the room before he could move a step.

'Just watch me.'

Alessandro stood on the private terrace of his suite, watching the dark-clad workers scurry across the bridge and swarm the streets. Morning peak hour and he'd already been at work for several hours.

Habitually he started early and finished late. But this morning…he raked a hand through his hair as frustration filled him.

He'd slept even less than usual, bedevilled by tantalising dreams of luscious pale limbs entwined with his, of generous feminine curves and silky smooth skin, of smoky blue-grey eyes enticing him to the brink of sexual fulfilment. Each time he'd woken, sweating, gasping for breath and formidably aroused, to the realisation Carys Wells had fled rather than allow them the release they both craved.

He rubbed a hand over his freshly shaved jaw, as if to dispel the tension there.

Even in sleep she denied him.

He could barely believe she'd run. Especially after he'd felt the hunger in her, a hunger as ravening as his own. It was a wonder their clothes hadn't disintegrated around them, their passion had been so combustible.

He grasped the iron balustrade savagely. Could it have been a tactic to tease him into wanting more then leave him aching with need? What could she hope to gain?

He shook his head. No woman was that good an actress. Besides, he knew every trick in the book when it came to conniving women, and Carys hadn't played the tease. He remembered the scent of her arousal, sharp and musky.

Oh, no, Carys Wells had wanted him all right.

Why had she denied them both?

A stiff breeze blew up from the river and chilled his skin. He should have taken things slower, scoped out the situation rather than allowing his driving need free rein.

One of the first things he'd learned when he entered the commercial world was to plan carefully and unemotionally and only strike at the most opportune moment.

Last night it hadn't been his brain doing the thinking.

He'd frightened her off. Her wide eyes had been desperate as she backed to the door. For an instant he'd even suspected they shone overbright.

A ripple of regret passed through him and he frowned.

His security team assured him she'd got home safely, unaware of their surveillance or their orders to keep her safe. Yet still Alessandro felt the weight of guilt. It was his fault she'd fled.

He should have controlled himself and conquered his animal instincts. Yet he'd been unable to comprehend anything but the need to possess her.

Alessandro scrubbed his palm over his face again, grimacing. He couldn't remember ever acting with less forethought. He'd been like a starving man set before a banquet, unable to summon even a shred of restraint.

Was he always like that with her?

The question tantalised him. The frustration of not knowing ate like acid into his gut.

He was so close, and still the answers eluded him.

A discreet ringtone interrupted his thoughts and he drew his cellphone from his pocket.

It was Bruno, head of his security team, reporting on Carys' movements this morning. Alessandro froze into immobility at the report, delivered in a carefully uninflected tone.

Eventually he roused himself enough to issue a few more orders. Then he took the phone from his ear and waited for the image Bruno was sending.

There it was. A little blurry with movement, but unmistakeable. Carys Wells, in a familiar dark suit and not a hair out of place. But what held Alessandro's attention wasn't his erstwhile lover. It was the burden she carried in her arms.

Small, rounded, riveting his attention.

A baby.

Carys had a child.

The air purged from Alessandro's lungs in a hiss of disbelief. His jaw tightened so hard his head began to throb as he stared at the image before him.

Whose child? The boyfriend from whom she'd been separated? Some other man? A long-term lover or a passing stranger?

Pain roused him from his turbulent thoughts. Alessandro looked down to discover he'd grasped the railing so hard the decorative ironwork had drawn blood on the fleshy part of his palm.

Dispassionately he stared at the welling redness, then back at the picture of Carys and her child.

Only then did Alessandro recognise the emotion surging so high it threatened to choke him. Fury. Raw sizzling wrath that she'd been with another man.

It didn't matter how or why they'd separated. Every instinct screamed that Carys belonged to *him*. Could it be any clearer after the way they'd been together? The intensity of their passion made every other liaison pale into insignificance.

He'd come seeking answers. Last night he'd discovered answers weren't enough. He wanted Carys too, for as long as the attraction between them held.

Looking at her holding another man's child in her arms sent spears of flame through his chest and gut.

The sight should have cured him of his lust.

Instead he felt a burning desire to discover the identity of the man who'd fathered Carys' baby and mash him into a pulp with his bare hands.

CHAPTER FOUR

CARYS pulled her long, flapping coat tight around herself as she left the staff entrance. A cheap second-hand purchase, it helped combat Melbourne's cold, but it was a size too large, billowing out in the wind and allowing chill draughts to tease her.

A glance at the louring sky made her pick up her pace, scurrying to avoid the blur of rain already washing over the city. With luck her train would be on time and she'd get home at a reasonable hour. Two of her colleagues had returned to work today, so she didn't have to stay back.

Carys looked forward to the luxury of some quiet time with Leo then a long luxurious soak and a good night's sleep.

Resolutely she avoided the knowledge that she'd probably spend another sleepless night tossing and turning.

She'd made it through the day in a state of numb shock, working like an automaton, except when the sight of a tall dark-haired man, or an unexpected call, froze the blood in her veins.

She'd expected him to come after her. If not last night when she'd left him high and dry, then today.

He knew where she worked. He knew far too much. Why had he left her alone?

Foreboding crept through her. He was biding his time.

It could only be Leo he wanted. Her precious boy. What else would drag Alessandro here from Italy?

The realisation was like a knife at her neck. A man with Alessandro's resources could get anything he wanted.

If he wanted Leo…

Carys had no illusions that he was here for anything else. For Alessandro, last night had simply been about the chance for hot sex.

Absence from his wife must be wearing on him.

Bile rose in Carys' throat, a savage, scouring bitterness. Shame flooded her and she ducked her head.

She hadn't even remembered he was tied to another woman! The overwhelming reality of his presence had blasted Carys back to a time when she'd been his, body and soul. When she'd believed he was hers. Before he had married his blue-blooded heiress.

Carys tasted salt on her tongue as she bit her lip.

Distress filled her at how close she'd come to compounding her stupidity in an act that would shatter her principles.

She hadn't been able to meet her eyes in the mirror this morning, recalling her uninhibited response to him.

Fury, disbelief and disappointment filled her. At him for using her as a convenience to assuage his physical needs. For not being the honourable man she'd once thought him. At herself for abandoning her pride and principles in letting him sweep her into his tempestuous embrace.

Carys squared her shoulders. She'd played the fool for the last time. Besides, he'd relinquished all rights when he—

A pair of massive mirror-polished black shoes blocked the pavement before her. Carys side-stepped to skirt the man, but with one long stride he moved too, forcing her to stop.

Her gaze climbed a pair of bulky legs in pin-striped trousers so beautifully tailored they almost tamed the rampantly muscled solidity of the man. Neat shirt, dark tie, perfectly fitting jacket and a swarthy face topped by pepper and salt hair. Gold winked in the man's earlobe as he turned his head and Carys stared, sure she'd seen him before.

'*Scusa, signorina.* This way, please.'

He extended one arm, gesturing towards the kerb.

Carys turned to see a limousine with tinted windows drawn up beside her, its back door open.

Her pulse sped up to thunder in her ears. A sprawl of long masculine limbs filled her vision of the interior and her heart rate spiked. The last thing she wanted was to share such an intimate space with Alessandro Mattani.

'You've got to be kidding,' she muttered, automatically stepping back from the road.

The large Italian moved closer, shepherding her towards the vehicle. Resolutely she planted her feet on the pavement, refusing to budge.

She looked around, hoping to find the street filled with people, but the few she saw were racing for cover as big fat drops of rain spattered the pavement. There was no one to interfere if Alessandro's goon tried to manhandle her into the car.

'Why don't you get in before you both get soaked?' asked a cool voice from the back of the limo.

Outraged dignity came to her rescue. 'And if I'd prefer to get drenched than share a car with you?'

'I'd say it was very selfish of you to force Bruno to suffer the same fate just for the sake of your pride.'

Her eyes rounded. Pride? Alessandro thought this was simply about pride?

The man beside her moved, closing in beside her, and Carys darted a glance at him, wondering if she had any hope of getting away. He was built like a rugby player, all dense-packed muscle. Right now he had that grim, blank-eyed set to his face that she'd seen on the super-tough minders of the rich and famous.

'Per favore, signorina.'

Drops splattered his jacket as the rain fell faster. He didn't bat an eyelid, just watched her with the stony countenance of a man ready to deal with anything.

She'd bet five feet six of female, hampered by heels and a skirt, would be the work of a moment to overpower.

'Don't let his looks fool you, Carys,' came a laconic voice from the limo's interior. 'Bruno has a weak chest. He's just got over a bout of bronchitis. I wouldn't like him to have a relapse. And you wouldn't want that on your conscience.'

Carys blinked, catching the merest flicker of expression on the security man's face. A smile? Surely not.

Movement to one side caught her eye, and she turned to find

Alessandro had slid to the edge of the seat and was regarding her with a peculiarly unreadable expression.

'His wife would flay me alive if I brought him home with pneumonia.'

Despite her anger, Carys felt her lips twitch. Once, long ago, Alessandro's dry wit had been one of the things that had drawn her to him. She'd almost forgotten that, her memories skewed by those final, unhappy days when banter and teasing had been absent between them.

'I would have thought blackmail was more your style,' she jeered. 'Or threats, rather than an appeal to my conscience.'

Rain trickled into her collar, but she stood ramrod straight. This man was dangerous.

A shrug of those lean shoulders and he said something in Italian that made Bruno move away to give them space. Carys barely had time to register the chance for escape when Alessandro's voice curled around her, silkily smooth. 'I regret last night, Carys. It wasn't planned.'

He paused, awaiting a response that she steadfastly refused to give. If that was his idea of an apology he had a lot to learn.

Alessandro's eyes narrowed as she stood rigid under his scrutiny. Something glittered in that forest-dark gaze that sent shivers of trepidation running through her. Despite his earlier light-hearted words, his stare sizzled. She guessed his deadpan expression disguised an anger almost as great as her own. Now she looked more closely, she read tension in his shoulders and grim mouth.

Too bad. She tilted her chin up, wishing she had a long aristocratic nose like his so she could look down it.

'But if that's the way you'd prefer to do this,' he purred, 'then I can oblige.'

She'd opened her mouth to say she preferred to have nothing to do with him, when his next words forestalled her.

'I'm sure the hotel management would be interested in the security camera footage of the lobby outside the presidential suite last night, and in the lift. If they cared to check the recording they'd find it…illuminating.'

'You wouldn't!' Shock hammered her like a physical blow, sucking out her breath. That tape would show her emerging from his suite in the early hours looking like…like…

'Wouldn't I?' His stare was unnervingly blank. 'I'm sure they frown on staff providing *personal* services to guests.' His tongue dripped with hateful innuendo and Carys burned with frustration and fury. Her hands clenched around the shoulder strap of her bag.

'I wasn't providing a service, you—'

'It doesn't matter what you were doing, Carys. All that matters is how the evidence appears.' He leaned back with a smug glimmer in his eyes.

Evidence. It sounded so formal.

It *would* be formal if anyone decided to check the recording. Formal enough to get her the sack.

Her heart dived and she shivered, but not from the rain's chill. She needed this job. How else could she support Leo? Good positions were hard to find for someone with limited qualifications.

Would Alessandro make good on his threat?

Once she'd thought she'd known this man. Had trusted him. Had even believed he was falling in love with her.

What a naïve innocent she'd been.

She'd learned the hard way not to trust her judgement with him. Better to assume him capable of anything to get his own way. He'd already made a fool of her once.

He was her enemy, threatening the life she'd begun to build, her independence, even, she feared, her child.

'What do you want?' She didn't care that her voice was scratchy with distress, despite her attempt to appear calm.

'To talk. We have unfinished business.'

He didn't wait for her to assent but slid back across the wide leather seat, making space for her.

Unfinished business.

That was how he described one little boy?

Her throat closed convulsively as the fight bled out of her. She couldn't ignore Alessandro. She had to face him and hope against hope she could retain some control of the situation.

She tottered forward on numb legs and entered the limousine, her wet coat sliding along a leather seat that looked and smelled fresh from the factory.

Only the best for the Conte Mattani.

Under no circumstances would she, an ordinary single mum with not an ounce of glamour, be classed as *the best*. Alessandro had made that abundantly clear in Italy.

Her heart bumped against her ribs. Had Alessandro decided her little boy was a different matter?

The limo door shut with a quiet click and she sagged back, shutting her eyes. She was cold to the bone.

There was no escape now.

Moments later the front door closed and the vehicle accelerated. Belatedly she remembered to do up her seatbelt. A swift sideways glance told her Alessandro wasn't happy, despite having got her where he wanted her.

The proud, spare lines of his face seemed austere and forbidding silhouetted against the city streets. He looked as approachable as some ancient king, brooding over judgement.

The flicker of unease inside her magnified into a hundred fluttering wings. She was at a disadvantage to him in so many ways.

His silence reinforced that she was here at his pleasure.

Carys flicked her gaze away, not deigning to ask where they were going. Two could play the silent game. It would give her time to marshal her resources.

As she stared straight ahead, trying to control her frantic, jumbled thoughts, she found herself looking through a smoky glass privacy-screen at the back of Bruno's head.

Recognition smote her.

'He was on my street. Last night!' Carys leaned forward to make sure. There was no mistaking the bunched-muscle silhouette of the minder's neck and shoulders, or the shape of his head.

As she'd walked up the ill-lit street to her block of flats in the early hours, she'd faltered, her heart skipping as she noticed a brawny man in jeans and a leather jacket just ahead. He looked to be waiting for someone. But as she'd hesitated he'd turned to stroll away in the opposite direction.

Nevertheless, she'd scurried inside as fast as possible. Her street was peaceful by day, but the shopping strip a few blocks away had been attracting unsavoury characters at night.

'Bruno, your bodyguard. He was outside my home.'

She swung round to find Alessandro watching her steadily. His lack of response infuriated her.

'You're not even bothering to deny it!'

'Why would I?' His brow furrowed in a hint of a frown that, annoyingly, didn't detract from his handsome looks.

'You had him follow me?' Already Alessandro had pried into her personnel records. Now his stooge had been scoping out her home. He had no qualms about invading her privacy.

'Of course.' He stared coolly as if wondering what the fuss was about. 'It was late. I had to make sure you got back all right.'

His explanation took the wind out of her sails and she slumped in her seat, her mind whirling.

'You were trying to *protect* me?'

Something indefinable flickered in his eyes. 'You were out alone at an hour when you should have been safely home.'

At least he didn't mention her state of disarray. Even in a pair of shoes borrowed from the staffroom, and with her shirt buttoned again, she'd felt as if the few people she'd met on her journey took one look and knew exactly what she'd been up to in the presidential suite.

Alessandro made her sound like a teenager in need of parental guidance. Not a twenty-five-year-old woman supporting herself and her son.

Yet it wasn't indignation Carys felt rise like a tide inside her. It was warmth, a furtive spark of pleasure, that he'd cared enough to worry about her safety.

In the old days she'd been thrilled by the way he'd looked after her, showing what she'd thought was a strongly protective nature.

Until she'd discovered her mistake. What she'd seen as caring had been his way of keeping her isolated, separate from the rest of his life. It had been a deliberate tactic to ensure she didn't know how he used her.

The lush melting warmth inside her dissipated as a chill blast of reality struck right to the bone.

'I'm perfectly capable of looking after myself! I was doing it long before you turned up.' Carys wrapped her arms around the faux-leather bag on her lap and turned away.

She was proud of what she'd achieved. When she'd arrived in Australia she'd been a mess, her heart in tatters, her confidence shattered. Even her destination of Melbourne was unplanned. She'd been too distraught to do more than turn up at the airport and board the first available flight home.

Now she'd built a new life for herself and Leo. She was working hard to achieve the financial security they needed.

'Is that so?' Scepticism dripped from each syllable as he held her with a glacial green stare. 'You really think that the best neighbourhood to bring up a child?'

Her fingers, busy fiddling with the zipper on her bag, froze. Every muscle tensed.

Now they'd come to the crux of the matter.

She waited for him to accuse her of being a bad mother, to demand his rights and push his case. Yet he remained silent, only his lowered brows hinting at displeasure.

'The flat is sunny and comfortable. And affordable.' It went against the grain to hint at her lack of funds, but no doubt he knew about her precarious finances.

Despite working right up till she went into labour, Carys had used all her meagre savings in the months after Leo's birth. If it hadn't been for the money her father had sent long-distance, she wouldn't have been able to support them. When the going had got really tough, she'd even thought of moving to be with her dad. Till she imagined his horror at the idea.

Only now, with her job at the Landford, could she make ends meet, though most of her wages went on childcare and rent and there was precious little for other necessities.

'And the location? Your neighbourhood is becoming a hub for drug dealing and prostitution.'

He didn't bother to hide his disapproval. If she hadn't been wearing a thick coat, his coruscating glare would have scraped off layers of skin.

'The reports are exaggerated,' she bluffed, refusing to admit he'd tapped into her own fear. That the cosy nest she'd created for her son grew less desirable by the week.

Only days ago there'd been more syringes found in the park and another bashing in the street. Carys had decided that, despite the friends she'd made locally, she'd look for somewhere else to bring up Leo.

'If you say so.' His tone implied boredom.

Carys was puzzled. This was his opportunity to weigh in with comments about her inability to care for Leo. To make a case that she shouldn't have sole custody.

Yet Alessandro seemed totally uninterested. Had she got it wrong? Hope rose shakily in her breast.

But if he wasn't here for her little boy, what did he want from her?

Alessandro tamped down the fury he'd felt ever since receiving this morning's report. Fury that Carys should live in such a neighbourhood. That she'd hooked up with a man who obviously refused to take care of her and her child.

That he, Alessandro, had let her get under his skin enough to be concerned for her!

He cursed himself for a fool. She'd walked out on him, moved on from whatever relationship they'd had. He should do the same. Dignity and pride demanded it.

He *would,* he vowed, once he knew all he needed to about those blank months.

Yet that sense of intimate connection still hammered at him. It was stronger even than the cool logic around which he built his life.

Despite her antipathy and her child by another man, Alessandro couldn't banish the possessiveness that swamped him when he was with her. It consumed him.

Never had he experienced such feelings.

His fists tightened as his temples throbbed. Flickers of images taunted him. Whether remnants of last night's erotic dreams or snippets of memory, he didn't know.

He wanted to hate her for the unaccustomed weakness she wrought in him. Yet the bruised violet smudges under her eyes snagged his attention. It had taken more than one sleepless night to put them there.

His belly clenched as he took in her pallor and the way her worn coat dwarfed her. Last night he'd seen she was tired, but he'd been too overwhelmed by his own cataclysmic response to register what looked now like utter exhaustion.

He'd been impatient to solve the riddle that had haunted him so long. Too busy losing himself in her lush curves and feminine promise to admit the extent of her vulnerability.

That vulnerability clawed at his conscience. He should never have unleashed the beast of sexual hunger that roared into life when she was near.

'Where's this boyfriend of yours? Why doesn't he help you?' He snapped the words out, surprising himself. It wasn't his way to blurt his thoughts.

Wary eyes met his. They darkened like storm clouds and instinctively he knew she concealed something.

Carys blinked and looked away. 'I'm fine by myself. I don't need anyone to—'

'Of course you do. You shouldn't be living in this area. Not with a baby.' He spared the run-down neighbourhood the briefest of glances. It was seedy, an area of urban decline. 'He should help you.'

Her mouth remained mutinously closed.

Alessandro knew a wholly uncharacteristic desire for hot-blooded argument. He, who never let anything ruffle his equanimity! Who was a master at sublimating useless emotions and pursuing his goals with single-minded purpose.

How this woman unsettled him. The last twenty-four hours had been a roller coaster of unfamiliar feelings that made a mockery of his habitual control.

He resented that more than anything.

'Who is he, Carys? Why do you protect him?'

Because she loved him? Alessandro's mouth flattened. This should be none of his business, yet he couldn't let go.

'I'm not protecting anyone!' she muttered. 'There's no one. What I told you—'

'You said you'd argued. That's no excuse for him walking out on his child and its mother.'

Alessandro's nostrils filled with pungent distaste. His reaction to the idea of any man getting Carys pregnant was bone-deep rage. His belly cramped as he strove to master his feelings.

Who *was* this woman that she made him react so?

She stared silently, an arrested expression on her face.

'Is he someone you work with?' The words shot out through gritted teeth.

She shook her head. 'Don't be absurd.'

There was nothing absurd about it. Working side by side led too easily to intimacy. He'd had to move his PA elsewhere after she'd mistaken their working relationship for something else. He'd lost count of the female employees and business associates who'd thought work the perfect way into his bed.

Silently he cursed himself for needing to know.

'He's married? Is that it?'

Carys stared into his glowering face and struggled against a sense of unreality. He looked genuinely perplexed. Deep grooves bracketed a mouth that morphed from sensual perfection into a wrathful line.

She shook her head as if to clear it. She mustn't have heard right.

'There *is* no man in my life.' She hesitated, knowing a craven urge to avoid the truth. 'I made that up so you'd leave me alone.'

Alessandro's brow furrowed, his eyebrows disapproving black slashes that tilted down in the centre. And still he looked better than any man she knew.

'Don't deny it. Of course there's a man.'

'Are you calling me a liar?' His refusal to accept her word reopened a wound that had never healed. He hadn't believed her before. Why should things be different now? Her word wasn't good enough.

Pain mixed with Carys' fury. Her distress was all the more potent for having been suppressed so long.

'Spare me the show of innocence,' he sneered. 'You didn't get pregnant all by yourself. Or are you trying to tell me it was an immaculate conception?'

'You bastard!' Her arm shot out faster than thought. An instant later her hand snapped across his cheek as her fury finally boiled over.

Her palm tingled. Her whole arm trembled with the force of the slap. Her breath came in hard, shallow pants. She barely noticed the dangerous glint in his narrowing eyes or the way he loomed closer.

Then, out of the blue, the implication of his words sank in. Relief swamped her, making her shake as she sagged back in her seat.

He wasn't here to take Leo away.

Hysterical laughter swelled inside at her stupidity. Alessandro didn't want to take her boy. Of course he didn't! He'd made his disinterest and disapproval clear from the start. He'd left her in no doubt both she and her baby weren't good enough for him and his rarefied circle of moneyed friends.

Why had she thought he'd changed? Because part of her still foolishly ached to believe he was the fantasy man she'd fallen in love with?

Pain welled.

It felt as if Alessandro had taken her last precious fragment of hope and callously ground it underfoot, shattering a fragile part of her.

'You really are some piece of work, Alessandro Mattani.' Her voice was hoarse with distress, her throat raw with pain as if she'd swallowed broken glass. 'I should have known you hadn't changed.'

'Me, change?' Astonishment coloured his voice, at odds with his look of rigid control.

'Yes, you. You coward.' Carys pressed a palm to her stomach, trying to prevent the churn of nausea. 'Even after all this time you refuse to acknowledge your own son.'

CHAPTER FIVE

THE woman was mad.

Or conniving.

Alessandro met her glittering eyes, dark now as a thunder storm, and saw lightning flash.

Did she even notice that he'd grabbed her wrist and yanked it from his face? That he still held it in an implacable grip?

She didn't seem to notice anything except her own fury.

His cheek burned from her slap and pride demanded instant retribution. No one, man or woman, insulted Alessandro Mattani.

Yet he held himself in check. He would not resort to violence against a woman.

More importantly, he needed to know what she was up to, this mad woman with the wild accusations and glorious eyes.

'Don't be absurd. I don't have a child.' That was one thing he'd never forget, no matter how severe his injuries.

Besides, he'd always taken care not to lay himself open to paternity claims. He enjoyed short-term liaisons, but that didn't mean he took risks with his health or his family honour.

'Spare me the act, Alessandro,' she hissed. 'Others might be impressed, but I'm not. I gave up being impressed the day I left you.'

He frowned as he felt tremors rack her body and her pulse catapult into overdrive.

'You're angry because our relationship ended?'

Women never liked knowing they held a temporary place in his life. Too often they set their sights on becoming the Contessa

Mattani. But he had no illusions about matrimony. For him it would be a duty, to carry on the family name. A duty he was happy to postpone.

Her mouth opened in a short, humourless laugh. 'I wouldn't have stayed if you'd paid me,' she spat out. 'Not once I knew what you were really like.'

Such vehemence, such hatred, was new to Alessandro. The shock of it ran through him like a jolt of electricity. It felt as if he held a jumping live wire in his hand, liable to twist unpredictably at any moment and burn him to cinders.

She was unlike anything or anyone in his well-ordered life. *She fascinated him.*

'What's this about a child?' *That* sort of claim was one he would never take lightly.

Her mouth twisted in a grimace. 'Forget it,' she muttered, turning her head away. Her dismissive tone would anger a less controlled man.

Carys tried to tug her hand free, but he held her easily. He had no intention of letting her take another swipe at him. Swiftly he captured her other hand, holding both effortlessly till she gave up trying to escape and subsided, chest heaving, against the back of the seat.

'I can hardly forget it.' He pulled her hands, making her turn. Studiously he ignored the way her rapid breathing emphasised the swell of her breasts. 'Tell me.'

Thick dark lashes rose to reveal silvery-blue eyes that flashed with repressed emotion. Her pulse pounded beneath his fingers and she swiped the tip of her tongue over her lips as if to moisten them.

Instantly desire flared in his belly.

Just like that.

The immediacy of his response would have stunned him if he hadn't experienced it last night. Whatever the secret of her feminine allure, he responded to it with every particle of testosterone in his body.

He watched her hesitate and kept his expression unreadable. All the while he was aware of the way her moist pink lips unconsciously invited him to plunder her mouth. His fingers tightened on her hands, as if ready to tug her close.

'There's nothing to tell.' Her look was pure belligerence. 'You have a child. But you already know that.' She paused; for the first time the heat in her expression disappeared and her eyes turned glacial, stabbing him with invisible icy shards. 'Why make me repeat what you know?'

'I want the truth. Is that too much to ask?' Finally anger exploded behind Alessandro's façade of calm. A roaring flame of wrath at this woman who turned his life inside out. He strove to resist shaking the truth out of her.

He couldn't remember ever being so irate.

But then no woman had ever dared make such accusations. Plus the frustration of not knowing his own past would drive any man wild. Alessandro abhorred that sneaking sense of powerlessness, not remembering.

Her chin lifted. 'Is it too much to ask that you stop crushing my hands?'

Instantly he released her, flexing fingers rigid with tension. He hadn't intended to hurt her. Another disturbing sign that his control was close to shattering.

'Thank you.' She paused, her gaze skating sideways. 'I promise not to slap you again. That was…unintentional.' She turned. 'We're here.' She spoke quickly, relief evident in every syllable.

Already Bruno was opening the door to the pavement. The driver stood at Alessandro's door, waiting for him to alight.

'We'll finish this discussion inside.'

'I'm not sure I want you in my home,' she countered.

'You think I *want* to be there?' Being with Carys opened a Pandora's Box of conflicting feelings he could do without.

But he needed to fill the gaps and banish once and for all the nagging sense of something missing in his life. Besides, he had to end this nonsense about fathering a child. He would not countenance such allegations.

Alessandro unfolded his legs from the car and stood up. He felt stiff, as if his muscles had cramped during the drive. He pushed his shoulders back and looked around the street. Graffiti marred the building opposite and a couple of ground-floor windows were boarded up further down the block.

Carys scurried ahead into an ugly square building, not looking back. Her shoulders were hunched and her head bent.

But she couldn't avoid him. He stepped forward.

'Signor Conte.' Bruno waited on the pavement for him.

'Yes?' Alessandro paused, his eyes on Carys.

'On the way here I received answers to the enquiries I made this morning. I didn't like to interrupt your discussion with *la signorina*.'

Bruno's careful tone snared Alessandro's attention, dragging it from his furious thoughts. He turned to meet his security chief's blank stare, sensing he wouldn't like this.

'And?'

'There's no record of a marriage. Signorina Wells is single.'

So, she hadn't bothered to marry the baby's father.

Alessandro shoved his hands deep into his pockets, refusing to examine the emotions stirring at that news.

'There's more?'

Bruno nodded. 'The birth was just over a year ago here in Melbourne.' There wasn't a hint of expression in his voice and a tickle of premonition feathered Alessandro's spine.

'What other details did you get?'

'The mother is given as Carys Antoinette Wells, receptionist, of this address.' Bruno gestured to the tired red-brick block of flats.

Alessandro waited, instinct making his skin crawl. 'And the rest?'

Bruno's eyes flickered away. He drew himself up straighter. 'The father is listed as Alessandro Leonardo Daniele Mattani of Como, Italy.'

Despite the fact that by now he'd half expected it, each word slammed into Alessandro's gut with the force of a sledgehammer.

His name. His identity.

His honour.

Damn her for using him in this way! She'd taken his name and dragged it in the mud with her petty manipulations.

What did she hope to achieve? Money? Position? A hint of respectability even though her child was born out of wedlock?

But why hadn't she come forward if she'd wanted to try screwing cash from him? Was she waiting for the most auspicious time to approach him?

As if there would ever be a good time for such a plan!

He felt his lips stretch in a grimace of distaste that bared his teeth. His nostrils flared and the blood pounded loud and fast in his ears.

'Wait here,' he barked. Without waiting for a response, he strode up the cement pavement to the eyesore of a building. A red mist hazed his vision. The need for justice, for retribution, spurred him on.

This was about far more now than curiosity. More even than the stirring of a libido that had been dormant since he'd woken in hospital twenty-two months ago.

Carys Wells had gone too far. She'd sullied his honour.

For that she would pay.

Carys had only just collected Leo from next door and put him down, still sleeping.

The rap on her door came too soon. She looked at Leo's peaceful form and felt a tug of intense protectiveness. There'd been no time to decide how to deal with Alessandro.

Who was she kidding? She'd always been putty in his hands. Even now when she almost hated him, she had no illusions about that.

She'd never be rid of him until they had this out.

Reluctantly she walked through the miniscule flat, wiping her damp hands on her skirt. Her legs shook as another tattoo of raps sounded.

The glorious surge of anger had seeped away, leaving her prey to nerves and bone-melting exhaustion.

Fumbling, she unlatched the door and swung it wide.

Alessandro stood there, vibrating with a dangerous energy that wrapped right round her, squeezing her lungs. His eyes sizzled with a fury she'd seen only once before. The day he'd told her, with arctic composure, she'd outstayed her welcome.

Yet even now his potent charisma tugged at her. She bit down hard on her lip, desperate for the strength to face him.

Wordlessly he strode past her into the small sitting room-cum-kitchen. For such a big man he still managed to avoid brushing against her which, given the size of the entry, was a feat in itself.

Her lips turned up in a grimace as she pushed the door shut. He couldn't bear to touch her now she'd called him on his behaviour. How different from last night when his hands had been all over her, marking her with his own special brand of sensual possession.

Hot shame suffused her.

'You used my name for your bastard child.'

She spun round to find him towering over her, the image of disdain. But his anger was no match for hers.

'Don't ever talk about him like that!' She ignored the blast of his disapproval and jabbed an accusing finger.

'What? You're telling me you married after all?'

'No! Why would I go looking for a husband after my child's father had already rejected us?'

Alessandro leaned forward, using his superior height to intimidate her. 'For the same reason you perjured yourself, listing me as the father on the birth certificate. To try to claim some measure of respectability. Or financial support.'

The irony of his accusation hit her full force. If she'd expected support of any kind from Alessandro she'd been grossly mistaken.

She might have harboured a fatal weakness for this overbearing, arrogant, gorgeous man, but, where her son was concerned, she refused to be bullied. She stuck her hands on her hips and stared back, glare for glare.

'It was for Leo. He has a right to know who his father is.'

'Have you no shame?' Alessandro's dark green eyes sliced right through her self-possession.

'Only about the fact that I was once foolish enough to…' She stopped herself in time. She would not lay herself open to derision by admitting the feelings she'd once held for him. 'To believe in you.'

But she sensed he wasn't listening. He was absorbed in his own thoughts.

'Leo? You called him—'

'Leonardo. After your father.' She hesitated, aware now of her sentimental folly in choosing a family name for her son. She'd wanted to give him a link to his paternal family, even though that family had roundly rejected him.

Had she secretly thought one day Alessandro might be pleased to have the baby named after the father he'd lost? How misguided she'd been. He looked as she imagined some aristocrat of old must have when confronted with a troublesome serf.

'You dared to—'

'I'm not ashamed of what I did,' she bit out between clenched teeth. 'Live with it, Alessandro!'

A muffled wail sounded. Immediately Carys spun round and hurried to the bedroom she shared with Leo. She refused to stay and be reviled by Alessandro Mattani of all men.

Moments later Leo was in her arms, a warm cuddly bundle smelling of baby powder and sunshine and little boy. Carys held him against her and shut her eyes, feeling the serenity and joy she always experienced holding him.

'Mumum!' He reached up and patted her face.

Carys nuzzled his soft cheek then held him away. 'Hello, sweetie. Did you have a good day?'

His face split in a broad smile. 'Mum!' Then something over her shoulder caught his attention and he stared, his grin fading.

The skin on her neck prickled as she sensed Alessandro's presence in the room. She didn't have to turn to know he stood behind her.

She froze.

For so long she'd daydreamed about him coming to find her and Leo. He'd admit he'd been wrong and be devastated by the pain he'd caused. Carys would even find it in her heart to forgive him once he realised his true feelings for her and changed his ways. He'd take one look at Leo and his heart would melt like hers had when she'd first seen her son.

But that would never be.

There was no warmth in his heart for either of them.

Apprehension trickled like hot ice down her backbone. She couldn't bear it if he took out his anger on Leo. She cuddled her son tighter, but he leaned sideways, craning to keep Alessandro in view.

'Mumum!'

'No, darling. Not mummy.' For a split second she knew a hysterical urge to tell him it was daddy. But she wouldn't invite Alessandro's wrath.

She turned, shoulders braced and chin up, holding her baby close. If Alessandro dared make one more disparaging remark—

But she needn't have worried. All trace of arrogance and anger had vanished. Instead her tormentor stood curiously still, arms loose at his sides. His brows were knitted and he stared at Leo as if he'd never seen a baby before.

Instinctively Carys cuddled her son nearer. She smoothed back his glossy dark hair, almost long enough to be cut. But Leo paid her no heed. He was busy gazing up at the man who refused to be called his father.

She remembered how Alessandro's collar-length hair had once been like sable under her hands, just like Leo's. Their eyes were the same too. Though Leo's reminded her of a cheeky pixie's, with their twinkle, and Alessandro's showed no warmth at all. They might have been made of rock crystal.

She watched Alessandro's hands clench. The tendons in his neck stretched taut.

And still he stared at Leo.

A shiver raced down her spine.

'How old is he?' Alessandro's voice was curiously husky.

'He had his first birthday six weeks ago.'

'He was born early?'

'No. He went to full term.' Why all the questions?

Leo's sudden movement took her by surprise. He wriggled in her arms and lunged forward with all his weight as if trying to swim across the gap between himself and Alessandro.

'Mumum!' His hands opened and closed as if trying to grasp the big man before him. But Alessandro didn't move.

Carys felt her heart spasm at the sight of her little boy reaching for his father. He was doomed to disappointment.

Alessandro would never acknowledge him.

Would never love him. Or her.

Finally, after all this time, she shrugged off the last tarnished remnants of hope. The ache in her throat nearly choked her, but she felt freer than she had in almost two years. Surely, in time, the wounds would heal.

Meanwhile she had to protect Leo from the pain of knowing his dad didn't want him. She'd make up for the lack of a father, she decided fiercely. Leo would never want for love or encouragement or kindness. Not like she had.

Her arms tightened and he wailed, turning accusing eyes on her. 'Mum!'

'Yes, sweetheart. I'm sorry. Are you hungry? Are you ready for something to eat?' She took a step towards the door, studiously ignoring the tall man, standing as if riveted to the spot. 'Let's get you some food, shall we?'

It seemed a lifetime before Alessandro moved. Finally he stepped aside. 'After you.'

Carys didn't deign to respond.

She'd made it to the kitchen, Leo clamped safely on her hip, when a deep voice halted her in her tracks.

'Tell me how you came to be pregnant.'

He had to be kidding!

She whirled round to find him only a metre away, his eyes glued to her son. The intensity of his gaze unnerved her and she stroked her palm protectively over Leo's cheek.

'Oh, come *on,* Alessandro!' Her lips were stiff with fury. 'I don't know what sort of game you're playing, but I've had enough. This stops now.'

Dark green eyes lifted to pinion hers. Banked heat flared in that hooded gaze. Instantly a coil of reaction twisted in the pit of her stomach. Fear and something else she refused to name.

'No, Carys.' His words fell like blows, slow and heavy. 'It's just starting.'

Abruptly he turned to pace the room, but not before she read the bleak emptiness in his eyes.

'Because as far as I know for certain, we met for the first time last night.'

CHAPTER SIX

'SO THAT'S it? We met in the Alps, where you had a job in a ski resort. We had an affair and I invited you back to my home.' Alessandro kept his voice neutral, as emotionless as if he were reading a company report rather than repeating the most astonishing thing he'd heard in years.

The whole idea was absurd.

He'd never invited any woman to share his home. The only woman he could imagine living there was the woman he'd one day make his wife. A woman he hadn't yet met.

He'd spent his adult years ensuring the women he dated understood he wasn't interested in deep, meaningful relationships. That was just female-speak for snaring a rich man gullible enough to believe she wanted him for his character and personality!

'We lived together, but it didn't work out, and you came back to Australia,' he continued, watching her avoid his gaze. 'You discovered you were pregnant and you called my home repeatedly, eventually spoke to my stepmother and as a result, believed I wanted nothing further to do with you?'

'That's about the size of it.'

Her offhand response fuelled the remnants of his earlier temper. Didn't she realise how vital this was?

Alessandro's fists clenched tight. He abhorred the need to share the fact of his memory loss with a stranger. Even a stranger with whom he'd once been intimate.

He'd been brought up never to show vulnerability, never to

feel it. No wonder his discomfort now was marrow deep. His certainties, his sense of order, his grasp of the situation were far too shaky for a man accustomed to taking charge.

Still Carys didn't look at him but busied herself feeding the tot in the high chair. Was it his imagination or was she taking far too long fussing with cloths and dishes?

Alessandro kept his eyes on her, rather than her son. Meeting those big green eyes so like his own made him uneasy. And the way the boy kept staring at him, surely that wasn't normal.

The child wasn't his. He'd *know* if he had a son.

He'd always been careful about contraception. He would have children at the appropriate time, when he'd found a suitable bride. She'd be clever, chic, at home in his world, sexy. She wouldn't bore him after two weeks as most females did.

The harsh overhead light caught rich colour as Carys bent her head and the child tugged a lock of burnished hair loose from her prim bun.

Something snagged in Alessandro's chest, looking at her. And her son.

No!

He refused to feel anything except annoyance that her story didn't trigger any memories. It was all still an infuriating blank.

She turned and lifted the baby high in her arms, her prim white blouse dragging taut with the movement.

Something plunged in the pit of Alessandro's belly and heat spread in his lower body.

At least one thing was explained: his sense of possessiveness when he looked at Carys. She'd been his and, if her story was true, they'd shared a relationship unlike his usual liaisons. He'd desired her enough, trusted her enough, to install her in his own home.

Incredible! Yet it would be easy to check.

Had he planned to keep her as a long-term mistress? The idea fascinated him.

Watching the tight material of her skirt mould her thighs, the thin cotton of her blouse stretch over her breasts, the idea didn't seem quite as absurd as it should.

If it weren't for the baby, he'd be tempted to take up right now where they'd left off last night.

Sudden pain slashed behind his eyes and through his temple as he struggled to remember. The headache he'd fought in the car hovered. He was well now. Recovered. Only occasionally did the pain recur, a reminder of the past.

'Are you all right?' Smoky eyes held his. He dropped his hand from his temple and stretched his legs in front of him, shifting his weight on the lumpy sofa.

'Perfectly.' He paused, following the movement of a chubby little starfish hand that patted her breast then tugged at one of her buttons. A moment later she caught the baby's hand in hers.

Alessandro raised his eyes. Her cheeks were delicately flushed, her lips barely parted.

'You haven't told me why we split up.'

The colour in her cheeks intensified. But not, he'd swear, with sexual awareness. Her nostrils pinched, and her lips firmed.

'I don't want to talk about this. There's no point.'

'Humour me,' he murmured, leaning forward.

He wanted his pound of flesh. But what choice did she have? He looked as immovable as Uluru. Instinctively she knew he wouldn't leave till his curiosity was satisfied.

Carys believed him about his missing memory. He looked so uncomfortable she knew it was a truth he didn't want to share. She'd heard of such amnesia from her medico eldest brother. And it explained so much that had puzzled her. Like why Alessandro had come round the globe to find her.

What other reason could he have for going to such lengths? Especially since he'd dumped her so unceremoniously.

She bit her lip, glad she was the only one to remember every ignominious detail of that scene.

'You don't remember *anything?*' Pointless to ask, given his patent lack of knowledge about her, about them. Yet it seemed impossible she'd been wiped totally from his memory.

Once they'd been close. Not just physically intimate, but close as soulmates, or so it had seemed.

How could all that just disappear completely?

Because what they'd shared was far less important to Alessandro than it had been to her?

'My memory stops several months before my father's death.' His words were terse. She guessed he viewed amnesia as a weakness he should be able to master. 'I don't remember meeting you.' His tone implied he still doubted what she'd told him. 'Those months are blank. I don't even remember driving before the accident. Just waking up in hospital.'

Slowly Carys lowered herself into the rocking chair. She let Leo stand on her thighs while she held his hands. It was a game he loved, marching on the spot.

Besides, it gave her a chance to rest her shaky legs. The shock of Alessandro's revelations was a stunning blow. She still felt faintly nauseous and her limbs trembled, thinking of him injured seriously enough to cause amnesia.

'You didn't tell me how the accident happened.' She paused, wondering if her concern was too obvious. But she had to know. She avoided staring at the scar reaching up to his temple. Instead she fixed her attention on a spot over his shoulder.

His shrug was fluid and easy.

'I was driving to Milan. The car skidded in the wet when I swerved to avoid a driver on the wrong side of the road.'

On the way to the office, then. Of course. He preferred to drive himself, claiming it helped him sort out his priorities for the day's business. From the rough timeline he'd mentioned, it must have happened soon after she left.

Had she thought, even for an instant, that her departure would disrupt his precious business schedule?

Her ridiculous naivety still stunned her.

'And you're all right?' Her heart pounded, imagining the scene. Carys swallowed hard on a jagged splinter of regret and fear. 'No other after-effects? No pain?'

No matter what she told herself, she hadn't completely severed her feelings for this man. She should despise him for the way he'd treated her, yet her conflicting emotions weren't so straightforward.

Carys refused to meet his intent gaze, choosing instead to watch Leo as he babbled to her.

'I'm perfectly healthy.'

Alessandro paused so long she looked up. He stared straight into her eyes as if reading her hunger for every detail. Her need for reassurance. Eventually he continued, his clipped words indicating how little he cared to dwell on his injuries.

'I was lucky. I had lacerations and a couple of fractures.'

At her hissed indrawn breath he shrugged. 'I mended quickly. I was only in hospital a few weeks. The main concern was my memory loss.' Darkening eyes bored into hers. 'But the specialists say there's nothing I can do about that except let nature take its course. There's no other brain damage.'

Carys slumped back, only now acknowledging the full depth of her fears. Relief warred with a sense of unreality.

'I see.' This strange, constrained conversation didn't seem real given the past they shared. But it gave Carys a little time to work through the implications of his news.

He mightn't remember her, but last night in his suite he'd seduced her with a combustible passion that had sheared straight through every defence she'd painstakingly erected in the last two years.

How had he done that if he couldn't even recall her?

Was he such an awesome lover he could make any woman feel the heady, mind-blowing certainty that she wanted nothing more than Alessandro Mattani, unbridled and consummately masculine? Were the intimacies she'd shared with him and always thought so special, the wondrous sensations, something he shared with countless women?

Her weakness mortified her.

'And your wife?' Carys failed to keep the bitterness from her voice as she choked out the word. 'I assume she's not with you?'

'Wife?' The single syllable slashed through the heavy atmosphere in the room. 'You're not saying I have a wife?'

Did she imagine it or had he paled? His lazy sprawl morphed into stark rigidity as he sat up, staring.

Carys hesitated. 'You were single when I left, but you were

seeing someone else, planning to marry her. Principessa Carlotta.' She couldn't prevent distaste colouring her voice.

Of course Alessandro would only marry one of his own, a rich, privileged aristocrat.

Carys swallowed bile as memories surged. Of how she'd obstinately disregarded his stepmother's warnings about Alessandro's intentions. And about her true, temporary place in his world. Of how she'd foolishly pinned her belief and hopes on the tender passionate words he whispered in her ear. On the rapture of being with him, being loved by him.

No! Having sex with him. The love had been all on her side.

'You seem to imply I did more than just *see* her.' His tone was outraged; his eyes flashed a furious warning. 'And that I did so while you and I were…together.'

If the cap fits, buddy. 'So you did.' Deliberately she turned away to focus on Leo, happily jouncing on her knees.

'You're mistaken.' Alessandro didn't raise his voice, but his whisper was lethally quiet, an unmistakeable warning. 'I would never stoop to such despicable behaviour.' Green eyes clashed with hers. They were so vibrant with indignation she expected to see sparks shoot from their depths.

'I was there, remember.' Carys took a slow breath, forcing down the rabid, useless jealousy that even now clawed to the surface. She concentrated on keeping her voice even. 'And unlike you I have perfect recall.'

Silence. His stare would have stripped paint at twenty paces. It scoured her mercilessly.

Yet Carys refused to back down. He might believe he was incapable of such behaviour, but if his memory ever returned he was doomed to disillusionment.

'I don't need to remember to know the truth, Carys.' He leaned forward, all semblance of relaxation gone. His voice echoed an unshakeable certainty. 'No matter what you think you understand about that time, I would never betray one lover with another. Never have two lovers at the same time. It wouldn't be honourable.'

Not honourable!

Carys suppressed an anguished laugh.

Was it honourable to have a lover share his bed but exclude her from the rest of his life because she wasn't good enough for his aristocratic friends? To use her for temporary sex while he courted another woman?

Whatever had gone wrong between Alessandro and the *principessa* to prevent the marriage, that was exactly what he'd been up to.

Carys had simply been convenient, gullible, expendable.

She swung her head away, refusing to look at him. Even now the pain was too raw. A cold, leaden lump rose in her throat, but she refused to reveal her vulnerability.

She drew a slow breath. 'When I tried to contact you about the pregnancy, your stepmother said you were preparing for your wedding. She made it clear you had no time to spare for an ex-mistress.'

'Livia said that?' His astonished tone drew her unwilling gaze. His eyebrows jammed together in a V of puzzlement. 'I can't believe it.'

No. That was the problem. He hadn't believed her before either. Her word meant nothing against his suspicions. The reminder stiffened her backbone.

'Frankly, Alessandro, I don't care what you believe.'

'It's true Livia is fond of Carlotta,' he murmured as if to himself. 'And that she wants me to marry. But arranging a wedding? It never went that far.'

How convenient his loss of memory was.

Carys had confirmation of the betrothal from another source too. But most convincing of all had been the sight of Alessandro with the glamorous, blue-blooded Carlotta. Even now the recollection stabbed, sharp as a twisting stiletto in her abdomen, making her hunch involuntarily.

The princess had stared up at him with exactly the same besotted expression Carys knew she herself had worn since the day he'd swept her off her feet and into his bed. Alessandro had kept the other woman close, his arm protectively around her as if she were made of delicate porcelain. He'd gazed into her eyes, utterly absorbed in their intimate conversation as if she were the only woman in the world.

As if he didn't have a convenient lover waiting obediently at home for him.

Carys blinked to banish the heat glazing the back of her eyes. Resolutely she focused instead on Livia's dismissive words when Carys had rung to tell Alessandro about her pregnancy.

Alessandro will do what is necessary to provide for the child if it's his. But don't expect him to contact you in person. Her tone had made it clear Carys was too socially inferior to warrant anything more than a settlement engineered by his formidable legal team. *The past is the past. And questions about your, shall we say...extra-curricular activities raise suspicions about the identity of the child's father.*

That slur, above all, had been hard to swallow.

How furious Alessandro's stepmother would have been if she'd known Carys hadn't accepted her word. Instead she'd left numerous messages on Alessandro's private phone and sent emails, even a hand-written letter. She'd been so desperate for personal contact.

Only after months of deliberate, deafening silence had she finally accepted he wanted nothing to do with either her or her unborn child. Then she'd determined to turn her back on the past and start afresh, not even considering a legal bid to win child support. Leo was better off without a father like that.

Yet now it seemed Alessandro hadn't known about her pregnancy.

Her breath jammed in her throat. All this time he hadn't known! He hadn't rejected Leo at all.

Nor was he married.

Her head spun, trying to take in the implications, her emotions a whirling jumble. Once she might have believed that would change everything.

Now she knew better.

One glance at Alessandro confirmed it. He was absorbed in his thoughts, totally oblivious to the little boy perched on her lap, twisting around time and again to try catching the attention of the big man who so effortlessly dominated their flat.

Alessandro had no interest in her either. She was nothing but a source of information.

Or an easy lay.

A shudder passed through her as memories of last night's passion stirred. Carys stiffened her resolve.

She looked into her baby's excited green gaze. He twinkled back at her mischievously as he nattered away in a language all his own. *He* was the important thing in her life. Not ancient dreams of happily ever after with the wrong man.

Whether Alessandro had known about the pregnancy or not didn't matter. What mattered was that the grand passion they'd shared had been a cheap affair, not a love on which to build a future. And he couldn't have made it clearer he had no interest in Leo.

Bridges burned. End of story.

Carys ignored the ache welling deep inside at the finality of it all and summoned a wobbly smile for Leo.

'Time for a bath, young man.' She gathered him close and stood on creaky legs. Suddenly she felt old beyond her years. Old with grief for what her son would never have, and with a stupid, obstinate hurt at being rejected again. After a lifetime of not measuring up, not being quite good enough, it was stupid to feel so wounded, but there it was.

'Why did I tell you to leave my home? You still haven't told me.'

She looked across to see Alessandro on his feet, hands jammed deep in his trouser pockets. He stood as far from her as he could while remaining in the same room.

Didn't that say it all?

'I'd decided to go anyway.' She lifted her chin. After learning about Alessandro and Carlotta the scales had fallen from her eyes. Carys knew she had to get as far away from him as she could. 'But you accused me of having an affair, of betraying your trust.'

The irony should have been laughable. But Carys had never felt less like laughing. She jiggled Leo higher in her weary arms and straightened her back.

'An affair? With whom?' His brows furrowed and his features took on a remote, hawk-like cast. Condemnation radiated from him.

'With Stefano Manzoni. He's—'

'I know who he is.' If anything, Alessandro's scowl deepened. His jaw set like stone and a pulse worked in his temple.

'Nice company you keep,' he said after a moment, his voice coolly disapproving.

Talk about double standards!

Carys jerked her chin higher. 'I thought he *was* nice. At first.' Until he wouldn't take no for an answer. He was another macho Italian male who couldn't cope with rejection. Though, to be fair, she'd never felt unsafe with Alessandro. 'I would have thought that as your Princess Carlotta's cousin he'd be utterly respectable.'

'She's not *my* Carlotta.' The words emerged through taut lips.

'Whatever.' Carys hunched stiff shoulders. 'Now, it's time for me to bathe Leo.' Her composure was in tatters and her limbs trembled with exhaustion. She felt like a wrung-out dishrag. 'I'd appreciate it if you'd go now.' She couldn't take any more.

Alessandro's appearance had dredged up emotions she thought she'd vanquished. Emotions that threatened to undo her. She needed desperately to be alone.

All she had left was the torn remnants of her pride, and Carys refused to collapse in a heap while he was here.

Head high, she walked on unsteady legs towards the front door, intending to show him out.

Leo's sudden sideways dive out of her arms took her completely unawares. One minute she was holding him. The next he was plunging headlong towards the floor when his bid to throw himself at Alessandro failed.

'Leo!'

Belatedly Carys grabbed for him, her weariness banished as adrenaline pumped hard and fast through her bloodstream, but her reactions were too slow.

'It's all right. I've got him.' How Alessandro got there so fast she didn't know, but he scooped Leo up in his arms just before he hit the floor.

Her heart catapulted against her ribs, slowing only when she saw he had the baby safe in his large hands. Relief shook her so hard her legs wobbled.

He held Leo awkwardly, at a distance from himself.

As if he couldn't bear to touch him? Or as a man would who'd never had experience with babies?

Carys hesitated, trying to decide which. In that moment Leo latched onto Alessandro's suit-clad arm, plucking at the fabric as if trying to climb closer. Green eyes met green, and Leo frowned, his chubby face puckering as he regarded the unsmiling man before him.

Finally, like the sun emerging from behind a cloud, Leo smiled. His whole face lit up. His hands thumped on Alessandro's arm and he crowed with delight.

Terrific! Her son had developed a soft spot for a man who never wanted to see him.

Obstinately Carys shied from dwelling on the sight of her son in his father's arms. It would be the only time. It was foolish to feel even a jot of sentimentality over the image of the tall, strong man holding her precious baby so ineptly yet so securely.

Carys hurried forward, arms outstretched.

'I'll take him.'

Alessandro didn't even turn his head. He was busy regarding Leo, not even flinching when the child's rhythmic thumps against his arm became real whacks as he grew impatient with the adult's lack of response.

'Alessandro?' Her voice was husky. The intensity of his stare as he looked down at his son made something flip over in her stomach. Anxiety walked its fingers down her spine.

'I'll arrange for the necessary tests to be done as soon as possible. Someone will ring you tomorrow with the details.'

'Tests?'

He didn't even turn at the sound of her voice, but he did lift Leo a little closer, winning himself a gurgle of approval and a spate of excited Leo-speak.

Carys watched Leo lean up, patting both hands over Alessandro's square, scrupulously shaved jaw. A squiggle of emotion unsettled her, seeing her little boy with the man she'd once loved.

If only circumstances had been different.

No! It was better she knew what sort of man Alessandro was and that in his eyes she could never measure up.

'DNA tests, of course.' He flashed an assessing look from slitted eyes. 'You can't expect me to take your word this is my son.'

Her stomach went into freefall.

She'd fought so hard to have Alessandro acknowledge his son before giving up in despair. Yet now she felt fear at his sudden interest. Fear at what this might mean.

Leo was hers. But if Alessandro decided he wanted him…

She found refuge in stormy anger. 'Distrust must be your middle name, Alessandro.'

The idea of him seeking independent scientific proof was a slap in the face.

Especially as he'd been her only lover.

His distrust tainted what they'd shared, reducing it to something tawdry. Her skin crawled as she met his glittering gaze and felt the weight of his doubt.

His fiery green stare scorched her. 'Better distrustful than gullible.'

CHAPTER SEVEN

THREE days later Carys received a summons to the presidential suite. David, her manager, relayed the news with a quizzical look that made the blood rise hot in her cheeks.

'Moving in exalted circles, Carys,' he murmured. 'Don't hurry back.'

She was aware of the other staff, watching surreptitiously as she pushed her chair back and stood up.

Carys had been a bundle of nerves for the past few days, ever since Alessandro had pulled strings to have the DNA tests taken in the privacy of her flat. Another reminder, if she'd needed it, of his enormous wealth. His ability to get what he wanted.

The technician had been friendly, talkative despite the marked silence between Carys and Alessandro. She'd seemed oblivious to the atmosphere laden with unspoken challenges and questions. Or maybe the woman was used to the high-octane emotions such circumstances engendered. After all, there'd be no need for mouth swabs and scientific proof if there was trust between a couple.

If a man believed his lover.

Sucking in her breath, Carys straightened her shoulders and took her time walking to the lift.

Alessandro must have received advice from the pathology company. Surely that was why she'd been summoned. No doubt he'd paid for the privilege of getting an ultra-fast turnaround on the lab results.

Her stomach cramped in anxiety.

What would he do now that he knew Leo was his?

The question had haunted her for days so that even when she finally slept, stress dreams plagued her. She woke feeling even more tired than when she went to bed.

The butler was waiting at the door for her, his smile friendly but impersonal.

Had he seen her desperate flight from the suite several days ago? Carys kept her chin high as she forced an answering smile to her lips and walked in.

The lush quiet of the suite engulfed her. Its understated opulence showcased fine furnishings and every modern convenience provided just for one man. It had been designed for the mega-wealthy, the vastly important.

No wonder she felt wretchedly small and nervous as she approached the silent man who dominated the room.

He might fit in here, but she didn't. Carys was completely, unalterably ordinary. Not by any stretch of the imagination could she be considered special. She'd faced that long ago, before Alessandro had tempted her for a brief, crazy time to believe in miracles.

'Carys.' The sound of his deep, slightly husky voice rippled like a sensual caress across her skin. Her reaction, her physical weakness for him, made her hackles rise.

'Alessandro.' She nodded. 'You demanded my presence?'

His head tilted slightly as he watched her, his look assessing but his face unreadable.

'I *requested* your presence.'

'Ah, but when the request comes from the presidential suite we staff tend to jump.' For some reason she found safety in emphasising the huge gulf between them. As if she could magically erase the memory of the madness that had gripped them last time she was here.

Her gaze flickered to the plump lounges, the wall where he'd held her and caressed her and almost…

'Please, take a seat.'

To her surprise, he gestured to an upright chair in front of an antique desk. Carys shot him a startled glance but complied. Better this than the intimacy of the sofas.

It was only as she sat that she noticed the papers spread across the desk. 'You've had the test results, then.'

'I have.'

Carys could read nothing in his voice or in his face. Was he disappointed, angry, excited to discover he had a son? Or, she thought with a sinking sensation, didn't he feel anything at all?

'Coffee, Robson. Or—' Alessandro paused to catch her eye '—would you prefer tea?'

'Nothing, thank you.' The idea of swallowing anything made her stomach curdle.

'That will be all, Robson.' Alessandro waited till the butler left before he turned to her again.

Instead of taking a chair, he lounged, arms crossed, against the desk. He was near enough for her to register his cologne. Her nerves reacted with a shimmy of excitement that made her grit her teeth in annoyance. She wished he'd move away. Far enough that she wasn't plagued by remnants of the physical attraction that had been so strong between them.

'What is it you want, Alessandro?' After days of silence from him, now he expected her jump to do his bidding. It infuriated her.

'We have arrangements to make. And you need to sign this.' He waved a hand towards the paper on the desk then reached into his jacket pocket, eyes still holding hers. 'You can use this when you've read it.'

Casually he laid a gold fountain pen on the desk beside a wad of papers.

Carys turned to face the desk. Not lab results after all. A quick look showed her long numbered paragraphs. Dense typescript. Pages and pages of legalese.

Her heart sank. Just the sort of document she hated. She couldn't deal with this while Alessandro stood so close.

A flutter of panic flared in her breast and she reached out one clammy hand to flick through the wad. The last page had space for her signature and Alessandro's.

As the pages settled again, she tried to concentrate on the

first paragraph, but one of the lines kept jumping sideways so she lost her place.

Damn. Had she brought her glasses? She fumbled in her jacket pocket, aware of Alessandro's silent scrutiny.

'What is it you want me to sign?'

His eyes blazed green fire as he watched her from his superior height. Did she imagine a hint of tension around his mouth? A faint tightness between his brows?

'A prenuptial agreement.'

'*A what?*' Carys' reading glasses slid from numb fingers as she swung round to face him.

The sober light in his eyes told her she wasn't hearing things.

'An agreement setting out both parties' entitlements—'

'I know what a prenuptial agreement is.' She dragged in a deep breath to fill her suddenly constricted lungs, her pulse racing jaggedly. 'We don't need one. It's for people who plan to marry.'

He smiled then. Not a grin. Not even a real smile. Just a brief quirk of the lips that might have signalled amusement or impatience or even annoyance.

And still his eyes bored into her like lasers.

'We need it, Carys.' His words were crisp, clear and unmistakeable. 'Because we're getting married.'

He reached out and stroked a finger down her cheek. Fire streaked across her skin and blasted through her hard won calm. 'It's the only possible course of action. You must have known we'd marry once I discovered the child is mine.'

For an eternity the words hung between them. She stared up at him, lush mouth sagging, bright eyes stunned. Then, like the flick of a switch, animation returned.

'*The child* has a name, damn you!'

Carys jerked from his touch, catapulting from the chair and almost knocking it over in her haste. She stood defiant and furious, feet planted squarely and chest heaving.

'Don't you *ever* talk about Leo again as if he were some… some commodity!'

Madonna mia! With her eyes flashing and high colour in her softly-rounded cheeks, energy radiating from her in angry waves, she was stunning. More than pretty. Or beautiful. Something far more profound.

Enough almost to distract him from the important business of securing his child.

Alessandro felt the drag of attraction in his belly, his limbs, his mind. It was the possessive hunger he'd felt for days but mixed with another sensation so deep-seated it rocked him where he stood.

In that moment the careful logic that dictated his decision to marry faded. This was no longer about simple logic. The force that drove him was purely visceral.

She would be his. He would accept no other alternative.

He would have Carys *and* his son. A wave of hot pleasure suffused him.

'Of course he's not a commodity. He's Leonardo.' Alessandro inclined his head, savouring the name. 'Leo Mattani.'

An image of intelligent jade eyes, handsome dark hair and a small determined chin surfaced. His son.

His son!

Satisfaction and pride welled in his chest and—

'No! Leo Wells, not Leo Mattani. And that won't change. Marriage is a preposterous idea, so you can forget it.' Carys took a step closer, her chin rising.

Once more a blast of white-hot hunger shot through him.

What a woman she was! So fiercely protective and proud.

And as a lover…? Alessandro inhaled sharply, breathing in her skin's warm cinnamon scent. He looked forward to rediscovering the passion they'd shared. It must have been spectacular for him to take the unprecedented step of inviting her to live with him.

But first, most important, he would secure his son.

A twist of deep-seated memory skewered Alessandro, ripping a familiar hole through his belly. Of the feckless way his own mother had abandoned her '*caro Sandro*' without a backward glance. How selfish greed had triumphed over the supposedly unbreakable bonds of maternal love. She'd put her own salacious desires and hunger for wealth above her son.

Despite Carys' fiery attitude and her protectiveness, Alessandro knew the frailty of maternal love. The fickleness of women.

He would safeguard his son. Shield him and ensure he never wanted for anything.

The terms of the prenuptial agreement, with its hefty allowance for Carys while she stayed with him and his son, would ensure stability in Leo's life.

Alessandro's legal team had worked night and day to make it watertight. The obscene amount of money Alessandro had allocated to buy his wife would keep her just where he wanted her. Where Leo needed her.

With Alessandro.

'My son will grow up as Leo Mattani. That is not open to debate.' Alessandro waved his hand dismissively, his expression remote. 'Any other alternative is unthinkable.'

'Unthinkable?' Carys planted her hands on her hips as she stared into the proud, arrogant face of the man she'd once loved. 'He's been Leo Wells since he was born and he's been just fine, thank you very much.'

'Just fine?' Alessandro shook his head abruptly, voice deepening and nostrils flaring with disapproval, the epitome of masculine scorn. 'You think it fine that my son is born illegitimate?'

For a moment Carys stared helplessly into his dark, heated gaze, reading indignation and outrage.

In a perfect world Leo would have been born into a loving family with parents who were permanently committed to each other. But that hadn't been an option.

'There are worse things in the world,' she said quietly, wrapping her arms round her torso as old pain tore through her. The pain of lacerated dreams.

She'd done everything she could to ensure Alessandro had known about her pregnancy. But even if he'd known, even if he'd proposed marriage, nothing could change the fact that he wasn't a man she could trust with her heart. Or that she'd never fit into his world.

Silence hung between them as he stared down at her.

'And you think my son will continue to be *just fine* growing up in a run-down tenement among thieves and pimps?' One haughty eyebrow rose to a lofty height and Carys felt the weight of his disapproval push down on her.

'You're exaggerating,' she countered, ignoring a twinge of guilt that she hadn't been able to find somewhere better. 'It's not that bad. Besides, I'm planning to move.'

'Really? And how will you find better premises on your wage?'

His supercilious tone made Carys bite her lip in frustration. It didn't matter that her salary was the best she could get with her qualifications or that she worked hard for the money she earned. In the long term her prospects were good for promotion. But in the meantime…

'I will provide for Leo. I always have.'

For a moment Alessandro's gaze seemed to soften. 'It must have been difficult, managing on your own.'

Carys shrugged. She didn't dwell on that. On the fact that her siblings and father, scattered as they were around the globe, hadn't found time to visit when Leo was born, or afterwards. They'd sent gifts instead. A money box from her advertising executive sister in Perth. A set of children's books Leo couldn't read for years from her physicist brother in New Zealand. An oversized fluffy rabbit from her brother at a medical outpost in New Guinea. And from her dad in Canada money to secure the bond on her flat.

They meant well and they cared in their distant, uninvolved way. But how she'd longed for one of them to make the effort to be with her when she'd felt so alone. When depression had vied with excitement and determination as she struggled on her own.

Defiantly Carys met the eyes of the one person who'd had the right to be at her side when Leo came into the world.

But that time was past.

'I'm used to managing alone.' Years younger than her siblings, the late child of parents engrossed in demanding careers, she'd virtually brought herself up. 'Leo and I are OK.'

'OK isn't enough for my son. He deserves more.'

Carys compressed her lips, fighting the urge to agree. The

doting mother in her wanted Leo to have the best opportunities. The sort of opportunities a working single mum couldn't provide.

'What Leo needs is love and a secure, nurturing environment. I give him that.' She defied him to disagree.

'Of course he does. And we'll provide it. Together.'

Had Alessandro stepped closer? His eyes mesmerised and his persuasive dark coffee tone made the impossible sound almost sensible.

Carys gave herself a mental shake.

'There's no question of *together*. What we had is over.'

It died two years ago, when you betrayed me with another woman then accused me of being unfaithful. She didn't say it out loud. There was no point in revisiting the past. Carys had to focus on the future, on what was best for Leo.

'It will never be over, Carys.' His voice dropped to a caress, like the stroke of velvet on bare, shivery skin. 'We have a child together.'

She clasped her hands before her, horrified to find them shaking. His words conjured images that were too vivid, too enticing, of what it had been like when they'd been lovers.

'But that's no reason for marriage! You'll have access to him, see him as he grows.' It was a father's right. Besides, despite the emotional turmoil it would cause her to see Alessandro regularly, it was a relief that Leo would grow up knowing his father. Every boy deserved—

'*Access?*' The word shot out like bullet. 'You think that's what I want? What my son needs?'

This time it wasn't her imagination. Alessandro obliterated the space between them with a single stride. He loomed above her like an impregnable mountain citadel. Unmoving and unforgiving. Utterly forbidding.

She trembled at the impact of his powerful presence. Energy radiated from him. A dangerous undercurrent of power.

'You have strange ideas about fatherhood. I've already missed the first year of my son's life. I don't intend to miss any more.' His clipped words revealed gleaming white teeth as they bit out each word. Involuntarily Carys shrank a little.

'I just meant—'

'I know what you meant.' He paused, scrutinising her as if she came from another planet. 'Leo is my son. My flesh, my blood. I refuse to be a part-time visitor in his life while he grows up on the other side of the world.'

'But marriage!' Her tongue stuck to the roof of her mouth on the word. 'The idea is absurd.'

Alessandro's eyes darkened. His face stiffened and his lips thinned. 'I assumed you'd prefer that to the alternative.'

'Alternative?' Carys' voice was a cracked whisper as foreboding slammed into her. That look in his eyes…

'A legal battle for custody.'

CHAPTER EIGHT

CARYS' fingers twisted into knots as he said the words she'd been dreading. She swallowed convulsively, forcing down fear. 'I'm his mother. Any court would give me custody.'

'You're sure, Carys?' An infinitesimal shake of his dark head accompanied the words, as if he pitied her naivety. 'You have a good lawyer? As good as my legal team?'

Plus the Mattani millions to back them up. The words were unspoken, but Carys heard them nonetheless.

'You wouldn't...' Her voice petered out as she met his un-blinking stare. He would. He'd do what it took to get Leo.

Jerkily she swung away, frantic for breathing space. For time to marshal her jumbled thoughts. Her chest cramped so she could barely breathe and her head pounded as tension crawled up her spine and wrapped clammy fingers around her temples.

He was wrong. He must be! No court would take a child from his mother.

And yet...Carys stumbled to a stop in front of a massive window commanding a view of the city. Alessandro's wealth and power were far beyond anything she or her family, if they were so inclined, could gather. He lived in a world of stratospherically rich, privileged and well-connected families. The normal rules didn't apply to them.

Did she dare take Alessandro on? She should have nothing to worry about. She was a good mother. Leo was thriving.

Yet the poisonous seed of doubt grew.

The thought of their cramped flat in a run-down neighbourhood, the best she could provide on her meagre wage, haunted her. Would that be held against her? Contrasted to the vast resources of the Mattani family?

There were so many ways Alessandro could get what he wanted, even without gaining sole custody. What if he refused to return Leo after a visit? If he kept him in Italy?

Carys didn't have the resources to go there and demand her son back. She didn't have the power to force Alessandro's hand. She'd be at his mercy. Who knew what delays Alessandro could throw up to stop her seeing Leo while their lawyers slogged it out?

A shiver rippled through her and she lifted a hand to her throbbing temple. This was the stuff of nightmares.

The man she'd loved wouldn't have threatened her like this, no matter how they'd parted. He'd never have robbed her of her baby.

But that man was gone. The realisation felt like someone had carved a part out of her heart. Alessandro had no memory of the happiness they'd once shared. To him she was merely a stranger who had what he wanted.

She longed to hold Leo, safe and warm in her arms. Hide away from Alessandro and his demands.

But there was no hiding.

'My preference is to keep this between us, Carys.' His deep voice came from just behind her, making her jump. 'I wouldn't *choose* a court battle. That would be a last resort.'

He expected her to be grateful for that? Hurt and fear coalesced in a surge of desperate anger till her body hummed with the effort of containing it.

'Well, that's a comfort! I feel so much better now.'

Long fingers grasped her shoulder, their heat branding through her clothes. She resisted but his grip firmed and she turned.

Was that compassion in his gaze?

She blinked and the illusion disappeared. Alessandro's face was angular, hard, powerful. He would never back down.

'You come swanning into our lives and think you can run roughshod over everyone.' Her words tumbled out so fast they slurred. 'As if only you know best.' Carys drew herself up to her full height. 'Your demands are outrageous. You've got no right—'

'I have the right of a father.' His cool words stopped her tirade. 'Remember that, Carys. You are no longer the only one with a say in how our son is brought up.'

Our son. The words were a douche of cold water dousing her indignation. Reminding her how vulnerable she was.

'I offer you marriage, Carys. Position, wealth, a life of ease. And—' he paused '—a home for our son. He will grow up with both parents. In a secure, stable home. What objection can you have to that?'

'But we don't care for each other. How can we—?'

'We have the best possible reason to marry. To bring up our child. That's something worthwhile and enduring.' The words sank into the silence between them as his touch warmed her shoulder. She wanted to pull away, but his intense gaze pinioned her. 'There is no better reason to wed.'

Except love. The futile little voice rang in her ears.

Carys ignored it. She'd given up believing in seductive fantasies of romance two years ago.

Yet she couldn't douse her dismay at the matter-of-fact way Alessandro spoke of marriage for the sake of their child. Perhaps the aristocracy were accustomed to convenient marriages, brokered for family or business reasons.

How could she marry a man she didn't love? A man who'd betrayed her trust?

Her lips twisted ruefully. Look where her fantasies of love had got her!

'Unless…' His fingers tightened then dropped away. His head jerked up and he regarded her down the length of his aristocratic nose, his look coldly accusing. 'Unless you've become attached to someone here?'

Carys hesitated, tempted to grab at the excuse. But she couldn't lie. Once already she'd tried to deflect Alessandro's interest by pretending to have a boyfriend, but she hadn't been able to maintain the pretence.

She shook her head, shifting back a pace and turning her head away. He was too close for comfort.

Did he know how distracting he was, standing in her personal space, radiating energy like a human generator? The hairs on her arms prickled just being so near him.

'Good, then there's no reason to refuse.'

'But what if...?' Carys bit her tongue, furious that she'd begun to blurt out her wayward thoughts. Furious she was even listening to his bizarre reasoning. She must be mad.

'What if...?' His whisper made her shiver and stiffen as the warmth of his breath caressed her cheek.

For three heartbeats, for four, Carys remained silent. Then unwillingly she continued. 'What if one day you meet someone you...care for? Someone you want to marry?'

Even now, cured of the love she'd felt for Alessandro, the thought of him with someone else squeezed her insides into a tortured knot of distress.

'That won't happen.' Certainty throbbed in his words and she turned, curiosity stirring at his instantaneous response.

'You can't know that.'

Alessandro's beautiful, sensuous mouth kicked up at the corner in a mirthless smile that made a mockery of the heat she'd imagined in his eyes moments before.

'I know it absolutely.' His gaze held hers till her chest tightened and she remembered to breathe. And still his expression of weary cynicism didn't change. 'Romantic love is a fallacy invented for the gullible. Only a fool would consider himself in love, much less marry for it.'

Carys felt her eyes widen, staring up at the man she'd once believed she'd known. He'd been considerate, witty, urbane and, above all, passionate. The sort of lover a woman dreamed about. A lover who tempted a woman to believe in the most outrageously wonderful happily ever afters.

She'd always understood he kept something of himself back. She'd sensed his deep-seated reserve despite the intimacies they shared. A sense of aloneness she'd never quite breached. An aloneness that intensified after his father died and Alessandro withdrew, devoting himself to business. Yet it shocked her to discover the hardened kernel of scepticism behind his charming exterior.

It made him seem so *empty*.

Had he always been like that? Or was this the result of the trauma he'd been through?

Distress and unwilling compassion burgeoned for this man who seemed to have so much, yet apparently felt so little.

Absurdly she wanted to reach out to him.

And what? Comfort him? Show him compassion? Love?

No! She reeled back, stunned at the depth of feelings he engendered even now.

Her hand, half raised as if to reach out to him, dropped noiselessly to her side.

'Marriage is a duty,' he continued, oblivious to her reaction. 'There was never any question of me marrying for love.' His scornful tone almost made her wince, recalling how blithely she'd believed he was falling in love with her as she'd fallen for him.

Acidly she wondered how he'd class his interest in other women. Even if he were married, there would be other women. Alessandro was a man who enjoyed sex. He wouldn't stay celibate just because he'd married a woman he didn't love. He'd have no qualms about pursuing someone who took his fancy. After all, she'd been his bit on the side, hadn't she?

'I believe in marriage for life.' His words cut through her stark thoughts. 'Once married there would be no divorce.'

'A life sentence, in fact.'

'You would not find it so hard, believe me, Carys.' A hint of mellow honey edged his words and Carys shut her eyes, fighting the insidious weakness in her bones. He was talking about money, luxury, position, that was all. Not anything important, like the emotions he so despised.

'You're not worried I might fall for someone else and want a divorce?' The words tumbled out in self-defence.

Taut silence reigned as his displeasure vibrated on the air between them.

'There will be no divorce.' His words were adamant, his tone rough-edged. 'As for believing yourself in love...'

Abruptly he stepped in front of her and lifted her chin with his hand. She felt herself fall into the shaded depths of his green gaze. Heat sparked in her abdomen as he leaned closer. A thrill of excitement skimmed down her backbone.

No! She wasn't making a fool of herself like that again. If he thought he could seduce her into falling for him all over again, he had another thing coming.

Furiously she jerked out of his hold. 'Don't worry,' her voice was icy with disdain. 'There's no danger of me falling in love with *anyone*.'

Once bitten, now cured for life!

His eyes blazed with curiosity. Then those heavy lids dropped, hiding his expression.

'Good. Then we have an understanding.'

'Now, just a minute! I didn't say I—'

'I'll leave you to read the agreement.' He gestured to the papers on the desk as he turned away, obviously eager to go. 'There are arrangements to be made.' He paused, spearing her with a look. 'Consider well what I've said, Carys. I'll be back soon for your answer.'

She hadn't meant to, but finally Carys was drawn to the elegant regency desk with its fateful document. The thickly worded pages taunted her, evidence of Alessandro's superior position, of his lawyers and his precious money.

She wasn't really considering marriage. Was she? Fear swooped through her stomach and her damp hands clenched.

Alessandro couldn't force her to marry.

He was gambling that a judge would give him custody. More, he was probably bluffing about court action. He wouldn't...

The memory of eyes flashing like jade daggers in the sun pulled her up short.

He would. To get his son, of course he would.

How had she ever imagined Alessandro would settle for part-time fatherhood?

Stiffly she raised a hand and drew the papers towards her. She settled her glasses on her nose and began reading.

By the third page panic welled. It had taken twenty minutes of desperate concentration and still some of the text eluded her.

She was exhausted after so many sleepless nights and emo-
tionally drained. Even at the best of times her dyslexia made
reading solid text like this a challenge. But now…she bit her lip,
fighting down angry tears of frustration.

Leo's future was at stake and she didn't have the skills to
ensure he was protected! What sort of mother was she?

The old, jeering voice in her head told her she was a failure,
and for a moment she was tempted to believe it.

She slammed her palms on the table and pushed her chair
away. It wasn't a matter of skills or intelligence. It was simply a
disability, exacerbated by tiredness and stress.

Besides—it suddenly hit her—the prenup wasn't about Leo.
It was about her rights and Alessandro's.

She flicked to the end and found a section, mercifully short,
that declared she would get nothing, either in cash or interest in
Alessandro's fortune, in the case of divorce. Relief filled her. That
was the heart of it. All the rest was legal bumph of conditions
and counter-conditions.

Still, caution warned she should have a lawyer read this before
she signed.

Hell! Caution warned her to run a mile rather than consider
marrying Alessandro Mattani! Even in a convenient marriage
where they'd be virtual strangers, he had the power to turn her
world on its head.

But this wasn't about her. This was about Leo. Leo who had
the right to both his parents. Who didn't deserve to be fought over
in a tug-of-love battle. Whom she loved so much she couldn't
bear the risk of Alessandro taking him from her.

Carys blinked glazing hot eyes and straightened her spine.

She didn't have a lawyer to check the document, but that
didn't matter. She didn't have a choice.

Heart heavy, fingers tense, she picked up Alessandro's
custom-made pen and turned to the final page.

Carys Antoinette Wells. Such a pompous document deserved
her full name. But instead of writing with a flourish, her hand
shook so much it looked like the signature of an inexperienced
teenager, pretending to be someone else.

The pen clattered to the desk. Carys got slowly to her feet, stiff like an old woman, her heart leaden.

A muffled sound drew Alessandro's attention. He lifted his head, all too ready for a distraction from paperwork.

These last days Alessandro had found it extraordinarily difficult to give business his full attention. To be expected since he'd just discovered he had a son and was in the process of acquiring a wife.

A renegade spurt of pleasure shot through him. At the thought of Leo. And, more surprisingly, at the idea of Carys, soon to be his wife.

His lips twisted in self-mockery. Two years of celibacy had honed his libido to a razor-sharp edge. That explained the anticipation surging in his blood. Even the freshly recovered memory, visited again and again, of her lying in his bed, dark russet hair spread in sensual abandon, seized his muscles in potent sexual excitement.

Since the accident his sex drive had been dormant. At first he hadn't given it a thought. All his physical and mental strength had been directed to recovery. Then there were the gruelling hours he'd put in day after day, month after month, to turn around the family company that had careened towards disaster.

Yet as the months passed, he'd realised something fundamental had altered. Despite the temptations around him, he barely found the energy to take out a pretty girl, much less summon the enthusiasm to have one in his bed.

He'd always been a discriminating but active lover. Twenty-two months of celibacy was unheard of.

Was it any wonder he fretted over those lost months, as if something in that time had reduced his drive? Somehow weakened his very masculinity?

Not even to himself had he admitted anxiety that the change in him might be permanent.

Now though, there was no doubt everything was in working order. There was a permanent ache in his groin as he fought to stifle the lustful desires Carys provoked.

His lips stretched taut in a smile of hungry anticipation.

The sound came again. A whimper, drawing Alessandro's attention. He turned to find Leo stirring in his mother's arms. She'd refused to let the cabin crew take the boy but had stretched out on her bed with the tot in her arms. They'd looked so comfortable together Alessandro saw no reason to object.

Now the little one was fidgeting and twisting in his mother's loose embrace.

Alessandro watched his son's vigorous movements and felt again the cataclysmic surge of wonder that had overcome him when he'd held the boy in his arms. The idea that he had a child still stunned him.

Green eyes caught green and Leo stopped his restless jigging.

'Ba,' Leo said solemnly. 'Ba, ba, ba.'

Alessandro put his laptop aside. 'No. It's papa.'

'Baba!' One small arm stretched towards him and pride flared. His son was intelligent, that was obvious.

Alessandro stood, scooped the boy off the bed and held him carefully in both arms. An only child himself, Alessandro had virtually no experience with young children. But he'd learn fast, for his son's sake.

He'd been brought up by nannies and tutors, following a strict regimen designed to ensure he grew early into self-reliance and emotional independence. Alessandro didn't intend to spoil his son, but he'd ensure Leo spent time with his father—a luxury Alessandro had rarely enjoyed.

He lifted his son higher, registering the elusive scent he'd noticed before, of baby, sunshine and talc. He inhaled deeply and found himself staring into a small bright face.

'I'm Papa,' he murmured, brushing dark hair back from his son's forehead. It was silky and warm under his palm.

'Baba!' Leo's grin was infectious and Alessandro's lips tilted in an answering curve.

'Come. It's time to get better acquainted.' He turned towards his seat but paused as he caught sight of Carys. She lay on her side, arms outstretched invitingly.

In sleep she looked serene, gentle, tempting.

What was it about her that tempted him when so many

beauties hadn't? That turned him on so that just standing looking down at her, he was hard as granite with wanting. Desire was a slow unmistakeable throb in his blood.

She was the mother of his child, and that was a definite turn on. The thought of her body swelling and ripening with his baby was intensely erotic and satisfying.

But he'd lusted after her before he knew about Leo. When she was a stranger in a photograph.

Why was she different?

Because she challenged him and provoked him and got under his skin till he wanted to kiss her into submission?

Or because of something they'd shared?

Something about Carys Wells made him hanker to believe she was different.

Different! Ha!

She'd admitted she had left him because he'd found out about her with another man. Stefano Manzoni. The very shark who'd been circling, aiming to take a fatal bite out of Alessandro's company after Leonardo Mattani's death. That added insult to injury.

The idea of Carys with Stefano made Alessandro sick to the stomach. Had the affair been consummated? Fury pounded through him at the images his mind conjured.

He'd make absolutely sure from now on that Carys had no time to think of looking at another man.

Then there was the way she'd pored over the prenup in Melbourne. Proof, if he'd needed any, that she was just like the rest. She'd been so absorbed, she hadn't heard him enter then leave again.

Of course she'd signed without any further demur. As soon as she'd read the size of the outrageously large allowance he'd grant her while she lived with him and Leo, she'd been hooked. Just as he'd intended.

The generosity of that allowance had caused a stir with his advisers, but Alessandro knew what he was doing. He'd make sure Leo had the stability of a mother who stayed. Alessandro's son wouldn't be left, abandoned, as he had been.

No. Despite her strange allure, Carys wasn't different.

And yet...there would be compensations.

He looked from her abandoned sprawl and enticingly sensual lips to the chubby face of the son in his arms.

He'd made the right decision.

Carys didn't know whether to be relieved or astonished that Alessandro didn't take them to his home in the hills above Lake Como. She'd loved the spare elegance of his modern architect-designed house, built to catch every view with spectacular windows and an innovative design.

Now though, he drove his snarling, low-slung car to the massive family villa. *The villa to which she'd never been invited during her months living with him.*

She hadn't been good enough for his family.

The knowledge stuck like a jagged block of ice in her chest as he turned into a wide gravel drive. Her breathing slowed as trepidation filled her.

They passed lawns and garden beds, artfully planted shrubberies, and emerged before a spectacular view of the lake. To the left the villa rose serenely, like a sugar-encrusted period fantasy. To the right stretched Lake Como: indigo water rimmed by small towns and sunlit slopes.

Beside her sat Alessandro in silent magnificence. Six feet two of brooding Italian male. His straight brows and thinned lips made it clear how he felt about bringing her to the family mansion. Clearly she wasn't the sort of bride he'd have chosen in other circumstances.

The knowledge ate at her like acid. She hadn't been good enough before. Now only Leo's presence in the back seat elevated her enough to enter the Mattani inner sanctum.

Carys sensed old doubts circling, the belief that she really was second best, not able to live up to her family's exacting standards, let alone Alessandro's.

The sight of the villa, redolent with generations of power and wealth, only reinforced the sinking sense of inadequacy she'd striven all her life to overcome.

'Your home is very imposing,' she murmured as she shoved the traitorous thoughts away. She would *not* go down that track. Only tiredness made her think that way.

Plus nerves about what lay ahead.

'You think so?' Alessandro shrugged. 'I've always thought it overdone, as if trying too hard to impress.' He waved towards one end of the villa, thickly encrusted with pillars, balconies, decorative arched windows and even what looked from this angle like a turret.

'I hadn't thought about it like that.' She scanned the pale silvery-pink façade, taking in every quaint architectural device, every ostentatious finish. Alessandro was right. Yet with its mellow stone bathed in morning sun it was beautiful. 'Now you mention it, it's rather like an ageing showgirl, a little overdone, a little too obvious. But appealing anyway.'

A shout of laughter made her turn. Alessandro leaned back in his seat. He grinned as he met her startled gaze. That grin brought back crazy, wonderful memories. Her heart jumped then began pounding against her ribcage as heat sizzled, a long slow burn, right to her heart.

'You've hit the nail on the head. I'd never have described it that way, but you're absolutely right.' His gaze met hers and a shock wave hit her at the glint of approval and pleasure in his eyes. 'Just don't let Livia hear you say that. It's her pride and joy.'

'Livia?' The surge of jubilation Carys had felt in the unexpected shared moment ebbed. 'Is your stepmother here?'

'She no longer lives here. She spends her time in Milan or Rome. But you'll see her. She'll give you advice on what's expected of you. Fill you in on the social background you need to know.'

And you can't? The thought remained unspoken.

Of course he couldn't. Alessandro would be too busy with business or with other interests to spare time for his new fiancée. Swiftly Carys thrust aside the idea of his 'other interests' and schooled her face into a calm façade.

'Is that necessary?' She met his steady look then turned away to fumble with her seat belt. 'I'm sure she's busy.'

And she never liked me anyway.

Spending time teaching the ropes to a gauche plebeian whose sense of style began and ended with chain-store bargains would be hell for Livia. And worse for Carys.

'Not too busy to assist my bride.' His cool tone reinforced what Carys already knew, that this would be a duty for the older woman, not a pleasure.

'I'll look forward to it,' Carys said through gritted teeth and turned away, only to find her door already open. A man in a butler's uniform bowed, waiting for her to step out.

'*Grazie,*' she murmured, dredging up her rusty Italian.

He smiled and bowed deeper. 'Welcome, madam. It's a pleasure to have you here.'

Delight warmed her as she realised she could understand his clear, precise Italian. It had been almost two years since she'd spoken it, but she had an ear for languages. Perhaps because she'd spent so many years honing her memory and learning by heart at school. She'd discovered that was the best way to avoid revising with reams of written notes.

Hesitantly she tried out a little more Italian as she got out of the car. She was gratified when Paulo, the butler, encouraged her faltering attempts. Soon he was telling her about the comforts of the villa awaiting her, including a lavish morning tea, and she was responding.

Carys let him usher her from the car, only to pull up short at the sight of Alessandro waiting for her.

He held Leo, still slumbering, in his arms. For a moment the sight of her son, flushed with sleep and hair tousled, snuggled up against the wide shoulder of his magnificent, handsome father, made her heart falter in its rhythm.

Then Alessandro spoke, fortunately in a voice pitched only for her ears. 'If you've finished practising your charm on my staff we can go in.'

Confused, Carys met his searing dark scrutiny.

'Now we're marrying, you need to forget about winning other men's smiles.' His grim tone made it clear he wasn't joking. 'My wife needs to be above reproach.'

'You think I was *flirting?*' Amazement coloured her voice.

She could scarcely credit it. Alessandro sounded almost...
jealous.

The idea was preposterous. But the glitter of disapproval in
his eyes intrigued her.

She imagined things. Alessandro had wanted her sexually in
Melbourne only because she was convenient and shamingly
willing. But that was past. Now he saw her solely as Leo's
mother. He hadn't touched her since he'd discovered his son.
Clearly he wanted her for Leo not himself.

Carys thanked her lucky stars for that. It gave her distance.
Safety. For if he ever decided to seduce her again, she wasn't sure
she had the strength to resist.

'I think it's time we went in and settled our son,' he said,
ignoring her blurted question. He breached the distance between
them, consuming her personal space till she found it almost impossible to draw a steady breath. 'You'll be tired after the journey
and you need rest before this afternoon.'

'This afternoon?' Bemused, Carys shook her head.

'Livia has arranged a designer to fit you for your wedding dress.'
His lips curved up in a tight smile that could have signalled either
pleasure or stoic acceptance. 'We marry at the end of the week.'

CHAPTER NINE

FOUR hours later Carys waited, palms damp with trepidation, for the haute couture designer who'd been brought in to produce her wedding gown.

The fact that Alessandro's name could procure a top designer to dress her in such a short time only reinforced his enormous wealth and the huge gulf between them. Carys had never had anything made to order in her life.

The few high-fashion gurus she'd met while working had been condescending creatures. Perhaps because they took one look at her: average height, average face, unfashionably rounded figure, and knew she was no clothes horse.

At least this one already knew the worst. Alessandro had insisted on having her measurements taken in Melbourne and sent through to Milan, with a rather unflattering photo.

Carys glanced at her watch. Maybe the designer wouldn't show. Maybe they'd decided the challenge of passing her off as anything approaching chic was too hard.

She grimaced as she paced the salon, wishing the appointment was somewhere less imposing. The luxurious formality of the reception rooms stifled. Carefully she avoided the gilt-edged antique mirrors and stiff, silk-upholstered chairs. She felt like an ugly duckling, plucked out of her comfortable little pond and plonked in a palace.

If only she'd been allowed to buy a ready-made dress.

Despite her nerves, her lips twitched as she remembered

Alessandro's look of astonishment when she suggested it. Only a big formal wedding would do for the Conte Mattani and his bride. No quick civil ceremony was permitted.

So now she had to face a temperamental artiste, no doubt disappointed the bride wouldn't live up to their designs. Carys stood straighter, preparing for the worst.

A knock sounded on the massive double doors and Paulo's voice introduced her visitor. Carys felt her jaw lock as his words rolled over her. Her body stiffened with disbelief.

Impossible as it seemed, the worst was even more horrendous than she could have anticipated.

Her stomach went into a freefall of shock.

How could Livia have done it? How could she have chosen this designer of all people? She must have known—

'Signorina Wells?' The softly spoken words finally penetrated. Reluctantly, stiffly, Carys turned.

The woman before her was just as she remembered. Slim, elegant, huge dark eyes in a gorgeous elfin face. Dressed with a casual grace and a fortune in pearls that accentuated her delicate appeal.

Was it any wonder Alessandro had planned to marry her?

Pain, razor sharp and vicious, sheared through Carys. She grabbed the back of a nearby chair rather than double up in anguish. Desperate tension crawled up her spine as she strove to school her expression.

'Principessa Carlotta.' The words were rusty, thick, the product of a throat aching with distress.

Did they really expect her to submit to this woman's ministrations?

'Carlotta, please.' Her smile was warm, her husky voice appealing. Carys registered surprise that she seemed so approachable. So apparently ready to befriend the woman Alessandro had chosen over her.

Carys knew if their places were reversed she couldn't behave so blithely.

'Forgive me.' The other woman stopped a few paces away, her

smile disappearing as concern etched her brow. 'But are you all right? You look very pale.'

Carys wasn't surprised. It felt as if all her blood had drained away. She clamped her hand tighter around the chair back, summoning the strength she needed to stay upright.

'I'm…' What? Surprised to find my husband's ex-lover here? *Or was she still his lover?*

The thought smashed through her rigid self-control and Carys found her knees crumpling. Abruptly she sat, grateful to discover an antique sofa behind her.

'You're unwell. I'll call for assistance.'

'No!' Carys cringed at the idea of a fuss. She couldn't believe her own weakness. She'd faced this years ago. It was just the shock of meeting her rival face to face. 'It's jet lag,' she murmured. 'We only arrived a few hours ago.'

Despite her exhaustion, she hadn't been able to sleep in the vast gold-on-cream bedroom suite she'd been given. She'd felt out of place and on edge, her mind whirring.

'Forgive me, *signorina*, but I think it's more than that.' Dark eyes scrutinised her carefully. It was clear the princess was an astute woman.

Carys released the breath she'd been holding. She couldn't play this charade. She'd never been good at dissembling. She'd rather face facts, however unpalatable.

'Won't you sit down?' Her voice sounded choked.

After a moment the princess took a chair opposite, every movement a study in fluid grace and elegance.

Carys felt like a country bumpkin in her presence. Carefully she locked her hands in her lap to stop them shaking, then drew another sustaining breath.

'The truth is it was a shock to see you.' She paused, watching the other woman tilt her head in curiosity. 'I saw you once with Alessandro, two years ago.'

Pride screamed at her to stop there, to retain her dignity. But despite the craven impulse to keep quiet, Carys refused to play games of innuendo and unspoken secrets. She wasn't that sophisticated. If her blunt unrefined ways didn't fit her husband's milieu, then so be it. If she was going to live here she had to face this.

'I was Alessandro's lover,' she said, her voice stretched thin like fine wire. 'But then I discovered he was planning to marry you.'

There. It was in the open. No hiding from the truth now.

The other woman's mouth sagged and her eyes widened. There was shock in her expression and the taut lines of her neck. Now, this close, Carys wondered if she'd been unwell. She seemed almost gaunt, suddenly fragile rather than chic.

'It was you? I thought there was someone, but Alessandro never said.'

'No.' Bitterness filled her mouth. 'Alessandro kept me very much to himself.'

'But you've got it wrong.' The other woman leaned forward, one thin hand stretched out.

'No, *principessa*. I know exactly how it was.'

'Please. You must call me Carlotta!' There was such tension in her small frame and wide eyes Carys didn't demur. 'And Alessandro and I were *not* planning to marry.'

What? Carys sat bolt upright in her seat, torn from welling self-pity in an instant.

'Nor were we lovers,' Carlotta said. 'Ah, I can see from your expression that's what you thought. But we were never more than friends.'

Carys remained silent. 'Friends' was often a euphemism for something more. Was Carlotta trying to gull her? What reason could she have?

'You must believe me, *signorina*—'

'Carys,' she said abruptly. Formality seemed absurd now.

'Carys.' Carlotta gave her a faltering smile. 'There was no marriage plan, except as a notion put forward between our families. Alessandro's stepmother and my father resurrected the idea. It had been discussed years ago when we were just teenagers, but it never came to anything. Alessandro and I…' She shrugged. 'We grew up together, but there was never that special spark between us. You know?'

Carys knew. The spark Alessandro ignited in her had blazed

like wildfire, instantaneous and all-consuming, incinerating everything in its path. Her doubts, her natural reticence, every defence she had. Oh, but it had been glorious. Heat drenched her chilled body, just remembering.

She looked into the other woman's earnest face. Could it really be true?

'But Livia told me…'

Carlotta nodded. 'Livia promoted the match. She and my family thought a marriage would be in all our interests.'

Something about her diffident tone caught Carys' attention. 'Interests?'

The other woman shrugged one shoulder. 'Business. You know how bad things were after Alessandro's father died. It was touch and go whether Alessandro would lose the company.'

No. Carys hadn't known. She'd guessed things were grim. Had tried to offer support, but the more she'd tried the more he'd turned from her, isolating himself.

'There was talk of a merger, saving Alessandro's company and boosting my family's.' She paused and looked down at her hands. 'Plus I'd been through a difficult time and they thought marriage to Alessandro would save me from myself.'

'I'm sorry. I don't understand.' This was beyond Carys.

Carlotta raised her head and met her gaze squarely. 'I was recovering from anorexia nervosa.' Her liquid dark eyes dared Carys to condemn her, but Carys felt only horror that anyone, much less this beautiful woman, should be struck down by the insidious condition.

'Two years ago I was barely out of hospital. With my family's help, and with Alessandro's, I was just beginning to find my confidence. To go out and even think of starting work again.' She shook her head. 'It took Alessandro's strength and persistence to force me out into society. Even at that worst of times for him, he found time to help me. If it hadn't been for him beside me those first few times, even my parents' support wouldn't have got me out the door.'

'I saw you with him,' Carys found herself saying, 'at a hotel in town. You wore full-length gold. You looked like a fairy princess.' And Carys had never felt more an outsider, standing in the shadows looking in at the glittering world she'd never be part of. At the man she'd lost.

'I remember that night.' Carlotta nodded. 'The gown had to be altered so much. But the full length and long sleeves hid the worst of my condition.'

'I'd never have guessed. You were breathtaking.' Carys sank back in her chair, her head reeling as she digested Carlotta's news.

Was that why Alessandro had seemed so protective? Because he was worried about Carlotta's health? But why had he never said anything to Carys?

'You don't believe me.'

Carys looked up to find Carlotta watching her. 'I do. I just…Livia deliberately let me believe…' The older woman had told her baldly that Alessandro was engaged to marry someone of his own social circle. That he was simply with Carys as a final fling before settling down. She'd even dropped by unannounced with a box of printers' samples for him. It had been full of wedding invitations.

'Livia wanted the marriage quite badly. At one stage it looked as if the company might go under. Which, if you forgive me saying, would impact on her own wealth.'

Livia as a desperate woman? The idea hadn't occurred to Carys. She seemed so assured, so regal, so in control. But perhaps if her position was threatened…

'I heard about the engagement elsewhere too,' Carys said slowly. At the time the evidence seemed insurmountable, especially when Alessandro had refused to explain, merely stating baldly he would never behave so badly and accusing *her* of infidelity! 'I met your cousin, Stefano Manzoni.'

'You know Stefano?'

'Not know, precisely. He took me for coffee and drove me home.' Carys refrained from adding Stefano had viewed her disillusionment with Alessandro as an invitation to sexual dalliance. For all his charm and flattery he'd had more arms than an octopus.

'Ah, Stefano had hopes of that merger. When it became clear it wouldn't happen, he spent a lot of energy aiming for a hostile takeover. But he didn't succeed. He was no match for Alessandro.'

The pride in Carlotta's voice made Carys watch her carefully, but she read no sign of possessiveness. No hint of intimacy in the way she spoke of Alessandro.

'I'm sorry my friendship with Alessandro hurt you. If I'd known—'

'It wasn't you.' Carys leaned forward at the other woman's obvious distress, instinctively accepting what she said as true. It was far more likely that Livia, jealous of her position and eager to shore up the family wealth, had gone all out to scare off an upstart foreigner.

And how little effort it had taken! Carys had been her own worst enemy, only too ready to believe her. The knowledge made her stomach churn in self-disgust and regret.

Alessandro had grown unapproachable, shunning her attempts to comfort him, but if Carlotta was right, he'd never betrayed Carys!

Excitement buzzed through her veins. A crazy delight that he had been loyal to her, though he hadn't loved her. That meant so much.

It meant that though all personal feelings were at an end between them, Carys was marrying a man she could respect.

'But now everything is right between you both,' Carlotta said with such a sweet smile Carys didn't have the heart to disabuse her. 'I'm glad. Alessandro deserves happiness.' She stood, and for the first time Carys noticed the large portfolio resting against her chair. 'And now perhaps we can discuss your gown. I have ideas I hope you'll approve.'

Alessandro replaced the phone with careful precision, a scowl dragging at his brow. The sound of Livia, so rarely flustered, still gabbling her excuses, rang in his ears.

He wasn't in the mood for excuses.

While in Australia he'd been unable to contact his stepmother in person. Frustration had built with each passing day till he'd simply left news that he was bringing home his fiancée and requesting she start the wedding preparations.

It still galled him to discover he'd lived with Carys Wells prior to his accident but hadn't been told about her after his coma. That Livia had kept it from him and told his staff not to refer to the woman who'd been his lover.

As if he needed protecting from his past!

He shot to his feet and paced the room.

Livia's explanations didn't alleviate his thwarted fury at being kept in the dark. It didn't matter that Livia thought Carys on the make, out to snare a wealthy man. Or that Carys had already walked out of his life. Or even that the doctors had said it was best if he were left to recover his memory without prompting.

He should have been told.

Livia's talk of a possible match at the time with Carlotta meant nothing. Alessandro knew without being told what had prompted that—Livia searching for an easy way to shore up the family finances. As if he and Carlotta would ever make a match of it. And, more to the point, as if he'd abrogate his responsibility to salvage the company by buying his way out of trouble with his wife's money!

He rubbed his jaw, realising he now had an explanation for Carys' belief he'd two-timed her with Carlotta. Livia had no doubt blown their friendship out of all proportion.

For a moment he considered enlightening Carys, proving he was innocent of her accusations. But she wouldn't believe him. The distrust flashing in her eyes was too easy to read.

He turned and strode back across the room, unable to ignore any longer Livia's most important revelation.

She'd hinted the affair had been a casual fling, because he'd kept Carys to himself and refused social invitations.

But that only stirred his curiosity. There had been plenty of lovers in his life, yet he'd never been reluctant to take them out publicly. That was one of the functions they performed—company at the many social events he attended.

His skin prickled with preternatural awareness as he remembered Livia saying while Carys was in residence he'd shunned the social whirl, preferring to stay home with his lover. Such behaviour was unprecedented.

And the only reason he could fathom was unthinkable.

That he'd been totally absorbed by her, unwilling to share her with others.

His ability to fixate on what interested him had been one of the keys to his business success. And though he hid it well, his possessive streak was well developed. He hadn't liked to share his toys as a child, and as an adult what he had he held on to.

If he'd felt…attached to Carys, he'd have kept her to himself rather than parade her before the sharks ready to pursue an attractive woman.

If he'd felt attached.

Alessandro shook his head. He didn't do serious relationships. Didn't believe in romantic love. It should be impossible.

Should be.

Yet that frisson of instinct told its own story.

He scrubbed his hand across his jaw, knowing a moment's unfamiliar hesitation.

There were too many unanswered questions, and Carys alone held the key to every answer.

Even his fiancée's relationship with her family puzzled him. Not one of them would attend the wedding. That wasn't like any family he knew.

The woman was an enigma as well as a temptation.

He turned on his heel and strode to the door.

He found her in the grand salon, leaning into the corner of one of the uncomfortable antique sofas Livia had installed.

In her crumpled aqua skirt and matching beaded top, her hair in a ponytail, Carys was a breath of fresh air in the stuffy, formal room.

He walked closer.

She didn't move. Her head rested on one arm as if she'd leaned sideways and fallen instantly asleep. One beaded sandal dangled precariously from her toes. The other lay discarded and his gaze moved to her slim, bare foot, pale and shapely and ridiculously enticing with its painted pink toenails.

A tremor of heat ricocheted through his belly as he followed the lissom curve of her ankle to her calf, her knee and, where her skirt had rucked up, to her thigh.

He remembered the feel of her supple legs encasing him as he thrust her back against the wall of his suite at the Landford. The musky scent of her arousal. The sound of her whimpering mews for more. The sheer erotic blaze of glory that had been him and Carys, on the verge of consummating this...need between them.

Just the echo of that memory had him hard and wanting and ready, feet planted wide and breathing constricted.

Yet instinctively he resisted.

Livia's news made him pause.

It *couldn't* be true that Carys had become so important to him before his accident. He, who'd learnt early not to trust in love or the fidelity of the female sex!

No. There was some other explanation behind his relationship with Carys.

And for the way she made him feel now.

Protective. It was ludicrous. This was the woman he'd told to leave because she'd been with another man. And yet...

Alessandro shook his head, adrift on a sea of turbulent, unfamiliar emotions. He was used to his life proceeding in the pattern he designed. Emotions had no place there. Or they hadn't before Carys.

His shoulders cramped as he fought the tug of feelings, weaknesses, he preferred not to acknowledge.

Despite a few hours' sleep on the long flight from Melbourne, dark smudges were still visible beneath her eyes.

Unwilling concern twisted in his belly.

This woman got to him as no other!

Without giving himself time to think, he bent and scooped Carys into his arms, ignoring the sense of familiarity that rose and crested, like a wave of warmth, as he tucked her close to his torso. Clearly he'd carried her before.

His body knew hers, only too intimately.

He turned for the door. She'd rest better in her own bed. He'd leave her there and then look in on Leo.

Alessandro lengthened his stride as he headed for the main staircase. That time alone with Leo on the flight had whetted his appetite for his son's company. He found the boy more fascinating than any other child of his acquaintance.

Alessandro had reached the top of the stairs when Carys

woke. Her lips parted in a sleepy smile, and heat doused him. Eyes as bright as stars met his and instantly desire exploded into life, tightening his groin, tensing every muscle. In that moment he veered automatically towards the master suite rather than the rooms where she'd been installed.

An afternoon of pleasure, rediscovering her feminine delights beckoned. He quickened his pace.

Then the misty soft smile disappeared, and alarm filled her eyes. Her mouth tightened and she jerked as if trying to wriggle out of his hold.

The heat in his belly fizzed out as quickly as it had ignited. He slammed to a stop. No other woman had ever looked at him in such horror.

'What are you doing?' It was an accusatory gasp. Automatically Alessandro lifted his chin, unaccustomed to such a tone.

'Carrying you to bed. You need rest.'

If anything her tension increased. He felt her stiffen. Her eyes blazed.

'No! I need to see to Leo. He—'

'Our son—' Alessandro paused, savouring the words '—is being looked after by a very capable and pleasant carer.' Carys opened her mouth, to object no doubt. He overrode her. 'In the longer term we will look for a more permanent carer to help with him, but for now be assured he's in safe hands.'

She drew in a deep breath and Alessandro wished he weren't so aware of the soft inviting press of her breast against his chest. It was the most refined torment.

'I can walk from here.'

'But we're almost there.' He stepped forward again, this time towards her guest bedroom. Still he felt her tension. She was stiff as a board, rigid with…anxiety? Distress?

Concern twisted in his belly, a flare of regret for what had happened this afternoon.

'I'm sorry you weren't warned it would be Carlotta coming to discuss your wedding gown today.' He said it slowly, unused to apologising. He'd always prided himself on behaving honourably. 'I only just found out myself.'

It had been Livia's little surprise to confront Carys with the woman she believed had been her rival.

Even now Alessandro found it hard to believe Livia had done anything so crass. He mightn't trust Carys, might have been betrayed by her, but his behaviour and his family's must always be above reproach.

From now on Alessandro would have his personal staff oversee all the wedding arrangements. His stepmother could attend and kiss the bride, but he no longer trusted her with anything more.

'It's all right,' Carys said quickly. 'We had a…useful discussion.' For a moment her gaze clung to his, then she turned her head abruptly, as if dismissing him.

Clearly she didn't accept his apology.

Alessandro registered a curious feeling of emptiness, as if something inside his chest shrivelled. An instant later he put the nonsensical notion from his mind. Resentment stirred at having his word doubted.

'She will do an excellent job,' he said tersely. 'Carlotta is one of Italy's most talented new designers.'

'I'm sure she is,' his bride-to-be said in a hollow voice. 'Her ideas are very clever.'

She sounded as enthusiastic as a woman being measured for her shroud. The idea slashed at his pride.

And this the woman he'd wanted to take to his room and ravish! It shamed him that even now he craved her.

He pushed open her bedroom door and quickly lowered her to the bed, stepping back as if her very touch contaminated.

Separate rooms until after the wedding were preferable after all. Carys needed time to accustom herself to marriage. And he needed space to master these unwanted feelings.

'I'll leave you now to rest.'

Alessandro spun round without waiting for a response and strode from the room.

He didn't see the longing or the anguish in her eyes as she watched him go.

CHAPTER TEN

CARYS drew a deep breath and paused before stepping into the church. The clamour of photographers and sightseers unsettled her, another reminder that she was marrying one of Italy's richest, most eligible men.

Only the presence of Alessandro's security staff kept the eager throng back.

She wished now she'd accepted Alessandro's suggestion that one of his cousins escort her down the aisle.

Foolishly she'd kept alive the faint hope her father would come to give her away. It wasn't a romantic match, but this marriage was for keeps. For Leo's sake. And because once wed she knew Alessandro would never relinquish his wife.

This ceremony would change her life for ever.

Her lips tightened as she smoothed shaky fingers over rich silk skirts. Even after all these years the pain of her dad's rebuff was as strong as ever.

All those missed school plays and speech days where her performances and athletic awards failed to measure up to parental expectations of academic brilliance. She should have realised he wouldn't come, just as her siblings had perfectly sound reasons for not attending, even with Alessandro's offer of free travel. They'd been too busy, promising to visit sometime in the future when life was less hectic.

'Are you ready, *signorina*?' Bruno's familiar husky voice interrupted her reverie. 'Is anything wrong?'

Everything!

She was marrying the man she'd once adored. Not for love, but in a bloodless marriage to keep her son. She had no friends here to support her. She was out of her depth, marrying into an aristocratic world she'd never fit into.

Worst of all, she suspected that despite all that had gone before, she might still…care for Alessandro.

Being with him had awoken so many memories.

More, Carlotta's news that he'd never betrayed Carys, hadn't been unfaithful, had opened the floodgates to emotions she thought she'd eradicated.

He might not love her, but he was essentially the same man she'd fallen for years ago. More impatient, more ruthless, yet just as charismatic and intriguing. And not the lying cheat she'd believed when she'd left him.

Guilt plagued her that she'd believed the worst of him. Her own insecurities had made her too ready to doubt.

Regret gave way to longing, and she found herself wishing this marriage was for real. For love, not expediency.

No! Alessandro wasn't looking for love.

And nor was she.

'Signorina?' Bruno stepped close, his tone concerned.

'Sorry, Bruno.' Carys directed a wobbly smile at the bodyguard. 'I'm just…gathering myself. It's a little overwhelming.'

'It will be all right, *signorina.* You'll see. The *conte* will take care of you.'

As he'd taken care of all the wedding arrangements, with a ruthless efficiency that brooked no delay. She was merely an item to be checked off his list.

Acquired: one wife, ditto mother for my son.

Carys repressed a hysterical giggle and lifted her bouquet. The rich scent of orange blossom filled her nostrils, and she swayed, stupidly unsettled by the evocative perfume.

'So he will, Bruno. Thank you.'

She was stronger than this. She didn't do self-pity.

This was for Leo. She had to focus on that. Pushing back her shoulders, she stepped through the door Bruno held open.

Music swelled, the sound of murmuring voices faded, and she was aware of a sea of faces turned towards her. She let her gaze trawl the congregation rather than look down the aisle to where Alessandro stood, waiting to make her his wife.

Pain constricted her chest and she faltered, but curious stares prompted her to move on. They were all strangers, friends of Alessandro. No doubt assessing the bride to see if she lived up to expectations.

Carys lifted her chin, knowing at least she was dressed the part. Carlotta had done a superb job creating a stylish gown that made Carys look feminine and almost elegant.

In grey silk so pale it almost passed for cream, the dress was closely fitted from neck to hips, turning her curves into an almost hourglass figure. From there it flared into lush folds and a rippling train studded with azure beads like hundreds of flashing stars. Long, fitted sleeves and a high collar gave it a severe, almost medieval style, belied by the deep, slit neckline, embroidered with azure sapphires.

The effect was austere yet sumptuous. It was the most flattering, gorgeous thing Carys had ever owned.

She heard whispers as she passed, saw the envy in female eyes, and a tiny thrill of pleasure skimmed her spine.

Now she noticed smiles, one or two familiar faces. And suddenly, there were Alessandro's three female cousins, whom she'd met only two days ago. Accompanied by their husbands and their brood of handsome children. All smiled broadly, nodding encouragement.

They'd chosen pews on the bride's side of the church. Warmth invaded her chilled body at the thoughtfulness of the gesture. It made her feel she wasn't quite so alone.

Then came Carlotta, beaming and gorgeous in ruby red, delight in her dark eyes. And Leo, clapping excitedly and calling to her from his carer's arms. Carys leaned over and gave him a quick cuddle, gaining strength from the flood of love that rose within her.

The buzz of whispered conversation began again and she straightened, feeling the curious stares stabbing into her back. She turned and there was Livia, her fixed smile cool.

This was the woman who'd tried to keep Alessandro and

Carys apart. How would she react if she knew that, despite this charade, they were virtually strangers? That the ceremony was a cruel parody of the dreams Carys had once cherished?

Momentary pleasure faded as reality slammed into Carys. It obliterated her tentative poise and transfixed her with a knife-blade of regret through the chest.

Finally she couldn't ignore any longer the tall man looming before her. Impatience radiated from every superbly tailored inch.

Her fingers clenched on the bouquet as she fought the impulse to run pell-mell back up the aisle and away to freedom. Blood rushed in her ears and her body tensed for flight.

Then he extended one powerful arm, his hand outstretched towards her. She felt his regard like a lick of flame on her face and her body. Her skin prickled in response.

There was no escape. He sucked the air from her lungs and shattered the remnants of her defiant courage.

Like an automaton she stepped forward, letting Alessandro capture her hand. Feeling in that moment the inevitable thrill of energy his touch always evoked.

Yet even that couldn't thaw the chill around her heart.

If only they were marrying for any other reason. If this was about caring instead of custody.

Desolation swept her. If only Alessandro remembered the past, remembered even a little of what they'd shared. But he didn't. Probably never would. Only she recalled the glory as well as the pain, the companionship and the ecstasy and the sense of belonging that had made their relationship unique.

What good were such memories when she couldn't share them? They might as well be figments of her imagination, torturing rather than comforting. She'd never again experience that closeness with the man she was about to marry.

'Carys.' The word feathered across her nerves like the stroke of his hand. His sexy accent invested the name with undercurrents that made her tremble. He turned her towards him and inevitably her eyes lifted to his face.

Her breath caught in astonishment as she met his deep green gaze. Its intensity scorched.

She tried to draw breath, but the incendiary flare in his eyes arrested her. Instead her breathing shallowed, became rapid and unsteady. Her knees trembled and tattered hope rose at what she read in his face.

Alessandro's expression almost made her believe…

The priest spoke and instantly, like a curtain descending to hide a stage, Alessandro's face became blank, wiped of all expression. No heat, no vibrancy, no emotion.

Had she imagined it? Wanted so much to believe he felt something, anything for her that she'd invented that look of fixation and wonder?

Looking now into shadowed dark eyes, Carys felt that tiny seed of hope shrivel in her breast.

The past was the past. What they'd once shared was dead.

In its place she gave herself in a farce of marriage.

Carys tasted the ashes of old dreams on her tongue as she turned to face the priest. Instinct screamed that she was making a terrible, terrible mistake.

But, for the sake of her son, she'd go through with it.

Hours later, drooping with fatigue, face stiff from pinning on a smile, Carys was too weary to object when Alessandro swept her off her feet and into his arms in front of their guests.

'There's no need for pantomime,' she whispered, attempting to ignore the insidious melting sensation as his arms closed round her. 'My legs work perfectly.'

'No pantomime, *wife*,' he murmured as he carried her from the enormous marquee and across the lawn to the sound of applause. 'In Italy men carry their brides across the threshold.'

Carys eyed the hundred metres between them and the villa and kept her lips closed. If Alessandro wanted to indulge in a show of machismo, she had little chance of dissuading him. She'd just have to pretend being held in his arms didn't evoke a cascade of tingling awareness she couldn't control.

She stiffened in his hold.

'You could try smiling,' he said under his breath. 'People expect a bride to look happy.'

Carys bared her teeth in what she guessed was more of a grimace than a smile of joy. The strain of acting the happy bride had taken its toll, shredding her frayed nerves.

'I'm a hotel management trainee, not an actress.'

Not for anything would she let him guess how deeply his embrace affected her. How that terrible gnawing sensation ate once more at her belly, and how her arms ached with the effort not to lift them around his neck so she could sink against the broad cushion of his chest.

'Little viper.' There was no heat in the look he gave her. But there was…something.

Her heart raced faster.

'You can put me down now. We've crossed the threshold.'

He didn't answer, just made for the sweeping central staircase and climbed it with a speed that belied the burden he carried.

Dimly Carys was aware of more applause and laughter from the few staff gathered in the foyer.

But nothing could distract her from the look on Alessandro's face. The determined set of his jaw and the hooded, unreadable expression in his eyes. He was so *focused*.

'Alessandro?'

He didn't answer as he reached the top of the staircase and plunged down a wide hallway.

'My room is to the left.' Was that her voice? That wisp of sound? Her hands clenched together so hard the pulse throbbed through her palms like a beaten drum. Her chest hollowed with an emotion that should have been trepidation.

Ahead wide double doors stood open. Alessandro strode through them then paused to kick them shut with a thud that reverberated right through her.

Slowly the sound died away to echoing silence. A silence taut with rising tension.

Still he held her.

She felt the rise and fall of his chest against her, surely more pronounced than when he'd climbed the stairs.

Did she imagine the shift of those long-fingered hands? The tightening of his embrace, drawing her more firmly against his powerful torso? Heat radiated from him, seeped into her flesh and bones, melting the tightness of her tensed muscles.

Craven, she turned her head, unable to meet his stare. Afraid he might see in her face traces of the crazy yearning that still plagued her. The yearning for *him*. No matter what she'd told herself, she'd never been able to obliterate it.

But she had to hide it.

Her breath hitched audibly as she saw the wide bed that took up one end of the vast room. Canopied in emerald green silk, perfectly centred between French doors that gave on to a balcony overlooking the lake, it took her breath away.

A long garland of roses was strung across the bed head, and rich velvety petals, like a shower of cream and blush and crimson, lay scattered across the sheets.

It looked like nothing so much as…

'Our wedding bed.' Alessandro's deep voice was resonant with an inflection she could almost swear was satisfaction.

Except she knew he had no desire for intimacy. No desire for her. This union was pragmatic, necessary. A legality.

Carys opened her mouth, but no words came. She drew a difficult breath, suddenly aware of how the tight silken bodice cupped her breasts and of the delicate scratch of her new bra's hand-made lace against peaking nipples.

Hot embarrassment flooded her. And more heat that wasn't embarrassment, creating an unsettling, pooling sensation way down low in her womb.

She shifted in his hold, praying he wouldn't notice her traitorous body's reaction to him.

'Your cousins have been busy,' she said in a scratchy, unfamiliar voice. Now she understood the presence of the other women in the house this morning, whispering and laughing over some secret as they made their way upstairs.

She felt the shrug of powerful shoulders. 'Another tradition. It's supposed to bring luck to a marriage. Blessings and, who knows, maybe even fertility.'

Carys wriggled, now desperate to escape. She couldn't keep up this façade of composure. Not when she felt his heart thudding against her, the warm tickle of his breath in her hair and the heat of his hands cradling her.

He made her want things she shouldn't. Things that could never be.

'The union is already fertile. We have Leo. We don't—'

Her words died as, instead of releasing her, Alessandro carried her to the bridal bed. A moment later she was sprawled across the mattress, the rich, sensual perfume of damask roses rising from the petals crushed beneath her.

Automatically she struggled against the encumbering long skirts and the veil dragging her down.

Then she looked up and froze. The expression of feral hunger in Alessandro's face made her heart hammer in her chest. Adrenaline spiked her bloodstream.

She told herself it was from fear. But she didn't believe it.

'You wouldn't condemn Leo to being an only child, would you?'

Alessandro looked down at the woman who was now incontrovertibly *his* and felt a satisfaction such as he'd never experienced.

It outstripped the pleasure of finally wresting the family company back to a secure footing. Even the recollection of his first major business coup, the difficult and astoundingly successful acquisition of a rival manufacturing firm, couldn't match the exultant surge of pleasure that shot through him as he looked down at his woman.

His wife.

It wasn't supposed to be like this. It was supposed to be convenient, sensible, a considered option to safeguard the interests of his son. But right now only his own interests were at the fore of Alessandro's mind.

This week had been a test of endurance such as he'd never known. Time and again he'd reined in the impulse to reach for her and make her his, assuage the physical hunger and, more, the edgy sensation that she could fill the nameless void at the core of his world.

When she'd walked down the aisle, an ice-cool, delicious vision of femininity, his temperature had soared and his libido had leapt into urgent life. It had taken all his resolve to stand and wait, not to throw her over his shoulder and abduct her to some-place private.

Laid out before him like a delicacy awaiting his approval, Carys stoked a fire in his blood for which he knew there could be only one solution.

Sex. Hot and satisfying.

Alessandro drew a slow breath, inhaling the scent of flowers and woman that had haunted him all afternoon.

Damn it. Carlotta had done her job too well. That dress em-phasised every sultry line and curve of the woman he'd married. It had driven him crazy from the moment he saw her.

His gaze skimmed the perfect swell of her breasts, hidden yet accentuated by the shadowy V of a neckline that had dragged his attention back again and again. With those scintillating blue stones on the bodice drawing his gaze, he'd spent half the recep-tion ogling his new wife instead of speaking to guests.

When they'd danced he'd put his hands around a waist that was surely too tiny for a woman who'd given birth, and felt a powerful surge of possessiveness overwhelm him.

It didn't matter that he couldn't recall the past between them. It was the present that mattered. Not even his doubts about her trustworthiness impinged on his thinking. Right now nothing mattered more than slaking his desperate lust for his brand new wife.

The self-imposed wait was over at last.

He lifted a hand to his tie and tugged it undone.

'Alessandro!'

His eyes had a glazed look: too intense, too febrile. As if the cool, utterly controlled man she knew had been replaced by a being only half tame. His scar complemented his lawless air. He looked dangerous, rapacious. He'd turned from magnate to pirate in the blink of an eye.

A delicious shiver shot through her, even as she tried to be sensible.

Sleeping with Alessandro would solve nothing. Not when his

heart wasn't engaged. Experience proved she was too vulnerable to him, too hungry for more.

But it's not sleep he wants, purred a demon voice inside her head.

She watched in fascination and dawning horror as his bow tie slid from his neck to the floor. Dark olive fingers flicked open his shirt.

Carys scrabbled backwards on the bed, hampered by the long veil underneath her and the voluminous skirts.

'What do you think you're doing? This wasn't part of our bargain.' If only her voice was strident rather than breathless. Instead it sounded like an invitation.

'Our bargain was marriage, *piccolina.* You're my woman now.' His voice had dropped to a throaty growl that should have warned but instead thrilled her.

She squeezed her eyes shut, seeking the strength she needed.

A dip in the mattress had her eyes popping open to discover Alessandro kneeling astride her thighs, pinning her wide skirt to the bed.

His glittering gaze raked her as if there was no exquisite gown covering her. As if she was his for the taking.

A shiver of pure carnal anticipation ripped through Carys, making a mockery of all her logical protests.

The truth was that, stripped of the varnish of urbane sophistication, Alessandro held an even more potent allure. His untrammelled machismo sent her hormones into overdrive.

'Alessandro.' Her voice was a telltale husky quiver, but she pressed on. 'You don't really want this.'

Or me. Her throat closed convulsively before she could blurt that out.

He'd turned away from her totally once he had discovered Leo. The completeness of his withdrawal, from hot pursuit to cold distance in the blink of an eye, had left her in no doubt she'd been a convenience, easy to use and easy to discard. Of no intrinsic value.

Hot, familiar pain suffused her and she dropped her eyes. She fought against a lifetime's experience of rejection, telling herself she *was* important.

'Not want this?' His words were sharp as the crack of a gun firing. His nimble fingers paused from reefing his shirt undone. 'What are you talking about?'

'You want to make it appear as if we're a real married couple, for the benefit of the guests,' she said in a low, cramped voice, her eyes fixed on his hands rather than his face. 'But carrying me all the way up here did the trick. There's no need to continue the charade.'

'Trick? Charade?' He spoke softly, yet the words throbbed with outrage. 'We are *really* married. You are *really* my wife. And I am now your husband. The *only* man in your life. Remember that.'

'There are no other men in my life.' She wished he'd move. Being caged by his long, lithe, hot body was doing terrible things to her pulse. It throbbed deep between her legs, in the place that suddenly felt so empty and needy. Her lovely dress felt too constricting, the bodice cramping her breath. If only he'd move away.

'And there will be no others from now on. Remember that.'

'I don't need a man in my life.' All she needed was Leo.

'Then you should not have married me, Carys.'

The finality of his tone penetrated, yanking her gaze back to his. Her mouth dried as she looked into his proud, severe, gorgeous face. Clear intent was etched in every angle and curve as well as in the glint of green fire in his deep-set eyes.

'I will not be used as a convenience, Alessandro. We might have married for our son's sake, but you can't have me on tap.' Her jaw ached with tension and she fought to keep her words calm, despite the emotions jangling through her.

'Convenience!' His eyes flared wide. 'You think *this* is convenient?' He snatched her hand up and pressed it, palm down, against his groin.

A massive erection throbbed against her touch. Hot and powerful, it filled her hand. Carys gulped at the memory of all that power unleashed inside her. Need spiralled deep within and she clenched her thighs against the moist proof that he still turned her on as no man ever had.

She tried to pull back, but he wouldn't let her.

Her pulse rocketed as he loomed over her, an autocratic, sexy captor, trapping her with his superior strength. And more, with the raw promise of pleasure in his eyes.

Heat exploded in her belly. The heat of sexual excitement.

She shouldn't want him, but she did. Badly. Despite pride. Despite everything.

'From the moment I saw your photo I've been hard.' He shook his head and she saw a fleeting glimpse of confusion in his eyes. It almost matched her own disbelief at the revelation. He'd wanted her? Not just seen her as a source of information for the memory he'd lost?

Could it be true? Part of her needed to believe that he'd wanted her, even if only on the most superficial level. That she was special to him.

'Hungry for a woman I didn't even know! And in Melbourne…' His eyes flickered half closed as he tilted his body, pushing right into her hold with a jerky thrust that ended in a low masculine groan of need.

The sound aroused her terribly. Memories swamped her of Alessandro gasping out his desire and his pleasure as they melded together in passion. She squirmed beneath him, fruitlessly trying to ease the wanton ache in her womb.

'Do you know what it did to me, letting you go?'

Dumbly she shook her head. He'd seemed so controlled. Yet now, looking into a face drawn tight with barely bridled hunger, a face of pain, Carys began to doubt her certainty.

'For the first time in two years I wanted a woman, but it was obvious you weren't ready. You were exhausted and overwhelmed by the changes in your life.'

He leaned forward, braced on one hand above her, the other hand still clasping her to him. Part of her revelled in his dominance, even as she fought to clear her mind. 'I thought you needed time, Carys. That's why I pulled back.'

For the first time in two years? Her brain stuck on that statement.

She couldn't have heard right. Alessandro was a virile man who revelled in physical pleasure. When all else had bled away, and their relationship grew empty, he'd still been a passionate lover, almost ferocious in his need for her. And in his need to give her equal pleasure.

A shudder of pure longing rippled through her.

'Don't soft soap me, Alessandro. I don't care how many lovers you've had since we were together,' she lied. 'So you don't have to pretend to—'

'Celibacy?' His mouth twisted in derision. 'And what if it's true? What if there's been no one since you?'

Her mind boggled at the idea of Alessandro celibate without her, only feeling desire when he saw her again.

As if his subconscious had kept him for her alone.

No! That was nonsense. The inane imaginings of a woman who'd once been too much in love.

'You can't mean it.'

'You know,' he growled, 'I'm getting tired of you telling me what it is I mean or feel.'

CHAPTER ELEVEN

WITHOUT warning he moved back. Carys was free, her skirts no longer pinned beneath his knees, her hand no longer pressed against that most intimate part of him.

She was relieved. Of course she was. She drew a long, shaky breath. In a minute she'd move and—

Her skirts bunched as strong hands slipped up from her ankles over silk-stockinged calves and knees. By the time Carys collected her stunned thoughts his fingers had reached her thighs, pausing to circle the tops of the stockings Carlotta had insisted she wear with her new underwear and glamorous gown.

Dumbfounded, Carys stared up over a froth of silk to Alessandro's stern face. He was looking down to where his hands played with her suspender straps. Her breath jammed in her lungs at the incredibly erotic sensations his feather-light caresses evoked.

She leaned up, intending to push him away, but it was too late. Already he'd thrust the fabric higher, baring her to his gaze. She felt a waft of air as, with a single tug, he ripped the delicate fabric of her panties away.

The look on his face stopped her instantaneous move to cover herself. Heat sizzled in her blood at the way he stared. Hungry. Possessive. Intense.

The air thickened, making breathing difficult. All she heard was the throb of her pulse, heavy and quick.

The soft wool of Alessandro's trousers brushed her thighs as he knelt between her legs, pushing them wider. Desire exploded as her blood rushed faster in her shaking limbs.

She needed to resist the lure of his seduction. But now, faced with the reality of Alessandro, rampant with desire, her longings obliterated every sensible reason for resistance.

All she could think of was that he hadn't betrayed her. Hadn't taken another lover when they were together, and, if he were serious, not even since they'd parted.

What she'd felt for him hadn't died. It had only been dormant. Even her heartache hadn't killed it off.

'The only thing that would stop me now is if you said you didn't want this.' He lifted his head and pinioned her with his gaze.

She lay supine before the blaze of power she read there, stunned by the immensity of the feelings rising within her.

'Can you tell me you don't want this?'

On the words one long finger slid unerringly through moist folds of skin where she was most vulnerable and sensitive.

Carys shook at the riot of sensations radiating out from his intimate caress. She felt so vibrantly alive. So needy.

Hands in tight fists, she opened her mouth to make him stop, summoning her shattered resistance. But with mind-numbing ease his finger slipped inside, pushing past muscles that clenched hungrily around him.

She almost sobbed with pleasure at the gentle, insistent, seductive slide. Just that alone felt so good. Too good. It had been so long and—

'Carys? I'm waiting for you to tell me.'

From under weighted lids she saw him watch her and felt a flush cover her breasts and cheeks. This was her last chance.

'I…' The tempo of his caress changed, the angle of his touch, and all at once the world shattered around her in a storm of ecstatic energy. She felt it splinter into tiny fragments as she bucked up against his palm, tidal waves of unstoppable sensation radiating out from his touch.

Heat drenched her as the sudden climax, as complete and mind-numbing as any she'd known, blasted her apart.

Only Alessandro's jade gaze held her together. Through the

maelstrom of exquisite delight and overwhelmed senses, his eyes locked with hers. The connection between them sparked like a live wire.

An instant later he moved, surging forward in a powerful motion that thrust her back into the mattress, her legs around his already pumping hips.

Better, so much better than before. The heavy, satisfying length of him filled her completely. His breath was hot at her neck, his broad chest flattening hers, rubbing against her sensitive breasts. His arms curled beneath her and lifted her up so that each rapid thrust slid further and further till surely he touched her very centre.

Her spasming muscles had begun to ease, but now, pummelled by the unstoppable force that was Alessandro, spent nerve endings came abruptly to life again. Hearing him growl her name, feeling his teeth graze her neck at its most sensitive point only heightened the intensity of his raw, earthy loving. Tension spiralled anew as she responded to a passion so primitive she'd never experienced its like before.

The force driving him was so elemental Carys felt as if he branded her for life. She revelled in it.

One last thrust, the slide of eager hands, and she looked up into dazed green eyes as an explosion, more cataclysmic than the first, shook them both.

She heard her name, heard her own high-pitched scream, felt the satisfying hot pulse of his seed inside her as the wave took them, and then they collapsed together.

Alessandro couldn't believe he'd so lost control. One minute they were arguing and the next Carys was tipped up on the bed and he was pounding into her with all the finesse of a rampant stallion.

The sight of her coming apart at his touch, the look of bemused wonder, of yearning on her face, had tipped him over the edge. And shattered every claim he had to be a civilised man.

He had no control where this woman was concerned. Not one iota of subtlety or restraint.

For weeks he'd harnessed a desperate, growing hunger, but

not for a moment had he thought the outcome would be so rough or so barbaric.

Alessandro scrubbed a hand across his face and met his hooded eyes in the bathroom mirror. Even now they glittered with unrepentant satisfaction and excitement. Because Carys, his wife, lay in the next room. In his bed.

He should be ashamed he'd taken her with such unskilled abandon. Yet even that wouldn't stop him a second time.

He reached out for a flannel and turned back towards the bathroom door.

She lay as he'd left her, limp and sated, long legs still encased in stockings and high-heeled satin shoes. The sight of those legs, the rucked up, crumpled dress, and the dark triangle of hair sent a bolt of electricity straight to his groin. His breath whistled out of his lungs as need, instant and consuming, swamped him again.

Had it always been like this with Carys?

Again that tantalising memory teased him, of Carys lying sated in another bed. This time, though, it wasn't her image that caught his attention but the emotions the scene evoked. As if he could feel what he'd felt then. Satisfaction tinged with stirring sexual anticipation. Blatant possessiveness. And…contentment.

It was the latter, the curious sense of absolute rightness, that unsettled him. The suspicion that along with his memory he'd lost something precious.

He'd never responded to another woman so. That made him wary. But he couldn't keep away. Didn't want to.

Already he hungered for her again. This time he'd put her needs first and prove he wasn't a barbaric lout who didn't know how to seduce a woman.

Alessandro avoided her eyes. Heat lashed his cheeks at the way he'd treated her.

She didn't move as he settled himself, naked, on the bed beside her. The dress he'd paid a fortune for was probably un-salvageable, but he didn't care. Didn't care about anything but the hunger thrumming again in his veins like a horde of locusts sweeping down to devour him.

She was barely dozing, worn out by his rough handling. He

should let her rest. She'd been wound tight as a top at the wedding. But in conscience he couldn't let her sleep in her clothes and shoes. She was bound to be uncomfortable and wake.

He reached out and took one slim foot in his hand.

Carys stretched, half aware of something behind her, something moving down her back. But she felt deliciously replete and she clung to sleep.

It was only as hot palms slid against her bare skin that she woke fully.

She lay in bed, still in her wedding gown, and Alessandro had undone each tiny button down her spine. His hands were inside the dress, massaging and soothing so she instinctively arched against his touch.

'You're awake.' His deep voice throbbed with an expression she couldn't identify.

Cravenly she wished she'd woken alone. The memory of what they'd done scoured her brain. The hot musk smell of sex permeated the air, reminding her of how she'd climaxed so easily at his touch. Without even a move to escape!

For all her protests, her fine talk about not being a convenience, she'd succumbed without a fight. Just lay there and given herself up to the ecstasy he wrought.

Carys bowed her head into upturned hands, hunching away from him. What had she done? How could she face herself?

'Carys? Are you all right?' His roving hands stopped, gripping her shoulders beneath her dress.

'I'm fine,' she lied.

She fought the tremors of delight spreading from his touch. The secret excitement hoarded close in her heart that he'd wanted her, and no one else, in all that time. Had she no pride?

It would be too easy to fall in love with Alessandro again. Where would that get her? A one-sided relationship where she gave all and he only as much as it suited him.

But she feared it was too late. That there was no turning back. Emotion filled the bitter void she'd lived with so long.

She needed time to work out what this all meant.

Yet there was no mistaking the sizzle of anticipation in her blood as his hands wandered, evoking magic.

Was she doomed to be enraptured by him all over again?

'Let me help you out of that dress. It can't be comfortable.'

Carys slithered forward out of his reach. 'I can do it myself.' It was too soon to meet his assessing eyes. If she didn't gather her wits, he'd have no trouble reading the effect he had on her.

She made it to the edge of the bed, sitting up and holding the sagging bodice against her breasts with one palm. She stopped there, rigid, as Alessandro walked around to stand before her.

Naked.

Long-limbed, muscle-toned, a tall Adonis come to life.

An *aroused* Adonis.

Her body prickled at nape, breast and forehead as heat bloomed. She swallowed hard and tried to control her wayward pulse.

She'd just experienced the most intense climax of her life. Twice. She should not be interested in sex right now.

He shifted his weight, and she watched, fascinated as muscles flexed in broad thighs and across his taut abdomen. A dart of fire pierced her chest and spiralled lazily down into her womb.

She shut her eyes, trying to banish the heady image of Alessandro, pure potent male, before her. But there was no escape. The picture was branded on her brain.

She tried to think of Leo, of the guests beginning to leave the wedding reception. Of—

'It will be easier if I help, Carys.'

Mutely she sat as he unpinned the veil that hung haphazardly from her hair. She felt the fine lace drop away but didn't open her eyes. Not when Alessandro stood before her so close his heat invaded her space.

His hands at her elbows urged her to her feet and she complied.

She snapped her eyes open, keeping them trained on his shuttered face. What had she expected? To see a reflection of the stunned delight that had consumed her such a short time ago? Instead his hooded gaze and flattened mouth gave nothing away. Only the merest hint of a frown suggested he wasn't quite satisfied with how this had played out.

What more could he want? She'd been putty in his hands, so eager she hadn't even managed to remove her precious gown. Her cheeks burned. She was so easy where he was concerned.

It had always been like that with Alessandro.

'I can take it from there, thanks,' she said in a clipped voice. But as she sidestepped he was already dragging the bodice from her shoulders.

With a shush of silk the dress fell to wedge at her elbows. She darted a look at Alessandro, but, contrary to expectations, he wasn't scrutinising the bare flesh he'd exposed. Instead he watched her face. That look sent her stomach plunging on a rollercoaster ride.

'Let me.' As simply as that, when his hands slipped down her sleeves and tugged, she allowed him to pull the dress away. It dropped in rumpled folds around her feet and he helped her step out. Only now did she realise he'd removed her shoes. She stood before him in bra, suspender belt and stockings. Totally vulnerable.

Yet the glow in his eyes warmed her to the core and stopped her from covering herself.

She felt something swell inside. She felt almost powerful. Felt desired. Even, for a crazy moment, cherished.

'Did you mean that?' Carys found herself asking before she could think twice. 'About there not being anyone since the accident?'

It was so unlikely, especially given his cold fury when he'd accused her of betraying him. But the Alessandro she'd known had never lied. If he said it was so…

He leaned close, holding her with his gaze, and with his hands, large and warm, grasping her upper arms.

For a moment she thought he wouldn't answer. She read a play of unfathomable expressions in his shadowed eyes and felt his fingers stiffen against her bare skin.

Finally he nodded. '*Si*. There was no one.' He didn't look happy about the admission, as if it impinged somehow on his masculinity. But Carys was so elated she barely registered it. A fizzing, as if of a hundred champagne bottles, flooded her bloodstream, making her dizzy. All this time…had he been subconsciously waiting for her?

She tried to blank the preposterous notion from her head, but it lodged there, insidiously tempting.

It meant nothing. He'd been recuperating from injury, or busy with business. Yet a stubborn part of her clung to the idea his celibacy had been because he hadn't had *her*.

'Carlotta told me you hadn't been lovers,' she blurted out. 'She said you hadn't planned to marry her.'

He shrugged, still holding her, yet his face took on a more rigid cast. 'I told you I would not behave in such a way. Carlotta is a childhood friend, nothing more.'

Even now, without remembering the details himself, he was so sure of himself, so positive about his actions!

Carys wished she had half his self-belief. She'd striven a lifetime to overcome the ingrained idea she was second best, fostered by being the 'slow' member of an academically high-achieving family. And by being all but ignored by her busy parents. Even now it was so easy to let doubt take hold.

'I'm sorry I didn't trust you, Alessandro.' Tentatively she raised her hand and pressed it over his where he held her. The feel of her hand on his seemed so right.

It wasn't her fault alone their relationship had unravelled at the seams. But she realised now her readiness to believe the worst, fed by her own sense of inadequacy, as much as Livia's lies, had been a major part of it.

Her throat clogged in mixed hope and fear as she waited for his response. Tension buzzed her rigid body.

'Now you know the truth,' he said dismissively. 'The past doesn't matter.'

But it does, she wanted to cry as pent up feelings lashed her. If they'd been able to trust, to believe in each other, they might still be together. Truly together, not yoked in a marriage of convenience.

Bitterness welled on her tongue as regrets swamped her.

'I believe you didn't betray me, Alessandro. Is it so hard for you to believe I didn't betray you?'

Alessandro stared down into her earnest, flushed face and felt again the stab of unfamiliar emotion in his gut. This woman twisted him inside out. With her words as well as her delectable body.

Automatically he shied from the emotions she sought to awaken. They were too confronting, too foreign to a man who built his life on logic and self-sufficiency. Too dangerous.

'I believe, *piccolina,* that the past is the past. There is nothing to be gained in revisiting it. Instead we have our future with our son to create. Our future together.'

She blinked and he could have sworn he saw tears well in eyes that had turned from hopeful blue to dull slate-grey in a moment. Heat corkscrewed through his chest at the knowledge he was responsible. But he refused to lie, even to placate the woman he intended to live with for life.

His trust only went so far. Taking any woman's word without proof was as foreign to him as breathing underwater.

She could not seriously ask him to accept, on the word of a woman he couldn't remember, that he'd been wrong to accuse her of infidelity. He must have had excellent reasons for the accusations.

Until he knew more, he would reserve judgement. Any sane man would.

Carys shifted, trying to shrug off his hold.

'I need to hang this dress up.' Her voice was as cool and colourless as a mountain stream and she avoided his eyes.

Though she didn't berate or accuse, he felt her disappointment as a tangible force. His belly clenched with a sensation that might have been regret.

Alessandro didn't like it.

'Later.' The word emerged roughly, dragging her stunned gaze to his face.

Didn't she understand that he gave her as much as any man could in the circumstances? That he'd already gone out on a limb tying himself to a woman he didn't know simply for the sake of their son?

And for the shimmering inexplicable force that hovered between them.

No! Now he was buying into that female territory where emotions rather than sense ruled the world.

'This is more important than your dress.' His hands slid round her bare shoulders and he yanked her close, revelling in the bare heat of her torso, the delicate scratch of her lace bra and soft breasts against his thudding chest.

Without giving her time to protest he covered her mouth with his, taking advantage of her parted lips to thrust inside and claim her. She tasted of hot summer days, sun-ripened cherries and warm, luscious woman.

This was real, tangible. The attraction between them sizzled and snarled like a live current. He sank into her sweet depths with something suspiciously like relief. One hand splayed in her hair, holding her so he could ravage her mouth. The other pressed her close.

Hunger rose, raw and untrammelled, making a mockery of every resolution to remain in control. Need consumed him.

Dimly he was aware he'd unleashed an onslaught on her, not a slow seduction. But he couldn't stop, couldn't think, until gradually the rigidity left her bones and she melted into him, her hands sliding up to cup his neck. He shuddered with pleasure when she pressed into him as if she too couldn't get enough of the powerful passion driving them.

Only much later, when their chests heaved from lack of oxygen and her lax form told him she was his for the taking, did he remember his vow to seduce and not simply ravage.

Moments later he'd flicked her bra open and dragged it off. He bent and cupped one luscious breast in his hand. Its weight was perfect, made for his palm. She sighed as he closed his lips around one peak and suckled, cried out when he bit gently on her nipple. Her hands dug into his skull, keeping him close as he lavished attention on one breast then the other. And all the while his body clamoured for more.

She swayed in his hold and he nudged her back a step till she collapsed on the bed. Perfect. Before she could protest he was between her knees, shoulders spreading her thighs, his hunger an unstoppable force.

'I—' Her words died as he cupped her with his palm, gently applying pressure till he felt a response shudder through her. He nudged aside her hands that had sought to stop him. Then he took his time, stroking and teasing till her body lifted off the mattress to meet his hand.

Relief scoured him. She was as needy as he. As hungry for this passion. His body felt gripped by a vice, too tight, too hard, too impossibly aroused, just by the sight and sound of Carys responding to his ministrations.

Never had a lover's pleasure affected him so profoundly. He wanted to give her more and more, even as his whole being thrummed with the need for release.

'Alessandro!' Her protest died as he parted her folds and licked her, tasting the dewy salt tang that was pure Carys. It was addictive, as was the delicate shiver of her legs enfolding him.

It didn't take much to push her over the edge and he revelled in the sound of her gasping breath, the feel of her body curving up around him, the shudders racking her from top to toe. He smiled his satisfaction even as he forced down a desperate hunger for his own release.

He needed to show Carys that here, now, was the beginning of their life together. That it was more important than the past she clung to and that he couldn't recall.

That yawning blank disturbed him more than he'd admit, but he was determined to carve a life with his child. And, therefore, his bride. He wanted to please her, sate her, till she was completely, absolutely *his*. Till she didn't hanker for anything else. So Carys understood the magnitude of this passion between them.

And gave up badgering him with emotions and tests of trust.
What they had was enough. More than enough.

Carys surely would attest to that as he brought her to climax again. This time he leaned over her, watching her eyes shine like a starry night.

Then, only when she was spent, did he slowly join with her, careful of her exhausted body. He trembled, almost undone by the depth of pleasure at being inside her. She tugged him close and held him to her. Instantly desperate energy rose and swamped him. He gave up all pretence at control and lost himself in the ecstasy of being at one with his wife.

Impossibly, it was as good as before. Better.

He didn't understand.

But he ceased thinking as Carys wrapped her legs around his hips and told him exactly how much she wanted him.

Aeons later Alessandro's drumming heartbeat slowed and he recovered enough to roll his weight off Carys and pull her onto him. Only then did his brain engage.

Despite the incredible pleasure they'd shared, his thoughts were nothing but trouble.

Above all was the niggling, astonishing idea that sex with Carys felt too good to be just about physical release.

That it felt profoundly important.

Like coming home.

CHAPTER TWELVE

'Papa! Papa!' Leo's screams of delight resounded in the glassed-in room that housed the villa's full-length pool.

Carys looked up from her paper to see Alessandro rise out of the water like a sleek, mighty sea god, all honed muscle and heart-stopping virility. The kick of her heartbeat accelerating played havoc with her breathing.

Every night since their wedding Carys had shared a bed with him. She hadn't been able to resist. She'd learned again the feel, scent and taste of that superbly sculpted body. Learned too the passion and pleasure he could unleash in her. Yet familiarity with his magnificent body didn't lessen the intensity of her reactions. Just the sight of Alessandro, almost naked in low-slung swimming trunks, set a pulse thrumming deep in her womb.

With casual ease he threw Leo in the air then caught him again, spinning him round, toes dragging in the warm water. Leo squealed with glee, holding tight to Alessandro's sinewy forearms.

Her son. Her husband.

A flash of heat speared Carys at the sight of them together, delighting in each other's company.

Stupidly, emotion clogged her throat.

Alessandro and Leo were developing the sort of relationship she'd dreamed of for her son. At first Alessandro had been wary, almost diffident, as if dealing with a baby was tantamount to meeting an alien being. But gradually he'd become adept at handling his child and a camaraderie had begun to build between them, a relationship that was based on far more than duty.

She knew about that sort of relationship. Initially she'd feared that, though Alessandro had been adamant he wanted his son, adamant enough even to marry *her,* he'd be the sort of parent she'd suffered. The sort who provided the necessities of life, and even some of the comforts, but never quite connected with their child. The sort who saw parenting as an obligation, especially when their child was a cuckoo in the nest, unlike them or their other offspring.

'Papa!' Leo's voice grew shriller as he demanded another aerial stunt.

Carys lowered her newspaper and turned more fully towards the pool, looking over her glasses. That high-pitched tone was a sure sign that Leo was tired and over-stimulated by this exciting new game. If it continued he'd end in tears.

She opened her mouth to warn Alessandro and suggest it was time to finish, but he forestalled her. He lowered Leo into the water and gently towed him along, pointing out the richly coloured sea creatures featured at the bottom of the enormous mural covering the end wall. After a few grizzly moments Leo became intrigued, leaning forward in his dad's arms and trying to repeat some of the words.

Carys leant back. Alessandro really was developing an understanding of his son. It was there in his eyes when he looked at Leo, in the calm encouragement and occasional firm reprimands he gave. He had a natural aptitude for parenting.

He enjoyed being with Leo. Why else would he spend so much time here at the villa, ignoring the lure of the office?

Alessandro still drove himself, working long hours, but increasingly those hours became flexible. Today he'd arrived mid-afternoon, at a time when Carys and Leo were always in the pool. Instead of closeting himself in his office or taking important calls, he'd spent the last half hour in the water with Leo.

She'd done the right thing. Leo and Alessandro were building something that would last a lifetime. Respect and love. The sort of relationship she'd longed for as a kid. The sort she'd vowed her son would have. Now he'd have it with both parents.

Even if all that kept those parents together was their child. And lust.

She grimaced, ashamed to admit the all-consuming hunger Alessandro sparked in her.

The lust would fade, on Alessandro's part, at least. Carys was a novelty still, and she was here, available, all too ready to accede to his every sensual demand.

Heaven help her when he lost interest in her!

For with every day spent here in his home, every night cocooned in his arms, sated from his lovemaking, Carys felt the tendrils of her old feelings bud again. She tried to resist, to remind herself that what she felt wasn't reciprocated, that this was a marriage of convenience.

The trouble was it *felt* like more.

She squeezed her eyes shut, pinching the bridge of her nose, reminding herself she'd given up on self-delusion.

She'd made her decision: to settle for a loveless marriage. To settle for what was best for Leo.

It didn't matter that deep inside she knew 'settling' meant accepting second best, accepting the sort of inferior status she'd fought against all her life. 'Settling' felt dangerously like slicing her innermost self apart, day by day. Till one day, perhaps, there'd be nothing of the real Carys left, just the façade of a woman who was nothing more than Leo Mattani's mother and Alessandro Mattani's wife.

She couldn't allow herself to think like that!

Clearly she'd made the right choice. Seeing Leo and Alessandro together made that obvious.

It didn't matter that she still secretly yearned for—

'Carys?' Alessandro's deep voice slid over her like the caress of warm hands on bare flesh.

She looked up to discover him standing before her, legs planted wide in an assured stance that spoke of masculine power. In his arms Leo smiled down at her.

'Mumum.'

Carys thrust her newspaper and reading glasses aside and held her hands out for Leo. After a quick glance, she avoided Alessandro's penetrating stare. Sometimes, as now, his regard was so intense it felt as if he delved right inside her.

'Here, sweetie.' She cuddled Leo close when Alessandro passed him to her, undoing her towelling robe and wrapping it around him, rubbing him dry. 'Did you have a good time?'

Leo grinned sleepily, his eyelids already drooping. 'Papa.' He turned and waved an arm at Alessandro.

'Yes, you swam with papa, didn't you?'

For the life of her Carys still couldn't meet her husband's hooded green gaze. There'd been a hint of something far too unsettling in it. She felt it flick over her, tangible as a touch.

Carys repressed a shiver of unwanted awareness and concentrated on drying Leo.

'It's time Leo had his nap,' she said eventually, sliding forward on her seat, ready to stand. Hopefully once she was in Leo's room the trembling eagerness for Alessandro's touch would abate. If she stayed any longer Alessandro would surely pick up on her edginess and guess the cause. When it came to understanding the demands of her body, he had more expertise than she!

'I just called Anna on the house phone. She'll be here in a minute to collect him and put him down for a rest.'

Carys frowned as Alessandro scooped Leo from her arms.

'I can settle him.'

Broad shoulders shrugged. 'We pay Anna to help with Leo. Let her do this while you finish reading. See? Leo's happy.'

He was right. Leo was calling out to Anna as she entered the room. There was no logical reason for Carys to insist on settling Leo herself. To do so would only arouse Alessandro's curiosity. Besides, as soon as Leo left, so would Alessandro. No doubt he'd taken enough time away from his work.

'OK,' Carys said at last, smiling to Anna and waving to Leo. Her heart swelled when Leo blew her a smacking kiss as he was carried from the room.

Her son was so happy here. She *had* done the right thing.

Carys eased back in her seat and picked up her newspaper.

It was only as she rested her head on the lounge that she realised Alessandro hadn't moved. He stood a few metres away, watching her.

Heat crawled up her throat and across her breasts. She realised her robe was wide open where she'd snuggled Leo and quickly closed it, knotting the belt tightly. There was something too unsettling about Alessandro's regard.

Instead of leaving, he took the lounge beside hers. Yet he didn't lean back to face the pool, and beyond it the manicured garden and lake. He sat sideways, facing her.

Too close! Far too close!

Those shivery little tremors inside Carys intensified, as did the hollow sensation in the region of her pelvis. He only had to look at her and desire consumed her. The realisation made a mockery of her hard-won self-control.

She searched for something to break the silence that felt too weighty for comfort.

'I haven't seen much of Livia since the wedding.' Carys could have kicked herself as soon as the words were out, for the last thing she wanted was to talk about her mother-in-law, or suggest she wanted to see more of her.

The relationship between Carys and Livia was polite and stiffly cordial, no more. Carys saw no point in confronting her about her lie that Alessandro had intended to marry Carlotta, but nor could she forget the way the older woman had deliberately misled her.

Alessandro's brows rose. 'Livia has been…busy lately.'

Carys paused, digesting the curious inflection in his tone. It sounded almost like disapproval. Alessandro and his stepmother weren't particularly close, but they had always seemed to get on.

'Really?'

'Yes.' This time there was no mistaking the spark of anger in Alessandro's eyes or the firming of his jaw. Had there been a falling out between him and Livia? Had he finally grown tired of her snobby, manipulative ways? It was too much to hope for.

'She has commitments elsewhere.'

Carys would have to be blind and deaf not to notice the

warning in his tone, but she refused to back off. She knew to her cost just how much damage Livia could do. She needed to understand what was happening.

'You said she'd come to advise me on how to play the role of *contessa*.' Carys was proud of the way she kept the bitterness from her voice. Of course she needed to learn, but the implication that she was so way below standard still hurt.

His gaze narrowed and he sat straighter, shoulders seeming to broaden before her eyes. 'You're not playing a role, Carys. You *are* the Contessa Mattani. Remember that.'

'Oh, I'm hardly likely to forget.' Surrounded by luxury acquired by the Mattani family over generations, Carys felt like an intruder, an impostor. She still couldn't get used to having servants at her beck and call.

Sometimes as she walked past the family portraits in the upstairs gallery, she felt the accusing eyes of long dead Mattanis, as if they wondered how someone as ordinary as she came to be in their home.

Carys shook her head. She had to get out of this place. She was going stir crazy.

She hadn't ventured out of the grounds in the weeks since the wedding, too busy ensuring Leo settled in to his new home. And with the memory of paparazzi surrounding the church on her wedding day, too nervous to face the press on her own. Alessandro hadn't offered to take her out, but nor had she expected him to. She had no illusions about her place in his life.

'Don't worry, Livia will perform the responsibilities of the Contessa Mattani until you're ready to take over.' The steel in his eyes made her wonder if she'd have to pass some test to convince him she was ready. Obviously he doubted her ability to make the grade. 'But I think it better if someone more compatible and…reliable is your mentor in the meantime.'

Reliable? It sounded as if dear Livia had blotted her copy book. Carys was human enough to feel a surge of satisfaction at the thought of the woman's schemes coming undone just a little.

'Who did you have in mind?' For one electrifying moment she thought he was going to take on the role himself.

Then common sense returned. Even as his wife she wouldn't merit that much claim on Alessandro's time.

'I thought perhaps Carlotta.' He sat back, watching her reaction.

'Carlotta?' Carys felt relief sweep her. 'I'd like that.' After the initial stiffness they'd got on well. Carys was attracted to the other woman's honesty and dry wit. She'd enjoy spending time with the princess. 'As long as that's OK with her,' she added diffidently.

'I'm sure it will be. She's already mentioned the idea of coming to see you.'

Carys frowned. 'But I haven't heard from her.'

Alessandro leaned forward a fraction, elbows on thighs and hands between his knees. 'No doubt she was allowing the newly-wed couple time alone before making social calls.'

Carys looked dumbfounded at his words. As if the idea of a honeymoon period was a foreign concept.

Alessandro felt frustration rise again. No matter how hot and heavy their lovemaking, afterwards Carys somehow managed to put a distance between them. Just as she'd done since he'd arrived at the pool today.

Of course he didn't want her hanging on his sleeve, pretending to dote on him, but the perpetual distance between them whenever they were out of the bedroom annoyed him.

He wanted…

He didn't know quite what he wanted. But it was definitely not a wife who treated him like a polite stranger unless he was naked and inside her. *Then* she responded with all the enthusiasm he could wish for.

Fire ignited in his groin and spread, tightening thighs and buttocks, curling fingers into fists and drawing the tendons in his back and neck unbearably taut.

Just thinking about sex with Carys made him hard. While she sat there, cool as a cucumber, quizzing him about Livia!

He'd thought marriage would bring respite from the surge of hormones that made him crave Carys like a fire in his blood. Yet the more he had her, the more he wanted her. And not just in bed.

Even watching her pull her robe open to nestle their son against her breast as she dried him made Alessandro rigid with desire.

What did that say about him?

He scrubbed a hand over his jaw, trying to ease the escalating tension there.

She didn't even dress provocatively to entice him. Despite the massive injection of funds to her new bank account, she still wore the simple, cheap clothes she'd brought with her.

There were no designer gowns or expensive shoes. No new handbags or hairstyles. Not even sexy new lingerie. Each night he found himself discarding her plain cotton night shirts. She didn't even bother to acquire a skerrick of lace or silk to entice her husband.

And somehow he still found her more alluring than any silk-clad siren of his memory.

Swaddled in thick towelling, her hair drying around her shoulders, and her face washed clean of make-up, Carys made his heart thud faster and his libido claw for release.

He told himself he'd come home to spend time with Leo, and he *had* enjoyed his son's company. Young Leo had an energy and an enquiring mind as well as an open, loving disposition that made him a pleasure to be with. Yet Alessandro had been distracted time and again by the enigmatic woman at the poolside. She'd been so engrossed in her reading it was clear her husband didn't hold her interest.

He didn't understand her.

'You haven't been away from the house,' he found himself saying.

She angled her chin a fraction, in that unconscious gesture of defiance he found ridiculously appealing.

'I didn't want to brave the press. I'm not used to that sort of attention.'

Guilt punched him. Why hadn't he thought of that? He'd been so busy adjusting to his ready-made family while trying to maintain his usual constant work schedule, it hadn't occurred to him.

'I'll arrange for a quick photo opportunity in the next few days. We'll give them a chance to snap shots of the happy couple.' He paused on the thought of how inappropriate the phrase seemed. 'Then the pressure will ease. Tell the staff when you want to go out and security will be arranged. You need have no fear. You'll be well taken care of.'

'Thank you.'

Again she avoided eye contact. Frustration returned. He felt an unfamiliar desire to provoke a reaction, any reaction from her. He refused to be ignored.

'The staff can tell you the best places to shop. No doubt that's high on your agenda.' After all, she now had a substantial fortune to spend.

Cool grey eyes met his as she frowned. 'Why would I need to shop? Do you mean for an outfit to wear for this press session?' She shook her head. 'There's no need. Carlotta already had two extra outfits made for me, a suit and a dress. I'm sure one of them will do. They're both lovely.'

Alessandro waved a dismissive hand. 'No doubt whatever Carlotta provided will be suitable. But you'll want to start enjoying your money and buy a new wardrobe.' On his instructions one of his secretaries had already provided her with a card linked to her new bank account.

Carys sat back in her seat, her brow clearing. 'There's no need. I've got plenty to last me till the cooler weather comes. Then I'll have to invest in a new winter coat.'

'A new winter coat?' His voice trailed off. Winter was months away. Summer was just starting. Who did she think she was fooling? 'With all that money at your disposal you expect me to believe you have no interest in spending it?'

'I know you're providing money for expenses, but—'

'Money for expenses!' This woman was something else. She reduced her new-found wealth to the status of grocery funds. 'It's far more than that, Carys. Remember, I know exactly how much since I'm paying it.'

'There's no need to sound so accusing.' A flash of fire in her eyes sent shards of ice-hot need splintering through him. That only intensified his anger.

'And there's no need to pretend your outrageously lavish allowance is a mere pittance.' The games women played!

Carys stiffened, looking more like an ice queen than the ordinary working girl he'd plucked from drudgery. 'I don't know what you're talking about.'

Alessandro shot to his feet, trying to work off his anger at her games by pacing the length of the pool and back. This pretence was the sort of thing he abhorred. Next she'd be complaining the funds he provided weren't enough.

'Of course you know. You read the prenup in such detail you must have checked every word twice. You have enough money in your personal account now to keep you in Gucci, Versace and Yves Saint Laurent every day of the year.'

Clouds must have passed over the sun, giving the illusion she'd paled.

Then, as he approached, Alessandro saw the way her hands gripped the arms of her chair, the stiffness in her small frame as she sat up. And in her eyes, what looked like shock.

'You're kidding.' Even her voice sounded different. Light and breathless. 'Why would you do that?'

He shrugged, refusing to put into words the suspicion that without such a financial incentive, she might one day walk out on Leo. And him.

'You need to dress as befits my wife.' Even to his own ears it sounded unconvincing. 'But you know all about it. You signed the agreement before we married. That set it all out.'

The sight of her gaze sliding guiltily from his, the way her hands tightened even more till they resembled talons clawing at the padded chair arms, brought him up short.

Instinct honed over years of business dealings told him something was wrong. Something important. The hairs at his neck rose and he stilled.

'Yes. Yes, I signed it.'

Alessandro's gaze strayed from her mouth, distorted as she bit hard into her bottom lip, to her knees, now pressed up to her chest. She looked so *vulnerable*. What on earth?

Eventually he followed the direction of her stare, to her folded newspaper and glasses. It was a prestigious English-language paper, open at the international news. He recognised the large picture of the United Nations Secretary General in one corner.

The same page she'd been reading over half an hour ago when he'd arrived.

'Carys?' He took a step closer till she turned to face him. Her expression was closed, rigid with something that looked like fear.

'What is it?' He glanced again at the newspaper. It was impossible that, even with the noise in the pool distracting her, it could take so long to read a single page.

Then he remembered the way Carys had hesitated over some passport control forms as they'd travelled.

'You *did* read the prenup,' he said to himself as much as her. 'I saw you.' He watched her swallow, almost wincing as the motion looked so difficult.

'I...started to.' Still she didn't face him. 'But in the end I decided it was just saying I'd get nothing of yours if we divorced.' She lifted her shoulders in a jerky shrug. 'So I signed. I didn't know anything about a big allowance.'

'Liar,' he whispered. 'I saw you. You were reading the last page just before you signed.'

Her head whipped around and he saw high colour flag her cheeks. Yet her face was chalky pale.

An appalling notion smote him. An unbelievable one.

'You *can* read, can't you?'

Had she been sitting there all this time, pretending to examine an article that made no sense? His stomach plunged heavily as an alien emotion kicked him hard.

'Of course I can read!' She drew herself up straighter in her chair, eyes brilliant with fury. 'How do you think I did my job if I couldn't read? Just because I...'

'Just because you...?' Alessandro stepped forward to stand before her, hands planted akimbo.

He watched her wrap her hands around her bare legs, rocking forward in the age-old motion of someone seeking comfort.

'I didn't read your precious papers.' She almost spat the words at him, they came out so fast. 'I began to but I was exhausted and stressed and...' She paused so long he thought she wouldn't continue. 'And I have dyslexia,' she said on a surge of breath. 'That's why I wear tinted glasses; they help me focus. But sometimes, especially when I'm tired or when the text is a solid mass, it's almost impossible to read, because whole lines keep disappearing and the words turn into a jumble. Legal papers are the worst.'

Silence. A silence ringing with the echo of her defiant tones.

Alessandro's heart twisted in his chest as he saw what it had cost her to share the truth. He wanted to reach out and soothe the hurt so evident in her drawn features, but guessed his touch wouldn't be welcome.

Her lips trembled into a heart-wrenching parody of a smile. 'It's not something I tell many people about.'

'But you told me, didn't you? When we were together before?' He knew it, sensed it, even though he didn't remember.

'I… Yes. You knew. Of course you did.'

Of course he did.

They'd been that close, sharing secrets as well as passion. Once again Alessandro had that sickening sense of taking a step straight into a yawning abyss. His damned memory loss had robbed him of so much. Robbed them both.

He took a deep breath, trying to make sense of what Carys had revealed.

'But you're reading the international news page.' In a paper renowned for in-depth, incisive journalism. It was no lightweight read.

Carys moved so swiftly, surging to her feet, that he stepped back a pace. Her eyes glittered blue fire as her gaze clashed with his.

'Just because I'm a slow reader doesn't mean I'm thick! You understood that before.' She paused, as if grappling for control over her hurt and disappointment.

Why couldn't he have remembered this one thing at least about her?

'I read the international news because I'm interested, even if it takes me longer than some people. Some days, like today, it's just slower than others, OK?'

'OK.' Alessandro watched the fire dim in her eyes as she wrapped her arms tight round her torso again.

Guilt carved a hole inside Alessandro's chest as he remembered how he'd all but forced her to sign the prenup on the spot. He'd already guessed she was exhausted and wrung out from stress. He'd had no compunction about seizing on her weakness and stampeding through her objections to get what he wanted, just as he would in any business deal.

But this wasn't business. It wasn't nearly so simple.

'I'm sorry,' he murmured, watching her rub her arms as if from cold. Clearly her dyslexia was an emotional issue. She was so defensive. 'I didn't mean to imply—'

'That I'm dumb?' Her lips curved up in a smile that held pain rather than humour.

'Of course not. No one would.' He didn't have any personal experience of the condition, but even he knew that.

Her laugh was hollow. 'You think not?'

'Carys?' Her distressed expression was too much. He reached out and took her by the shoulders. 'Talk to me,' he commanded as he massaged her stiff muscles, trying to ease their rigidity. Her pain made him feel uncomfortable…edgy…protective.

Again that bleak smile. 'Everyone thought I was slow-witted because I couldn't read well. *Everyone.* I was always bottom of the class. Even when I reached high school and a teacher suspected what was wrong, it was easier for people to think I was just slow.'

Alessandro frowned. 'Kids can be cruel.'

She lifted her shoulders in a weary gesture. 'Not just kids. My father is a professor; my mother ran her own business. My siblings are all academic over-achievers. They found it difficult to adjust to me. I didn't measure up.'

'Adjust to *you?*' Alessandro's jaw tightened. 'They should have been encouraging you, looking after you.'

She shook her head. 'They preferred to bury themselves in their own activities.' From the raw pain in her voice Alessandro guessed they had provided precious little support.

The idea infuriated him. Kids needed more from their parents than the bare necessities of life.

Suddenly it struck him that he and Carys had a lot in common— both had been left at too young an age to look after themselves.

'Even when I stopped working in dead-end jobs and finally found the nerve to sign up for a hotel management degree, they saw it as second best.' She paused, the dead chill in her eyes carving a chasm through his chest. 'That's all they ever expected from me…second best.'

'Carys.' He pulled her close, pushing her head down against his shoulder. His heart thumped unsteadily at the wild emotions running through him. He'd been angry and distrustful of her, yet now, seeing the hurt she tried so hard to hide, he felt compassion and a driving need to make things better.

Her pain felt like his. Sharp as a blade, it transfixed him.

He'd never experienced such empathy for anyone else. Or such a strong impulse to protect.

Automatically he rocked her against him, feeling shudder after shudder rack her taut frame.

'You're not second best, Carys. You're a wonderful mother. Anyone seeing Leo would know that. Plus you excel at your work.' He'd taken the time to find that out in Melbourne. 'And you haven't let dyslexia hold you back from tertiary study.' How she'd coped with that he had no idea. His own ability to read and quickly absorb huge amounts of information was something he'd always taken for granted.

'You're a special woman, *tesoro*. Never forget it.'

Slowly he stroked her back, feeling her tension begin to ease. But he didn't release her. He wanted to hold her. And not just because she was the woman at the centre of every erotic daydream he'd had for months.

He wanted to comfort her. The tenderness and regret that welled inside him at her story, the tide of anger on her behalf, overwhelmed him.

His mind shied from the realisation that he'd so easily misread her. Because if he dwelled on that too long, he might have to consider that he'd misjudged her in other things.

Her question on their wedding night echoed too clearly for comfort.

I believe you didn't betray me, Alessandro. Is it so hard for you to believe I didn't betray you?

CHAPTER THIRTEEN

ALESSANDRO nuzzled the silk tresses on his pillow, inhaling the scent of flowers. He wound a strand round his fingers, then brushed the end across her bare breast.

Carys shivered. Even now, exhausted from lovemaking, she responded to him. As he did to her.

It was as if she'd got into his blood, his bones.

Still it wasn't enough. 'Tell me about us,' he murmured, finally confronting the need that had gnawed at him so long. 'What did we do together…before? What was it like?'

He watched her breathing falter. Raising his gaze, he found her biting her lip. Wary eyes met his.

'You really want to know?'

He nodded. More than ever he needed to understand. Knowing the past might help him understand the present.

Huge eyes surveyed him carefully, as if seeking a hidden trap. Then she looked down to where he caressed her. Long eyelashes shielded her eyes from his gaze.

'It was like a summer storm. Like a lightning strike out of the blue.' Her lips tilted up. 'It was sudden and overwhelming. Wonderful and scary and…undeniable.'

'The sex, you mean?' She described perfectly the marrow-melting intensity of their loving.

Her moue of disappointment told him he'd got it wrong. 'No.' She tugged the sheet up, dislodging his hand. He ignored the tiny splinter of hurt that jabbed him.

'So tell me. What did we do together?'

She shrugged. 'Everything. You taught me to ski and snowboard. We went climbing and hiked some of the hills here. I cooked you Aussie style roast lamb and pavlova for dessert, and you taught me about Italian wines and the history of the area.' Her voice was so wistful he felt a pang of discomfort.

But greater still was his confusion. He'd taken her climbing and hiking? He slid a hand around her hip, lodging her concretely against him as the world started to spin.

'Alessandro? What is it? Have I sparked a memory?'

Numbly his shook his head. 'No memory.' The words were curt, but he couldn't help it. He still couldn't face with equanimity the fact he'd probably never remember.

Yet that wasn't what shocked him.

Climbing, hiking, constituted his rare, private time away from the high-pressure business world. He climbed with a friend or two. Male friends. He hiked alone. Always. Most of his acquaintances had no notion he loved the mountains even more than his fast cars. The idea of sharing that most precious private time with a woman was astonishing.

'We hiked together?' His voice sounded rusty.

Carys nodded. 'It was glorious. The countryside's so lovely. In the evening we'd sit together and discuss where we'd head the next weekend.'

'Really?' The picture she conjured was completely foreign. Yet it seemed…right. He frowned, wondering how he knew that so definitely when he remembered nothing.

'You don't believe me.' She shuffled away to prop herself against the bed head, hurt shimmering in her eyes.

He reached out to cup her face, stunned by what he'd learned. He needed to know more. But this wasn't the time.

'I believe you, Carys.' He paused. 'Tell me about Leo. What was he like as a newborn? Did you know from the first how intelligent he was?'

The sound of his son's laughter warmed Alessandro, but it was the sight of his wife, smiling as she held Leo up to look out the

ferry window, that made something shift inside him. Something
he hadn't ever acknowledged before.

The barrier that had kept him safely separate and self-
contained from those who tried to get too close.

Alessandro drew a slow breath and exhaled, battling the turmoil inside.

This shift wasn't a sudden event. The barrier had been crum-
bling for weeks. Day by day the connection with Leo and Carys
had strengthened, growing into something he'd never expected
to feel. There was protectiveness, possessiveness, caring. Joy and
acceptance.

Despite the ferry's smooth progress across the lake, Alessandro rocked back on his feet as if struck off balance.

He should have expected it, he supposed, with Leo.

His son.

Though his own parents had never indicated they felt anything
for Alessandro except mild pleasure if he did well and cold dismissal if he intruded at an inopportune time, he knew what the
bond between parent and child should be. When he discovered
his son, he'd acted instantly to get custody, desperate to ensure
Leo was in the care of a loving parent.

Even though Alessandro knew he had everything to learn
about how to love.

He'd never expected it would come so easily.

He watched Leo point out the window and babble, talking to
both Carys and Bruno, standing protectively beside them. Something warm inside Alessandro's chest expanded and his lips
twitched as he watched his boy's animated face.

His boy.

The happiness Leo had brought into Alessandro's life, and the
weighty sense of responsibility, were unprecedented.

He wouldn't change them for anything.

His gaze shifted to Carys and the way her gentle smile lit her
face. She did things to him he didn't understand.

A lifetime's lessons in the ways of women had taught him he'd
be a fool to give any woman his heart on a platter.

And yet, these past weeks he'd grown…comfortable with

her. Never comfortable enough to ignore the effervescent bubble of lust that was now a constant in his life. But relaxed as he'd never been with any other woman.

So relaxed he had to force himself to remember that, like the rest of her sex, she wasn't above cheating on a man.

Yet looking at her now, so thrilled that he'd given in to her request to do something 'normal' like spend the afternoon sightseeing around the lake, without a limo or a Lamborghini or any other of his 'rich man's toys', he found it hard to believe she could be selfishly calculating.

He didn't want to believe it. That was the most astonishing of all.

He found himself trusting her in so many ways. *Liking* her. Not merely desiring her.

She *was* different.

Her disinterest in cash was genuine. She really did prefer a picnic by the lake to the ostentation of Milan's top restaurants. And though she now spent money from her account, it was mainly on toys and books for Leo rather than fashion for herself.

She was completely different to his mother, who'd had barely a maternal bone in her body. Carys was a wonderful mother.

Alessandro realised his insurance policy, the prenup that provided her with a fortune if she stayed with Leo, hadn't been necessary. Nothing on this earth would drag Carys from her son. Alessandro approved of her for that alone.

And, he realised, for so many other things.

For her indomitable spirit, conquering what he realised were wounds as old and deep as his. Overcoming dyslexia and the ingrained sense of not measuring up, to get on with her life.

Her intelligence. Her quiet dignity.

Carys was the sort of wife a man could be proud of in many ways. With her warmth and generosity of spirit, he saw her taking her place beside him in the public aspects of his life. Livia had fulfilled the public responsibilities of the Contessa Mattani with panache, but with a cool intolerance for what she termed 'the ordinary people' that made him grit his teeth.

Across the cabin Carys stretched and her sundress grew

taut across her breasts. Predictably his body tightened in a spasm of hunger.

Alessandro thought of their slow, languorous lovemaking this morning, of the wonder in her eyes as he brought her to climax and pumped his life essence inside her.

His gaze dipped to her flat belly and excitement stirred. For all they knew she could even now be carrying another of his children. Raw, primal satisfaction smote him at the idea of watching her grow big with his baby. He'd missed that the first time. But now…they could build a family together and he'd participate in every moment.

'Signor Conte.'

Alessandro dragged himself from his thoughts to focus on the small, grey-haired woman before him.

Some sixth sense made Carys turn and look for Alessandro. He stood not far away, head tilted down as he listened to the rotund woman before him. The intensity of his expression, the stillness of his rangy frame, sent a skitter of prescience up her spine.

The woman looked vaguely familiar.

At her side Bruno also watched the pair, making no move to intervene. Yet something was wrong. She sensed it.

'Bruno, would you please take Leo?' She met the minder's startled gaze as she thrust Leo towards him. Barely waiting to see her son settled, she turned towards Alessandro. The woman leaned in, gripping his arm.

Begging? No, that wouldn't leach the colour from Alessandro's face. The woman tilted her head and finally Carys recognised her: Rosina, who'd been Alessandro's housekeeper when he'd lived in his home in the hills behind the lake.

Rosina had been so friendly and warm. She'd encouraged Carys in her tentative attempts to learn Italian. More, she'd provided comfort in the form of a cup of tea or a plate of fruit and admonishment not to starve herself when Carys felt her relationship with Alessandro shatter around her.

Carys squeezed through the seats, eager to greet her, but more than ever concerned by Alessandro's frozen expression. She regretted now that she'd requested they come by ferry instead of private boat or car.

After being surrounded by servants, getting used to her new life as the Contessa Mattani, and absorbing the overwhelming reality of her role as Alessandro's wife, she'd been eager for a 'normal' day with people who hadn't a clue who she was. Had it been a mistake?

By the time she reached the aisle, Rosina had gone and the ferry was coming in to dock. People rose, ready to stream ashore.

Yet Alessandro stood unmoving, as if riveted to the spot. Fear made her heart thump so hard it seemed to catapult around her chest.

She hadn't wanted to care for him, but somehow he'd deviously wormed his way back into her heart. He pleasured her to within an inch of her sanity, comforted her when she needed it, made her feel…special.

She could no longer pretend she didn't care. *Didn't love.*

Carys swallowed a welling knot of anxiety. 'Alessandro?'

He turned and for a moment it seemed as if he didn't see her. His gaze was blank, inward looking. Then he blinked, focused, and snagged her close, away from the people thronging towards the door.

'Bruno has Leo? Good.' He sounded just the same as ever, but he looked…different.

'What is it, Alessandro?' He met her eyes for a moment before looking away, towards the passengers. Somewhere in that crowd was the woman who'd talked to him so earnestly.

'Come.' He curved his arm around her back and led her to the door. 'It's all right. Leo and Bruno are on their way.'

It wasn't all right; Carys could see the pinched line of his mouth and the deep crease in his forehead.

Yet it wasn't till they were ashore and a waiting car had delivered them to the villa, that Carys got any answers. Alessandro gave a sleepy Leo into his nanny's arms, and as if too edgy to settle indoors, led the way to the private path along the lake. He seemed distracted, forgetting to shorten his long pace so she had to scurry to keep up.

'Please, Alessandro.' The look on his face, as if he'd just seen a ghost, frightened her. 'What's wrong? What did Rosina want?'

He turned then, the expression in his shadowed eyes unreadable. 'You remember her?'

'Of course. She was kind to me.' At a time when Carys had felt lost. 'Does she still work for you?' Carys realised she didn't even know if he'd kept his mountain home.

He shook his head. 'When I went to hospital, the house was shut up. She took the retirement she'd put off and moved away to be near her daughter. When I came out of hospital I settled into the family villa instead.'

Was that wistfulness in his voice? The home he'd built had been so like him, vibrantly unique and attractive. Did he miss it?

'But she said something to you.' Something significant.

Alessandro shrugged, walking ahead as her steps slowed.

'She said it was good to see me again, all recovered. Good to see us,' he added after a moment.

Carys started forward. 'She remembered me?' He nodded. 'What else did she say?' There was more. Shadows darkened Alessandro's face, each line etched as if on a lifeless mask.

'She congratulated us on our wedding. She read about it in the papers.'

'And?' Alessandro was stonewalling. After living with him she knew that much.

Suddenly he stopped and turned. 'She was there the day you left.'

The day Alessandro had told her to go. The day he'd found her, dishevelled from holding Stefano Manzoni at bay, and leapt to the conclusion she'd been fooling with her lover, not fighting off a predator. Alessandro's fury had been instantaneous and all consuming, as if the incident had thrown fuel on a long-smouldering fire.

Carys groped for the balustrade between her and the water as memories she'd tried to forget came rushing back.

'I see.'

'No. You don't.' Something in his voice made her turn. His expression baffled her. 'She said that after you left, I couldn't settle. I paced the house from end to end.'

That didn't surprise her. He'd been in a towering rage, for all that he'd kept it tightly leashed. Even his order to leave had been delivered in a lethally quiet whisper that had cut Carys to the bone and slashed through her last hopes that he could ever love her.

'Twenty minutes later I raced out to the car. Apparently I said I was going to bring you back.'

Carys gasped. Her heart stuttered then eventually took up something like its usual rhythm.

Alessandro had gone after her? He'd wanted her back?

Her eyes opened so wide they stung. Did that mean he'd realised his accusations were baseless? Now her heart pounded like a locomotive and adrenaline pulsed in her blood.

He'd chased after her...

Heat flooded Carys at the thought of him racing to stop her leaving. *Of him realising his mistake.*

'But you didn't go to the station.' She'd waited ages for a train.

'No.' Penetrating green eyes met hers. 'That was when I had the accident, speeding along the road after you.'

Dumbfounded, Carys met his shuttered gaze. Guilt replaced the buoyant surge of elation in her veins and she slumped against the balustrade as shock hit her in the knees.

'Carys!' Strong arms dragged her up against a familiar, hard torso and she shut her eyes, unwilling to face just yet the dislike which surely must be in his face now.

Did he blame her for the accident?

She did. Guilt seeped through her bones. She clutched him close, reliving the horror she'd experienced when she'd heard about his accident. But this was worse. So much worse.

Alessandro widened his stance, wrapping Carys closer to his pounding chest. Fear spiked at her sudden pallor. He told himself it was shock, expected in the circumstances, but that didn't ease his concern. He rubbed a hand down her back, willing warmth back into her trembling, chilled form.

It would be OK, he assured himself.

OK? His world had turned upside down!

You were so much in love, both of you. Of course you went to fetch her back.

The words rang in Alessandro's head, pounding in time with the heavy rush of blood surging through his temples.

No! She had that wrong. Must have.

Yet the words resonated, shocking him with their familiarity.

Love? Romantic love?

He tried to reject the notion, as he'd rejected it all his life. But the emotions Carys evoked lodged deep inside and wouldn't be removed.

The fact remained that he'd gone after Carys. He'd been wild-eyed and desperate if his former housekeeper was to be believed. Though clearly she had a romantic disposition. No doubt her memory embroidered the event.

That wasn't important. What mattered was knowing if he'd changed his mind because he'd realised he'd been wrong about Carys, or whether he'd decided he didn't care what she'd done—simply had to have her back.

Either option revealed him as emotional, too strongly affected by his lover to think straight.

He didn't want to believe it.

Yet here he was, tied in knots because of this same woman. Feeling so much because of her. Even now her fresh cinnamon scent tangled in his senses, a heady distraction.

He thought through the few concrete facts he'd pieced together about her infidelity. He'd come home to find Stefano Manzoni, a man he'd never trusted, accelerating recklessly down the driveway. He'd found Carys with her blouse undone, her hair down and a fresh love bite on her neck. She'd admitted meeting Manzoni in town and letting him bring her home. Then she'd tried to deflect Alessandro's anger by accusing him instead of infidelity with Carlotta.

What else had there been that he couldn't recall? Was there any more? Had his accusation been as misguided as her belief he'd planned to marry Carlotta?

That didn't seem believable. Yet honesty made him face the possibility he'd jumped to conclusions.

Had Alessandro subconsciously waited for Carys to prove it was his money that really attracted her? That she would dump him for a man who could give her more once the going got tough? As his mother had left his father years before, hooking up with a man whose bank account made the Mattani wealth at that time look insipid by comparison.

Had Alessandro primed himself to expect Carys' betrayal?

He drew a steadying breath, tightening his hold on her, feeling her rapid heartbeat near his, the way her soft form moulded so perfectly to his.

Reluctantly he faced the truth he'd been avoiding.

Despite those few wisps of memory, the gap in his mind was as real as ever. Intimacy with Carys hadn't restored it. He could no longer kid himself that would happen.

He would never remember that part of his past. Never have his memory as absolute proof about her behaviour. He had only the comments of those, like his housekeeper and Carys, who'd been there.

He had logic.

Above all he had his own gut instinct.

What did they tell him?

Carys felt the heavy thud of Alessandro's heart, strong and steady, against her. The way he held her, as if welded to her, made her heart sing, but couldn't blot out her distress.

'I'm sorry,' she murmured at last, clutching his shirt as if to stop him retreating.

'Pardon?' He stepped back a fraction so her voice wasn't muffled against his chest. Carys only just resisted the impulse to burrow back into him, seeking comfort.

'I'm sorry.' Finally she lifted her face. 'If it weren't for me, you wouldn't have crashed. You wouldn't have…' Even now the thought of him in a coma paralysed her larynx.

'You blame yourself?' He tilted his head.

'Don't you?' She remembered the steady rain that day—that was why she'd accepted a man's offer of a lift rather than waiting for a bus. That and the fact that the evening before she'd seen Alessandro with Carlotta. He'd spent the night in town rather than return home, and Carys had finally grown tired of waiting meekly for him to appear. No wonder she'd been distracted enough to fall into Stefano's clutches.

If only she hadn't been so gullible, so ready to believe Livia's plausible lies.

'Of course I don't. Don't be absurd.' Alessandro's eyes flashed dark fire. 'How could you be to blame? I was the one speeding, and the driver that forced me off the road was on the wrong side. It had nothing to do with you.' His gaze held hers so long Carys felt his certainty pulse through her.

'Don't take that upon your conscience, *tesoro*,' he said more gently and cupped her chin in one warm palm. Her heart squeezed tight at such tenderness. It reminded her of how he'd looked, and sounded, so long ago.

'Carys.' He bent his head and touched his lips to hers. Instantly she melted into him, her body alive with the tingle of magic only Alessandro could create. 'Sweet Carys.'

Kisses, soft yet fervent, covered her cheeks, brow, even her nose. Large hands cupped her head, holding her still. Her heart rose in her mouth. These weren't the caresses of a man desperate to bed her. They weren't about sex. They were about emotion. The sort of emotion she'd nurtured so long.

'Forgive me, Carys?'

The kisses stopped, though he didn't release her. Dazedly Carys opened her eyes. The look on her husband's face stole her breath right away. It would have claimed her heart too, if she hadn't already given that to him.

She blinked. 'What are you talking about?'

He didn't speak immediately and she had the bizarre feeling he was gathering his courage. He, the man who felt no qualms about anything, not billion-dollar deals or handling a hungry media scrum.

He breathed deep, his chest expanding so mightily it brushed hers, sparking inevitable flickers of awareness in every erogenous zone.

'These past years have been hard for you,' he murmured, his voice a suede caress that unravelled the ribbon of tension in her stomach. 'I sent you away, and because of that you were alone through your pregnancy and Leo's birth. Alone bringing up our son and making a home for him.' He paused and squeezed his eyes shut as if in pain.

Carys reached out, sliding her trembling fingers over his shoulders, feeling the tension vibrate within him.

'We survived.'

'I deprived myself of you and Leo.' Alessandro's mouth twisted up in a mirthless smile, and when he opened his eyes they were darker than she'd ever seen them. So dark it felt as if she looked right into his soul.

'I should never have let you go. Never have doubted.'

'Sorry?' His admission struck Carys dumb. She read the remorse in his face, felt the powerful energy hum through his body as if he kept a lid on a force too great to be released. But still she couldn't believe.

Long fingers slid round to cradle her face. His gentle touch set a thousand butterflies dancing inside her. A sense of something precious, something miraculous, filled her.

'I'm to blame, Carys. It's my fault. I should never have accused you of betraying me.'

She looked into his eyes and read emotion there, bare and powerful. Remorse. Guilt. Pain. And hope.

The shock of it, of having him reveal such depth of feelings rocked her on her heels. She clung to his shoulders, trying to marshal stunned thoughts.

'You weren't to know,' she found herself saying tentatively, not even questioning her need to ease his pain. 'After all, I believed Livia when she told me you were getting married.'

He shook his head abruptly. 'You weren't to know Livia had her own agenda. Whereas I…I have no one but myself to blame for leaping to conclusions.'

Carys' heart accelerated. 'Rosina told you on the boat? Told you there was nothing between me and Stefano Manzoni?'

Once more Alessandro shook his head. 'No.'

'But then…?'

'How do I know?' Again that raw, self-deprecating smile.

He reached up and took her hand, slid it from his shoulder, past the spot where his heart thundered, then pressed it down against his abdomen. 'I feel it here. Gut instinct, if you like.' He shrugged, still holding her palm against his belly. 'My sixth sense has been telling me all along that you weren't the woman I thought, but I ignored it.'

His eyes glowed emerald fire that melted the last of her defences.

'Two years ago I was wrapped up in saving the company, fixing the mess my father had left behind. I know that much, at least. Plus I'd decided all women were treacherous. I was probably waiting for you to slip up and prove me right.' He shook his head in obvious self-disgust.

Carys remembered the speed with which he'd put two and two together and made five, assuming infidelity where there was none. It *had* seemed as if he'd been all too ready to believe the worst.

She felt as if she'd whirled into an alternate universe, where nothing made sense. For a crazy instant, as he'd dragged her palm down his chest, she'd thought he was going to say it was his heart dictating this change in him. That he loved her.

Now she battled a queasy sensation of burgeoning hope and fear roiling together inside her.

'I don't understand.'

Alessandro was silent so long her nerves screamed with tension. Eventually he shrugged, a tense movement that only reinforced her awareness of his pain.

'Let's just say I've spent too many years as a target for women interested in acquiring wealth and prestige.'

Carys stared. Was it possible Alessandro thought women threw themselves at him for material things they could get from him? Didn't he understand the pull of a devastatingly sexy, macho man? She'd been a sucker for him the moment she saw him, and she'd known nothing of his wealth or position.

'And earlier...' He paused a moment before continuing. She watched his nostrils flare as if he stole a sustaining breath. 'My mother left when I was five. Dumped my father and went off to become the partner of a man whose fortune and prestige was even greater than his. I never saw her again.'

'Your father kept you apart?' Despite the rift between man and wife, to deprive a son of his mother was—

Alessandro snorted. 'My dear mama wasn't interested in me. She'd palmed me off to nannies from the first. In some ways it wasn't such a blow when she left.'

Despite his tight smile, Carys read the lie in his words. Her heart turned inside out, recognising the ancient scars he hid: the knowledge that his mother hadn't wanted him. How devastating that must have been.

Fellow feeling stirred. She felt his hurt deep in her psyche.

'After that it was a succession of nannies, most of them more interested in snaring a man with a title than looking after his son.' Alessandro didn't hide his bitterness for all that his words were clipped. 'I learned not to trust anyone.'

Carys wanted to soothe away the years of built up pain and distrust. To cradle him in her arms as if he were still that little boy distressed at losing his mother.

'But that's no excuse for my behaviour.'

Alessandro lifted her hand and pressed a kiss on her wrist. Another on her palm. Heat juddered through her and suddenly her need to comfort turned into something else. The familiar electrical current flowed from him to her and back again.

His smouldering eyes held her fast.

'Carys. I can't remember what happened between us. I probably never will. But I understand now that I jumped to conclusions and acted rashly.'

Her pulse leapt at the admission.

'Living with you these past couple of months, I realise I misjudged you. I should never have ended it the way I did.'

Her heart swelled as if it would burst as she read the warmth in his gaze.

'Sandro!' It was what she used to call him. The name she'd kept locked away in her heart for so long. Now it slipped out easily. 'Sandro, I—'

He pressed his index finger to her mouth. The male musk scent of his skin teased her. 'Let me say this first, Carys.'

He drew a deep breath and, stunned, she read hesitancy in his expression. Instinct told her this was serious. Her muscles tightened and she almost stopped breathing.

Was it possible her secret hopes were coming true?

'I never expected to feel like this about any woman. You're honest, direct, caring.' He smiled and the impact scrambled her brain. 'And we're good together. Aren't we?'

He looked so serious as he watched for her reaction, almost vulnerable, despite his innate strength.

Carys nodded carefully, trying to remain calm as a high-octane mix of excitement, love and desire ignited inside.

She tugged his hand from her mouth and squeezed it, willing him to say the words she'd waited so long to hear. The words she wanted to share with him.

I love you.

His face was sober as he pulled her close.

'I…trust you, Carys.'

CHAPTER FOURTEEN

'DID you hear me, Carys?' Carlotta tilted her head to one side, looking like an inquisitive little bird.

'Of course I heard.' Carys mustered a smile for her friend, trying to drag her mind back to the conversation.

She spent too much time fretting over what couldn't be changed. Life with Alessandro was good. More than good. He was a great father to Leo, a stupendous lover. Even now the memory of his hands and mouth on her body quickened her pulse. He was kind, attentive.

And he trusted her. Her lips twisted, remembering his words and the depths of her disappointment.

He gave her more than he'd given any other woman. All he had to give.

It wasn't Alessandro's fault he'd never learned what love was. That he couldn't offer it to her.

She would learn, one day, to be content. It didn't matter that she'd craved love all her life. Or that she bestowed it on him unstintingly. She was thankful for what she had, and soon she'd stop wishing for the moon.

The best way to do that was to keep herself busy, as she had these past couple of months.

'Yes, the tutor is terrific. I'm so glad I took your advice about hiring him.' This time her smile was more convincing. If she was going to live here, she had to master the language, which was why she and Carlotta spoke Italian when they were alone. 'I'm improving, don't you think?'

'You're a marvel,' Carlotta said with a smile. 'Your pronunciation is great, even if your vocab has a way to go. You'll be a hit when Alessandro starts entertaining on a large scale again. With that cute hint of an accent everyone will find you enchanting.'

'You think?' Carys glanced around the exclusive hotel restaurant Carlotta had chosen for lunch. Despite her new clothes and her determination to fit into Alessandro's life, she felt a ripple of unease sometimes, as if she didn't belong and everyone knew it.

The fact that Alessandro seemed to keep her apart from the demands of his social schedule didn't help either. Yes, they went out, even had friends to dine occasionally, but it was obvious he turned down a lot of invitations he would normally accept. Because he wasn't sure she'd cope?

'I *know,* Carys. According to the grapevine, the young *contessa* is charming, refreshing and beautifully dressed.' Carlotta laughed. It was she who'd steered Carys through the acquisition of a new wardrobe.

Carys smiled. 'You can take a lot of credit there.'

'Don't be so modest. Now, tell me, how are you going with your speech for the annual charity lunch? Any ideas?'

Carys nodded. 'A few.' In truth, she'd been thinking of little else since she'd heard about it. Each year the Contessa Mattani hosted a charity luncheon in the ballroom of the Mattani villa. Proceeds, along with a sizeable donation from Mattani Enterprises, went to a charity of her choosing, a different one each year. It was a tradition dating back to the time of Alessandro's grandmother.

Now it was a major event on the calendar of Italy's social elite. Anxiety skipped down her spine as she thought of hosting it and delivering a speech to a throng of the country's rich and famous.

'You *will* be there, won't you?'

'I wouldn't miss it for the world. And you'll have Alessandro by your side too.'

Alessandro hadn't spoken to her about it yet. Instead she'd learned about it from Carlotta, then had the date confirmed by the housekeeper. Tonight she'd finally remember to ask him for more details. She'd been meaning to for weeks, but somehow she often found herself...distracted around him.

Carlotta signalled for the bill. 'I'm afraid I have to rush off. Special meeting with a special client.'

'Then you go and I'll pay.'

'Sure?'

'Of course. Don't be late. I'll just sit here a little longer.' Because it was back again, that slight queasiness she'd experienced on and off lately.

'*Ciao, bella.*' Carlotta kissed her on both cheeks. 'I'll call when I'm back from Paris.'

Carys said goodbye and sat back, willing her stomach to settle. She paid the bill, sipping water, trying to stifle excitement that rose even stronger than the nausea.

She'd only felt like this once before. When she'd been pregnant with Leo. Her breasts were tender too. Or was that from Alessandro's thorough loving last night?

A ripple of pleasure tingled through her as she remembered their passion. And at the possibility she could no longer ignore. *Was she pregnant?*

A brother or sister for Leo. Another child to love and cherish. Only this time with Alessandro at her side from the start. Would he be happy? They hadn't taken precautions, so presumably he wasn't averse to the idea.

Surreptitiously she rubbed her palm over her stomach, wonder growing at the possibility.

Eventually she pushed her chair back and made for the foyer, only to falter as she saw a group of well-dressed older women in a group ahead of her.

A familiar voice spoke; a familiar elegantly tall figure blocked her path.

'Of course, I expected it. Poor Alessandro, what choice did he have? The girl was the mother of his child. But now he's stuck with the consequences.' A shrug of bony shoulders emphasised the point.

Carys put her hand to the door jamb, clinging tight as nausea hit again, stronger this time, preventing her from turning and walking away. Besides, her feet were welded to the spot by the scalding venom in Livia's voice.

'She has no breeding, no class, no idea of how to go on. How she's going to fill her responsibilities as *contessa* I can't imagine. Thank goodness I'm in the country for the day of the gala charity luncheon.' She shook her head. 'He asked me to step in and host it. Begged me. I couldn't let him down. We both know his wife would make a hash of it, and the Mattani name is too important to be made a laughing stock.'

Carys didn't hear any more vitriol. She'd finally unlocked her feet and prised her hand from the wall.

'Since the family name is so important to you, I'm surprised to hear you doing your best to taint it.'

Despite the bile rising in her throat, Carys somehow managed to sound cool and in control. Each word emerged with a crystal-clear diction that would have made her language tutor proud.

Amazing what shock and fury could produce. Especially since Carys wanted only to retreat and give in to the nausea.

Instead she stood straighter in her heels and smoke-blue suit of finest local silk. She told herself she looked elegant, even chic, like the countess she now was.

Livia spun round, hectic colour rimming her artfully made-up cheeks.

Carys looked up at the woman who'd tried to destroy what Alessandro and she had shared. For the first time she saw beyond the careful grooming and exquisite sophistication to the ugly greed and discontent beneath.

'Anyone would think you had an axe to grind,' Carys said softly and heard a collective intake of breath from the women watching so avidly. 'That you had your nose put out of joint because you'd been supplanted by Alessandro's wife.' She let a pause lengthen. 'Supplanted by a younger woman.'

The widening of Livia's eyes and a single muffled laugh from the group told Carys she was right.

She was tempted to confront Livia with her lies and machinations. But she refused to play her game and feed gossip to the curious. Instead she summoned a stiff-lipped smile. 'But we know that's nonsense, don't we?'

Livia opened her mouth then shut it, nodding abruptly.

'As for my charity lunch,' Carys continued, 'no doubt there was some misunderstanding about the arrangements. I'll ensure it's sorted and send you an invitation, Livia. I hope your friends will all attend too.'

Dimly she was aware of nods and agreement, but her focus was on the woman before her, who suddenly looked smaller and less assured. Carys didn't feel satisfaction or triumph, just a cold lump of distress in the pit of her belly.

'I must go, but I'll talk to Alessandro about having you to the villa for a meal soon. *Ciao,* Livia.' She pressed obligatory kisses to the other woman's cheeks, heard her automatic responses, then turned and concentrated on putting one foot in front of the other all the way to the entrance.

By the time she was alone in the back of the limo, her rigid control had cracked. She was shaking, her skin clammy, and her stomach heaved anew.

She tried to concentrate on the shock and defeat in Livia's eyes but instead remembered only her words.

What choice did he have? His wife would make a hash of it...he begged me...

No, Carys didn't believe it. Alessandro wouldn't do that to her. Livia had lied again. Carys wouldn't trust her as far as she could lift Alessandro's favourite Lamborghini. As soon as the shaking passed, she'd ring him and he'd confirm it.

He'd told her he trusted her.

He'd looked so sincere she'd believed him without hesitation.

But now that old doubting voice whispered again in her head. Had he said it just to woo her into compliance? To make things easier between them? Pain lanced her chest.

No! He'd meant every word.

Yet maybe trust came in different forms. He might trust her word but not think she was fit for the role of wife to a mega-wealthy industrialist.

Who could blame him?

She hadn't grown up in his world. Didn't know all the rules. And maybe—the thought sneaked up out of nowhere—he secretly believed, as others had, that her reading problems reflected on her capacity in other things.

Another surge of nausea made her hunch in her seat. She spent the next few wretched minutes riding wave after wave of pain, trying to blot out the voice of doubt.

Finally, she sat up straight, staring blind-eyed out the window. The roiling in her stomach was vanquished for now, yet she trembled in the aftermath of distress.

She lifted her chin. No matter that a craven part of her was tempted to agree with Livia, that she didn't know how to go on in these rarefied social circles. Carys was here to stay. She was Alessandro Mattani's wife and she'd prove to everyone, herself included, that she could handle whatever that entailed. She owed it to herself, and to Leo.

Her hand slid to her stomach. If she was going to bring up her family in this place, she couldn't afford to let herself sink into the shadows as she'd done when she was young. She knew what that was like, and it was a place she didn't want to visit again.

She'd worked all her adult life to make something of herself, prove to herself that she was as good as everyone else, and not live down to her family's expectations. She refused to let anyone put her in that position again.

She was tired of being made to feel second best. Even by herself.

Carys slipped her cellphone from her handbag and punched in the number for Alessandro's office. She ignored the tingle of fear running through her. Instead she reminded herself Alessandro trusted her.

Alessandro was out of his car and loping up the front steps before the echo of the Lamborghini's engine died. The front door swung silently open before he reached it.

'Where's my wife?'

Paulo moved back to let him enter. 'I believe madam is still at the pool. Master Leo has had his swim and gone up for a nap.'

'Good.' What needed saying was better done in private. Alessandro strode towards the fitness wing, his sense of urgency growing with each step.

He'd been driving home when his efficient new assistant called, explaining that the *contessa* had rung to ask about arrangements for the charity lunch. When she'd checked, it was to find the fool of a woman who'd been his temporary PA had arranged for Livia to host the event. Despite his express instructions that his step-mother no longer be invited to represent the family or his company.

He speared a hand through his hair, frustration rising. At Livia. At incompetent temps. At himself for not double-checking.

He stalked down the corridor. All the while his assistant's voice echoed in his head. 'No, she didn't leave a message. No, she didn't say anything. She hung up after I told her about the luncheon.'

Alessandro had a bad feeling about this. He knew Carys sometimes felt unsure of herself. That was why he'd taken it slowly introducing her to society. He guessed at the scars her family's treatment of her had caused. Scars he suspected had never truly healed.

He thrust open the door to the pool, shrugging out of his jacket and tie as the warmth hit him. He dropped them on a chair, eyes fixed on the small form swimming in the pool. Usually she swam gracefully. This time there was a dogged de-termination about her freestyle stroke that spoke more of churning emotion than the need for exercise.

Carys let her palm slam onto the tiles at the end of the pool. She was too tired to make a proper racing turn. Her chest heaved, but still the hurt and anger bubbled inside. She'd do a few more laps, till her mind cleared.

A shadow fell on the tiles. Hands reached down.

'Let me help you out.'

Automatically she kicked out off the wall, propelling herself away. But Alessandro forestalled her by grasping her upper arms and using his extraordinary strength to haul her out to stand before him.

She didn't want to talk to him yet. Not till she was calm. Not till she'd got over the sense of betrayal. It was just a lunch, for goodness sake. Nothing to get worked up about.

Yet it felt like more. Like once again she hadn't measured up.

Like last time when he'd kept her to himself rather than trust her to socialise with his friends. Like all the times her parents hadn't showed, or hadn't remembered or just weren't interested. Like she was doomed to be second best still.

'Look at me, Carys.'

She looked. He stood in a puddle as water sluiced off her body. His trousers were wet from where he'd lifted her, and his shirt clung in a way that made her want to run needy hands over his sculpted chest and torso. The knowledge fuelled her anger just as she was aiming for calm.

'You're home early.' It emerged as an accusation, belying the rapture she'd found so often when he returned in time to play with Leo, then take his wife to bed for some late afternoon loving. She bit her lip and looked over his shoulder.

A finger at her chin inexorably lifted her face towards his. There was no escaping his dark gaze or the sympathy she read there.

She didn't want his sympathy! She wanted so much more.

The futility of it hit her. She'd married Alessandro pretending not to care for him, but she'd known, deep in her heart, that she was fated to love this man no matter how unequal their circumstances or the feelings between them.

Alessandro's heart jammed against his ribs, almost stopped beating, as he saw her reddened eyes.

His indomitable Carys had been crying. The realisation gutted him. His hold on her tightened, but he resisted the need to pull her close. The set of her jaw and the flash of her ice-bright eyes were pure warning.

'I can explain—'

'I'm sure you can.' Bitterness laced her words. 'I suppose your office warned you I'd rung. That I knew you'd asked Livia to take my place.'

'It wasn't like that.' Not in the way she thought. His hands gentled on her shoulders, sliding down her slick arms in an instinctive gesture of comfort.

'Wasn't it?' Her gaze shifted. She didn't want to look at him. 'You think I'm not up to playing the role of *contessa*.'

'Don't say that!' He hated it when she talked of playing a role. As if at any moment she might decide she was tired of the act and simply leave. His fingers tightened and he planted his feet wider, instinctively ready to fight for what was his.

'So you asked Livia, *begged* her to step in.'

'That was a mistake, Carys.'

'You can say that again!' She tried to shrug out of his grip, but he refused to release her. He watched temper war with pain as her lips trembled and her eyes glowed bright with slow burning anger. He wanted to fold her close and soothe her.

'I'm you're *wife*, Alessandro. Not some employee you can put aside if you think they're not up to a job.' The words poured out in a rush. 'You *manipulated* me into this marriage. Gave me no choice in the matter. It's too late to decide now that you didn't get a good bargain when you married me.'

'Now hold on.' She'd hit on a sore spot. He knew a sneaking guilt that he'd forced her into marriage. That he'd taken unfair advantage of a woman who hadn't the resources to withstand him. He'd been utterly ruthless in getting this woman into his home and his bed.

'No, I won't hold on!' She straightened, glaring at him with something akin to hatred in her eyes. That look set his heart pounding and fear skimming through him. A fear such as he'd never known.

He couldn't lose Carys. It was impossible. Not now.

'I'm not some prop to be pulled out and shown to the public when you want a compliant wife, then shoved aside when you think I'm not up to dealing with your aristocratic friends.'

'You can't believe that's what I've been doing!' Indignation warred with sympathy. 'I've been giving you time to adjust, trying not to overwhelm you. I know this is different to what you're used to.'

She wasn't listening, just shook her head and planted her hands dead centre on his chest, pushing as if to make him move away.

He stayed planted exactly where he was. No one, not even Carys, dismissed him.

'I'm tired of this, Alessandro. Tired of being treated as second best. Tired of settling for less.'

'Settling?' His brow knotted. 'What do you mean settling?'

'This *convenient* arrangement of ours,' she said, distaste dripping from every syllable. 'It can't go on like this. I can't—'

'Convenient?' Alessandro tried to obliterate burgeoning panic, funnelling his fears instead into the wrath that surfaced when she spoke of ending their marriage. 'You accused me of that the night we got married, didn't you? You were wrong then and you're wrong now.' After all this time they were back where they'd started. Why couldn't she see how important this was? How important *they* were. 'You think this marriage is *convenient* for me?'

Azure eyes met his, unblinking. Her gaze pierced him to the soul. 'I think you got what you wanted, Alessandro. But it's not enough for me. I—'

He refused to listen to Carys request a divorce. Feelings, more tumultuous than he'd ever experienced, exploded within him, shattering the last of his iron-clad control, leaving him defenceless against the pain that ripped him apart.

'You think *this* is convenient, Carys?' He swooped down and took her mouth with his. The kiss was hard, demanding, proprietorial, almost brutal, but he could no longer hold himself in check.

She was *his*. Absolutely incontrovertibly *his*. Nothing had ever felt as right as holding Carys, kissing her. He pulled her close, enfolded her in an embrace that nothing could break.

He needed her. Wouldn't be whole without her.

The feel of her there, her heart hammering in time with his, her soft lips yielding, even giving back kiss for furious kiss, only strengthened his certainty.

'Or this?' He drew back enough to lick a line from her collarbone to her ear, feeling her judder in response, her breath catch in a gasp of pure pleasure.

'There's nothing convenient about what I feel for you, Carys.' He drew back just enough to hold her dazed eyes with his. 'I refuse to give up the woman I love. Do you hear me? There will be no talk of divorce. I won't accept it. I won't give you up.'

This time when he kissed her, he lifted her right off the ground, securing her with one arm around her bottom, the other around her torso, pulling her to him as if he could meld her wet form into his own.

They were one, damn it. They belonged together.

'Sandro?'

'No.' The coward in him didn't want to hear her pleas to be released from their marriage. Instead he kissed her again, turning and walking the few paces till he felt the wall against his arm. He held her there, secure in his arms, her back to the wall, unable to escape, as he concentrated on ravaging her senses with all the passion welling inside him.

He could swear she responded as ardently as ever. More so. Perhaps, after all, she could be persuaded.

'Sandro.' Only lack of oxygen, the need to breathe again, allowed her to speak.

Her fingers against his lips stopped him when he would have kissed her again to stop the flow of words he didn't want to hear.

'Please, Sandro.' Such emotion in her husky voice. His heart squeezed in sheer terror as he knew he couldn't put off the moment any longer. He drew back enough to look down into her face. But he didn't relinquish his hold. He held her clamped hard against him.

'You love me?' There was wonder in her eyes, and doubt.

He was a proud man. From childhood he'd learned not to share himself, not to trust his heart to anyone else. But what he felt was too big to be hidden.

'Can you doubt it, Carys?' He lifted his hand to stroke her brow, her cheek, her swollen lips. 'I think I loved you even before I saw your picture in that brochure. Definitely from the moment I held you in my arms in my hotel suite, and almost died from the sheer ecstasy of you there, with me.' He swallowed a rising lump in his throat.

'And when I saw you holding our son...' This time his kiss was tender, soft and fleeting. Reluctantly he pulled back, watching her eyes widen.

'I didn't know what love was till I met you, *tesoro mio*. But now I do. It's the glorious warmth I feel just thinking about you. Just remembering your smile when you're not there. It's the desire to keep you safe, to protect you and care for you every day of the rest of our lives. To share my life with you. It would kill me if you left.'

His heartbeat slowed to a sombre, waiting pulse. 'I was only half alive before I found you again. Please...' He didn't care that he laid his innermost self open and vulnerable before her. All that mattered was having Carys in his life.

'Oh, Sandro!' Her kiss was fervent but almost clumsy as she pressed her lips feverishly to his. He felt hot tears slide down his cheek and realised she was crying in earnest.

Guilt scorched him. Did he really want to trap her with sympathy?

'Sandro.' She pressed kisses to his chin, his lips, his face. 'I love you so much. I've always loved you. I thought you'd never feel the same.'

He shuddered with the shock of it. But lifting his head, he saw the truth in her eyes. She glowed incandescently as if lit from within. Even then he couldn't believe.

'But you wanted to leave me. You said so.'

Her smile, through drenched eyes and a tear-stained face, was the most beautiful thing he'd ever seen.

'No. I couldn't do that. Ever.' The words sank into his soul and settled there. A tentative sense of peace washed through him. He lowered his head to kiss her again, but she stopped him.

'I'm here for good, Sandro. I just meant I couldn't put up with accepting less than a real marriage with real responsibilities. I couldn't bear thinking you were ashamed of me, that I wasn't good enough to be your *contessa*.'

'Never say that, *piccolina*.' He hitched her higher so they were at eye level. 'You are the perfect wife for me. In every way.' He let the words echo around the tiled walls, satisfaction filling him.

'The luncheon arrangements were a mistake. I didn't invite Livia to take your place. I—'

Her lips against his stopped his words. Stopped thought. She kissed him with all the sweet pleasure and tenderness love could bestow. Alessandro felt it seep into his very bones. He cradled her close and gave back what she offered so unstintingly.

He loved this woman. Would love her till his dying day. The knowledge was glorious, terrifying and wonderful.

When eventually they pulled apart a fraction, she whispered, 'Tell me later. Much later.'

'But it's important for you to understand.'

She smiled and his heart stopped.

'And I will, Sandro.' Alessandro felt his pulse start again, rocketing into life. 'But it can wait. Nothing is more important than this.' She cupped his face in her hands and gazed into his eyes. 'I love you Alessandro Leonardo Daniele Mattani. We're going to be so happy together.'

CHAPTER FIFTEEN

'ONCE again, thank you all for your generosity.' Carys looked across the crowded ballroom, acknowledging smiles from her audience. Relief sighed through her.

Far from being an unresponsive group, those attending the lunch had embraced her and her chosen charities with disarming enthusiasm.

'And please, when you've finished your meal, feel free to come outside and enjoy the fair.'

At a nod from her, the light curtains covering the series of French doors were pushed aside and the doors flung open.

On the afternoon breeze, children's laughter mingled with the sound of music. A fairground had been set up on the lawns and those who would be the recipients of today's fundraising were enjoying themselves: children. Some from orphanages, some with disabilities and others recuperating from serious illnesses.

Carys stepped down from the small podium, acknowledging applause from all sides.

Her gaze kept straying to the tall figure at the back of the room. His nod and smile confirmed what she saw herself. That the lunch and the speech she'd sweated over so long had been successful.

She guessed he was proud of her. But it was the love in his eyes, clear even from here, that warmed her to the core.

Walking between the tables took for ever as she stopped to talk to those she knew and others eager to introduce themselves.

By the time she reached Sandro, Carys felt as if she'd shaken hundreds of hands, answered thousands of questions. And she revelled in it. The guests' support of the charities she'd chosen touched her heart.

'You're a natural,' said a warm voice as she left the final table. She stopped, looking up into familiar hooded eyes alive with approval. Sandro took her hand and raised it to his lips. Inevitably she shivered in response and he smiled, recognising the effect he had on her.

'You made them laugh and even made them cry,' he added. 'I've never seen such unabashed enthusiasm for our fundraising before.'

Carys looked at Leo, bright-eyed and excited, on his father's hip. Her heart swelled seeing him so happy. Feeling the bond between the three of them.

She shrugged. 'A lot of them are parents. Besides, who wouldn't want to help those kids and make life a little easier for them?'

Alessandro gathered her close with his free arm and she went willingly, content to be in her husband's strong embrace. Content, at last, to be home.

'The hotel industry lost a treasure when you left,' he murmured. 'But I'm not giving you back. You make the perfect Contessa Mattani.' His voice dropped to a low purr. 'You're perfect for me, *piccolina*.' He lowered his head.

'Sandro,' she hissed. 'We can't! Not here.'

His response was to kiss her till her bones tingled and she clung to him.

Some time later she became aware of Leo leaning in for a hug, and sound swelling around them. The sound of laughter and more applause.

Alessandro looked over her head and waved to their guests, then led her out into the gardens.

'We can't just leave them,' she protested.

'Of course we can,' he assured her. 'Today is a treat for the local children.' His gaze dropped to her still-flat stomach, and he smiled, a secret, possessive smile that turned her limbs to jelly.

'Let's give ours a treat too, before we sneak away for a

weekend at our place in the mountains.' He hitched Leo higher and drew Carys further into the balmy afternoon.

She went willingly, knowing there was nowhere else on earth she'd rather be.

* * * * *

THE SECRET
BABY BARGAIN

MELANIE
MILBURNE

From as soon as **Melanie Milburne** could pick up a pen she knew she wanted to write. It was when she picked up her first Mills & Boon® novel at seventeen that she realised she wanted to write romance. Distracted for a few years by meeting and marrying her own handsome hero, surgeon husband Steve, and having two boys, plus completing a Masters of Education and becoming a nationally ranked athlete (masters swimming), she decided to write. Five submissions later she sold her first book and is now a multi-published, award-winning *USA TODAY* bestselling author. In 2008 she won the Australian Readers Association's most popular category/series romance and in 2011 she won the prestigious Romance Writers of Australia R*BY award.

Melanie loves to hear from her readers via her website www.melaniemilburne.com.au, or on Facebook http://wwwfacebook.com/pages/ Melanie-Milburne/351594482609.

CHAPTER ONE

ASHLEIGH knew something was wrong as soon as she entered her parents' house on Friday evening after work.

'Mum?' She dropped her bag to the floor, her gaze sweeping the hall for her three-, nearly four-year-old son before turning back to her mother's agitated expression. 'What's going on? Where's Lachlan?'

Gwen Forrester twisted her hands together, her usually cheerful features visibly contorted with strain. 'Darling…' She gave a quick nervous swallow. 'Lachlan is fine… Your father took him fishing a couple of hours ago.'

Ashleigh's frown deepened. 'Then what on earth is the matter? You look as if you've just seen a ghost.'

'I don't quite know how to tell you this…' Gwen took her daughter's hands in hers and gave them a gentle squeeze.

Ashleigh felt her heart begin to thud with alarm. The last time she'd seen her mother this upset had been when she'd returned from London to deliver her bombshell news.

Her heart gave another sickening thump and her breathing came to a stumbling halt. Surely this wasn't about Jake Marriott? Not after all this time… It had been years…four and a half years…

'Mum, come on, you're really freaking me out. Whatever's the matter with you?'

'Ashleigh…he's back.'

Ashleigh felt the cold stream of icy dread begin to flow through her veins, her limbs suddenly freezing and her stomach folding over in panic.

'He called in a short while ago,' Gwen said, her soft blue eyes communicating her concern.

'What?' Ashleigh finally found her voice. *'Here? In person?'*

'Don't worry.' Gwen gave her daughter's hands another reassuring squeeze. 'Lachlan had already left with your father. He didn't see him.'

'But what about the photos?' Ashleigh's stomach gave another savage twist when she thought of the virtual gallery of photographs her parents had set up in the lounge room, each and every one of them documenting their young grandson's life to date. Then, as another thought hit her like a sledgehammer, she gasped, 'Oh, my God, what about his toys?'

'He didn't see anything. I didn't let Jake past the hallway and I'd already done a clean-up after your father left with Lachlan.'

'Thank God…' She slipped out of her mother's hold and sank to the telephone table chair, putting her head in her hands in an attempt to collect her spinning thoughts.

Jake was back!

Four and a half lonely heartbreaking years and he was back in Australia.

Here.

In Sydney.

She lifted her head from her hands and faced her mother once more. 'What did he want?'

'He wants to see you,' Gwen said. 'He wouldn't take no for an answer.'

So that much hadn't changed, she thought cynically. Jake Marriott was a man well used to getting his way and was often unashamedly ruthless in going about it.

'I can't see him.' She sprang to her feet in agitation and began to pace the hall. 'I just can't.'

'Darling…' Her mother's tone held a touch of gentle but unmistakable reproach. 'You really should have told him about Lachlan by now. He has a right to know he fathered a child.'

'He has no right!' Ashleigh turned on her mother in sudden anger. 'He never wanted a child. He made that clear from the word go. No marriage—no kids. That was the deal.'

'All the same, he still should have been informed.'

Ashleigh drew in a scalding breath as the pain of the past assaulted her afresh. 'You don't get it, do you, Mum? Even after all these years you still want to make him out to be the good guy.' She gave her mother an embittered glance and continued, 'Well, for your information, if I had told Jake I was pregnant he would've steamrollered me into having a termination. I just know he would've insisted on it.'

'That choice would have been yours, surely?' Gwen offered, her expression still clouded with motherly concern. 'He could hardly have forced you into it.'

'I was barely twenty years old!' Ashleigh said, perilously close to tears. 'I was living overseas with a man nine years older than me, for whom I would have done anything. If he had told me to jump off the Tower of London I probably would have done it.' She let out a ragged breath. 'I loved him so much…'

Gwen sighed as she took her daughter in her arms, one of her hands stroking the silky ash-blonde head as she had done for almost all of Ashleigh's twenty-four years.

'Oh, Mum…' Ashleigh choked on a sob as she lifted her head. 'What am I going to do?'

Gwen put her from her gently but firmly, her inbuilt pragmatism yet again coming to the fore. 'You will see him because, if nothing else, you owe him that. He mentioned his father has recently passed away. I suppose that's why he's returned to Sydney, to put his father's affairs in order.'

Ashleigh's brow creased in a puzzled little frown as she followed her mother into the kitchen. When she'd asked Jake about his family in the past he'd told her that both his parents were dead. During the time they'd been together he had rarely spoken of his childhood and had deliberately shied away from the topic whenever she'd probed him. She'd put it down to the grief he must have felt at losing both his parents so young.

Why had he lied to her?

'Did he say where he was staying?' she asked as she dragged out one of the breakfast bar stools in the kitchen and sat down.

Gwen busied herself with filling the kettle as she answered. 'At a hotel at the moment, but I got the impression he was moving somewhere here on the North Shore.'

She stared at her mother in shock. 'That close?'

'I'm afraid so,' Gwen said. 'You're going to have a hard time keeping Lachlan's existence a secret if he ends up living in a neighbouring suburb.'

Ashleigh didn't answer but her expression communicated her worry.

'You really have no choice but to see him and get it over with,' Gwen said as she handed her a cup. 'Anyway, for all you know he might have changed.'

Ashleigh bit back a snort of cynicism. 'I don't think people like Jake Marriott ever change. It's not in their nature.'

'You know you can be pretty stubborn yourself at times, Ashleigh,' her mother chided. 'I know you've needed to be strong to be a single mother, but sometimes I think you chop off your nose to spite your face. You should have been well and truly married by now. I don't know why poor Howard puts up with it, really I don't.'

Ashleigh rolled her eyes, gearing herself up for one of her mother's lectures on why she should push the wedding forward a few months. Howard Caule had made it more than clear that he wanted to bring up Lachlan as his own, but every time he'd tried to set a closer date for their wedding she'd baulked. She still wasn't entirely sure why.

'You do love him, don't you, Ashleigh?'

'Who?' She looked at her mother blankly.

'Howard,' Gwen said, her expression shadowed with a little frown. 'Who else?'

Ashleigh wasn't sure how to answer.

She cared for Howard, very deeply, in fact. He'd been a wonderful friend to her—standing by her while she got back on her feet, offering her a part-time position as a buyer for his small chain of antique stores. But as for love... Well, she didn't really trust such volatile feelings any more. It was much safer for her to care for people in an affectionate, friendly but slightly distant manner.

'Howard understands I'm not quite ready for marriage,' she said. 'Anyway, he knows I want to wait until Lachlan settles into his first year at school before I disrupt his life with any further changes to his routine.'

'Are you sleeping with him?'

'Mum!' Ashleigh's face flamed with heated colour.

Gwen folded her arms across her chest. 'You've known Howard for over three years. How long did you know Jake before you went to bed with him?'

Ashleigh refused to answer; instead she sent her mother a glowering look.

'Three days, wasn't it?' Gwen asked, ignoring her daughter's fiery glare.

'I've learnt my lesson since then,' Ashleigh bit out.

'Darling, I'm not lecturing you on what's right and wrong.' She gave a deep and expressive sigh. 'I just think you might be better able to handle seeing Jake again if things were a little more permanent in your relationship with Howard. I don't want to see you hurt all over again.'

'I won't allow Jake to hurt me again,' Ashleigh said with much more confidence than she had any hope of feeling. 'I will see him but that's all. I can't possibly tell him about Lachlan.'

'But surely Lachlan has the right to meet his father at some point? If Jake stays in Sydney for any length of time you will have no choice but to tell him of his son's existence. Imagine what he would think if he were to find out some other way.'

'I hate to disillusion you, Mum, but this is one thing Jake will never budge on. He would be absolutely furious to find out he had a son. I just know it. It was one of the things we argued about the most.' She bit her lip as the memory of their bitter parting scored her brutally, before she continued. 'He would be so angry…so terribly angry…'

Gwen reached into her pocket and handed Ashleigh a card. 'He left this card so you can contact him. He's staying at a hotel in the city. He apparently wants some work done on his father's house before he moves in. I think it would be wise to see him on neutral territory.'

Ashleigh looked down at the card in her hand, her stomach clenching painfully as she saw his name printed there in silver writing.

Jake Marriott CEO Marriott Architecture.

She lifted her gaze back to her mother, resignation heavy in her tone. 'Will you and Dad be all right with minding Lachlan if I go now?'

Gwen gave her a soft smile. 'That's my girl. Go and get it over with, then you can get on with your life knowing you did the right thing in the end.'

Ashleigh stood outside the plush city hotel half an hour later and wondered if she was even in her right mind, let alone doing the right thing. She hadn't rung the mobile number printed on Jake's business card to inform him of her intention to see him. She told herself it was because she didn't want him to have the advantage of preparing himself for her arrival, but deep down she knew it had more to do with her own cowardice.

In the end she had to wait for him, because the reception desk attendant refused to give Jake's room number without authorisation from him first.

She decided against sitting on one of the comfortable-looking leather sofas in the piano lounge area and took a stool at the bar instead, perching on the edge of it with a glass of soda water in her hand, which she knew she'd never be able to swallow past the lump of dread blocking her throat.

As if she could sense his arrival, she found her gaze tracking towards the bank of lifts, his tall unmistakable figure stepping out of the far right one, every scrap of air going out of her lungs as he came into full view.

She knew she was staring at him but just couldn't help it. In four and a half years he had not changed other than to look even more devastatingly handsome.

His imposing height gave him a proud, almost aristocratic bearing and his long lean limbs displayed the physical evidence of his continued passion for endurance sports. His clothes hung on his frame with lazy grace; he had never been the designer type but whatever he wore managed to look top of the range regardless. His wavy black hair was neither long nor short but brushed back in a careless manner which could have indicated the recent use of a hairbrush; however she thought it was more likely to have been the rake of his long tanned fingers that had achieved that just-out-of-bed look.

She was surprised at how painful it was to look at him again.

She'd known every nuance of his face, her fingers had traced over every hard contour of his body, her gentle touch lingering over the inch-long scar above his right eyebrow, her lips kissing him in every intimate place, and yet as he strode towards her she felt as if she had never known him at all.

He had simply not allowed her to.

'Hello, Ashleigh.'

Ashleigh had trouble disguising her reaction to his deep voice, the smooth velvet tones with just a hint of an English accent woven through it. How she had longed to hear it over the years!

'Hello.' She met his dark eyes briefly, hoping he wouldn't see the guilt reflected in hers at the thought of what she had kept hidden from him for all this time.

'You're looking well,' Jake said, his gaze running over her in a sweeping but all-encompassing glance. 'Have you put on weight?'

Ashleigh pursed her lips for a moment before responding with a touch of tartness. 'I see your idea of what constitutes a compliment is still rather twisted.'

One eyebrow rose and his mouth lifted in a small mocking smile. 'I see you're still as touchy as ever.' His eyes dipped to her breasts for a moment before returning slowly to hers. 'I think it suits you. You were always so bone-thin.'

'It must have been the stress of living with you,' she shot back before she could stop herself, reaching for her drink with an unsteady hand.

A tight little silence fell in the space between them.

Ashleigh felt like kicking herself for betraying her bitterness so unguardedly. She stared at a floating ice cube in her glass, wishing she was able to see Jake without it doing permanent damage to her emotional well-being.

'You're probably right,' Jake said, a tiny frown settling between his brows and, as he took the stool beside her, lifted his hand to get the barman's attention.

Ashleigh swivelled on her stool to stare at him. Was that regret she could hear in his tone?

She waited until he'd given the barman his order and his drink had arrived before speaking again.

'My mother told me why you're here.'

His gaze met hers but he didn't answer. Something indefinable flickered in the depths of his coal-black eyes before he turned back to his drink and took a deep draught.

Ashleigh watched the up and down movement of his throat as he swallowed. He was sitting so close she could touch him but it felt as if there was an invisible wall around him.

'Why did you tell me when we met that both your parents were dead?' she asked when she could stand the silence no longer.

'It seemed the easiest thing to say at the time.'

'Yes, well, lying was always something that came very naturally to you,' she bit out resentfully.

He turned to look at her, his darker-than-night eyes holding hers. 'It might surprise you to hear this, but I didn't like lying to you, Ashleigh. I just thought it was less complicated than explaining everything.'

Ashleigh stared at him as he took another sip of his drink, her heart feeling too tight, as if the space allocated for it had suddenly been drastically reduced. What did he mean—'explain everything'?

She let another silence pass before she asked, 'When did you arrive?'

'A couple of weeks ago. I thought I'd wait until after the funeral to see if he left me anything in his will.' He drained his glass and set it back down with a nerve-jangling crack on the bar in front of him.

There was a trace of something in his voice that suggested he hadn't been all that certain of his father's intentions regarding his estate. Ashleigh was surprised at how tempted she was to reach out and touch him, to offer him some sort of comfort for what he was going through. She had to hold on to her glass with both hands to stop herself from doing so, knowing he wouldn't welcome it in the bitter context of their past relationship.

'And did he?' She met his eyes once more. 'Leave you anything?'

A cynical half smile twisted his mouth as his eyes meshed with hers. 'He left me everything he didn't want for himself.'

She had to look away from the burning heat of his eyes. She stared down at the slice of lemon in her glass. 'It must be very hard for you…just now.'

Jake gave an inward grimace as he watched her toy with her straw, her small neat fingers demonstrating her unease in his company.

The hardest thing he'd ever had to do was to look her up that afternoon. His pride, his damned pride, had insisted he was a fool for doing so, but in the end he'd overridden it for just one look at her.

When he'd seen her mother at the house he'd considered waiting for however long it took for Ashleigh to return, but sensing Mrs Forrester's discomfiture had reluctantly left. He hadn't been entirely sure she would have even told Ashleigh of his call. He could hardly blame her, of course. No doubt Ashleigh had told her family what a pig-headed selfish bastard he'd been to her all the time they'd been together.

But he *had* to see her.

He had to see her to remind himself of what he'd thrown away.

'Yes…it's not been easy,' he admitted, staring into his empty glass.

He felt her shift beside him and had to stop himself from turning to her and hauling her into his arms.

She looked fantastic.

She'd grown into her body in a way few women these days did. Her figure had pleased him no end in the past, but now it was riper, more womanly, her softer curves making him ache to mould her to him as he had done in the past.

If only they had just met now, without the spectre of their previous relationship dividing them. But it wasn't *their* past that had divided them—it had been his. And it was only now that he was finally coming to terms with it.

'Your mother looks the same,' he said, sending her another quick glance, taking in her ringless fingers with immeasurable relief.

'Yes…'

'How is your father?'

'Retired now,' Ashleigh answered. 'Enjoying being able to play with…er…'

Jake swung his gaze back to hers at her sudden vocal stall. 'Golf?'

Ashleigh clutched at the sudden lifeline with relief. 'Yes… golf. He plays a lot of golf.'

'I always liked your dad,' he said, looking back at his empty glass again.

The undisguised warmth in his statement moved her very deeply. Ashleigh's family had come over to London for Christmas the second year she'd been living with Jake, and she had watched how Jake had done his best to fit in with her family. When he hadn't been hiding away at work he'd spent a bit of time with her father, choosing his company instead of the boisterous and giggling presence of her younger sisters, Mia and Ellie, and her trying-too-hard mother. She had been touched by his effort to include himself in her family's activities, his tall, somewhat aloof, presence often seeming out of place and awkward amidst the rough and tumble of the family interactions that she had always taken for granted.

'How are your sisters?' he asked after another little pause.

A small smile of pride flickered on her mouth. 'Mia is trying her best to get into acting, with some limited success.

She was a pot plant in a musical a month ago; we were all incredibly proud of her. And Ellie… Well, you know Ellie.' Her expression softened at the thought of her adopted youngest sister. 'She is still the world's biggest champion for the underdog. She works part-time in a café and spends every other available minute at a dogs' home as a volunteer.'

'And what about you?' Jake asked, looking at her intently.

'Me?' She gave him a startled look, her pulses racing at the intensity of his dark eyes as they rested on her face. His smile had softened his normally harsh features, the simple upward movement of his lips unleashing a flood of memories about how that mouth had felt on hers…

'Yes, you,' he said. 'What are you doing with yourself these days?'

'I…' She swallowed and tried to appear unfazed by his question. 'Not much.' She twirled her straw a couple of times and continued. 'I work as a buyer for an antique dealer.' She pushed her glass away and met his eyes again. 'Howard Caule Antiques.'

He gestured to the barman to refresh their drinks, taking his time to turn back to her to respond. 'I've heard of him.' He picked up his glass as soon as it was placed in front of him. 'What's he like to work for?'

For some reason Ashleigh found it difficult to meet his eyes with any equanimity. She moistened her lips, her stomach doing a funny little somersault when she saw the way his eyes followed the nervous movement of her tongue.

'He's…he's nice.'

Damn it! She chided herself as she saw the way Jake's lip instantly curled. Why couldn't she have thought of a better adjective than that?

'A nice guy, huh?'

She had to look away. 'Yes. He's also one of my closest friends.'

'Are you sleeping with him?'

Her eyes flew back to his, her cheeks flaming for the second time that day. 'That's absolutely no business of yours.'

He didn't respond immediately, which made her tension go up another excruciating notch. She watched him as he surveyed her with those dark unreadable eyes, every nerve in her body jumping in sharp awareness at his proximity.

She could even *smell* him.

Her nostrils flared to take in more of that evocative scent, the combination of full-blooded-late-in-the-day active male and his particular choice of aftershave that had always reminded her of sun-warmed lemons and exotic spices.

'My my my, you are touchy, aren't you?' he asked, the mocking smile still in place.

She set her mouth and turned to stare at the full glass in front of her, wishing herself a million miles away.

She couldn't do this.

She couldn't be calm and cool in Jake Marriott's presence. He unsettled her in every way possible.

'I'm not being touchy.' Her tone was brittle and on edge. 'I just don't see what my private life has to do with you…*now.*'

His continued silence drew her gaze back as if he'd pulled it towards him with invisible strings.

'Ashleigh…' He reached out to graze her cheek with the back of his knuckles in a touch so gentle she felt a great wave of emotion swamp her for what they'd had and subsequently lost.

She fought her feelings down with an effort, her teeth tearing at the inside of her mouth as she held his unwavering gaze.

'I'd like to see you again while I'm here in Sydney,' he said, his deep voice sounding ragged and uneven. 'I'm here for a few weeks and I thought we could—' he deliberately paused over the words '—catch up.'

Ashleigh inwardly seethed. She could just imagine what he meant by catching up; a bit of casual sex to fill in the time before he left the country to go back to whoever was waiting for him back in London.

'I can't see you.'

His eyes hardened momentarily and his hand fell away. 'Why not?'

She bit her lip, hunting her brain for the right words to describe her relationship with Howard.

'Is there someone else?' he asked before she could respond, his eyes dipping to her bare fingers once more.

She drew in a tight breath. 'Yes…yes there is.'

'You're not wearing a ring.'

She gave him an ironic look and clipped back, 'I lived and slept with you for two whole years without needing one.'

Jake shifted slightly as he considered her pert response. Her cheeks were bright with colour, her eyes flashing him a warning he had no intention of heeding.

He knew it bordered on the arrogant to assume that no one had taken his place after four and a half years, but he'd hoped for it all the same. His own copybook wasn't too pristine, of course; he'd replaced her numerous times, but not one of his subsequent lovers had affected him the way Ashleigh had, and, God help him, still did.

'What would you say if I told you I've had a rethink of a few of my old standpoints?' he asked. 'That I'd changed?'

Ashleigh got to her feet, rummaging in her purse, placed some money on the counter for her drink, her eyes when they returned to his like twin points of angry blue flame.

'I'd say you were four and a half years too late, Jake Marriott.' She hoisted her bag back on her shoulder. 'I have to go. I have someone waiting for me.'

She turned to leave but one of his hands came down on

her wrist and turned her round to face him. She felt the velvet-covered steel bracelet of his fingers and suppressed an inward shiver of reaction at feeling his warm flesh on hers once more.

'Let me go, Jake.' Her voice came out husky instead of de-termined, making her hate him for affecting her so.

He rose to his full height, his body within a whisper of hers. She felt as if she couldn't breathe, for if she so much as drew in one small breath her chest would expand and bring her breasts into contact with the hard wall of his chest. Dark eyes locked with blue in a battle she knew she was never going to win, but she had to fight regardless.

'I can't see you, Jake,' she said in a tight voice. 'I am en-gaged to be married.' She took another shaky breath and added, 'To my boss, Howard Caule.'

She saw the sudden flare of heat in his eyes at the same time the pressure of his fingers subtly increased about her wrist.

'You're not married yet,' he said, before dropping her wrist and stepping back from her.

Ashleigh wasn't sure if his statement was a threat or an ob-servation. She didn't stay around to find out. Instead, she turned on her heel and stalked out of the bar with long pur-poseful strides that she hoped gave no hint of her inner distress.

Jake watched her go, his chest feeling as if some giant hand had just plunged between his ribs and wrenched out his heart and slapped it down on the bar next to the ten dollar note she'd placed beside her untouched drink…

CHAPTER TWO

ASHLEIGH drove back to her parents' house with her bottom lip between her teeth for the entire journey.

It had *hurt* to see Jake again.

It had *hurt* her to hear his voice, to see his hands grip his glass—the hands that had once caressed her and with his very male body brought her to the highest pinnacle of human pleasure.

It had *hurt* to see his mouth tilt in a smile—the mouth that had kissed her all over but had never once spoken of his love.

Damn it! It had *hurt* to turn him down, but what other choice did she have? She could hardly pick up where they'd left off. How could she, with the secret of Lachlan's existence lying between them? Jake had made it clear he never wanted to have children. She could hardly tap him on the shoulder and announce, *By the way, here is your son. Don't you think he looks a bit like you?*

'Mummee!' Lachlan rushed towards her as soon as she opened the door, throwing his little arms around her middle and squeezing tightly.

'Hey, why aren't you in bed?' She pretended to frown down at him.

His chocolate-brown eyes twinkled as he looked up at her.

'Grandad promised me I could show you what we caught first.'

She looked up at her father, who had followed his young grandson out into the hall. 'Hi, Dad. Good day at the bay?'

Heath Forrester grinned. 'You should have seen the ones we let get away.'

Ashleigh smiled and stood on tiptoe to plant a soft kiss on his raspy cheek. 'Thanks,' she said, her one word speaking a hundred for her.

Heath turned to Lachlan. 'Go and get our bounty out of the fridge while I have a quick word with your mum.'

Lachlan raced off, the sound of his footsteps echoing down the hall as Heath turned to his eldest daughter. 'How was Jake?'

'He was…' she let out a little betraying sigh '…Jake.'

'What did he want?'

'I got the distinct impression he wanted to resume our past relationship—temporarily.'

Her father's bushy brows rose slightly. 'Same old Jake then?'

She gave him a world-weary sigh. 'Same old Jake.'

'You didn't tell him about Lachlan?'

Ashleigh hunted her father's expression for the reproach she privately dreaded, but found none and was immensely grateful for it.

'No…' She inspected her hands for a moment. 'No, I didn't.'

'Howard called while you were out.' Heath changed the subject tactfully. 'He said something about taking you out to dinner. I told him you'd call but if you want me to put him off I can always—'

Ashleigh forced her mouth into a smile and tucked her arm through one of his. 'Why don't we go and look at that fish first?'

'What a good idea,' he said and led her towards the kitchen.

An hour later Lachlan was fast asleep upstairs and Ashleigh made her way downstairs again, only to be halted by her

sister Mia who had not long come in from an actors and per-
formers' workshop.

'Is it true?' Mia ushered her into the study, out of the hearing of the rest of the Forrester family. 'Is Jake really back in
Sydney?'

Ashleigh gave a single nod. 'Yes…he's back.'

Mia let out a very unladylike phrase. 'Have you told him
about Lachlan?' she asked.

Ashleigh shook her head. 'No…'

Mia's eyes widened. 'What are you doing? Of course he
has to know now that he's back.'

'Listen, Mia. I've already had this sort of lecture from
Mum, so I don't need another one from you.'

Mia held up her hands in a gesture of surrender. 'Hey,
don't get all shirty with me, but have you actually listened to
that kid of yours lately? All he ever talks about is dad stuff.'

Ashleigh frowned. 'What do you mean?'

Mia gave her a sobering look. 'I read him a story the other
night when you were out with Howard. You know, the one
about the elephant with the broken trunk who was looking
for someone to fix it? Lachlan kept on and on about how if
he could find his real dad he was sure he would be able to fix
everything. How cute, but how sad, is that?'

Ashleigh turned away, her hands clenching in tension. 'I
can't deal with this right now. I have enough to think about
without you adding to it.'

'Come on, Ash,' Mia said. 'What's to think about? Jake
has come home to Sydney and he should be told the truth.
It's not like you can hide it from him. One close look at that
kid and he's going to see it for himself.'

Ashleigh felt the full force of her sister's words like a blow
to her mid-section. Lachlan was the spitting image of his
father. His darker-than-night eyes, his long rangy limbs, his
black hair that refused to stay in place, his temper that could

rise and fall with the weight of a timely smile or gentle caress…

The doorbell sounded and Ashleigh turned and walked down the hall to answer it rather than continue the conversation with her sister.

'Ashleigh,' Howard Caule greeted her warmly, pressing a quick kiss to her cheek as he came in. 'How's my girl?' He caught sight of Mia hovering. 'Hi, Mia, how are the auditions for the toilet paper advertisement going?'

'Great, I'm going to wipe the floor with the competition,' Mia answered with an insincere smile and a roll of her eyes before she walked away.

Ashleigh dampened down her annoyance at her sister's behaviour towards her fiancé, knowing it would be pointless to try and defend him. Mia and Ellie had never taken to him no matter how many times she highlighted his good points. It caused her a great deal of pain but there was nothing she could do about it. Howard was reliable and safe and more or less wanted the same things in life that she did. Her family would just have to get used to the idea of him being a permanent fixture in her life. Lachlan liked him and as far as she was concerned that counted for more than anything.

Once Mia had gone she closed the front door and leant back against it, her eyes going to Howard's. 'We have to talk.'

'Let's do it over dinner,' he suggested. Then, taking something out of his pocket, he added, 'Is Lachlan still awake? I brought him a little present.'

Ashleigh took the toy car he held out to her, her expression softening with gratitude. 'He's asleep but I'll leave it on his bedside table for him. Thank you; you're so good to him.'

'He's a good kid, Ashleigh,' he said. 'I can't wait until we're finally married so I can be a real father to him.'

She gave him a weak smile. 'I'll just tell my folks we're leaving.'

'I'll go and start the car,' he offered helpfully and bounded back out the front door.

Ashleigh spoke briefly with her parents before joining Howard in his car, all the time trying to think of a way to bring up the subject of Jake Marriott.

She had told Howard the barest details of her affair with Lachlan's father, preferring to keep that part of her life separate and distant from the here and now. She hadn't even once mentioned Jake's name. Howard hadn't pressed her, and in a way that was why she valued his friendship so much. He seemed to sense her pain in speaking of the past and always kept things on an upbeat keel to lift her spirits.

Howard was so different from Jake, and not just physically, although those differences were as marked as could ever be. Howard had the typically pale freckled skin that was common to most redheads, his height average and his figure tending towards stocky.

Jake's darkly handsome features combined with his imposing height and naturally athletic build were made all the more commanding by his somewhat aloof and brooding personality.

Howard, on the other hand, was uncomplicated. Mia and Ellie described him as boring but Ashleigh preferred to think of him as predictable.

She *liked* predictable.

She could handle predictable.

She liked knowing what to expect each day when she turned up to work. Howard was always cheerful and positive, nothing was too much trouble and even if it was he didn't let on but simply got on with the task without complaining.

She wished she was in love with him.

Truly in love.

He was worthy of so much more than she could give him but her experience with Jake had taught her the danger of loving too much and too deeply.

'You're very quiet.' Howard glanced her way as he pulled up at a set of traffic lights.

'Sorry…' She shifted her mouth into a semblance of a smile. 'I've got a lot on my mind.'

He reached over and patted her hand, his freckled fingers cool, nothing like the scorching heat of Jake's when he'd touched her earlier.

Her wrist still felt as if it had been burnt. She looked down at it to see if there were any marks but her creamy skin was surprisingly unblemished.

What a pity her heart hadn't been as lucky.

The restaurant he'd chosen was heavily booked and even though Howard had made a reservation they still had to wait for over half an hour for their table.

As Ashleigh sat with him at the bar she couldn't help thinking how different it would have been if it had been Jake with her. There was no way he would have sat patiently waiting for a table he'd pre-booked. He would have demanded the service he was paying for and, what was more, he would have got it.

'What did you want to talk to me about?' Howard asked as he reached for his mineral water.

Ashleigh took a steadying breath and met his light blue eyes. 'I met with Lachlan's father today.'

He gave her a worried look. 'Does he want to see him?'

'I didn't get around to telling him about Lachlan,' she answered. 'We talked about…other things.'

Howard put his glass down. 'You mean he still doesn't know anything about him? Nothing at all?'

'I know it seems wrong not to tell him, but at the time it was the right decision…and now…well…'

'What about now?' Howard asked. 'Shouldn't he be told at some point?'

Ashleigh had thought of nothing else, especially after what Mia had told her about Lachlan. It seemed wrong that her tiny son could never openly acknowledge his father. And yet after seeing Jake again it brought it home to her just what he had missed in knowing nothing of his son's existence. He had not been there for any of the milestones of Lachlan's life. His first smile, his first words and his very first 'I love you'. Jake had missed out on so much and those years could never be returned to him. But she had done what she had thought was right... She still thought it was right. But somehow...

'Lachlan's father hasn't changed a bit.' She gave a deep regretful sigh. 'I was young, far too young to even be in a relationship let alone with someone as intense as him. I lost myself when I was with him. I forgot how to stand up for myself, for what I believed in. I let him take control... It was a mistake... Our relationship was a mistake.'

'Did you tell him about us?' he asked. 'That we're engaged to be married?'

'Yes...'

He frowned as he looked at her bare hands. 'I wish you'd wear my mother's ring. I know you don't like the design but we could get it altered.'

Ashleigh wished she liked it, too. She wished she liked his mother as well, but nothing in life was perfect and she had learned the hard way to make the most of what was on offer and get on with it.

'I'll think about it,' she said. 'Anyway, it's only a symbol. It means nothing.' The words were not her own but some that Jake had used in the past but she didn't think Howard would appreciate that little detail.

'Come on, let's have dinner and forget all about Lachlan's

father for the rest of tonight,' Howard said as the waiter indicated for them to follow him to their table.

Ashleigh gave him a wan smile as she made her way with him to their seats, but even hours later when she was lying in her bed, willing herself to sleep, she still had not been able to drive all thought of Jake from her mind.

He was there.

Permanently.

His dark disturbing presence reminding her of all that had brought them together and what, in the end, had torn them apart.

Ashleigh had not long arrived at the main outlet of Howard Caule Antiques in Woollahra the next morning when Howard rushed towards her excitedly.

'Ashleigh, I have the most exciting news.'

'What?' She put her bag and sunglasses on the walnut desk before tilting her cheek for his customary kiss. 'Let me guess…you've won the lottery?'

His light blue eyes positively gleamed with excitement. 'No, but it sure feels like it. I have just spoken to a man who has recently inherited a veritable warehouse full of antiques. He wants to sell them all—to us! Can you believe it?' He rubbed his hands together in glee. 'Some of the stuff is priceless, Ashleigh. And he wants us to have it all and he's not even worried about how much we are prepared to pay for it.'

Ashleigh gave a small frown. 'There must be some sort of catch. Why would anyone sell off such valuable pieces to one dealer when he could play the market a bit and get top dollar?'

Howard shrugged one shoulder. 'I don't know, but who cares? You know how worried I've been about how things have been a bit tight lately and this is just the sort of boost I need right now.' He reached for a sheet of paper on his desk and handed it to her. 'I've made an appointment for you to meet with him later this morning at this address.'

'But why me?' she asked, glancing down at the paper, her heart missing a beat when she saw the name printed there.

Jake Marriott.

She lifted her tortured gaze to Howard's blissful one. 'I—I can't do this.' The paper crinkled in her tightening fingers.

'What are you doing?' Howard plucked the crumpled paper out of her hand and began straightening it as if it were a piece of priceless parchment. 'He particularly asked for you,' he said. 'He said he knew your family. I checked him out on a few details. I wouldn't allow you to deal with anyone who I thought was unsafe. He knew both your parents' names and—'

'That's because he's Lachlan's father,' she said bluntly.

Howard's eyes bulged. *'Jake Marriott is Lachlan's father?'*

She gave a single nod, her lips tightly compressed.

'Jake Marriott?' His throat convulsed. 'Jake Marriott as in the billionaire architect who's designed some of the most prestigious buildings around the globe?'

'That's the one,' she said.

'Oh, no…' Howard flopped into the nearest chair, the freckles on his face standing out against the pallor of his shocked face.

Ashleigh gnawed her bottom lip, fear turning her insides to liquid.

Howard sprang back to his feet. 'Well, for one thing, you can't possibly tell him about Lachlan,' he insisted, 'or at least not right now. If you do he'll withdraw the offer. I need this deal, Ashleigh.'

'I'll have to tell him sometime…' She let out a painful breath. 'Mia told me Lachlan has been asking about his father. He must have heard the other kids at crèche talking about their dads. I knew he would eventually want to know but I didn't expect it to be this soon.'

'Let's get married as quickly as possible,' he said, taking

both her hands in his. 'That way Lachlan can start calling me his dad.'

She eased herself out of his hold, suddenly unable to maintain eye contact. 'I don't want to get married yet. I'm not ready.'

'Are you ever going to be ready?' His tone held a trace of bitterness she'd never heard in it before.

She turned back to him, her expression wavering with uncertainty. 'It's such a big step. We haven't even…you know…' Her hands fluttered back to her sides, her face hot with embarrassment.

'I told you I don't believe in sex before marriage,' he said. 'I know it's old-fashioned, but my faith is important to me and I think it's a small sacrifice to make to show my loyalty to you and to God.'

Ashleigh couldn't help wondering what Jake would think of Howard's moral uprightness. Jake hadn't even believed in the sanctity of marriage, much less waiting a decent period before committing himself to a physical relationship. He'd had her in his bed within three days of meeting her and if it hadn't been for the prod of her conscience at the time, she knew he would have succeeded on the very first.

She was trapped by circumstances beyond her control and it terrified her. No matter how much she wished her past would go away and never come back she had a permanent living reminder in her little son. Even now Lachlan was a miniature of his biological father and even if a hundred Howards offered to step into his place no one could ever be the man Lachlan most needed.

Besides, she'd seen this played out before in her adopted sister Ellie's life. Ellie pretended to be unconcerned about who her biological parents were but Ashleigh knew how she secretly longed to find out why she had been relinquished when only a few days old. It didn't matter how loving her adoptive parents and she and Mia as her sisters were, Ellie was like a lost soul looking for a connection she both dreaded and desired.

She took the paper out of Howard's hand with dogged resignation. 'All right, I'll do it. I'll buy the goods from him and keep quiet, but I can't help feeling this could backfire on me.'

'Think about the money,' he said. 'This will take me to the top of the antiques market in Sydney.' He reached for the telephone. 'I have to ring my mother. This has been her dream ever since my father died.'

Ashleigh gave an inward sigh and picked up her bag and sunglasses from the desk. Jake had her in the palm of his hand and she could already feel the press of his fingers as they began to close in on her…

The drive to the address in the leafy northern suburb of Lindfield seemed all too short to Ashleigh in spite of the slow crawl of traffic on the Pacific Highway.

She kept glancing at the clock on the dashboard, the minutes ticking by, increasing her panic second by painful second.

The street she turned into as indicated on the paper Howard had given her was typical of the upper north shore, leafy private gardens shielding imposing homes, speaking quietly but unmistakably of very comfortable wealth.

She pulled up in front of the number of the house she'd been given but there was no sign of Jake. The driveway was empty, the scallop-edged blinds at the windows of the house pulled down low just like lashes over closed eyes.

The front garden was huge and looked a bit neglected, as if no one had bothered to tend it recently, the lawn still green but interspersed with dandelion heads, the soft little clouds of seeds looking as if the slightest breath of wind would disturb their spherical perfection for ever.

She walked up the pathway towards the front door, breathing in the scent of sun-warmed roses as she reached to press the tarnished brass bell.

There was no answer.

She didn't know whether to be relieved or annoyed. According to the information Howard had given her, she was to meet Jake here at eleven a.m. and here it was twelve minutes past and no sign of him.

Typical, she thought as she stepped away from the door. When had Jake ever been the punctual type?

She made her way around to the back of the house, curiosity finally getting the better of her. She wondered if this was the house where he had grown up. He had always been so vague about his childhood but she seemed to remember him mentioning a big garden with an elm tree in the backyard that he used to sometimes climb.

She found it along the tall back fence, its craggy limbs spreading long fingers of shade all over the rear corner of the massive garden. She stepped beneath its dappled shade and looked upwards, trying to picture Jake as a young child scrambling up those ancient limbs to get to the top. He wasn't the bottom branches type, a quality she could already see developing in her little son.

'I used to have a tree-house way up there,' Jake's deep voice said from just behind her.

Ashleigh spun around so quickly she felt light-headed, one of her hands going over her heart where she could feel it leaping towards her throat in shock. 'Y-you scared me!'

He gave her one of his lazy half smiles. 'Did I?'

He didn't seem too bothered about it, she noted with considerable resentment. His expression held a faint trace of amusement as his eyes took in her flustered form.

'You're late,' she said and stepped out of the intimacy of the overhanging branches to the brighter sunlight near a bed of blood-red roses.

'I know,' he answered without apology. 'I had a few things to see to first.'

She tightened her lips and folded her arms across her chest crossly. 'I suppose you think I've got nothing better to do all day than hang around waiting for you to show up. Why didn't you tell me yesterday about this arrangement?'

He joined her next to the roses, stopping for a moment to pick one perfect bloom and, holding it up to his nose, slowly drew in the fragrance.

Ashleigh found it impossible to look away.

The softness of the rose in his large, very male, hand had her instantly recalling his touch on her skin in the past, the velvet-covered steel of his fingers which could stroke like a feather in foreplay, or grasp like a vice in the throes of out of control passion.

She gave an inward shiver as his eyes moved back to meet hers.

He silently handed her the rose and, for some reason she couldn't entirely fathom at the time, she took it from him. She lowered her gaze from his and breathed in the heady scent, feeling the brush of the soft petals against her nose where his had so recently been.

'I'm glad you came,' he said after a little silence. 'I've always wanted you to see where I grew up.'

Ashleigh looked up at him, the rose still in her hand. 'Why?'

He shifted his gaze from hers and sent it to sweep across the garden before turning to look at the house. She watched the movement of his dark unfathomable eyes and couldn't help feeling intrigued by his sudden need to show her the previously private details of his childhood.

It didn't make any sense.

Why now?

Why had it taken him so long to finally reveal things she'd longed to know way back? She had asked him so many times

for anecdotes of his childhood but he had skirted around the
subject, even shutting her out for days with one of his stony
silences whenever she'd prodded him too much.

His eyes came back to hers. 'I used to really hate this
place.'

She felt a small frown tug at her forehead. 'Why?'

He seemed to give himself a mental shake, for he suddenly removed his line of vision from hers and began to
lead the way towards the house. Ashleigh followed silently,
stepping over the cracks in the pathway, wondering what
had led him home if it was so painful to revisit this place.

There was so much she didn't know about Jake.

She knew how he took his tea and coffee, she knew he
had a terrible sweet tooth attack at about four o'clock every
afternoon, she knew he loved his back rubbed and that he
had one very ticklish hip. But she didn't know what made
his eyes and face become almost mask-like whenever his
childhood was mentioned.

Jake unlocked the back door and, leaving Ashleigh hovering in the background, immediately began rolling up blinds
and opening windows to let the stale, musty air out.

Ashleigh wasn't sure if she should offer to help or not. She
was supposed to be here in a professional capacity but
nothing so far in Jake's manner or mood had indicated
anything at all businesslike.

'I'm sorry it's so stuffy in here,' he said, stepping past her
to reach for the last blind. 'I haven't been here since…well…'
He gave her a wry look. 'I haven't been here since I was about
sixteen.'

She knew her face was showing every sign of her intrigue
but she just couldn't help it. She looked around at the sun-room
they were in, but apart from a few uncomfortable-looking
chairs and a small table and a cheap self-assembly magazine
rack there was nothing that she could see of any great value.

'I know what you're thinking,' he said into the awkward silence.

She looked at him without responding but her eyes obviously communicated her scepticism.

'You're thinking I've led you here on a fool's errand, aren't you?' he asked.

She drew in a small breath and scanned the room once more. 'The contents of this room would barely pay for a cup of coffee and a sandwich at a decent café.' She met his eyes challengingly. 'What's this about, Jake? Why am I here and why now?'

'Come this way.'

He led her towards a door off the sun-room which, when he opened it, showed her a long dark, almost menacing, hallway, the lurking shadows seeming to leap out from the walls to brush at the bare skin of her arms as she followed him about halfway down to a door on the left.

The door opened with a creak of a hinge that protested at the sudden movement, the inner darkness of the room spilling out towards her. Jake flicked on a light switch as she stepped into the room with him, her eyes instantly widening as she saw what was contained within.

She sucked in a breath of wonder as her nostrils filled with the scent of old cedar. The room was stacked almost to the ceiling with priceless pieces of furniture. Tables, chairs, escritoires, chaise longues and bookcases and display cabinets, their dusty shelves filled with an array of porcelain figurines which she instinctively knew were beyond her level of expertise to value with any sort of accuracy. It would take days, if not weeks, to assess the value of each and every item.

She did her best to control her breathing as she stepped towards the first piece of polished cedar, her fingers running over the delicately carved edge as if in worship.

'What do you think?' Jake asked.

She turned to look at him, her hand falling away from the priceless heirloom. 'I think you've picked the wrong person to assess the value of all of this.' She chewed her lip for a moment before adding, 'Howard would be much better able to give you the right—'

'But I want you.'

There was something in his tone that suggested to Ashleigh he wasn't just talking about the furniture.

'I'm not able to help you…' She made to brush past him, suddenly desperate to get out of this house and away from his disturbing presence.

'Wait.' His hand came down on her arm and held her still, leaving her no choice but to meet his dark brooding gaze. 'Don't go.'

She dragged in a ragged breath, her head telling her to get the hell out while she still could, but somehow her treacherous heart insisted she stay.

'Jake…' Her voice sounded as if it had come through a vacuum, it didn't sound at all like her own.

His hand cupped her cheek, his thumb moving over the curve of her lips in a caress so poignantly tender she immediately felt the springing of tears in her eyes.

She watched as his mouth came down towards hers and, in spite of her inner convictions, did absolutely nothing to stop it.

She couldn't.

Her body felt frozen in time, her lips waiting for the imprint of his after four and a half years of deprivation. Her skin begged for his touch with goose-bumps of anticipation springing out all over her, her legs weakening with need as soon as his mouth met hers.

Heat coursed through her at that first blistering touch, her lips instantly swelling under the insistent pressure of his, her mouth opening to the command of his determined tongue as it sought her inner warmth.

She felt the sag of her knees as he crushed her close to his hard frame, the ridges of his body fitting so neatly into the soft curves of hers as if made to measure.

Desire surged through her as if sent on an electric circuit from his. She felt its charge from breast to hip, her body singing with awareness as his body leapt in response against her. She felt the hardening of his growing erection, the heat and length of him a heady, intoxicating reminder of all the intimacies they had shared in the past.

Her body was no mystery to him. He had known every crease and tender fold, had explored and tasted every delicacy with relish. Her body remembered with a desperate burning plea for more. She ached for him, inside and out, her emotions caught up in a maelstrom of feeling she had no control over. It was as if the past hadn't happened; she was his just as she had been all those years ago. He had only to look at her and she would melt into his arms and become whatever he wanted her to become…

She jerked herself out of his hold with a strength she had not known she was capable of and, thankfully for her, he was totally unprepared for.

'You have no right.' She clipped the words out past stiff lips. 'I'm engaged. You have no right to touch me.'

His eyes raked her mercilessly, his expression hinting at satire. 'You gave me the right as soon as you looked at me that way.'

'What way?' She glared at him defensively. 'I did not *look* at you in any way!'

His mouth tilted in a cynical smile. 'I wonder what your fiancé would say if he saw how you just responded to me?'

Ashleigh felt as if someone had switched on a radiator behind her cheeks. Guilty colour burnt through her skin, making her feel transparent, as if he could see right through her to where she hid her innermost secrets.

She had to turn away, her back rigid with fury, as she glared at a painting on the wall in her line of vision.

'Oh, my God…' She stepped towards the portrait, her eyes growing wide with amazement, incredulity and what only could be described as gobsmacked stupefaction as realisation gradually dawned. Her eyes dipped to look at the signature at the bottom of the painting, even her very fingertips icing up with excitement as she turned around to look at him.

'Do you realise what you have here?' she asked, her tone breathless with wonder. 'That painting alone is worth thousands!'

He gave the painting a dismissive glance and met her eyes once more. 'You can have it,' he said. 'And everything else. There's more in the other rooms.'

She stared at him for at least five heavy heartbeats. *'What?'*

'You heard,' he said. 'I'm giving it to you to sell; everything in this house.'

She felt like slapping the side of her head to make sure she wasn't imagining what she'd just heard. 'What did you say?'

'I said I'm giving you the lot,' he said.

She backed away, her instincts warning her that this was not a no-strings deal. 'Oh, no.' She held up her hands as if to warn him off. 'You can't bribe me with a whole bunch of priceless heirlooms.'

'I'm not bribing you, Ashleigh,' he said in an even tone. 'I'm simply giving you a choice.'

'A choice?' She eyeballed him suspiciously. 'What sort of choice?'

His eyes gave nothing away as they held her gaze.

'I told you I wanted to see you again,' he said. 'Regularly.'

Ashleigh's heart began to gallop behind the wall of her chest. 'And I told you I can't…' She took a prickly breath.

'Howard and I...' She couldn't finish the sentence, the words sticking together in her tightened throat.

He gave her a cynical little smile that darkened his eyes even further. 'I don't think Howard Caule will protest at you spending time with me sorting this house out. In fact, I think he will send you off each day with his blessing.'

Cold fear leaked into her bloodstream and it took several precious seconds to locate her voice. 'W-what are you talking about?'

'I want you to spend the next month with me, sorting out my father's possessions.'

'I can't do that!' she squeaked in protest.

'Fine, then.' He reached for his mobile phone and began punching in some numbers. 'I'll call up another antiques dealer I know who will be more than happy to take this lot off me.' His finger was poised over the last digit as he added, 'For free.'

Ashleigh swallowed as he raised the phone to his ear.

He was giving the lot away? *For nothing?*

She couldn't allow him to do that. It wouldn't be right. The place was stacked to the rafters with priceless heirlooms. She owed Howard this deal for all he had done for her and Lachlan. She couldn't back out of it, no matter what it cost her personally.

'No!' She pulled his arm down so he couldn't continue the call. 'Wait... Let me think about this...'

He pocketed the phone. 'I'll give you thirty minutes to think it over. I should at this point make it quite clear that I'm not expecting you to sleep with me.'

She blinked at him, her tingling fingers falling away from his arm as his words sank in.

He didn't want her.

She knew she should be feeling relief but instead she felt

regret. An aching, burning regret that what they'd had before was now gone…

He continued in an even tone. 'We parted on such bitter terms four and a half years ago. This is a way for both of us to get some much needed closure.'

'But…but I don't need closure,' she insisted. 'I'm well and truly over you.'

He held her defiant look with enviable ease while her pulse leapt beneath her skin as she stood uncertainly before him.

'But I do,' he said.

Her mouth opened and closed but no sound came out.

Jake stepped back towards the door, holding it open as he addressed her in a coolly detached tone. 'I will leave you to make your initial assessment in private. When the thirty minutes are up I'll be back for your decision.'

Ashleigh stared at the back of the door once he'd closed it behind him, the echo of its lock clicking into place ringing in her ears for endless minutes.

A month!

A month in Jake's presence, sorting through the house he'd spent his childhood in.

She turned back around and stared at the fortune of goods in front of her, each and every one of them seeming to conceal a tale about Jake's past, their secrets locked within the walls of this old neglected house.

Why was he as good as throwing it all away? What possible reason could he have for doing so? Surely he would want to keep something back for himself? She knew he was a rich man now, but surely even very wealthy people didn't walk away from a veritable fortune?

Ashleigh sighed and turned, her eyes meeting those of the subject in the portrait on the wall. She felt a little feather of unease brush over her skin, for it seemed that every time she tried to move out of range of the oil-painted sad eyes they continued to follow her.

She gave herself a mental shake and rummaged in her bag for her digital camera. The sooner she got started the sooner she would be finished.

Her stomach gave a little flutter of nerves. There was something about this house that unsettled her and the less time she spent in it the better.

Especially with Jake here with her...

Alone...

CHAPTER THREE

ONCE she'd taken some preliminary photos Ashleigh left the overcrowded room for some much needed air and found herself wandering down the long passage, her thoughts flying off in all directions.

This was Jake's childhood home, the place where he had been raised, but for some reason it didn't seem to her to be the sort of house where a child would be particularly welcome.

This house seemed to be almost seeping with the wounds of neglect; the walls spoke of it with their faded peeling paint, the floorboards with their protesting creaks, as if her very tread had caused them discomfort as she moved across their tired surface. She could sense it in the woodwork of the furniture, the heavy layer of dust lying over every surface speaking of long-term disregard. And she could feel it in the reflection of the dust-speckled glass at the windows, the crumpled drape of the worn curtains looking as if they were doing their best to shield the house's secrets from the rest of the quiet conservative street.

Ashleigh had never considered herself a particularly intuitive person. That had been Ellie's role in the Forrester family, but somehow, being in Jake's childhood home made her realise things about him that had escaped her notice before.

He hated the darkness.

Why hadn't she ever noticed the significance of that before?

He had always been the first one to turn on the lights when they got home, insisting the blinds be pulled up even when the sunlight was too strong and disrupted the television or computer screen.

He'd hated loud music with a passion, particularly classical music. She couldn't remember a time when he hadn't come in and snapped her music off, glaring at her furiously, telling her it was too loud for the neighbours and why wasn't she being more responsible?

What did it all mean?

She opened another door off the hall and stepped inside. Some pinpricks of light were shining through the worn blinds, giving the room an eerie atmosphere, the dust motes disturbed by the movement of air as the door opened rising in front of her face like a myriad miniature apparitions.

The air was stuffy and close but she could see as she turned on the nearest light that it was some sort of study-cum-library, two banks of bookshelves lining the walls from floor to ceiling.

She moved across the old carpet to examine some of the titles, her eyes widening at the age of some of them nearest her line of vision.

Jake's father had sure known how to collect valuable items, she mused as she reached for what looked like a first edition of Keats's poems.

She put the book back amongst the others and turned to look around the rest of the room. The solid cedar desk was littered with papers as if someone working there had been interrupted and hadn't returned to put things in order. She picked up the document nearest her and found it was a financial statement from a firm of investors, the value of the portfolio making her head spin.

She heard a sound behind her and turned to see Jake standing in the frame of the door, his dark gaze trained on her.

Her time was up.

She put the paper back down on the desk, her mouth suddenly dry and uncooperative when there was so much she wanted to ask him before she committed herself to the task he had assigned her.

'Jake…I…I don't know what to say.' She waved a weak hand to encompass the contents of the room, the house and the sense of unease she'd felt as she'd moved through each part but not really knowing why.

'What's to say?' he said, moving into the room. 'My father died a very rich man.'

She gave a small frown as she recalled their conversation at his hotel the day before. 'I thought you intimated he left you nothing in his will?'

His eyes held hers for a brief moment before moving away. He wandered over to the big desk and, pulling out the throne-like chair, sat down, one ankle across his thigh, his hands going behind his head as he leaned backwards.

'He left me nothing I particularly wanted,' he answered.

Her teeth caught her bottom lip for a moment, her eyes falling away from the mysterious depths of his.

'But…we're not talking about a few old kitchen utensils and second-hand books here, Jake. This place is worth a fortune. The house itself on current market value would be enough to set anyone up for life, let alone the contents I've seen so far.'

'I'm not getting rid of the house, just what's inside it,' he informed her.

'You plan to live here?' She stared at him in surprise.

He unfolded his leg and stood up, his sudden increase in height making her feel small and vulnerable in the over-crowded space of the room.

'I have set up a branch of my company here in Sydney. I plan to spend half the year in England and the other half here.'

She moistened her mouth. 'But you told me earlier you've always hated this house.'

'I do.' He gave her another inscrutable look. 'But that's not to say it can't have a serious makeover and be the sort of home it should have been in the first place. I'm looking forward to doing it, actually.'

Ashleigh knew there was a wealth of information behind his words but she wasn't sure she was up to the task of asking him exactly what he meant. After all, hadn't he been the one who'd insisted on living in a low maintenance one-bedroom apartment when they had lived in London? Whatever was he going to do with a house this size, which looked as if it had at least ten bedrooms, several formal rooms, including a ballroom, not to mention an extensive front and back garden with a tennis court thrown in for good measure?

'It seems a bit…a bit big for a man who…' She let her words trail away when he moved towards her.

'For a man who what, Ashleigh?' he asked, picking up a strand of her shoulder-length hair and coiling it gently around his finger.

She swallowed as her scalp tingled at the gentle intimate tether of his finger in her hair, her heart missing a beat as his darker-than-night eyes secured hers.

'You're…you're a c-confirmed bachelor,' she reminded him, her tone far more breathy than she'd intended. 'No wife, no kids, no encumbrances, remember?'

His mouth lifted at one corner. 'You don't think it's possible for people to change a little over time?'

Her heart gave another hard thump as she considered the most likely possibilities for his change of heart.

Perhaps he'd met someone…someone who was so perfect

for him he couldn't bear to live without her and was prepared to have her on any terms, even marriage—the formal state he had avoided so determinedly in the past.

She couldn't get the question past the blockage in her throat, but her mind tortured her by conjuring up an image of him standing at an altar with a beautiful bride stepping slowly towards him, his eyes alight with desire as the faceless woman drifted closer and closer to finally take his outstretched hand…

Jake uncoiled her hair but didn't move away.

Ashleigh tried to step backwards but her back and shoulders came up against the solid frame of the bookshelves. The old books shuffled on their shelves behind her and, imagining them about to tumble down all over her, she carefully edged away a fraction, but it brought her too close to Jake.

Way too close.

'W-what's…what's changed your mind?' she asked, surprised her voice came out sounding almost normal considering she couldn't inflate her lungs properly.

He stepped away from her and, picking up an old gold pen off the desk, began to twirl it in his fingers, his face averted from hers. It seemed to Ashleigh a very long time before he spoke.

'I have spent some time since my father's death thinking about my life. I want to make some changes now, changes I just wasn't ready to face before.' He put the pen down and faced her, his mouth twisted in a little rueful smile. 'It might sound strange to you, but you're the first person I've trusted enough to tell this to.'

Ashleigh felt her guilt claw at her insides with accusing fingers, sure if he looked too closely he would see the evidence of her betrayal splashed over her features.

She had kept from him the birth of his son.

What sort of trustworthiness had that demonstrated?

Jake turned away again as he continued heavily, 'But four

and a half years ago I just wasn't ready.' He raked a hand through his hair. 'I guess I'm only doing it now because my father is dead and buried.' He gave a humourless grunt of laughter and looked back at her. 'It's that closure I spoke of earlier.'

'So…' she ran her tongue over her desert-dry mouth '…have you changed your mind about…marriage?'

'I have given it some considerable thought,' he admitted, his eyes giving nothing away.

'What about the…the other things you were always so adamant about?' At his enquiring look she added, 'Kids, pets, that sort of thing.'

She picked up the faint sound of his breath being released as he turned to look out of the window over the huge back garden, the solid wall of his tall muscled frame instantly reminding her of an impenetrable fortress.

'No,' he said, reverting to the same flat emotionless tone he'd used earlier. 'I haven't changed my mind about that. I don't want children. Ever.'

Ashleigh felt the full force of his words as if he had punched them right through the tender flesh of her belly where his child had been curled for nine months. She hadn't realised how much she had hoped for a different answer until he'd given the one she'd most dreaded.

He didn't want children.

He *never* wanted children.

How could she tell him about his little son now?

Jake turned round to look at her. 'Have you decided to take me up on my offer, Ashleigh?' he asked.

'I—I need more time…'

'Sorry.' The hard glance he sent her held no trace of apology. 'Take it or leave it. If you want to have this stuff then you'll have to fulfil my terms. A month working nine to five in this house—alongside me.'

Panic set up an entire percussion section in Ashleigh's chest, the sickening thuds making her feel faint and the palms of her hands sticky with sweat.

'I—I don't usually work nine to five,' she said, avoiding his eyes.

'Oh, really?' There was a hint of surprise in his tone. 'Why ever not?'

'Howard doesn't like the thought of me working full-time,' she said, pleased with her response as it was as close to the truth as she could get.

'And you agreed to that?'

'I…' She lifted her chin a fraction. 'Yes. It frees me to do… other things.'

'What other things do you like doing?'

Ashleigh knew she had backed herself into a tight corner and the only way out of it was to lie. She averted her gaze once more and inspected a figurine near her with avid intent. 'I go to the gym.'

'The gym?' His tone was nothing short of incredulous.

Her chin went a bit higher as she met his eyes again. 'What are you saying, Jake? That I look unfit as well as fat?'

He held up his hands in a gesture of surrender. 'Hey, did I ever say you were fat?'

She threw him a resentful look and folded her arms across her chest. 'Yesterday when we met you said I'd put on weight. In my book that means you think I'm fat.'

She heard him mutter an expletive under his breath.

'I think you look fabulous.' His dark gaze swept over her, stalling a little too long for her comfort on the up-thrust of her breasts. 'You were a girl before, barely out of your teens. Now you're a woman. A sexy gorgeous-looking woman.'

Who has given birth to your son, Ashleigh wanted to add, but knew she couldn't.

Would she ever be able to?

'Thank you,' she mumbled grudgingly and looked away.

Jake gave an inward sigh.

He'd almost forgotten how sensitive she was. Her feelings had always seemed to him to be lying on the surface of her skin, not buried deep inside and out of reach as his mostly were.

But the Ashleigh he'd known in the past was certainly no gym junkie. Her idea of exercise had never been more than a leisurely walk, stopping every chance she could to smell any flowers that were hanging over the fence. It had driven him nuts at times. He needed the challenge of hard muscle-biting endurance exercise to keep his mind off the pain of things he didn't want to think about.

He still needed it.

'I'm prepared to negotiate on the hours you work,' he inserted into the silence.

Her head came up and he saw the relief in her blue eyes as they met his. 'Is…is ten to four all right?' she asked.

He pretended to think about it for a moment.

She shifted uncomfortably under his scrutiny and he wondered why she felt so ill at ease in his company. He'd expected a bit of residual anger, maybe even a good portion of bitterness, but not this outright nervousness. She was like a rabbit cornered in a yard full of ready-to-race greyhounds, her eyes skittering away from his, her small hands fluttering from time to time as if she didn't quite know what to do with them.

'Ten to four will be fine,' he said. 'Do you want me to pick you up each day?'

'*No!*'

One of his brows went upwards at her vehement response.

Ashleigh lowered her eyes and looked down at the twisting knot of her hands. 'I—I mean that won't be necessary. Besides—' she gave him a little speaking glance '—Howard wouldn't like that.'

'And what Howard wouldn't like good little Ashleigh wouldn't dream of doing, right?' he asked without bothering to disguise the full measure of scorn in his tone.

She clamped her lips shut, refusing to dignify his question with an answer.

'For Christ's sake, Ashleigh,' he said roughly. 'Can't you see he's all wrong for you?'

'Wrong?' She glared at him in sudden anger. 'How can you say that? It was you who was so wrong for me!'

'I wasn't wrong for you; I just—'

'You *were* wrong for me!' She threw the words at him heatedly. 'You ruined my life! You crushed my confidence and berated everything I held as important. I was your stupid plaything, something to pass the time with.'

'That's not true.' His voice was stripped of all emotion.

Ashleigh shut her eyes for a moment to hold back the threatening tears. She drew in a ragged breath and, opening her eyes again, sent him a glittering look. 'God damn you, Jake. How can you stand there and say Howard is all wrong for me when at least I can be myself with him? I could never be myself with you. You would never allow it.'

Jake found it hard to hold her accusing glare, his gut clenching at the vitriol in her words. As much as he hated admitting it, she was very probably right. He wasn't proud of how he had treated her in the past. He'd been insensitive and too overly protective of his own interests to take the time to truly consider hers.

The truth was she had threatened him from the word go.

He had always avoided the virginal, looking for hearth-home-and-cute hound-thrown-in types. He'd shied away from any form of commitment in relationships; the very fact that he'd let his guard down enough to allow her to move in with him demonstrated how much she had burrowed beneath his skin.

Her innocence had shocked him.

He had taken her roughly, their combined passion so strong and out of control he hadn't given a single thought to the possibility that it might have been her first time.

He'd hurt her and yet she hadn't cried. Instead she'd hugged him close and promised it would be better next time.

And it had been.

In fact, making love with Ashleigh had been an experience he was never likely to forget. She had given so freely of herself, the passion he'd awakened in her continually taking him by surprise. No one he'd been with since—and there had been many—had ever touched him quite the way she had touched him. Ashleigh had reached in with those small soft hands of hers to deep inside him where no one had ever been before. Sometimes, if he allowed himself, he could still feel where her gentle stroking fingertips had brushed along the torn edges of his soul.

'Ashleigh…' His voice sounded unfamiliar even to his own ears. He cleared his throat and continued. 'Can we just forget about the past and only deal with the here and now?'

Ashleigh brushed at her eyes with an angry gesture of her hand, hoping he wouldn't see how undone she really was. How could she possibly pretend the past hadn't happened when she had Lachlan to show for it?

'Why are you doing this?' she asked. 'What can you possibly hope to achieve by insisting I do this assessment for you? You say you don't want the money all this stuff is worth…' She drew in a scalding breath as her eyes scanned the goods in front of her before turning back to meet his steady gaze, her voice coming out a little unevenly. 'What exactly do you want?'

'This house is full of ghosts,' he said. 'I want you to help me get rid of them.'

She moistened her bone-dry lips. 'Why me?'

'I have my reasons,' he answered, his eyes telling her none of them.

Her gaze wavered on his for a long moment. This was all wrong. She couldn't help Jake deal with whatever issues he carried from his past. How could she when she had the most devastating secret of all, that at some point he would have to hear?

But he needs you, another voice inside her head insisted.

How could she turn away from the one man she had loved with all of her being? Surely she owed him this short period of time so he could achieve the closure he had spoken of earlier.

It was a risk she had to take. Spending any amount of time with Jake was courting trouble but as long as she stood her ground she would be fine.

She *had* to be fine.

'I think we need some ground rules then,' she said, attempting to be firm but falling well short of the mark.

'Rules?'

'Rules, Jake.' She sent him a reproachful look. 'Those moral parameters that all decent people live by.'

'All right, run them by me,' he said, the edge of his mouth lifted in a derisory smile.

She forced her shoulders back and met his gaze determinedly. 'There's to be no touching, for a start.'

'Fine by me.' He thrust his hands in his jeans pockets as if to remove the temptation right there and then.

Ashleigh had to drag her eyes away from the stretch of denim over his hands. 'And that includes kissing, of course,' she added somewhat primly.

He moistened his lips with his tongue as if removing the taste of her from his mouth. 'Of course.'

She straightened her spine, fighting to remain cool under that dark gaze as it ran over her. 'And none of those looks.'

'Which looks?' he asked, looking.

She set her mouth. *'That* look.'

'This look?' He pointed to his face, his expression all innocence.

She crossed her arms. 'You know exactly what I mean, Jake Marriott. You keep undressing me with your eyes.'

'I do?'

He did innocence far too well, she thought, but she could see the hunger reflected in his gaze and no way was she going to fuel it.

'You know you do and it has to stop. *Now.*'

He sent her one of his megawatt lazy smiles. 'If you say so.'

'I say so.'

He shifted his tongue inside his cheek for a moment. 'Are you done with your little rules?'

She gave him a schoolmarm look from down the delicate length of her nose. 'Yes. I think that just about covers it.'

'You want to hear my rules now?' he asked after a tiny heart-tripping pause.

Ashleigh gave a covert swallow and met his eyes with as much equanimity as she could muster. 'All right. If you must.'

'Good.'

Another little silence coiled around them.

Ashleigh didn't know where to look. For some strange reason, she wanted to do exactly what she'd just forbidden him to do.

She wanted to feast her eyes on his form.

She wanted to run her gaze over all the hot spots of his body, the hot spots she had set alight with her hands and mouth in the past.

She could almost hear the sound of his grunting pleasure in the silence throbbing between them, could almost feel the weight of him on her smaller frame as he pinned her beneath him.

She could almost feel the pulse of his spilling body between her legs, the essence of himself he had released at the moment of ecstasy, the full force of his desire tugging at her flesh both inside and out.

She forced herself to meet his coal-black gaze, her stomach instantly unravelling as she felt the heat coming off him towards her in searing scorching waves.

'I promise not to touch, kiss or even look if you promise to refrain from doing the same,' he stated.

I can do that, she thought. *I can be strong.*

I *have* to be strong.

'Not a problem,' she answered evenly. 'I have no interest in complicating things by revisiting our past relationship.'

'Fine. We'll start Monday at ten.' He took his hands out of his pockets and reached for a set of keys in the drawer of the desk and held them out to her like a lure.

'These are the keys to the house in case you get here before me,' he said.

She slowly reached out her opened palm and he dropped them into it.

'See? No touching.' He grinned down at her disarmingly.

She put the keys in her bag and straightened the strap on her shoulder to avoid his wry look. 'So far,' she muttered and turned towards the door.

'Ashleigh?'

She took an unsteady breath and turned back to face him. 'Yes?'

He held out the blood-red rose he'd picked for her earlier, the soft petals deprived of water for so long, already starting to wilt in thirst.

'You forgot this,' he said.

She found herself taking the four steps back to him to get her faded bloom, her fingers so meticulously avoiding his that she encountered a sharp thorn on the stem of the rose instead.

'Ouch!' She looked at the bright blood on her fingertip and began rummaging in her bag for a tissue, but before she could locate one Jake's hand came over hers and brought it slowly but inexorably up to his mouth.

She sucked in a tight little breath as he supped at the tiny pool of blood on her fingertip, her legs weakening as his eyes meshed with hers.

'Y-you promised…no t-touching…' she reminded him breathlessly but, for some inexplicable reason, didn't pull her finger out of his mouth.

She felt the slight rasp of his salving tongue, felt too the full thrust of her desire as it burst between her legs in hot liquid longing.

'I know.' He released her hand and stepped back from her. 'But you'll forgive me this once, won't you?'

She didn't answer.

Instead she turned on her heel and flew out the door and out of the house as if all the ghosts contained within were after her blood.

And not just one tiny little pin drop of it…

CHAPTER FOUR

LACHLAN flew out of the crèche playroom to greet her. 'Mummy! Guess what I did today?'

Ashleigh pressed a soft kiss to the top of his dark head and held him close for longer than normal, breathing in his small child smell. 'What did you do, my precious?'

He tugged on her hand and pulled her towards the painting room. 'I drewed a picture,' he announced proudly.

Ashleigh smiled and for once didn't correct his infant grammar. He would be four in a couple of months—plenty of time ahead to teach him. For now she wanted to treasure each and every moment of his toddlerhood.

It would all too soon be over.

'See?' He pressed a paint-splattered rectangle of paper into her hands.

She looked down at the stick-like figures he'd painted. 'Who's this?' she asked, bending down so she was on a level with him.

His chocolate-brown eyes met hers. 'That's Granny and Grandad.'

'And this one?' She pointed to another figure, who appeared to be doing some sort of dance.

'That's Auntie Mia,' he said.

I should have guessed that, Ashleigh thought wryly. Mia

was the Forrester fitness fanatic and was never still for a moment.

'And this one?' She knew who it was without asking. The dog-like drawing beside the blonde-haired human figure was a dead give-away but she wanted to extend his pleasure in showing off his work.

'That's Auntie Ellie.' He pointed to the yellow hair he'd painted. 'And that's one of the dogs she's wescued.'

Ashleigh's eyes centred on the last remaining figure who was standing behind all the others.

'Who is that?' she asked, not sure she really wanted to know.

'That's you,' he said, a touch of sadness creeping into his tone.

She swallowed the lump in the back of her throat and stared down at the picture. 'Really?'

'Yes.' He met her eyes with a look so like his father's she felt like crying.

'Why am I way back there?' She pointed to the background of his painting.

His eyes shifted away from hers, his small shoulders slumping as a small sigh escaped from his lips. 'I miss you, Mummy.'

'Oh, baby.' She clutched him to her chest, burying her head into the baby-shampoo softness of his hair, her eyes squeezing shut to hold the tears back. 'Mummy has to work, you know that, darling.' She eased him away from her and looked down into his up-tilted face. 'Aren't you happy at crèche and at the times you have with Granny and Grandad?'

His little chin wobbled for a moment before he got it under control. 'Yes…'

Ashleigh's stomach folded as she saw the insecurity played out on his features. Hadn't she seen that same look on Jake's face in the past, even though, like Lachlan, he had done his level best to hide it?

'I have to work, poppet,' she said. 'I have to provide for us. I can't expect Granny and Grandad to help us for ever.'

'But what about my daddy?' Lachlan asked. 'Doesn't he want to provide for me too?'

I will kill you, Mia, so help me God, she said under her breath. This was surely her sister's doing, for Lachlan had never mentioned anything about his father in the past.

'He doesn't know about you,' she said, deciding the truth was safer in the long run.

'Why not?'

She couldn't meet his eyes.

Was this how it was going to be for the rest of her life, guilt keeping her from looking at eyes that were the mirror image of his father's?

'I couldn't tell him…' she said at last.

'Why not, Mummy?'

She closed her eyes and counted to five before opening them again. 'Because he never wanted to be a daddy.'

'But I *want* a daddy,' he said, his big dark eyes tugging at Ashleigh's heartstrings. 'Do you think if I met him and asked him he would change his mind?'

She looked down at the tiny up-tilted face and smiled in spite of her pain. 'I just know he would. But you can't meet him, sweetie.'

'Why?'

She hugged him close, not sure how to answer.

'Mummy?'

'Mmm?' She bit the inside of her cheek to stop herself from falling apart.

'I still love my daddy even if he doesn't want to see me,' he said solemnly.

Ashleigh felt as if someone had just stomped on her heart.

* * *

Howard couldn't contain his delight at her decision to take on the assessment.

'You mean he wants to give us the whole lot?' he asked incredulously. *'For nothing?'*

She nodded, her expression unmistakably grim. 'That's the deal.'

'But on market value the whole load is probably worth…' He did a quick mental calculation from the notes Ashleigh had already prepared. 'Close to a couple of million, at the very least!'

'I know…' Her stomach tightened another notch. 'But he doesn't want any of it.'

'He's mad,' Howard said. 'Totally out of his mind, stark staring mad.'

Ashleigh didn't answer. She didn't think Jake was mad, just being incredibly tactical.

Howard frowned for a moment. 'Does he…' he cleared his throat as if even harbouring the thought offended him '…does he want something in exchange, apart from you working in the house to document everything?'

'What do you mean?' Ashleigh hoped her cheeks weren't as hot on the outside as they felt to her on the inside.

'Some men can be quite…er…ruthless at times, Ashleigh, in getting what they want,' he said. 'No one but no one gives away a fortune of goods without wanting something in return.'

'He doesn't want to sleep with me, if that's what's worrying you,' she said, wondering why it had hurt to say it out loud.

'He told you that?' Howard's red brows rose.

She nodded.

He let out a sigh of relief. 'You are doing me the biggest favour imaginable, Ashleigh.' He took her hands and squeezed them in his. 'This will secure our future. We can get married in grand style and never have to worry about making ends meet again. Think of it!' His face glowed with delight at this stroke of good fortune. 'My mother is thrilled. She wants you to come to dinner this evening to celebrate with us.'

Ashleigh felt like rolling her eyes. The one sticking point in her relationship with Howard, apart from his deeply ingrained conservatism, was his mother. No matter how hard she tried, she just did not like Marguerite Caule.

'I need to spend time with Lachlan,' she said carefully, removing her hands from his hold. 'He's been missing me lately.'

'Bring him with you,' Howard suggested. 'You know how much my mother enjoys seeing him.'

Seeing him, but not hearing him, Ashleigh added under her breath. Marguerite was definitely from the old school of child-rearing: children were to be seen not heard, and if it could possibly be avoided without direct insult, not interacted with at all.

'Maybe some other time,' she said, avoiding his pleading look. 'I have a lot on my mind just now.'

She heard him sigh.

'Is this all too much for you?' he asked. 'Do you want me to call Jake Marriott and pull out on the deal? I know it's a lot of money but if you aren't up to it then I won't force you.'

Ashleigh turned to look at him, privately moved by his concern. He was such a lovely person, no hint of malice about him. He loved Lachlan and he loved her.

Why, oh, why, couldn't she love him in return?

He had so much to lose on this. His business hung in the balance. It was up to her to save it. She couldn't walk away from Jake's deal without hurting Howard, and hurting him was the last thing she wanted to do.

Besides, it *was* a lot of money to throw away. How could

she live with herself if she turned her back on Jake's offer, no matter what motive had precipitated it?

'No…' She picked up her bag and keys resignedly. 'I'm going to see this through. I think Jake is right.' She gave a rough-edged sigh. 'I need closure.'

'Good luck.'

She gave him a rueful look as she reached for the door. 'Luck has been in short supply in my life. I hardly see it changing any time soon.'

'Don't worry, Ashleigh,' Howard reassured her. 'He's given you the opportunity of a lifetime. Don't let your past relationship with him get in the way of your future with me.'

Ashleigh found it hard to think of an answer. Instead she sent him a vague smile and left the showroom, somehow sensing that her future was always going to be inextricably linked with Jake.

Even if by some miracle he never found out about Lachlan.

The house and grounds were deserted when Ashleigh arrived. Jake's car was nowhere in sight and, although most of the blinds at the windows hadn't been pulled completely down, the house still gave off a deserted, abandoned look.

She walked up the cracked pathway to the front door, feeling as if she was stepping over an invisible barrier into the privacy of Jake's past.

She rang the doorbell just in case, but there was no answer. She listened as the bell echoed down the hall like an aching cry of loneliness, the sound bouncing off the walls and coming back to her as if to taunt her. She put the key into the lock and turned it, the door opening under her hand with a groan of protest.

At least it didn't smell as musty as before.

The movement of air in the hall indicated that Jake had left a window open and she couldn't help a soft sigh of remembrance. Hadn't he always insisted on sleeping with at least one window open, even when it had been freezing cold outside?

She wandered from room to room, taking a host of pictures with a digital camera, stopping occasionally to carefully document notes on the various pieces, her fingers flying over the notebook in her hand as she detailed the estimated date and value of each item.

As treasure troves went, this was one of the biggest she'd ever encountered. Priceless piece after priceless piece was noted on her list, her estimation growing by the minute. Howard's business would be lifted out of trouble once these babies hit the showroom floor.

She lifted the hair out of the back of her top and rolled her stiff shoulders as she finished the first room. She glanced at her watch and saw it was now well after twelve. Two hours had gone past and still no sign of Jake.

Deciding to take a break, she left her notebook and pen on a side table and wandered through to the kitchen at the back of the house.

It wasn't the sort of kitchen in which she felt comfortable. It was dark and old-fashioned, the appliances so out of date she wondered if they were still operational.

She picked up a lonesome cup that someone, she presumed Jake's father, had left on the kitchen sink. It was heavily stained with the tannin of tea, the chipped edge seeming out of place in a house so full of wealth. She ran her fingertip over the rough edge thoughtfully, wondering what sort of man Jake's father had been.

Ashleigh realised with a little jolt that she had never seen a picture of either of his parents, had never even been informed of their Christian names.

She thought of the stack of family albums her mother had lovingly put together. Every detail of family life was framed with openly adoring comments. There were shiny locks of hair and even tiny pearly baby teeth.

What had Jake's parents looked like? She hadn't a clue and yet their blood was surging through her son's veins.

'I'm sorry I'm so late,' Jake said from just behind her.

Ashleigh swung around, surprise beating its startled wings inside her chest. 'I wish you would stop doing that,' she said, clutching at her leaping throat.

'Do what?' He looked at her blankly.

She lowered her hand and gave herself a mental shake. 'You should announce your arrival a bit more audibly. I hate being sneaked up on like that.'

'I did not sneak up on you,' he said. 'I called out to you three times but you didn't answer.'

She bit her lip, wondering if what he said was true. It was certainly possible given that her thoughts had been located well in the past, but it still made her feel uncomfortable that he could slip through her firewall of defences undetected.

She put the cup she'd been holding down and turned away from his probing gaze. 'I've almost finished assessing one room.'

'And?'

Her eyes reluctantly came back to his. 'Your father certainly knew what he was doing when it came to collecting antiques.'

He gave a humourless smile. 'My father was an expert at many things.'

Again she sensed the wealth of information behind the coolly delivered statement.

'Would it help to…to talk about it?' she asked, somewhat tentatively.

His eyes hardened beneath his frowning brow. 'About what?'

'About your childhood.'

He swung away from her as if she'd slapped him. 'No, not right now.'

She bit her lip, not sure if she should push him. A part of her wanted to. She ached to know what had made him the man he was, but another part of her warned her to let well alone. His barriers were up again. She could see it in the tense line of his jaw and the way his eyes moved away from hers as if he was determined to shut her out.

'Which room would you like me to work on next?' She opted for a complete change of subject.

He gave a dismissive shrug and shoved at a dirty plate on the work table in front of him as if it had personally offended him.

'I don't care. You choose.'

'Which room was your bedroom?' she asked before she could stop herself.

She saw the way his shoulders stiffened, the rigidity of his stance warning her she had come just a little too close for comfort.

'I don't want you to go in there,' he said. 'The door is locked and it will stay that way. Understood?'

She forced herself to hold his glittering glare. 'If that's what you want.'

He gave her one diamond-hard look and moved past her to leave the room. 'I will be in the back garden. I have some digging to do.'

She sighed as the door snapped shut behind him.

What had she taken on?

It was well after three p.m. when she decided she needed a break. She had nibbled on a few crackers she'd brought with her and had a glass of water earlier, but her eyes were watering from all the dust she'd disturbed as she itemised the contents of the largest formal room.

She went out the back door, her eyes automatically searching the garden for Jake as she sat down on one of the steps, stretching her legs out to catch the sun.

He was down in the far corner, his back and chest bare as he dug up the ground beneath the shade of the elm tree. She saw the way his toned muscles bunched with each strike of the spade in the resisting earth, the fine layer of perspiration making his skin gleam in the warm spring sunshine.

He stopped and, leaning on the spade, wiped a hand across his sweaty brow, his eyes suddenly catching sight of her watching him.

He straightened and, stabbing the spade into the ground, walked towards her, wiping his hands on the sides of his jeans.

From her seated position on the back step she had to crane her neck to look up at him. 'That looks like hard work,' she said. 'Do you want me to get you a glass of water?'

He shook his head. 'I drank from the tap a while ago.'

She lowered her gaze, then wished she hadn't as she encountered the zipper of his jeans. She jerked upright off the step but her sandal caught in the old wire shoe-scraper and she pitched forwards.

Jake caught her easily, hauling her upright, his hands on her upper arms almost painfully firm.

'Are you OK?'

'I—I'm fine…' She tried to ease herself out of his hold but he countered it with a subtle tightening of his fingers.

She had no choice but to meet his eyes. 'You can let me go now, Jake.'

Tiny beads of perspiration were peppered over his upper lip, a dark smudge of soil slashed across the lean line of his jaw giving him an almost primitive look. Gone was the high-powered architect who had offices in several major cities of the world; in his place was a man who smelt of hard physical work and fitness, his chest so slick with sweat she wanted to press her mouth to his skin and taste his saltiness.

His hands dropped away from her and he stepped backwards. 'I've made you dirty,' he said without apology.

She glanced at each of her arms, her stomach doing a funny little tumble turn when she saw the full set of his earthy fingerprints on the creamy skin of her bare upper arms.

'It's all right,' she said. 'At least I wasn't wearing the jacket. I left it inside it was so…so hot…'

His eyes ran over her neat skirt and matching camisole and she wished she hadn't spoken. She could feel the weight of his gaze as it took in her shadowed cleavage, a cleavage she hadn't had four and a half years ago.

'I'd better get back to work…' she said, waving a hand at the house behind her, her feet searching blindly for the steps. 'There's still so…so much to do and I need to leave on time.'

'If you want to leave early, that's fine,' he said, narrowing his eyes against the sun as he looked back over the garden. 'I'm just about finished for the day myself.'

Ashleigh hovered on the first step. 'What are you going to plant in that garden bed you're digging?'

It seemed an age before his gaze turned back to meet hers, his eyes so dark and intense she felt the breath trip somewhere in the middle of her throat.

'I'm not going to plant anything.'

A nervous hand fluttered up to her neck, her fingers holding the fine silver chain hanging there, her expression clouded with confusion. 'Then what are you digging for?'

His mouth tilted into one of his humourless smiles.

'Memories, Ashleigh,' he said, his tone deep and husky. 'I'm digging for memories.'

Ashleigh watched him, her eyes taking in the angles and planes of his face, wondering what was going on behind the screen of his inscrutable gaze.

He'd always been so adept at concealing his true feelings; it had both frustrated and fascinated her in the past. She knew his aloofness was part of what fed her lingering attraction for him. She felt ashamed of how she felt, especially given her commitment to Howard, but every time she was in Jake's presence she felt the pull of something indefinable, as if he had set up a special radar to keep her tuned in to him, only him. She felt the waves of connection each time his gaze meshed with hers, the full charge zapping her whenever he touched her. His kiss had burnt her so much she was sure if it were to be repeated she would never have the strength to pull away. It wouldn't matter how committed she was elsewhere, when Jake Marriott's mouth came down on hers everyone else ceased to exist.

'You're breaking rule number three,' Jake's voice cut through her private rumination. 'No looks, remember?'

She dragged her eyes away from the amused line of his mouth and met his eyes, her cheeks heating from the inside like a stoked furnace.

'I wasn't *looking*, I was thinking,' she insisted.

'One wonders what was going on in that pretty little head of yours to make you blush so delightfully,' he mused.

'I'm not blushing!' She flung her hair back with a defiant toss of one hand. 'It's hot. You know how I can't stand the heat. You always said I…' She stopped speaking before she trawled up too many dangerous memories. She didn't want him thinking she had stored away every single word he'd ever spoken to her.

'I always said what?'

'Nothing; I can't remember.' She carefully avoided his eyes. 'It was all such a long time ago.'

'Four years is not such a long time.'

'Four and a half,' she said, meeting his eyes with gritty determination. 'Time to move on, don't you think?'

'That's why we're here,' he said. 'So we can both move on.'

'Then let's get on with it,' she suggested and turned towards the house.

'Ashleigh.'

She sent her eyes heavenward with a silent prayer for strength as she turned to look back at him. Because she was on the top step he was now at eye level. This close she could see the curling fringe of his sooty lashes, could even feel the movement of air against her lips when he let out a small breath. Her stomach muscles tightened, her legs going to water at his physical proximity. She had only to tilt her body a mere fraction and she would be touching him.

No touching, she reminded herself firmly.

Rule number one.

Her gaze dipped to the curve of his mouth and she mentally chanted rule number two, over and over again. *No kissing, no kissing, no kissing, no—*

'I want to visit your family,' Jake said, startling her out of her chant. 'I was thinking about coming over this evening.'

'What?' She choked. 'W-whatever for?'

He gave her a long studied look, taking in her flustered features and fluttering nervous hands.

Ashleigh fought her panic under some semblance of control as her mind whirled with a list of possible excuses for putting him off. She straightened her shoulders, controlled her hands by tying them together and forced herself to meet his eyes.

'We're all busy,' she said. 'No one's going to be home.'

'Tomorrow will do just as well.'

'That's no good either,' she said quickly—far too quickly.

He gave her a sceptical look. 'What happened to the happy-to-be-at-home-altogether-every-night Forrester family? I thought your family's idea of a big night out was once a month to the cinema.'

She set her mouth, knowing he was mocking the stable security of her family. 'My parents have regular evenings out and so do my sisters,' she said, not bothering to hide the defensiveness in her tone. 'Anyway, I will be out with Howard.'

'I don't need you to be there,' he said.

No, but if he were to see even a single toy of Lachlan's lying about the house he would begin to ask questions she wasn't prepared to answer. Not to mention all the photographs arranged on just about every surface and wall by her overly sentimental mother. She'd been lucky the first time when he'd called in unexpectedly but she could hardly strip the house of everything with Lachlan's name or face on it.

'All the same, I don't think it's such a good idea.' She bit her lip momentarily as she hunted her brain for a reasonable excuse. 'My parents are…very loyal and since we…I mean… you and I parted on such bitter terms they might not be all that open to seeing you now.'

'Your mother was fine with me the other day,' he said. 'Admittedly she didn't ask me in for tea and scones, but she was openly friendly and interested in how I was doing.'

I will throttle you, Mum, for being so damned nice all the time, she silently vowed.

'I don't think Howard would like the thought of you fraternising with my family,' she put in desperately.

The cynical smirk reappeared at the mention of her fiancé's name.

'We don't have to tell Howard,' he said, adding conspiratorially with the wink of one dark glittering eye, 'it can be our little secret.'

Ashleigh was already sick to death of secrets, her one and only one had caused enough anguish to last a lifetime. She felt as if her heart hadn't had a normal rhythm in days and even now her head was constantly pounding with the tension of trying to avoid a vocal slip in Jake's presence.

'I'd rather not do anything behind Howard's back,' she said.

'Good little Ashleigh,' he drawled with unmistakable mockery.

She ground her teeth and wished she could slap that insolent look off his face, but she knew if she did all three rules would end up being broken right there and then where they stood on the back door steps.

She straightened her spine, speaking through tight lips. 'I'll arrange a meeting for you with my family on neutral ground. A restaurant or something like that some time next week or the one after.'

He inclined his head at her in a gesture of old-world politeness. 'If you insist.'

'I do.'

'Why don't you and Howard join the party?' he suggested.

'I don't think so.'

He gave a soft chuckle of laughter. 'Why? Would he be frightened he might have to foot the bill?'

She sent him an arctic glare. 'Howard is a hard-working man. Sure, he doesn't have the sort of money that you do to throw around, but at least he is honest and up-front.'

'What are you implying? That I came by my fortune by less than honest means?' His eyes were hard as they lasered hers.

'How did you do it, Jake?' she asked. 'When we were living in London you hardly had a penny to your name.'

'I worked hard and had some lucky breaks,' he said. 'No shady deals, so you can take that look of disapproval off your face right now.'

'From living in squalor to billionaire in four and a half years?' she gave him a disbelieving look. 'You should write one of those how-to-be-successful books.'

'I didn't exactly live in squalor,' he said.

'No, not after I moved in and did all your housework for

you,' she bit out resentfully. 'How delightfully convenient for you, a housekeeper and lover all rolled into one.'

Ashleigh felt his continued silence as if it were crawling all the way up her spine to lift the fine hairs on the back of her neck.

She knew she was cornered. Her back was already up against the closed door behind her and his tall frame in front of her blocked any other chance of escape.

She could feel the air separating them pulsing with banked up emotions. Dangerous emotions, emotions that hadn't been unleashed in a very long time…

CHAPTER FIVE

ASHLEIGH could feel the weight of his dark gaze on her mouth, the sensitive skin of her lips lifting, swelling as if in search of the hard pressure of his, her heart fluttering behind her ribcage as his head came even closer.

'Don't even think about it...' she cautioned him, her voice a cracked whisper of sound as it passed through her tight throat.

His lips curved just above hers, hovering tantalisingly close, near enough to feel the brush of his warm breath as he asked, 'Is that to be another one of your little rules?'

She moistened her lips nervously. 'Yes...' She cleared her throat. 'Rule number four: don't think about me in that way.'

'How do you know what way I'm thinking about you?' His dark eyes gleamed with mystery.

'You're still a full-blooded man, aren't you?' she asked with considerable tartness. 'Or is that another one of those changes you insist you've undergone in the last four and a half years?'

He had timed silences down to a science, Ashleigh thought. He used them so tactically. She had forgotten just how tactically.

She held her breath, waiting for him to say something, her head getting lighter and lighter as each pulsing second passed.

'Want to check for yourself?' he finally asked.

'What?' Her indrawn breath half-inflated her lungs and her head swam alarmingly as his meaning gradually dawned on her.

He pointed to his groin, her eyes following the movement of his hand as if they had a mind of their own.

'You're the expert assessor. Why don't you head south to check out if the crown jewels are still in mint condition?'

Her eyes flew back to his in a flash of anger. 'This is all a big game to you, isn't it, Jake? You think this is so funny with your stupid double meanings and sexual hints.' She sucked in a much needed breath and continued, 'I'm not interested. Got that? Not in-ter-est-ed. Do I have to spell it out for you? Why can't you hear what I'm telling you?'

'There seems to be some interference from the transmission centre,' he said.

'Transmiss...' She rolled her eyes. 'Oh, for God's sake! Is your ego so gargantuan that you can't accept that what we had is over?'

'It would be a whole lot easier to accept if you didn't look at me with those hungry eyes of yours,' he said.

'Hungry eyes?' She gaped at him in affront. 'You're the one with the wandering eyes!'

'I said hungry, not wandering.'

'Don't split hairs with me!' she spat back. 'And back off a bit, will you?' She leant back even further against the door behind her until the door handle began to dig into the tender flesh of her lower back. 'I can practically see what you had for breakfast.'

'I didn't have breakfast.'

'Do you think I care?' she asked.

He gave her one of his lengthy contemplative looks. Ashleigh could feel herself dissolving under his scrutiny. She felt as if he could see through her skin to where her heart was beating erratically in response to his closeness.

'See?' He held up his hands as if he'd just read her mind. 'I'm not touching you.'

'You don't have to; just being close to you is enough to—' She clamped her wayward mouth shut and sent him another furious glare.

'Is enough to what, Ashleigh?' he asked, his deep voice like a length of sun-warmed silk being passed over too sensitive skin.

She refused to answer, tightening her mouth even further.

'Tempt you?' he prompted.

'I'm not the least bit tempted,' she said, wishing to God it was true.

'That's what the rules are for, aren't they, Ashleigh?' he taunted her softly. 'They're not for me at all. They're for you, to remind you of your commitment to dear old Howard.'

'He is not old!' she put in defensively. 'He's younger than you. He's thirty and you're thirty-three.'

'How very sweet of you to remember how old I am.'

Damn! She chided herself. She hadn't seen that coming and had fallen straight into it.

'If you don't mind I'd like to get on with what I'm supposed to be doing,' she said, hitching up her chin.

He stepped down a step and her breath whooshed out in relief. He didn't speak, but simply turned away to stride down to the back of the garden to the spade he'd dug into the earth under the elm, lifting it out of the ground and resuming his digging as if the last few minutes hadn't occurred.

Ashleigh tore her eyes away from the sculptured contours of his muscles and, wrenching open the back door, hurried inside where, for once, the dark lurking shadows of the house didn't seem quite so threatening.

Her father was the first person she saw when she got home that afternoon after picking up Lachlan from the crèche.

'I need to talk to you, Dad,' she said, hanging up Lachlan's backpack on the hook behind the kitchen door.

'Where's Lachlan?' Heath Forrester asked.

'He wanted to play outside for a while,' she informed him with undisguised relief. Her young son had been full of energy and endless chatter all the way home from the crèche and it had nearly driven her crazy.

Heath gave her a look of fatherly concern. 'What's on your mind, or should I say who?'

Her breath came out on the back of a deep sigh. 'Jake wants to have a family get-together of all things.'

Heath's bushy brow rose expressively. 'That could be a problem.'

She sent him a speaking glance as she reached for the kettle. 'He wanted to come here tonight but I managed to put him off. I said I'd organise a restaurant for some other evening in a week or two.' She leant her hips back against the bench as the kettle started heating. 'I just wish I didn't have to deal with this. I can't think straight when he's…when he's around.'

'You share a past with him,' her father said. 'It won't go away, especially with Lachlan lying between you.'

'You think I should tell him, don't you?'

Heath compressed his lips in thought for a moment. 'Jake's a difficult man, but not an unreasonable one, Ashleigh. For all you know he might turn out to be a great father if given the chance.'

'But he's always made it more than clear he never wanted to have children,' she said. 'He told me the very same thing again yesterday.'

'He might think differently if he met Lachlan,' Heath said.

Ashleigh smiled sadly in spite of her disquiet. 'You and Mum are the most devoted grandparents I know. Of course you would think that, but I know Jake. He would end up hating Lachlan for having the audacity to be born without his express permission.'

'I understand your concerns but you can't hide Lachlan from him for ever,' Heath pointed out. 'Attitudes have changed these days. He has a legal right to know he has fathered a child.'

'I know…' Ashleigh sighed. 'But I can't do it now. Not like this. I need more time. I need to prepare myself, not to mention Lachlan.'

'Who is going to prepare Jake?' Heath asked.

'That's not my responsibility,' she said.

Her father didn't answer but reached for two cups in silence. Ashleigh dropped two tea bags into the cups he put on the bench in front of her and poured the boiling water over them, watching as the clear liquid turned brown as the tea seeped from the bags into the water.

'I *will* tell him, Dad,' she addressed the cup nearest her, 'eventually.'

'I know you will,' her father answered, taking his cup. 'But I just hope it's not going to be too late.'

Ashleigh stared into the cup in her hands, the darkness of her tea reminding her of Jake's fathomless eyes—eyes that could cut one to the quick or melt the very soul.

'Better late than never…' she murmured.

'That's certainly a well-used adage,' Heath said. 'But I wonder what Jake will think?'

Ashleigh just gave her father a twisted grimace as she lifted her cup to her lips. She spent most of her sleepless nights tortured by imagining what Jake would think.

It wasn't a pretty picture.

'So how is your assessment going?' Howard asked her the next morning.

Ashleigh handed him the notes she'd made so far. 'I've

done one room, mostly the furniture as I think I'll need your help with the figurines. I've looked them up in the journals but I'd prefer your opinion. The painting, however, is certainly an Augustus Earle original. I think there are more but the one I've seen so far is worth a mint.'

'Good work,' Howard congratulated her as he glanced over her descriptions.

'I've taken some initial digital photos but I haven't downloaded them yet,' she said. 'It's a big house and the furniture is virtually stacked to the ceiling in some rooms. It will take me most of the next week to get everything photographed and documented.'

'So how is it working alongside your ex-boyfriend?'

Ashleigh found it hard to meet Howard's gently enquiring gaze. 'It's all right…I guess.'

'He hasn't—' he paused, as if searching for the right word '—made a move on you, has he?'

'Of course not!' she denied hotly.

Howard gave her a slightly shamefaced look. 'Sorry, just asking. You know I trust you implicitly.'

She stretched her mouth into a tight smile that physically hurt. 'Thank you.'

'However, I'm not sure I trust him,' he continued as if she hadn't spoken.

'You've only met him the once; surely that's not enough time to come to any sort of reasonable opinion on someone's character.' She found it strange springing to Jake's defence but it irked her to think her fiancé had made that sort of critical judgement without a fair trial.

'I know the type,' Howard answered. 'Too much money, too much power, not enough self-restraint.'

That about sums it up, she thought to herself, but decided against telling him how close he'd come to assessing her ex-lover's personality.

'I thought you were glad he was giving us this load of goods?' she said.

'I am,' he said. 'More than glad, to be honest. Who wouldn't be? It's a dream come true. Without this input of goods I was going to be sailing a little too close to the wind for my liking. The antiques fair coming up will time in nicely with this little haul. I will make a fortune out of it.'

'If it goes through,' she muttered darkly.

'What do you mean?' Howard looked at her in consternation.

'What if he pulls on the deal?'

'Why would he do that?' he asked. 'He gave us the exclusive. Well, at least he gave it to you.' He glanced at her narrowly. 'You're not making things difficult for him, are you?'

'Why would I do that?'

He gave a shrug. 'You're very bitter about him. Up until the other day you never once mentioned his name in the whole time I've known you.'

'You didn't ask.' She kept herself busy with shuffling some papers on her desk.

'That's because I sensed it was too painful for you,' he said.

Ashleigh looked at him, her expression softening as she recalled the way he had always considered her feelings. He was like the older brother she'd always wanted—caring, considerate and concerned for her at all times.

'I'm hoping he won't pull out of the deal.' She picked up a pen and rolled it beneath her fingers, the line of her mouth grim. 'But who knows what he might do if he finds out about Lachlan?' She stared at the pen for a moment before adding, 'He seems keen to get his father's house cleaned out so he can start renovating it.' She gave a tiny despondent sigh and added, 'I think I'm what you could call part of his clean-up process.'

'What do you mean?'

The pen rolled out of her reach. A small frown creased her brow as she lifted her gaze back to his. 'I can't quite work him out. Sometimes I think he wants to talk to me about his past…I mean *really* talk. You know, tell me every detail. But then he seems to close up and back off as if I've come too close.'

'It's a difficult time when a parent passes away,' Howard said. 'I remember when my father died how hard it was. I was torn between wanting to talk and needing to stay silent in case I couldn't handle the emotion.'

Ashleigh chewed her bottom lip for a moment. 'I could be wrong, but I can't help feeling he isn't exactly grieving his father's passing.'

'Oh?' Howard frowned. 'You mean they didn't get on or something?'

'I don't know…but why else would he be practically giving away everything his father left him?'

Howard let out a breath. 'I guess it wouldn't hurt to listen to him if he ever decides he wants to tell you about it. What harm could it do? You never know, you might come to see him in a totally new light.'

Ashleigh gave him a small wan smile by way of response. She didn't want to see Jake Marriott in a new light.

She didn't want to see Jake Marriott at all.

It wasn't safe.

'Come on!' Mia urged Ashleigh on the cross-training machine at the local gym early the next morning. 'Use those legs now, up and down, up and down.'

Ashleigh grimaced against the iron weight of her thighs and continued, sweat pouring off her reddened face and pooling between her breasts. 'I thought this was supposed to fun,' she gasped in between steps.

'It is once you get fit,' Mia said, springing on to the tread-mill alongside.

Ashleigh watched in silent envy as her trim and toned sister deftly punched in the directions on the treadmill and began running at a speed she'd thought only greyhounds could manage.

'You make me sick,' she said with mock sourness as she clung to the moving handles of the machine, her palms slippery and her legs feeling like dead pieces of wood.

Mia gave her a sweet smile as she continued running. 'It's your fault for fibbing to Jake about going to the gym regularly.'

'Yeah, don't remind me.'

'Anyway, I think it's a great idea for you to get some exercise,' Mia said without even puffing. 'You're so busy juggling work and Lachlan that you don't get any time on your own. You know how much Mum and Dad love to mind him for you so there's no excuse. The gym is a great place to switch off.'

Ashleigh looked at the sea of sweaty bodies around her and seriously wondered if her sister was completely nuts. Loud music was thumping, a row of televisions were transmitting several versions of early morning news shows, and a muscle-bound personal trainer who looked as if he'd been fed steroids from birth was adding to the cacophony of noise by shouting out instructions to a middle-aged man with a paunch, in tones just like a drill sergeant at Boot Camp.

'I can't believe people get addicted to this,' she said with a pointed look at her sister.

Mia grinned. 'It's also a great place to meet people.' She glanced at a tall, exceptionally handsome man who was doing bench presses on the other side of the room. 'Not a bad sight for this time of the morning, is it?'

Ashleigh couldn't help thinking that Jake's muscles as he'd dug the garden the previous day were much more

defined than the man in question; however, she had to accede
that her sister was right. There were certainly worse things
to be looking at first thing in the morning.

'How long do I have to do this for?' she asked after a few
more excruciating minutes of physical torture.

'Five more minutes and then we'll do some stomach
crunches,' Mia informed her cheerily.

Ashleigh slid a narrow-eyed glance her sister's way.
'How many?'

'Three hundred a day should do it,' Mia said determinedly.
'You're not overweight, just under-toned.'

'*Three hundred?*' Ashleigh groaned.

'Come on,' Mia said and, jumping off the treadmill, pulled
over a floor mat near the mirrored wall. 'Down on the floor
and let's get started.'

'One…two…three…four…five…'

When Ashleigh arrived at Jake's house later that morning the
temperature had risen to the late thirties and the air was thick
and cloying with humidity. A clutch of angry, bruised-looking
clouds was already gathering on the western horizon as if in
protest at the unseasonable heat.

She couldn't see Jake's car or any sign of him about the
house or garden so she let herself in and closed the door with
a sigh of relief as the coolness of the dark interior passed over
her like a chilled breath of air.

She lost track of time as she went to work in the second
of the two formal sitting rooms, this one smaller but no less
jam-packed. She ran her hand over a Regency rosewood
and brass-inlaid dwarf side cabinet in silent awe. The
cabinet had a frieze drawer and a pleated cupboard door
decorated with a brass grille and was on sabre supports.
She knew it would fetch a fabulous price at auction and the

very fact that Howard had it in his possession would lift his profile considerably.

Her gaze shifted to a George III mahogany cabinet, and then to a Victorian walnut credenza which was inlaid and gilt metal-mounted, the lugged serpentine top above a panelled cupboard door and flanked by glazed serpentine doors.

The scent of old wood stirred her nostrils as she took photo after photo, edging her body around the cluttered furniture to show each piece off to best advantage.

During her time working with Howard she had seen many wonderful pieces, had visited many stately homes and purchased deceased estates, but nothing in her experience came anywhere near what was in Jake's father's house. She'd completed enough courses by correspondence to recognise a genuine antique when she saw it and this house was practically filled floor to ceiling with them, most of them bordering on priceless.

It only begged the question why someone had collected such expensive showpieces when he'd clearly had no intention of ever showing them off. They were cheek by jowl in an old neglected house that needed more than a lick of paint on the outside and a great deal of it inside as well.

From the unfaded splendour of the furniture she could only assume the blinds at the windows had nearly always been kept down. She couldn't help thinking what sort of life Jake must have had as a young child in this mausoleum-like house. She couldn't imagine her little son lasting even a full minute without touching or breaking something valuable. She looked at a Prattware cat and wondered if Jake had ever broken anything in the boisterousness of youth. Lachlan had recently accidentally toppled over a vase at Howard's house and Marguerite Caule had torn strips off him, reducing him to tears even though the vase hadn't even been so much as chipped.

She gave an inward shudder and left the room.

The closed door of what used to be Jake's bedroom was three doors away down the hall. She looked at it for a long moment, wondering what secrets he kept locked there. She walked slowly towards the door, each of her footsteps making the floorboards creak as if they were warning her not to go any further. Jake had forbidden her to go in, telling her he kept it locked at all times, but she wouldn't be human or indeed even female if she didn't try the handle just the once…

It opened without a sound.

She stared at the open space before her for at least half a minute until the overwhelming temptation finally sent her feet forward, one after the other, until she was inside, the door as her hand left it, shifting soundlessly to a half-open position behind her.

It wasn't as dark as the rest of the rooms in the house. The blinds were not pulled all the way down and, although the sky outside was cloudy, enough light still came through for her to see the narrow single bed along one wall. Compared to the rest of the furniture in the house, Jake's bedroom was furnished roughly, almost cheaply. There was nothing of any significant value, that she could see. The wardrobe was little more than a chipboard affair and the chest of drawers not much better. There was a single mirror on the wall above the chest of drawers but it was cracked and crooked as if someone had bumped against it heavily but not bothered to straighten it again.

The bed was lumpy and looked uncomfortable, the ugly brown chenille spread bald in spots. The walls looked pock-marked, bits of poster glue still visible, although there was not a poster or photograph in sight. Again she thought of her childhood home with the walls covered with loving happy memories. Jake's childhood house was stripped of any such sentimentality. She had asked him once when they lived to-gether to show her a photo of himself as a child but he'd told her he hadn't bothered bringing any overseas with him. She had accepted his answer as reasonable and had thought nothing more about it. But now, in the aching emptiness of this room, she couldn't help wondering if anyone had ever taken one of him and cherished it the way her parents cherished the ones they had collected over the years.

There were no loving memories in this house.

The thought slipped into her head and once it took hold she couldn't erase it. The painful truth of it seemed to be seeping towards her, like a nasty stain that had been hidden for a long time but was now finally coming through the cracked paint on the walls to taint her with its dark shameful secret.

Jake had been abused by his father.

Her stomach clenched in anguish as the puzzle began to fall into sickening place. It all made sense now. No wonder he was getting rid of everything to do with his father. And no wonder he had never wanted children of his own.

Oh, Jake! Why didn't you tell me?

She looked again at the askew mirror on the wall and her stomach gave another painful lurch. Was that blood smeared in one corner?

Her eyes fell away from its mottled secrets and went to the chest of drawers beneath it. Almost of its own volition, her hand began to reach for the first drawer. She knew it was contravening Jake's rule but she had to find out what she could about his background. It was like a compulsion, an addiction she just had to feed, if only for the one time.

The drawer slid uneasily from its tracks as if it too was advising her against prying as the floorboards had seemed to do earlier, the scrape of rough-edged timber sounding like fingernails being dragged down the length of a chalk board.

She suppressed a tiny shiver and looked down at the odd socks tumbled in a heap, no two seemed to match or were even tucked together in the hope of being considered a pair. There was a bundle of underwear that looked faded and worn and a few unironed handkerchiefs not even folded.

The second drawer had a few old T-shirts, none of them ironed, only one or two folded haphazardly. A sweater was stuffed to one side, one of its exposed elbows showing a gaping hole.

Jeans were in the third drawer, only two pairs, both of them ragged and torn. She couldn't help a tiny smile. Both her sisters insisted on buying torn and ragged jeans; it was the fashion and they paid dearly for it, insisting they would *die* if anyone saw them in anything else.

She pushed against the drawer to shut it but it snagged and wouldn't close properly. She gave it another little shove but it refused to budge. She bent down and peered into the space between the second and third drawers but it was hard to see in the half light. She straightened and tugged the drawer right out of the chest in order to reinsert it, to check if anything was stuck behind.

A small package fell to the floor at her feet and, carefully sliding the drawer back into place, she bent down to retrieve it…

CHAPTER SIX

IT WAS an envelope, the edges well-worn as if it had been handled too many times. Ashleigh opened the flap and drew out the small wad of photographs it contained, her breath stalling in her throat as the first one appeared.

It was Jake as a small toddler and he looked exactly like Lachlan at the same age.

'I thought I told you this room was out of bounds.'

Ashleigh spun around so quickly she dropped the photographs, each of them fluttering to the floor around her quaking legs and feet.

'I…I…' She gave up on trying to apologise, knowing it was going to be impossible to get the words past the choking lump in her throat.

Jake moved into the room and she watched in a shocked silence as he retrieved the scattered photographs off the floor, slipping them back inside the old envelope and putting them to one side.

'There is nothing of value in this room.' He gave the room a sweeping scathing glance before his eyes turned back to hers. 'I told you before.'

She moistened her mouth, shifting from foot to foot, knowing he had every right to be angry with her for stepping across the boundary he had set down.

'You always were the curious little cat, weren't you?' he said, stepping towards her.

Ashleigh felt her breath hitch as he stopped just in front of her, not quite touching but close enough for her to feel the warmth of his body. It came towards her in waves, carrying with it the subtle scent of his essential maleness, his lemon-scented aftershave unable to totally disguise the fact that he'd been physically active at some point that morning. It was an intoxicating smell, suggestive of full-blooded male in his prime, testosterone pumped and charged, ready for action.

'The door…it wasn't locked…'

'It usually is, but I decided to trust you,' he said. 'But it seems I can no longer do so.'

She didn't know what to make of his expression. She didn't think he was angry with her but there was a hint of something indefinable in his gaze that unnerved her all the same.

'I was just checking…' she said lamely.

He gave a little snort of cynicism. 'I just bet you were.'

'I was!' she insisted. 'Was it my fault you left the door unlocked?'

'You didn't have to search through my things,' he pointed out.

'You haven't lived in this house for something like eighteen years,' she said. 'I'm surprised anything of yours is still here.'

He gave her an unreadable look. 'Quite frankly, so am I.'

She frowned at his words, her brain grappling with why his father had left things as they were. The room looked as if Jake had walked out of it all those years ago and yet it seemed as if nothing had been removed or changed since.

'Maybe he missed you,' she offered into the lengthy silence.

Jake's dark eyes hardened as they pinned hers. 'Yes, I suppose he did.'

She ached to ask why but the expression on his face warned her against it. Anger had suddenly tightened his jaw, sent fire to his eyes and tension to his hands as they fisted by his sides.

She couldn't hold his look. She turned and found herself looking at her own reflection in the cracked mirror on the wall. It was like looking at a stranger. Her blue eyes looked wild and agitated, her hair falling from the neat knot she had tied it in that morning, her cheeks flushed, her mouth trembling slightly.

She could see him just behind her. If she stepped back even half a step she would come into contact with the hard warmth of his very male body. Her workout in the gym that morning made her aware of her body in a way she had not been in years. She felt every used muscle, every single contraction reminding her of how she used to feel in his arms. Making love with Jake had been just like a heavy workout. He had been demanding and daring, taking her to the very limits of consciousness time after time until she hadn't known what was right and decent any more.

She met his eyes in the mirror and suppressed an inward shudder of reaction. Would she ever be able to look at him without feeling a rush of desire so strong it threatened to overturn every moral principle she had been taught to cling to?

She sucked in a breath as his hands came down on her shoulders, his eyes still locked on hers in the mirror. She did her best to control her reaction but the feel of his long fingers on her bare skin melted her resolve. She positively ached for him to slowly and sensually slide his hands down the length of her arms as he used to do, his fingers curling around the tender bones of her wrists in a hold that brooked no resistance. She wondered if he knew how he still affected her, that her heart was already racing at the solid presence of him standing so close behind her, the knowledge that in the past his hardened maleness, thick with desire, would be preparing to plunge between her legs and send every trace of gasping air out of her lungs.

'Y-you're touching me…' Her voice came out not much more than a croak.

'Mmm, so I am.' His hands moved slowly down her arms, his eyes never once leaving hers.

She moistened her parched lips when his fingers finally encircled her wrists, her breathing becoming ragged and uneven. 'Y-you're breaking the rules, Jake.'

'I know.' He gave her a lazy smile as his thumbs began a sensual stroking of the undersides of her wrists. 'But you broke my one and only rule and now I shall have to think of a suitable penalty.'

She wasn't sure if it was she who turned in his arms or if he turned her to face him, but suddenly she wasn't looking at his reflection in the mirror any more but into his darker than night gaze as it burned down into hers.

His body was too close.

She could feel the denim seam of the waistband of his jeans against her, and when his hands drew her even closer her stomach came into contact with his unmistakable arousal. No one else could make her feel this way. Her body remembered and hungered for what it had missed for so long.

When his mouth came down over hers a tiny involuntary whimper of pleasure escaped her already parted lips, and as his tongue began an arrogant and determined search for hers she gave no resistance but curled hers around his in a provocative dance which spoke of mutual blood-boiling desire.

Ashleigh vaguely registered the dart of lightning that suddenly lit the room and the distant sound of thunder, the low grumble not unlike the sounds coming from Jake's throat as he took the kiss even further, his body grinding against hers. She wound her arms around his neck, her fingers burrowing into his thick dark silky hair, her breasts tight with need as they were crushed against his chest.

Jake sucked on her bottom lip, a bone-melting act he'd perfected in the past, making her feel as if her body and mind were totally disconnected. She no longer felt like someone else's fiancé. She felt like Jake's lover, a lover who knew exactly how to please him. She remembered it all so well! How to make him groan with ecstasy as he spilled himself into her body, her mouth or wherever she chose to tempt him beyond the tight limits of his control.

Now she couldn't help relishing the feeling of power his reaction afforded her. She could sense his struggle to hold back as his tongue thrust back into her mouth, the sexy male rasp inciting her to give back even more. She bit down on his bottom lip, a tantalising little nip that made him growl deep in his throat. She wouldn't release him, supping on him as if she wanted to take him deep inside and never let him go.

She loved the feel of his hard mouth, the way his masculine stubble never seemed to be quite under smooth enough control, the rough scrape of skin against the softness of hers reminding her of all that was different between them.

How had she lived without his touch? This madness of blood racing through veins alight with passion, a frenzy of feeling that would not go away without the culmination of physical union.

And then only temporarily.

When she felt Jake's hands slide beneath her top she did nothing to stop him. She couldn't. Her breasts were aching too much for the cup of his warm hands, hands that in the past her too slim body hadn't quite been able to fill. But it did now.

Her flesh spilt into his hands as he released her simple bra, the stroke of his fingers over the tight buds of her nipples an almost unbearable pleasure. When he bent his head to place his hot mouth on her right nipple she nearly fainted with re-action, the slippery motion of his tongue stirring her into a madness of need that she knew had only one assuagement. He knew it too, for he did the same to her other breast, drawing little agonised gasping groans from her lips, her cheeks flushing with passion, her limbs weakening as she leant into his iron-strong hold.

He pressed her backwards until the backs of her knees came into contact with his narrow single bed. A distant corner of her conscience prodded her, reminding her of her commitment to Howard. But somehow when Jake's long strong body came down over hers and pinned her to the mattress, any notion of resistance disappeared on the tail end of a gasp as his thighs nudged between the quivering silk of hers.

'I have waited so long to do this,' Jake groaned as he lifted her skirt with impatient hands, his eyes like twin torches of fire as he looked down at her desire-flushed features. 'I have dreamt of it, ached for it, planned for it until I could think of nothing else.'

Planned for it? Ashleigh froze as his words sank in. She eased herself up on her elbows, dislodging his weight only because he hadn't expected it. 'What do you mean, *planned* for it?' she asked.

He began to press her back down but she pushed his hand away. 'No, Jake. Tell me what you mean.'

He gave her a frustrated look from beneath frowning brows. 'Do we have to talk *now?*'

'Yes.' She rolled off the bed and quickly rearranged her clothing with as much dignity as she could, and turned to face him determinedly. 'Tell me what you meant. Now.'

He drew in a harsh breath and got off the bed in a sin-gle movement, one of his hands marking a rough pathway through his hair. 'I have made no secret of my intention to see you again,' he said. 'I told you that the very first day.'

She gave him a reproachful glare. 'You also told me the following day that you had no intention of sleeping with me, or have you forgotten that little detail?'

His mouth curled up in one corner as he looked down at her. 'I was only responding to the invitation you've been sending out to me from the first moment we met in the hotel bar. You can deny it all you like, but you're as hungry for me as I am for you.'

'I. Am. Engaged.' She bit the words out with stiff force.

His cynical smile tilted even further. 'Just exactly who are you reminding of the fact, me or you?'

Ashleigh had never felt closer to violence in her entire life. Her hand twitched with the desire to take a swipe at the self-satisfied smirk on his darkly handsome face, and in the end only some tiny remnant of her conservative upbringing fore-stalled her.

She clenched her fists by her sides and berated him coldly. 'If you think you can replay our relationship just for the heck of it you're very much mistaken. I know what you're doing, Jake. As soon as you clean up this place you'll be back off to London or Paris or wherever you have some other stupid misguided woman waiting in vain for you to commit.'

'That has always been a sticking point with you, hasn't it?' he said, folding his arms in a casual unaffected pose. 'You don't think a relationship is genuine without some sort of for-mal commitment.'

She found it difficult to hold his very direct look but be-fore she could think of a response he continued, 'Which kind of makes me wonder why you don't wear an engagement ring. Can't poor old Howard even rustle up a second-hand one for you?'

It was all she could do to keep her temper under control.

Rage fired in her blood until she could see tiny red spots of it before her eyes. She so wanted to let fly at him with every gram of bitterness she'd stored up over the years, but instead of a stream of invective coming out of her mouth when she finally opened it, to her utter shock, shame and embarrassment a choked sob came out instead.

Jake stared at her, his own mouth dropping open as she bent her head to her hands, her slim shoulders visibly shaking as she tried to cover the sounds of her distress.

He muttered one short sharp curse and reached for her, pulling her into the shield of his chest, one of his hands cupping the back of her silky head as he brought it down against his heart.

'I'm sorry.' He was surprised it hadn't physically hurt to articulate the words, especially as he'd never said them to anyone before.

She didn't answer other than to burrow a bit closer, but after a moment or two he could feel the dampness of her tears through his thin cotton T-shirt.

He couldn't remember ever seeing her cry before. He'd always secretly admired her for it, actually. His childhood had taught him that tears were for the weak and powerless; he'd disciplined himself not to cry from an early age and, no matter what treatment had been dished out to him, he had been determined not to let his emotions get out of control. He had gritted his teeth, sent his mind elsewhere, planned revenge and grimly stored his anger, and for the most part he'd succeeded.

The only time he'd failed was the day his father had told him his dog had been sent away to the country. Jake had only been about ten and the little fox-terrier cross had been a stray he'd brought home. Her excited yaps when he'd come home from school each day had been the highlight of his young life.

The *only* highlight.

No one else had ever looked that happy to see him since… well…maybe Ashleigh had in their early days together, her eyes brightening like stars as he'd walked in the door.

Ashleigh eased herself out from his hold and brushed at her eyes with the back of her hand, her other hand hunting for a much-needed tissue without success.

Jake reached past her and opened the top drawer of the chest of drawers and handed her one of the crumpled handkerchiefs. 'Here,' he said, his tone a little gruff, 'it's more or less clean but I'm afraid it's not ironed.'

'It doesn't matter,' she said, turning away to blow her nose rather noisily.

Jake watched her in silence, wishing he could think of something to say to take away the gaping wound of their past so they could start again. He knew he didn't really deserve the chance, but if he could just explain…

He wanted to change. He wanted to be the sort of man she needed, the solid dependable type, the sort of man who would be a brilliant father to the children he knew she wanted to have. But what guarantee could he give her that he wouldn't turn out just like his father? Things might be fine for a year or two, maybe even a little longer, but he knew the patterning of his childhood and the imprint of his genes would win in the end.

He'd read the statistics.

Like father like son.

There was no getting away from it.

He just couldn't risk it.

Ashleigh scrunched the used handkerchief into a ball in her hand and turned back to meet his gaze. 'I'm sorry about that…' She bit her lip ruefully. 'Not my usual style at all.'

He smiled. Not cynically. Not sneeringly, but sadly, his coal-black eyes gentle, the normally harsh lines of his mouth soft. 'No,' he agreed, 'but everyone has their limits, I guess.'

She lowered her gaze, concentrating on the round neckline

of his close-fitting T-shirt. 'I think it's this house…' She rubbed at her upper arms as if she was suddenly cold. 'It seems sort of…sort of miserable…and…well…sad.'

Jake privately marvelled at the depth of her insight, but if only she knew even half of it! The walls could tell her a tale or two, even the mirror behind her bore the scar of his final fight with his father. He'd been fully expecting to see his blood still splattered like ink drops all over it and the wall but apparently his father had decided to clean up his handiwork, although it looked as if he'd missed a bit in one corner.

He forced his thoughts away from the past and, reaching for the envelope he'd put aside earlier, sat on the bed and patted the space beside him, indicating for her to sit alongside. 'Hey, come here for a minute.'

He saw the suspicion in her blue eyes and held up his hands. 'No touching, OK?'

She came and sat on the bed beside him, her hands in her lap and her legs pressed together tightly.

He opened the envelope with careful, almost reverent fingers and Ashleigh found herself holding her breath as he took out the first photograph.

It was the photo she'd seen earlier. It was the spitting image of Lachlan at the age of eighteen months or so—the engaging smile, the too long limbs and the olive skin the sun had kissed where summer clothes hadn't covered.

She didn't know what to say, so said nothing.

'I was about a year and a half old, I think,' Jake said, turning over the photo to read something scrawled in pencil on the back. 'Yeah…'

'What does it say?' she asked.

He tucked the photo to the back of the pile, his expression giving little away. 'Not much. Stuff about what I was doing, words I was saying, that sort of thing. My mother must have written it.'

Ashleigh felt the stabbing pain of her guilt as she thought about the many photographs she had with Lachlan's early life documented similarly.

Jake took out the next photograph and handed it to her. She felt the warm brush of his fingers against hers but didn't pull away. She held the photograph with him, as if the weight of the memories it contained was too heavy for one hand.

It was a photograph of a small dog.

Ashleigh wished she had her sister Ellie's knowledge of canine breeds but, taking a wild guess, she thought it looked like a fox-terrier with a little bit of something else thrown in. It had a patch of black and tan over one cheeky bright intelligent eye and another two or three on its body, its long narrow snout looking as if it was perpetually smiling.

She glanced at him, their fingers still linked on the picture. 'Was this your dog?'

He nodded and shifted his gaze back to the photograph. She sensed rather than heard his sigh.

'What happened to him?' she asked after what seemed an interminable silence.

'Her,' he corrected, without looking up from the image.

Ashleigh held her breath, instinctively knowing more was to come. Exactly what, she didn't know, but for now it was comforting that he trusted her enough to show her some precious relics of his past. Somehow she knew he hadn't done this before.

With anyone.

Jake tucked the photograph behind the others and closed the envelope. 'I called her Patch. She followed me home from school one day when I was about eight or so.'

'How long did you have her?'

'A year or two.'

'She died?'

He met her gaze briefly before turning away. 'My father sent her to live in the country.'

Ashleigh felt her stomach clench with sympathy for the child he had been and the loss he must have felt. 'Why?'

He gave another small shrug. 'I must have done something to annoy him.' He pushed the envelope away and stood up. 'As punishments went it was probably the best he'd ever come up with, not that I ever let on, of course.'

Ashleigh could just imagine how stoical he had been. His chin stiff, no hint of a wobble even though inside his heart would have been breaking. Hadn't she seen it in Lachlan when Purdy, the family's ancient but much loved budgerigar, had died not that long ago?

'Did you ever get to visit her?' she asked.

'No.' The single word was delivered like a punctuation mark on the subject, effectively closing it.

'Can I see the rest of the photos?' she asked after another stretching silence.

He pushed the envelope into the top drawer of the chest of drawers by way of answer. Ashleigh looked at the stiff line of his back as it was turned towards her, somehow sensing he'd let her past a previously well-guarded barrier and was now regretting his brief lapse into sentimentality. She could almost see the words Keep Out written across his face as he turned to look at her.

'Maybe some other time.' He moved past her to the door and held it open for her. 'Don't let me keep you from your work.'

Ashleigh brushed past him with her head down, not sure she wanted him to see the disappointment in her eyes at his curt dismissal. He'd allowed her into his inner sanctum for a moment, had made himself vulnerable to her in a way she'd never experienced with him before. It made it extremely difficult to use her bitterness as a barrier to what she really felt for him. The feelings she'd locked away for years were creeping out, finding gaps in the fences she'd constructed around herself. Her love for Jake was like a robust climbing vine that refused to die no matter how hard it was pruned or poisoned.

Ashleigh went into the first room she came to rather than have Jake's gaze follow her down the length of the hall. It was a dining room, the long table set with an array of dusty crockery and china, instantly reminding her of Miss Havisham's abandoned wedding breakfast in Charles Dickens's *Great Expectations*.

She reached for the light switch and watched as the ornate crystal chandeliers overhead flickered once or twice as if deciding whether to make the effort to throw some light in the room or not. The delicate drape of spiders' webs only added to the Dickensian atmosphere. She gave herself a mental shake and stepped further into the room to reach for the nearest blind, but just as she took hold of the tasselled cord a big furry black spider tiptoed over the back of her hand.

It was probably her best-ever scream.

Her mother had always said that Ashleigh held the record in the Forrester family for the scream that could not only wake the dead but everybody sleeping this side of the Blue Mountains as well.

The door behind her crashed open so roughly that the delicate glassware on the dining room table shivered in reaction as Jake came bursting in.

'What happened?' He rushed to her, his hands grasping her upper arms as he looked down at her pale face in concern.

'Nothing…' She gave a shaky little laugh of embarrassment and moved out of his hold. 'It was a spider, that's all.'

He frowned. 'I didn't know you were scared of spiders.'

'I'm not.' She rubbed the back of her hand on her skirt. 'I just don't like them using me as a pedestrian crossing.'

He glanced at what she was doing with her hand and grimaced. 'Where is it now?' He swept his gaze across the window-frame before looking back at her. 'Do you want me to get rid of it for you?'

'It's probably long gone,' she said. 'I think I screamed it into the next century.'

He gave her one of his rare genuine smiles. 'I thought you'd seen a ghost. I had no idea anyone so small could scream so loudly.'

Small? One gym workout and he already thought she was smaller? Thank you, Mia!

'I've had a lot of practice over the years,' she said. 'Mia and Ellie and I used to have screaming competitions.'

'Your poor parents,' Jake commiserated wryly.

'Yes…' A small laugh bubbled from her lips before she could stop it. 'The police were called once. Apparently one of the neighbours thought someone was being murdered or tortured at the very least. You should have heard the lecture we got for…' Her words trailed away as she saw the expression on Jake's face. It had gone from mildly amused to mask-like, as if something she had said had upset him and he didn't want to let her see how much.

'Jake?' She looked at him questioningly, her hand reaching out to touch him gently on the arm.

He moved out of her reach and turned to raise the blind.

The angry black clouds had by now crept right over the garden, their threatening presence casting the room in menacing, creeping shadows. The flickering light bulbs in the chandelier over the table made one last effort to keep the shadows at bay before finally giving up as a flash of sky-splitting lightning came through the window, momentarily illuminating the whole room in a ghostly lucency. The boom of thunder was close on its heels, the ominous sound filling Ashleigh's ears.

'Are you afraid of storms?' Jake asked without turning to look at her.

'No… not really,' she said, waiting a few seconds before adding, 'are you?'

She watched as he turned to look at her, the eerie light of the morning storm casting his face into silhouette.

'I used to be,' he answered, his voice sounding as if it had come from a distant place. 'But I'm not anymore.'

She waited a heartbeat before asking, 'How did you overcome your fear?'

It seemed an age before he responded. Ashleigh felt the silence stretching to breaking-point, her mind already rehearsing various phrases to relieve it, when he suddenly spoke, shocking her into vocal muteness.

'My father always used nature to his advantage. If a storm was loud and ferocious enough it would screen his activities from the neighbours.' He gave her a soulless look. 'Of course none of the neighbours called the police. They thought the booms and crashes going on were simply the effects of the storm.'

Ashleigh felt a wave of nausea so strong she could barely stand up. How had Jake survived such a childhood? She almost felt ashamed of how normal and loving her background was. She had been nurtured, along with her sisters, like precious hothouse flowers, while Jake had been consistently, cruelly crushed underfoot like a noxious weed.

'Oh, Jake…' She breathed his name. 'Why didn't you tell me?'

He gave a rough sound that was somewhere between scorn and dismissal. 'I'm over it, Ashleigh. My father's dead and I have to move on. Storms are just storms to me now. They hold no other significance.'

For some reason which she couldn't quite explain, her gaze went to the scar above his right eye. The white jagged line interrupted the aristocratic arc of his eyebrow like a bulldozed fire trail through a forest.

'Your eye…' she said. 'You always said you got that scar in a fight.' She took an unsteady breath and continued. 'Your father did it, didn't he?'

Jake lifted a hand and fingered the scar as if to make sure it was still there. 'Yes,' he said. 'It was the last chance he got to carve his signature on me. I was two days off my sixteenth birthday. I left and swore I'd never see him again.'

'You kept your promise…' She said the words for him.

He gave her a proud defiant look. 'Yes. I never saw him alive again.'

'I wish you'd told me all of this when we…when we were together,' she said. 'It would have helped me to understand how you—'

His lip curled into one of his keep-away-from-me snarls. 'What good would it have done? You with your perfect little family, everyone chanting how much they love each other every night as the night closed in like in all of those stupid TV shows. Do you know anything about what really goes on behind closed doors? Do you even know what it is like to go without a meal?' he asked, his tone suddenly savage, like a cornered neglected dog which had known nothing but cruelty all its life. 'Do you know what it is like to dread coming home at the end of the school day, wondering what punishment was in store if you so much as made a floorboard creak or a door swing shut too loudly?'

Ashleigh's eyes watered and she bit her lip until she could taste the metallic bitterness of blood.

Jake slashed one of his hands through the air like a knife and continued bitterly. 'I had no respite. From the day my mother died when I was three I lived with a madman. Not a day went past when I didn't have fear turning my guts to gravy while he watched and waited, timing his next hit for maximum effect.' He strode to the window once more, the next flash of angry lightning outlining his tall body as he stared out at the garden.

Ashleigh wanted to say something but knew this was not her turn to speak. Jake had been silent for most of his life; it was his turn to talk, to get what he could out of his system and he had chosen her to be witness to it.

He gave a deep sigh and she heard him rub his face with one hand, the slight raspy sound making her weak with her need to go to him in comfort. How she wanted to wrap her arms around him, to press soft healing kisses on all the spots on his body where his father had kicked, punched or brutalised him.

It was almost impossible for her to imagine someone wanting to harm their own child. She thought of Lachlan and how she would gladly give her life for his, had in fact given up so much for him already and not once complained. How could Jake's father have been so heartless? What possible motive could he have had to inflict such unspeakable cruelty on a defenceless child?

Jake turned around to look at her, his expression bleak. 'For most of my life I have done everything possible not to imitate my father. My life's single goal has been to avoid turning into a clone of him.'

She drew in a shaky little breath, hardly able to believe she was finally witnessing the confession she had always longed to hear.

'He remarried more often than he changed his shirts,' he continued in the same flat tone. 'I had a procession of stepmothers come in and out of my life, each of whom left as soon as they found out the sort of man my father was. I decided marriage was never going to be an option for me in case I ended up the same way, leaving a trail of emotional and physical destruction in my wake as my father did.'

'He abused you…didn't he?' Her voice came out on a thin thread of sound.

Jake's eyes shifted away from hers, his back turned towards her as he raised the ragged blind and stared out of the window.

'Not sexually,' he answered after what seemed another interminable pause.

Ashleigh felt her tense shoulders sag with instant relief.

'But he did just about everything else.'

Her stomach clenched, her throat closing over. 'Oh, Jake…'

He turned back to face her, his expression rueful. 'Do you realise you are the first person I've ever told this to?'

'I—I am?'

He gave her a sad smile. 'Every single day we lived together I wanted to tell you, but I thought if I did you would run a mile in case I turned out just like him.'

'You could never be like him, Jake…'

He turned back to the window, effectively shutting her out again.

'I have to go away for a few days,' he said into the silence, his voice sounding gut-wrenchingly empty.

After another little silence he turned around to look at her, the storm raging outside his backdrop. 'I have some things to see to interstate and I won't be back before the weekend.'

'That's OK,' she said softly. 'I can continue with the assessment on my own. There are quite a few things I'll need to do some research on anyway in order to give you some idea of valuation.'

'I don't care what this stuff is worth; I just want it out of here,' he said.

Ashleigh watched as he strode out of the room, his eyes avoiding hers as if he didn't want her to see the residual pain reflected there.

She didn't need to see it, she thought sadly, as the door clicked shut behind him.

She could *feel* it for him.

CHAPTER SEVEN

'BUT I don't want to go to crèche!' Lachlan whined for the fifth time a few days later on the Friday morning.

Ashleigh's patience was wearing thin. She hadn't slept properly in days, unable to erase the images of Jake's haunted past from her mind. Each day she'd spent in the old house seemed to make it worse, especially as he wasn't coming back until Monday to break the long aching silences. She knew it was disloyal to Howard, but she missed seeing Jake, missed hearing him move about the house and garden. God help her, she even missed his snarls and scornful digs.

'You have to go, Lachlan,' she insisted, stuffing his lunch box in his backpack.

'But I want to come wif you!' His chin wobbled and his dark eyes moistened.

Ashleigh felt the strings on her heart tighten; her son's little speech impediment always returned in moments of stress. She put the backpack to one side and squatted down in front of him, holding his thin shoulders so that he had to look at her.

'What's wrong, darling? Is someone making you unhappy at crèche?'

He shook his head, his bottom lip extended in a pout.

She gently pushed on his lip with the tip of her finger. 'You'll

trip over that if you poke it out any further.' She gave him a smile
as his lip returned to base. 'Now, what's all this about?'

He shuffled from one foot to the other. 'I just want to be
wif you.'

Ashleigh sighed. 'Darling, you know I have to work. We
can't live with Granny and Grandad for ever. They need time
alone and we need to have our own place too. As soon as
Howard and I get married…' She found it strange saying the
words and secretly wished she could take them back.

'Can I have a dog when we move to Uncle Howard's?'
Lachlan asked hopefully.

She forced her attention back to her son. His desire for a
dog had been so strong but her mother's allergy to cat and
dog hair had prevented it happening. However, Howard's
home with its pristine family heirloom décor was hardly the
family home a playful puppy would be welcomed into. She
could almost see Marguerite Caule's look of horrified distaste
at the first set of muddy pawprints on the pristine white carpet
or one of the linen-covered sofas.

'We'll see,' she said and straightened.

'We'll see means no,' Lachlan said with the sort of acuity
that marked him as Jake's son if nothing else. 'You always
say that, but it doesn't mean yes.'

She sighed and, zipping up his backpack, reached for his
hand. 'Come on, I'm late as it is.'

'I'm not going to crèche.' He snatched his hand away.

'Lachlan, I will not tolerate this from you,' she said
through tight lips. 'I have to go to…to that house I'm working
at and I have to leave now.'

'Take me to the house!' he begged. 'I'll be good. I won't
touch anyfing.'

Ashleigh closed her eyes as she pinched the bridge of
her nose.

Today of all days, she winced in frustration. Her mother

was out at a fundraising breakfast and wouldn't be back for hours. It was her father's annual heart check-up appointment in town and he'd left early to avoid the traffic and Mia had gone to an audition straight from the gym. Ellie, her last hope, hadn't come home yet from an all night sleep-in-the-park-for-homeless-dogs public awareness stunt that would probably see her on the front page of the morning's paper. It had happened before.

She let out her breath in a whoosh of tired resignation. 'All right, just this once. But if you so much as touch anything or break anything I won't let you watch *The Wiggles* or *Playschool* for a week.'

'Thank you, Mummy!' Lachlan rushed at her and buried himself against her, his arms around her waist, his cheek pressed to her stomach.

She eased him away to quickly scrawl a note for her mother who usually picked Lachlan up from the crèche on Friday afternoons to tell her about the change of plan.

'I love you, Mummy,' Lachlan said as she stuck the note on the fridge with a magnet.

'I love you, too, baby, but you're getting too big for pulling this sort of stunt.'

'What's a stunt?'

She tucked his hand in hers and shouldered open the door. 'Come on, I'll tell you in the car.'

Ashleigh was surprised and more than a little proud of the way Lachlan behaved at Jake's house. He had played quietly by her side as she worked in the library, never once complaining about being bored. He wheeled his little collection of toy cars across the floor, parking them in neat little rows on the squares on the Bakhtiari carpet with meticulous precision.

She knew she was taking a risk having him with her but

couldn't help feeling it had been worth it to see the simple joy on his little face every time she looked down at him.

She knew she was no different from every other working single mother, so often torn between the necessities to provide a reasonable living whilst allowing adequate time to nurture the child she'd brought into the world, but it still pained her to think how short-changed Lachlan was. Of late he'd been increasingly unsettled and clingy and she felt it was her fault. She'd thought her engagement to Howard would have offered him a bit more security but, while he liked Howard, she knew Marguerite intimidated him, although he did his very best not to show it.

'Can I go out into the garden for a while?' Lachlan got up from the floor with his little cars tucked into the old lunchbox container he kept them in, his dark eyes bright with hope.

Ashleigh pursed her lips as she thought about it. The garden, though large, was enclosed and the neighbourhood very quiet. The sun was shining, which it hadn't done properly in days, and she knew that—like most little boys his age—he needed lots of exercise and space.

'As long as you promise not to go through the side gate to the front; I can check on you while I'm working in this part of the house.'

'I promise,' he said solemnly.

A smile found its way to Ashleigh's mouth and she reached out a hand and ruffled his dark hair. 'Thanks for being so good this morning. It's really nice to have some company in this big old house.'

'Who lives here, Mummy?' Lachlan asked.

'No one at the moment,' she answered, fiddling with a gold shield-shaped bloodstone opening seal. 'The person who used to live here has…gone.'

'Did they die?'

It occurred to Ashleigh at that point that Lachlan had recently lost a blood relative, his paternal grandfather. It seemed unfair not to be able to tell her son who had actually lived in this house, when if things had been different he might have visited like any other grandson would have done, maybe even inherited some of the priceless pieces she was documenting.

But telling Lachlan would mean having to reveal the truth to Jake.

She wasn't ready to tell him and, given what she'd heard earlier that week about his childhood, Jake was nowhere near ready to hear.

'An old man used to live here,' she said.

'All by himself?' Lachlan asked, giving the imposing library a sweeping glance, his eyes wide with amazement.

'Yes…but a long time ago he used to live here with someone.'

'Who was it?' Lachlan's voice dropped, the sibilance of his childish whisper making Ashleigh feel slightly spooked.

'His…son.'

'Didn't he have a mummy too?'

'Yes…but she…she went away.' Ashleigh could see the stricken look come into Lachlan's eyes and wished she hadn't allowed the conversation to get to that point. As a child a few months off turning four who had grown up thus far without a father, his very worst nightmare was to have something take his mother away as well. She had always done her best to reassure him but still his fear lingered. She could see it in the way he looked at her at times, a wavering nervousness in his dark brown gaze, as if he wasn't sure if he would ever see her again once she walked out of the door.

She bent down and, tipping up his chin, pressed a soft kiss to the end of his nose. 'Why don't you go and explore the garden and in five minutes I'll join you. I'll bring out a drink and some fruit just like they do at crèche.'

His small smile brightened his features but did nothing to remove the shadow of uncertainty in his eyes. 'OK.'

She took his hand and led him back through the house to the back door, watching as he went down the steps with his car collection tucked under one small arm. He went straight to the elm tree, she noticed. The leafy shade was certainly an attraction on such a warm morning but she couldn't help wondering if it was somehow genetic.

She waited for a while, watching him set out his array of cars on the patches of earth where the lawn had grown threadbare, parking each of them neatly before selecting one to drive up and down the exposed tree root nearest him.

A pair of noisy currawongs passed overhead and a light warm breeze stirred the leaves of the old elm, making each one shiver.

'I'll be out to check on you in five minutes, poppet,' she called out to him.

He didn't answer, which in a way reassured her. He was happy playing under the tree with the sounds of the birds to keep him company.

After being in the outdoor sunshine it took a moment for Ashleigh's eyes to adjust when she went back to the library. She took a few photos of some Tunbridge Ware book slides and stands and wrote a few notes about each, unconsciously gnawing the end of her pen as her thoughts gradually drifted to Jake.

She wondered where he was and who he was seeing interstate. She drew in a painful breath as she thought of him with another lover. Over the years she'd forced herself not to think of him in the arms of other women and mostly she'd been successful. She'd been too busy looking after his little son to torture herself with images of leggy blondes, racy redheads or brunettes with the sort of assets that drew men like bees to a paddock full of pollen.

'You look pensive,' Jake's deep voice said from the door of the library.

Ashleigh nearly swallowed the pen she had in her mouth

as she spun around in shock. 'What are you doing here?' she gasped, the pen falling from her fingers.

He eased himself away from the door frame where he'd been leaning and came towards her, stooping to pick up the pen and handing it to her with a quirk of one dark satirical brow. 'My business was dealt with a whole lot earlier than I expected,' he said. 'I thought I'd surprise you.'

You certainly did that, she mused, even as her stomach rolled over at the thought of him taking a look out of the library window. One look and she would have hell to pay.

She forced her features into impassivity. 'I didn't hear you come in... Which door did you use?'

'The front door,' he answered as he picked up a Tunbridge Ware bookmark and began to turn it over in his hands.

Ashleigh edged towards the window, waiting until she was sure Jake was looking elsewhere before quickly checking on Lachlan. Her heart gave an extra beat when she couldn't see him under the tree. She glanced back at Jake but he appeared to be absorbed in the bookmark. Checking the elm tree once more, she found her son had come back into view. Her heart's pace had only just settled down again as she turned back to look at Jake.

He was watching her steadily, his dark intelligent gaze securing hers.

'So...' She forcibly relaxed her shoulders, a tight smile stretching her mouth as her heart began its rollercoaster run again. 'How was your business trip?'

'It was nothing out of the ordinary,' he responded, his eyes never once moving away from hers. 'How have you been while I've been away?'

'Me?' It came out like a squeak and she hastily cleared her throat and began again. 'I mean...I'm fine. Great, been to the gym and feeling pretty fit and...' She couldn't finish the sentence under his probing gaze. She was rambling but she knew that if she didn't go out to Lachlan soon he would come in to her. She didn't know which would be worse. Maybe she should just come right out and tell Jake now before he set eyes on Lachlan. It wasn't much of a warning for him, but what else could she do?

She straightened her spine and faced him squarely. 'Jake... I have something to tell you that...' She took a much needed breath and continued. '...that I should have told you before, but I just felt it was never the right time, and—'

'Mummee!' A child's voice rang out from the back of the house, closely followed by the sound of little footsteps running down the hall.

Ashleigh swallowed painfully as her son came rushing into the room, her breath stopping completely when he cannoned into Jake's long legs encased in dark trousers.

She watched in stricken silence as Jake's hands steadied Lachlan, his touch gentle but sure as he looked down at the small face staring up at him.

'J-Jake, this is Lachlan,' she said in a voice she hardly recognised as coming from her own mouth. 'Lachlan, this is...Jake.'

Lachlan, with the impulsiveness of youth on his side, got in first. 'Are you the boy who used to live here a long time ago?'

Jake stared down at the little child in front of him for what seemed like endless minutes until he registered that the boy had spoken to him. 'Yes...I am,' he said, hoping his tone wasn't showing how shell-shocked he felt.

Ashleigh had a child.

The child she'd always wanted.

The child he wouldn't give her, *refused* to give her.

He couldn't look at her. He knew if he did she would see his disappointment, his *unjustified* disappointment.

So she'd had Howard's child.

He assumed it was Howard's, although the child in front of him certainly didn't look much like Ashleigh's fiancé, he had to admit. The sick irony of it was that the kid looked more like him. Once the thought was there it tried to take hold but he just as quickly dismissed it, although it surprised him how much it hurt to let it go.

There was no way that kid could have been his. He'd watched Ashleigh take her pills every day; it had been part of their daily ritual. *He* had made it a part of it. She'd never missed a dose and if she had he would have insisted on using an alternative until things were safe.

It was hard to assess the kid's exact age. He'd deliberately avoided everything to do with children for most of his adult life and had very little idea of what age went with what stage in a child's life. On what limited knowledge he had, he thought the boy might have been about three and a half, which meant Ashleigh had dived pretty quickly into Howard Caule's bed, but then, hadn't she done the same with him?

The prospect of fathering a child had always terrified him. He had become almost paranoid about it. The thought of spreading his father's genes to the next generation had been too much for him to bear. How could he ever forgive himself if he turned on his own child the way his father had done to him? Parenting wasn't an easy task. How soon would it have been before a light tap of reproof became a closed-fist punch? How quickly would his gentle chastising tone have turned into full-blown self-esteem eroding castigation? How many unspeakable hurts would he have inflicted before the child was damaged beyond repair?

Nothing had ever been able to convince him it would be desirable to father a child, and yet one look at Ashleigh's little son had rocked his conviction as only flesh and blood reality could do. She'd had another man's child because he had been too much of a coward to confront his past and deal with it appropriately.

A burning pain knifed through him as a sudden flood of self-doubt assailed him. But what if he *hadn't* turned out like his father? What if, in spite of all that had been done to him, he could have rewritten the past and become a wonderful father, the sort of father he had longed for all his life? One who would listen to the childish insecurities that had plagued him, especially after his mother had died. Who would have listened and comforted him instead of berating him and punishing for simply being a lost, lonely little boy.

Other people had difficult backgrounds; there was hardly a person alive who didn't have some axe to grind about their past. Why had he let his take over his life and destroy his one chance at happiness? His father had been violent and cruel and totally unworthy of the role of parent, but in the end the person who had hurt Jake the most had been himself. When Ashleigh had walked out of his life four and a half years ago he had done absolutely nothing to stop her. Instead he had stood before her, stiff and uncommunicative, as she accused him of being unfaithful after she'd mistakenly read one of his e-mails about his recent trip to Paris. He could have told her then and there the real reason for his weekend away but he hadn't, for it would have meant revealing the filthy shame of his past to her. In the end his pride had not been able to stretch quite that far.

'I was going to tell you…' Ashleigh said, taking Lachlan's hand in hers and drawing him close to her.

Jake saw the way the child's eyes were watching him, the sombre depths quietly assessing him. It unnerved him a bit to have a kid so young look at him so intently, as if he were searching for something he'd been looking for a long time.

'It's none of my business,' he said, wishing his tone had sounded a little more detached.

Ashleigh had been waiting for the bomb to drop and found it hard to grasp the context of his words for a moment. She studied his expression and nervously disguised a swallow as his eyes went to Lachlan before returning to hers.

'I know it's probably very sexist of me, but it sure didn't take you long to replace me, did it?' he said.

It took her a nanosecond to get his meaning but she didn't know whether to be relieved or infuriated. Couldn't he see his own likeness standing before him in miniature form?

'I don't think this is a conversation we should be having at this time,' she said, indicating her son by her side with a pointed look.

'You're right,' Jake agreed.

There was a tense little silence. Ashleigh hunted her brain for something to fill it but nothing she wanted to say was suitable with her young son standing pressed to her side, facing his father for the very first time.

She wanted to blame someone.

She wanted to pin the responsibility for this situation on her mother for having a prior commitment, on her father for having a heart condition that needed regular monitoring, on her sister Mia for having an audition and Ellie for having a social conscience that was too big for her. If any of them had been free she wouldn't be standing in front of Jake now with his son, with a chasm of misunderstanding and bitterness separating them.

But in the end she knew there was no one to blame but herself. She should have told Jake four and a half years ago, given him the choice whether to be involved in his child's life or not.

Her mother was right. Even if he had pressed her to have a termination, the final decision would surely have been hers. She had thought she was being strong by walking away but, looking back with the wisdom of hindsight, she had to concede that she'd taken the weakling's way out. She had run for cover instead of facing life head on.

She turned to Lachlan, schooling her features into a serenity she was far from feeling. 'Poppet, why don't you go back out to the garden and we'll join you in a few minutes?'

Lachlan slipped his hand out of hers and scampered away without a single word of protest. He gave one last look over his shoulder before his footsteps sounded out down the hall as he made his way to the back door leading out to the garden.

This time the silence was excruciating.

Ashleigh felt each and every one of its invisible tentacles reaching out to squeeze something out of her but her throat had closed over as soon as Jake's eyes came back to hers.

'He doesn't look much like Howard,' he commented.

'That's because he's not Howard's son.'

'You surprise me.' The cynical smile reappeared. 'I didn't think you were the sleep-around type.'

'I had a very good teacher,' she returned, marginally satisfied when his smile tightened into something else entirely.

'How old is he?' he asked after another tense moment or two.

'Why do you ask?'

He shrugged one shoulder. 'Isn't it the usual question to ask?'

'As you said earlier, it's none of your business.'

'Maybe, but I'd still like to know,' he said.

'Why?'

It seemed an age before he answered.

'Because I need to be absolutely sure he's not mine.' He scraped a hand through his hair and added, 'You would have told me if he was, wouldn't you?'

It was all Ashleigh could do to hold his penetrating gaze. She felt herself squirming under the weight of its probe, the burden of her secret causing her a pain so intense she could scarcely draw in a breath.

'You can take a paternity test, if you'd like,' she said, taking a risk she wasn't sure would pay off. 'Then you can be absolutely sure.'

He gave her a long contemplative look before asking, 'Are you in any doubt of who the child's father is?'

'No,' she answered evenly. 'No, I know exactly who the father is.'

Jake moved away and went to the window she'd guarded so assiduously earlier. 'It was the one thing I could never give you, Ashleigh,' he said with his back still towards her. 'I told you that from day one.'

'I know…'

'I just couldn't risk it,' he said. He took a deep breath and added, 'My father…'

She bit her lip as she heard the slight catch in his voice, knowing how difficult this was for him.

'My father suffered from a rare but devastating personality disorder,' he said heavily. 'It's known to be genetic.'

'I understand…'

Jake squeezed his eyes shut, trying to block out the vision of Ashleigh's child playing underneath the tree he'd spent most of his own childhood sheltering beneath or in.

'No, you can't possibly understand,' he bit out, turning around to face her. 'Do you think I've wanted to have this burden all my life? I wish I could walk away from it, be a normal person for once instead of having to guard myself from having a re-run of my childhood played out in front of me every day.'

'I'm sorry…' She lowered her eyes from the fire of his, unable to withstand the pain reflected in his tortured gaze.

'But I couldn't risk it,' he went on. 'I couldn't put that intolerable burden on to another person. Not you, or whatever children we might have produced. My father was a madman who could switch at any moment. I'd rather die than have any child of mine suffer what I suffered.'

'But it might have skipped a generation…' she offered in vain hope.

'And then what?' His eyes burned into hers. 'I would have to watch it played out in the next or even the one after that but have no control over it whatsoever.' His expression grew embittered as he continued, 'How could I do that and live with myself?'

Ashleigh swallowed painfully. The burden of truth was almost more than she could bear but she knew she couldn't tell him about Lachlan's true parentage now. It would totally destroy him.

She watched as he sent his hand through his hair, his eyes losing their heat to grow dull and soulless as he turned to stare out of the window, the wall of his back like an impenetrable barrier.

'You don't know how much I've always envied you, Ashleigh,' he said after another long moment of silence. 'You have the sort of background that in fact most people today would envy. You have two parents who quite clearly love each other and have done so for many years exclusively, two sisters who adore you and not a trace of ill feeling to cast a shadow over the last twenty-odd years you've spent being a family.' He turned and looked at her, his expression grim. 'I'm sorry for what I couldn't give you, Ashleigh. If it's any comfort to your ego, I was tempted. Damn tempted. More tempted than I'd ever been previously and certainly more tempted than any time since.'

'Thank you...' she somehow managed to say, her eyes moving away from the steady surveillance of his.

She heard him give one of his trademark humourless grunts of laughter.

'Aren't you going to ask me how many lovers I've had over the years? Isn't that what most women would have asked by now?'

'I'm not interested,' she answered.

'How many lovers have you had?' he asked.

'I told you before, it's none of your business.'

'Well…' He stroked the line of his jaw for a moment, the raspy sound of his fingers on his unshaven skin making Ashleigh's toes curl involuntarily. 'One has to assume there have been at least two. Your son's father for one and then, of course, there's dear old Howard.'

Ashleigh felt increasingly uncomfortable under his lazy scrutiny. She kept her eyes averted in case he caught even a trace of the hunger she knew was there. She could feel it. It crawled beneath the surface of her skin, looking for a way out. Even her fingertips twitched with the need to feel his flesh under them once more. Behind the shield of her bra she could feel the heavy weight of her breasts secretly aching for the heat and fire of his mouth and tongue, and her legs were beginning to tremble with the effort of keeping her upright when all they wanted was to collapse so her body could cling to the strength and power of his.

'Tell me, Ashleigh.' Jake's voice was a deep velvet caress across her too sensitive skin. 'Does Howard make you scream the way I used to?'

She stared at him speechlessly, hot colour storming into her cheeks, her hands clenching into fists by her sides.

'How dare you ask such a thing?' she spat at him furiously.

His lip curled. 'You find my question offensive?'

She sent him a heated glare. 'Everything about you is offensive, Jake. You might think handing over your father's goods for free gives you automatic licence to offend me at every opportunity, but I won't allow you to speak to me that way.'

'It's a perfectly reasonable question, Ashleigh,' he said. 'You and I did, after all, have something pretty special going on there for a couple of years way back then. I was just wondering, as any other man would, if your future husband comes up to scratch in the sack.'

She folded her arms and set her mouth. 'Unlike you, Jake Marriott, Howard treats me with a little more respect.'

'You mean he hasn't had you up against the kitchen bench with your knickers around your ankles?' he asked with a sardonic gleam in his dark eyes. 'Or what about the lounge room floor with all the curtains opened? Has he done you there? Or what about the—'

'Stop it!' She flew at him in outrage, her hands flying at his face to stop the stream of words that shamed her cruelly. 'Stop it!'

Jake caught her flailing arms with consummate ease and pulled her roughly into his embrace, his mouth crashing down on hers smothering her protests, her cries, even her soft gasp of pleasure...

His tongue slid along the surface of hers, enticing it into a sensuous, dangerous, tempting dance that sent the blood instantly roaring through her veins, the rush of it making her head swim with uncontrollable need—a need that had lain hidden and dampened down for far too long.

Ashleigh vaguely registered the sound of movement in the hall, but was too far gone with the sensations of Jake's commanding kiss to break away from his iron hold.

So what if Lachlan came in and found her kissing Jake as if there was no tomorrow? The truth was that there was no tomorrow for her and Jake, and this kiss would very probably have to last a lifetime.

But in the end it wasn't Lachlan's voice that had her springing from Jake's arms in heart-stopping shock.

It was her sister's.

CHAPTER EIGHT

'ASHLEIGH, I just thought I'd let you know—' Ellie pulled up short when she came across her sister's stricken look '—that Mum couldn't make it to pick up Lachlan so...so I decided to come and take him off your hands.' She pointed in the general direction of the front door. 'I did try and knock but there was...no answer...'

Jake let his arms fall from Ashleigh and greeted Ellie with his customary somewhat detached politeness.

'Hello, Ellie.' He brushed her cheek briefly with a kiss. 'You're looking...er...very grown up.'

Ashleigh felt like groaning at his understatement. Ellie had the sort of figure that turned heads, male and female, her most attractive feature, however, being that she seemed totally unaware of how gorgeous she looked.

'Hi, Jake!' Ellie beamed up at him engagingly. 'You're looking pretty good yourself.' She glanced about the room and added, 'Wow, this sure is some mansion.' She turned back to look at him. 'I didn't know you had a thing for antiques.'

'I don't,' Jake answered. 'Ashleigh is helping me sort through everything.'

Ashleigh wanted the floor to open up and leave her to the spiders under the house's foundations. Surely it would be better than facing the knowing wink of her cheeky younger sister, who was quite obviously speculating on the interesting little tableau she'd just burst in on.

Ashleigh knew for a fact that Jake certainly wasn't suffering any embarrassment over it. She caught the tail-end of his glinting look, his dark eyes holding an unmistakable promise to finish what he'd started as soon as they were alone, rules or no rules.

'Ashleigh will do a fine job, I'm sure, won't you, Ash?' Ellie grinned. 'She'll have all your most valuable assets in her hot little hands in no time.'

Ashleigh threw her a fulminating look but just then Lachlan's footsteps could be heard coming along the hall.

'Auntie Ellie!' Lachlan came bounding in, instantly throwing his arms around Ellie's middle and squeezing tightly.

'Hi there, champ.' Ellie hugged him back and then bent down to kiss the tip of his nose, 'How did you get out of going to crèche, you monstrous little rascal?'

'I wanted to be with Mummy,' Lachlan answered, his cheeks tinged with pink as he lowered his eyes.

Ellie straightened and, giving his hair a quick ruffle, kept her hand on his little head as she turned to face her sister. 'I saw your note so I thought I would come instead. I took the bus so it will be a bit of a trek back, but Mum met up with an old school friend. I thought it best if I left her to catch up over a long lunch. Besides…' She tucked her spare hand into her torn jeans pocket and tilted her platinum blonde head at Jake. 'I wanted to check out what Jake thought of his son now that he's finally met him.'

Ashleigh felt every drop of blood in her veins come to a screeching, screaming halt. She even wondered if she was going to faint. She actually considered feigning it to get out of the way of the shockwaves of the bomb Ellie had unthinkingly just delivered.

Six sickening heartbeats of silence thrummed in her ears as she forced herself to look at Jake standing stiffly beside her.

'*My son?*' Jake stared at Ellie in stupefaction.

Ashleigh saw the up and down movement of her sister's throat as she gradually realised the mistake she'd just made.

'I—I thought you knew…' Ellie turned to Ashleigh for help but her older sister's expression was ashen, the line of her mouth tight with tension. She swivelled back to Jake's burning gaze. 'I kind of figured that since Lachlan was here at your house…' Her words trailed off, her eyes flickering nervously between the two adults. 'I sort of thought…she must have told you by now…'

'Mummy?' Lachlan piped up, his childish innocence a blessed relief in the tense atmosphere. 'Can I show Auntie Ellie the garage for my cars I made under the tree?'

Ashleigh gave herself a mental shake. 'Sure, baby, take her outside and show her what you've been up to.'

'Come on, Auntie Ellie.' Lachlan took Ellie's hand and tugged it towards the door. 'I made a garage out of sticks and a driveway and a real race track. Do you want to see?'

'I can hardly wait,' Ellie said, meaning it, and giving her sister one last please-forgive-me glance, closed the door firmly behind them.

As silences between them went, this one had to be the worst one she'd ever experienced, Ashleigh thought as she dragged her gaze back to the minefield of Jake's.

'My son?' He almost barked the words at her.

She closed her eyes on the hatred she could see in his eyes.

'*My son?*' he asked again, his tone making her eyes spring open in alarm. 'You calculating, lying, deceitful little bitch! How could you do this to me?'

Ashleigh had no defence. She felt crushed by his anger, totally disarmed by his pain, not one word of excuse making it past the scrambled disorder of her brain.

He swung away from her, his movements agitated and jerky as if he didn't trust himself not to shake her senseless.

She watched in silent anguish as his hand scored his hair, the long fingers separating the silky strands like vicious knives.

'I can't believe you did this to me,' he said. 'I told you from day one this must never happen.' He swung back to glare at her. 'Did you do it deliberately? To force me into something I've been avoiding for all of my god-damned life?'

'I didn't do it deliberately,' she said evenly, surprised her voice came out at all.

His heavy frown took over his entire face. 'You were on the pill, for Christ's sake!'

'I know…' She bit her lip. 'I had a stomach bug when you were in New York that time…I didn't think…I thought it would be all right…'

'Why didn't you tell me, for God's sake?'

She stared at him, a slow-burning anger coming to her defence at long last. 'How could I possibly tell you? You would have promptly escorted me off to the nearest abortion clinic!'

He opened his mouth to say something but nothing came out.

'You were always so adamant about no kids, no pets and no permanent ties,' she went on when he didn't speak. 'How was I supposed to deal with something like an unexpected pregnancy? I was just twenty years old, I was living in another country away from the security I'd taken for granted for most of my life, living with a man who had no time for sentimentality or indeed any of the ethics that had been drummed into me from the day I was born. How was I supposed to cope with such a heart-wrenching situation?' She drew in a ragged breath. 'For all I knew, you would have had me off to the nearest facility to get rid of "my mistake" before I could even think of an alternative. I wanted time to think of an alternative…'

'What sort of alternative were you thinking of?' he asked after a stiff pause.

She met his eyes for a brief moment. 'I couldn't face… getting rid of it…' She turned away and examined her hands. 'I considered adoption, but having seen Ellie go through the heartache of wondering whether to seek out her blood relatives or not, I just couldn't do it. I knew I would spend the rest of my life wondering what my child was doing. Whether his new parents would love him the way I loved him…whether he was happy…' She lifted her head and gave him an agonised look and continued. 'I knew that on his birth date for the rest of my life I would wonder… I would ache… I would want to know how he was… I couldn't go through with it. I had to have him. I had no other choice.'

She stared back down at the tight knot of her hands. 'I knew you wouldn't want to know about his existence, so I decided to go it alone. I knew it wouldn't be easy but my family have been wonderful. They love Lachlan so much…I can't imagine life without him now.'

Jake turned away, not sure he could cope with Ashleigh seeing how seriously he was affected.

A son!

His son!

His father's grandson…

His stomach churned with fear. This is what he had spent his lifetime avoiding and now here it was, inescapable. Ashleigh had given birth to his child without his permission and now he had to somehow deal with it.

'I want a paternity test,' he said. 'I want it done immediately and if you don't agree I'll engage legal help to bring it about.'

Ashleigh felt another corner of her heart break.

'If that's what you need I won't stop you.'

'I want it done,' he said, hating himself for saying it. 'I want it done so at least I know where I stand.'

'I don't want anything from you,' she said. 'I've never wanted anything from you. That's why I didn't tell you. I couldn't bear the thought of you thinking of me as some sort of grasping woman who wanted their pound of flesh on top of everything else.'

'Were you ever going to tell me?'

His words dropped into the silence like a bucket of ice-cold water on flames.

She seemed to have trouble meeting his eyes. He wasn't sure what to make of it but he assumed in the end it was guilt. Her shoulders were slumped, her head bowed, her hands twisting in front of her.

'Answer me, damn you!' he growled. 'Were you ever going to tell me?'

She lifted her head, her eyes glazed with moisture.

'I thought about telling you that first night…at the bar…' Her teeth caught her bottom lip for a moment before she continued raggedly. 'But you were so arrogant about insisting on seeing me again, as if I'd had no life of my own since we broke up. It didn't seem the right atmosphere to inform you of…of Lachlan's existence.'

Jake turned away from her, his back rigid with tension as he paced the floor a couple of times.

He couldn't take it in.

He tried to replay their conversation at the hotel bar, to see if there had been any hint of her well-kept secret, but as far as he could recall she had only met him under sufferance and had given every appearance of being immensely relieved to escape as soon as she possibly could.

'Jake, please believe me,' she appealed to him, her voice cracking under the pressure. 'I wanted to tell you so many times but you seemed so out of reach. And when you finally told me about your father I knew that if I told you it would only cause more hurt.'

'Hurt?' He swung back to glare at her. 'Do you have any idea of what you've done? How much you have hurt me by this?'

She tried her best to hold his fiery look but inside she felt herself falling apart, piece by piece.

'I know it seems wrong now but I thought I was doing the right thing at the time,' she said. 'I didn't want an innocent child to suffer just because his father didn't want to be a father. I thought I'd do my best…bring him up to be a good man and one day…'

Jake slammed his hand down on the nearest surface, the crash of flesh on old wood jarring her already overstretched nerves.

'Don't you see, Ashleigh? If things were different I would have gladly embraced fatherhood.' One of his hands moved over his face in a rubbing motion before he continued, his eyes dark with immeasurable pain. 'If I didn't have the sort of gene pool I have, do you not think I wouldn't have wanted a son, a daughter, maybe even several?'

She choked back a sob without answering.

He gave a serrated sigh and continued. 'I have spent my life avoiding exactly this sort of situation. I even went as far as insisting on a vasectomy but I couldn't find a surgeon who would willingly perform it on a man in his early thirties, let alone when I was in my twenties, especially a man who supposedly hadn't yet fathered a child.'

'I'm so sorry…'

He turned to look at her. 'Does your fiancé know I'm the boy's father?'

Ashleigh raised her eyes to his, her head set at a proud angle. 'His name is Lachlan. I would prefer it if you would refer to him as such instead of as "the boy".'

'Pardon me for being a bit out of touch with his name,' he shot back bitterly. 'I have only just been informed of his existence. I don't even know his birth date.'

'Christmas Eve,' she answered without hesitation.

Ashleigh could see him do the mental arithmetic and silently prepared herself for the fallout.

'You were almost *four months pregnant* when you left me?' he gasped incredulously.

She hitched up her chin even more defiantly. 'It wasn't as if you would have noticed. You were no doubt too busy with one of your other international fill-ins. Who was it now…Sigrid?'

He lowered his gaze a fraction. 'I wasn't unfaithful to you that weekend.'

'Why should I believe you?' she asked. 'I read her e-mails, don't forget. She said how much she was looking forward to seeing you, how much she had enjoyed meeting you that first time and how she hoped your "association" with her would continue for a long time.'

Jake closed his eyes in frustration and turned away, his hands clenched by his sides as he bit out, 'She means nothing to me. Absolutely nothing.'

'That's the whole point, isn't it, Jake?' she said. 'No one ever means anything to you. You won't allow them to. You keep everybody at arm's length; every relationship is on your terms and your terms only. You don't give, you just take. I was a fool to get involved with you in the first place.'

'Then why did you get involved with me?' he asked, turning around once more.

She let out a tiny, almost inaudible, sigh. 'I…I just couldn't help myself…'

Jake straightened to his full height, his eyes clear and focused as they held hers. 'I mean it, Ashleigh, when I say I wasn't involved in any way with Sigrid Flannigan.'

'Why should I believe you?'

'You don't have to believe me, but I would like you to hear my side of it before you jump to any more conclusions.'

'I asked you four and a half years ago and you refused to tell me a thing,' she pointed out stringently.

'I know.' He examined his hands for a moment before reconnecting with her gaze, a small sigh escaping the tight line of his lips. 'Sigrid is a distant cousin of mine. She was conducting some sort of family tree research. To put it bluntly, I wasn't interested. However, she was concerned about some health issues within the family line and I finally agreed to meet her. We met in Paris. She was there on some sort of work-related assignment and, as I was close by, I decided to get the meeting over and done with.'

'And?'

'And I hated every single minute of it.' He dragged his hand through his hair once more. 'She kept going on about how important family ties were and even though we were distantly related we should keep in touch. Apparently I have the questionable honour of being the one and only offspring of Harold Percival Chase Marriott, the last of the male line on that side of the family.' He sent her an accusing look and added, 'Or so I thought.'

'Why didn't you tell me the truth about her?' she asked, choosing to ignore his jibe. 'Why let me believe the worst?'

'I wasn't ready to talk to anyone about my background,' he said. 'I was tempted to tell you a couple of times but I couldn't help thinking that if I told you the truth of my upbringing it would in some way make the differences between us even more marked. Sigrid was an annoying reminder of where I'd come from and I wanted to forget it as soon as I could.'

'So you deliberately let me think she was your lover, even though in doing so it broke my heart?'

He gave an indolent shrug of one shoulder. 'I didn't tell

you what to believe. You believed it without the slightest input from me.'

She let out a choked gasp of outrage. 'How can you say that? You deliberately misled me! You were so cagey and obstructive. You wouldn't even look me in the eye for days on end, much less speak to me!'

'I was angry, for God's sake!' he threw back. 'I was sick to my back teeth with all your tales of how wonderful your family was and how much you missed them. I was sick and tired of being the dysfunctional jerk whose only memories were of being bashed senseless until I could barely stand upright. Do you think I wanted to hear how your mother and father tucked you into your god-dammed bed every night to read you a happy-ever-after story and tell you how much they loved you?'

Ashleigh had no answer.

She felt the full force of his embittered words like barbs in her most tender unprotected flesh. She had no personal hook to hang his experience on. She had never been shouted out; no one had ever raised a hand to her. Her parents had expressed their love for her and her sisters each and every day of their lives without exception. She was totally secure in their devotion. She had absolutely no idea of how Jake would have coped without such consistent assurances of belonging, no idea how he would have coped with nothing but harsh cruelty and the sort of vindictiveness which she suspected had at times known no bounds.

'Is this a good time to interrupt?' Ellie spoke from the doorway, for once her usually confident tone a little dented.

Jake recovered himself first and turned to face her, his expression giving away nothing of his inner turmoil.

'Sure, Ellie.' He stretched his mouth into a small smile. 'Do you need a lift back into town? I'm just about to leave.'

'No,' Ellie insisted. 'I've already promised Lachlan a ride on the bus. He's looking forward to it.'

'So you haven't got your licence yet?' he asked.

Ellie gave him a sheepish grin. 'I've failed the test ten times but I haven't entirely given up hope.'

Jake couldn't help an inward smile. Same old delightful Ellie.

'Is there an instructor left in the whole of Sydney who'll take you on?'

Ellie pretended to be offended. 'I'll have you know I've been with the very best of instructors but not one of them has been able to teach me to drive with any degree of safety.'

'Tell me when you're free and I'll give you a lesson,' he offered. 'After driving in most parts of Europe I can assure you I can drive under any conditions.'

Ellie grinned enthusiastically. 'It's a date. But don't tell me I didn't warn you. Ashleigh will vouch for me. She gave up on lesson two when I ploughed into the back of a taxi.'

Jake swung his gaze to Ashleigh. 'What did she do, rattle your nerves?'

No more than you do, Ashleigh felt like responding. No, she would much rather have Ellie trying to drive in the peak hour any day than face the sort of anger she could see reflected in his dark eyes.

'I have learnt over time to recognise when I am well and truly beaten,' she said instead. 'Ellie needs a much more experienced hand than mine.'

'I don't know...' He rubbed his jaw for a moment in a gesture of wry speculation. 'Seems to me you're pretty experienced at most things.'

Ellie interrupted with a subtle clearing of her throat, Lachlan standing silently by her side, his small hand in hers.

'Excuse me, but we really need to get going if we're going to make the next bus.'

'Are you sure you don't want a lift?' Jake asked again, his glance flicking to the small quiet child at her side.

Before Ellie could answer, Lachlan piped up determinedly, 'I want to go on the bus.'

Jake met the dark eyes of his son, the sombre depths staring back at him sending a wave of something indefinable right through him.

He knew a paternity test was going to be a complete waste of time. This was his flesh and blood and there was clearly no doubt about it. Even the way the boy's hair grew upon his head mimicked his. It was a wonder he hadn't recognised it from the first moment but his shock in discovering Ashleigh had a child had momentarily distracted him. He had still been getting used to the idea of her carrying someone else's progeny when Ellie had dropped her bombshell.

'Don't hurry home.' Ellie filled the small silence. 'You two must have lots to catch up on. I can mind Lachlan tonight. I'm not going out.'

'That won't be necess—'

'That's very kind of you, Ellie.' Jake cut across Ashleigh's rebuttal. 'Your sister and I do indeed have a lot of catching up to do.'

Ellie sent Ashleigh an overly bright smile. 'Well, then... Come on, Lachlan, let's go and get that bus. We'll leave Mummy and Daddy to have a chat all by themselves.'

'Daddy?' Lachlan stopped in his tracks, his expression confused as he looked between his mother and aunt and back again.

Ashleigh sent her sister a now-see-what-you've-done look before bending down to her son.

'Lachlan...'

'Is he my daddy?' Lachlan asked in a whisper, his glance going briefly to the tall silent figure standing beside his mother.

Ashleigh swallowed the lump of anguish in her throat. 'Yes... Jake is your daddy.'

Lachlan's smooth little brow furrowed in confusion. 'But you told me he didn't want to ever know about me.'

'I know…but that was before and now…' She couldn't finish the sentence as her emotions took over. She bit her lip and straightened, turning away to try to pull herself together.

'Lachlan…' Jake stepped into the breach with an out-stretched hand. 'I am very pleased to meet you.'

Lachlan slipped his hand out and touched Jake's briefly, his eyes wide with wonder. 'Are you going to live with Mummy and me now?' he asked.

Jake wasn't sure how to answer. He had never really spoken to a child this young before. How did one go about explaining such complicated relationship dynamics to one so young?

'No,' Ashleigh put in before he could speak. 'Remember I told you? As soon as you go to big school we are going to live with Howard and Mrs Caule.'

Lachlan's shoulders visibly slumped and his bottom lip began to protrude in a pout. 'But I don't like Mrs Caule. She scares me.'

'Lachlan!' she reprimanded him sternly. 'She will be like a pretend granny for you, so don't let me ever hear you speak like that again.'

Ellie tactfully tugged Lachlan towards the door, 'Time to leave, mate.'

Ashleigh opened her mouth to call them both back but caught Jake's warning glance. She let out her breath in a whoosh of frustration and flopped into the nearest seat, dropping her head into her hands.

Jake waited until he heard the front door close on Ellie and Lachlan's exit before he spoke.

'You cannot possibly marry Howard Caule.'

She lifted her head from her hands to stare up at him. *'Excuse me?'*

He met her diamond-sharp gaze with steely determination. 'I won't allow it.'

She sprang to her feet, her hands in fists by her sides.

'What do you mean, you won't allow it?' She threw him a blistering look. 'How the hell are you going to stop me?'

The line of his mouth was intractable as his eyes held hers.

'You cannot possibly marry Howard Caule because you are going to marry me instead,' he said. 'And I will not take no for an answer.'

CHAPTER NINE

ASHLEIGH stared at him for several chugging heartbeats.

'I'm asking you to marry me, Ashleigh,' Jake said into the tight silence.

'*Asking me?*' she shot back once she found her voice. 'No, you're not. You're demanding something you have no right to demand!'

'Don't speak to me of rights,' he bit out. 'I had a right to know I'd fathered a child and you kept that information from me. This is payback time, Ashleigh. You either marry me or face the consequences.'

What consequences? she thought with a sickening feeling in the pit of her stomach. Exactly what sort of consequences was he thinking of?

Jake was a rich man.

A *very* rich man.

How could she even begin to fight someone with his sort of financial influence? The best lawyers would be engaged and before she knew it she would be facing custodial arrangements that would jeopardise her peace of mind for the rest of her life. How would she cope with seeing Jake every second weekend when he came to collect his son on visitation access? How indeed would she cope if he were to gain full custody of Lachlan?

'How long do you think such a marriage would last?' she asked, hoping her panic wasn't too visible, even though her insides were turning to liquid.

'It will last for as long as it needs to last,' he said. 'Every child needs security and, from what little I've seen so far, that little kid is insecure and in need of a strong father figure.'

He'd seen all that in one meeting? His perspicuity amazed her but she didn't let on.

'He's not yet four years old,' she said. 'I would have thought it was a little early to have him written off as an anxious neurotic.'

He gave her a hardened look. 'What did you tell him about me?'

She faced him squarely. 'I told him the truth. I told him his father had never wanted to be a father.'

Jake opened his mouth to berate her but snapped it shut when he saw the defiant glitter in her eyes. He turned away, his stomach clenching painfully as he mentally replayed every conversation he'd had with her in the past on the subject.

No wonder she hadn't told him of the pregnancy.

She was right.

He would have very likely packed her off to the nearest abortion clinic, railroading her into a procedure he had never until this moment given the depth of thought it demanded. Seeing Lachlan this afternoon had made him realise that a foetus was not just a bunch of cells. It had the potential to become a real and living person.

Lachlan was a real and living person.

And he was *his* son.

'I can't change the past, Ashleigh,' he said after another lengthy silence. 'I never wanted this sort of situation to occur but it has occurred and I realise now you probably had little choice in the matter.' He took a steadying breath and continued. 'Given the sort of background you've had, I can see how you would be the very last person to rush off to have a pregnancy terminated. And, as you said earlier, given Ellie's situation, I guess adoption wasn't an option you would have embraced with any sense of enthusiasm.'

Ashleigh witnessed the play of tortured emotions on his face as he spoke and wished she could reach for him and somehow comfort him. They shared the bond of a living and breathing child and yet it seemed as if a chasm the width of the world divided them.

He was devastated by the knowledge of his son's existence; it was his biggest nightmare come true in stark, inescapable reality. It didn't matter how sweet Lachlan was or how endearing his personality, for in Jake's mind there was no escaping the fact that, along with his genetic input, Harold Marriott's blood also flowed through his son's veins.

'I'm sorry, Jake…' she said. 'I don't know what else to say.'

'You can say yes,' he said. 'You can agree to marry me and then this situation will be resolved.'

'How can it be resolved?' she asked. 'How can we pretend things are any way near normal between us?'

'I would hazard a guess that things between us will be very normal. Once we're married we will resume our previous relationship.'

She gaped at him in shock. 'You mean a physical relationship?'

'But of course,' he answered evenly.

'Aren't you forgetting the little but no less significant detail that I already have a fiancé?'

He gave her a cynical look. 'I don't consider Howard Caule your fiancé. He hasn't even convinced you to wear his ring and I can tell by that hungry look in your eyes that he hasn't yet convinced you to share his bed.'

'There are still some men in the world who have some measure of self-control,' she put in with a pointed glare his way. 'Howard has faith. I respect that, even though I don't necessarily share it.'

'Faith?' He let out a scathing snort. 'He would need more than faith to live with you. You are the devil's own temptation from the tip of your head to your toes. I've wanted to throw you onto the nearest flat surface from the first moment I walked into the bar and saw you sitting there twirling your straw in that glass with your fingers.'

His words shocked her into silence. She could feel her skin lifting in physical awareness, tiny goose-bumps breaking out all over her and the pulse of her blood stepping up a pace as her breathing rate accelerated.

'I am engaged.' She finally found her voice but she knew it sounded even less convincing than previously. She looked down at her ringless fingers and repeated, as if to remind herself, 'I am engaged to be married to Howard.'

Jake plucked his mobile phone from his waistband and held it out to her. 'Tell him it's off. Tell him you're marrying me instead.'

Ashleigh stared at the phone as if it were a deadly weapon set to go off at the merest touch.

'I can't do that!'

'Do it, Ashleigh,' he commanded. 'Or I'll do it for you.'

'You can't make me break off my engagement!'

'You don't think so?' he asked, his lip curling sardonically. 'How about if I call dear old Howard and tell him the deal is off?'

Her throat moved up and down in a convulsive swallow.

'There are any number of antique dealers who would gladly snatch up this little load,' he continued when she didn't speak, sending his free hand in an arc to encompass the price-less goods in the room.

'You think you can persuade Howard to release me with such a bribe?' she asked.

'Why don't you call him and find out?' he suggested and pushed the phone towards her again.

She took the phone, her fingers numbly pressing in the numbers.

'Howard?'

'Ashleigh!' Howard's tone was full of delight. 'How was your day?' He hardly paused for her to respond before he went on. 'Do you remember that consignment from Leura that I'd thought we'd lost to the opposition? Well, you'll be thrilled to know that the family of the deceased have decided to give us the deal after all. Isn't that wonderful news? With the consignment you're getting from Jake Marriott we'll be the toast of the town come the antiques fair!'

'Howard…Jake has met Lachlan.'

'My mother, of course, is beside herself,' Howard rambled on excitedly. 'She and my father never imagined the heights I would aspire to, but I have you to thank for that, for without your—'

'Howard—' she interrupted him '—Jake knows about Lachlan.'

'I know it is early days but it will be in all the papers. Howard Caule Antiques will be the premier…' Howard took a small breath. 'What did you say?'

Ashleigh's eyes avoided Jake's as she said into the phone, 'Jake knows Lachlan is his son.' She took an unsteady breath and continued, 'He has asked me to marry him.'

There was a tiny beat of silence before Howard asked, 'What answer did you give him?'

'How do you think I answered?'

Howard let out a long sigh. 'Ashleigh, I know you've done your very best to hide it from me, but I've known for a long time now that you don't really love me.'

'But I—'

'It's all right, Ashleigh—' he cut through her protest '—I understand, I really do. You still have feelings for—'

'Is this about the consignment?' she asked sharply.

'How could you think that of me, Ashleigh?' The hurt in his tone was unmistakable. 'I would gladly let them go to someone else if I thought by insisting you marry me instead of Jake you would be happy. You are never going to be happy until you sort out your past with Jake and we both know it.'

Ashleigh clutched the phone in her hand with rigid fingers, annoyed that Jake was quite clearly hearing every word of her fiancé's.

'You'll have to go through with it,' Howard insisted. 'If not for Lachlan's sake, then for mine.'

'What do you mean?' she asked, her heart plummeting in alarm.

'Jake has a prior claim. He's the child's father, after all. I could never stand in his way; it wouldn't be right. It wouldn't be decent. It wouldn't be moral.'

'But what about us?' she asked in an undertone, turning her back on Jake's cynical sneer.

'Ashleigh.' Howard's voice was steady with resignation. 'You know how much I care for you, but I've known for a long time you don't really feel the same way about me. My mother has been concerned about it for ages. We could have been married months ago, but you wouldn't commit. Doesn't that tell you something?'

She found it difficult to answer him. She *had* been stalling, almost dreading the day when her life would be legally tied to his, in spite of her very real gratitude for all he'd done for her both professionally and personally.

Ashleigh chanced a glance in Jake's direction and noted the self-satisfied curl of his lip with a sinking feeling in her belly.

She turned her back determinedly and spoke to Howard once more. 'I'm sorry about this, Howard…I didn't mean to hurt you like this. You've been so good to me and Lachlan.'

'Don't worry,' Howard said. 'We will always be friends. Anyway, it's not as if we won't see each other. You do still work for me, remember?'

'Yes…'

Jake reached across and took the phone out of her hand and spoke to Howard. 'Caule, Jake Marriott here. Ashleigh won't be working for you once this consignment is delivered to your showroom. I have other plans for her.'

'Oh…I see… Well, then, I wish you all the best, both of you, and Lachlan, too, of course…' Howard's words trailed off.

'We should have this deal stitched up in the next week. It's been good doing business with you, Caule,' Jake said.

'Yes, yes, of course…marvellous to do business with you, Mr Marriott. Absolutely marvellous. Goodbye.'

'What a prick,' Jake muttered as he clipped the phone back on his belt.

Ashleigh stood stiff with rage, her eyes flashing with sparks of fury.

'You arrogant jerk!' She pushed at his chest with one hand. 'How dare you take over my life? "I have other plans for her" indeed! Who the hell do you think you are?'

Jake captured her hand and held it against the wall of his chest.

'I am your son's father and as soon as I can arrange it I will be your husband.'

'You can't cancel my job just like that!'

'I just did.'

'Exactly what plans have you in store for me?' she sniped. 'Licking your boots every day?'

He gave her mouth a sizzling glance before raising his eyes back to her flashing ones.

'No. I was thinking of you going a little higher than that.'

She was incensed by his blatant sexual invitation, her cheeks flaming as a flood of intimate memories charged through her brain.

'I don't want to marry you! I hate you!'

His hand tightened as she tried to remove herself from his hold.

'You don't hate me, Ashleigh,' he said, tugging her even closer, the hard wall of his body shocking her into silence. 'You want me. That's why you've been constructing all those silly little barriers of no touching and no looking and so on because you are so seriously tempted to fall into bed with me. You know you are. It's always been the same between us. From the very first day we met in London, the chemistry between us took over. Neither of us had any chance of holding it back.'

'Your ego is morbidly obese!' she threw at him. 'I have no desire to fall into bed with you.'

'Do you think if you say that enough times you will eventually convince yourself?' he asked. 'Don't be a fool, Ashleigh. I can feel your desire for me right here and now; it's like a pulse in your blood, the same pulse that is beating in mine.' He pressed the flat of her palm over his heart. 'Can't you feel it?'

Ashleigh's eyes widened as his drumming heartbeat kicked against her palm, her mouth going dry as his coal-black eyes glinted down at her with undisguised desire.

She could feel his strong thighs against hers, her soft stomach flattened by the flat hard plane of his, the heat and throb of his growing arousal reaching towards her tantalisingly, temptingly and irresistibly.

Her eyes flickered to his mouth and her breath tripped in her throat as his head came down. She felt the brush of his breath over her mouth just before he touched down, the gentle pressure of his mouth on hers so unlike the hectic passion-driven kisses of the past. For some reason it made it all the more difficult for her to move away. It felt so wonderful to have her lips tingle and buzz with sensation as his caressed hers in a series of barely there kisses.

She felt the intimate coiling of their mingled breaths inside her mouth as he deepened the kiss, the sexy rasp of his tongue sliding along hers, rendering her legs useless.

Her tongue retreated and then flickered tentatively against his, a hot spurt of arrant desire shooting upwards from between her thighs, making her stomach instantly hollow out. She felt the smooth silk of desire anointing her inside as his hardened erection burned into her belly with insistent pressure. Her body remembered how he filled her so completely, privately preparing itself for the intimate onslaught of his passion-driven body surging into her with relentless clawing need.

Her thoughts and memories were in the end betraying her. She had been so determined to push him away. She had wanted to clutch at whatever rag of pride she could to cover herself but it was hopeless. He was right; the chemistry they felt was far too strong to ignore. The air almost crackled with it every time they were in the same room, let alone in each other's arms as they were now.

Jake scooped her up just as she thought her legs were going to fail, and carried her through to his childhood bedroom, coming down hard on the mattress with her, his weight on her a heavy but delicious burden.

He fed off her mouth like a man who had been starved for too long, his lips greedy, ravenous and relentless. Ashleigh kissed him back with the same grasping desperate hunger, her lips swelling beneath the pressure of his, her hands already tearing at his clothes. She tugged his T-shirt out of his jeans and he shrugged himself out of it and sent it hurling across the room, drawing in a ragged gasp as she went for the waist-band of his jeans.

Her eyes drank in the sight of him, the fully engorged length of him, as she pulled away the covering of his tight-fitting underwear. His sharp groan of pleasure as her fingers ran over him lightly sent another burst of liquid need between her legs.

He pushed her hand away and lifted her top, pushing her bra off her straining breasts without even stopping to unfasten it properly. She sucked in a scalding little breath as his mouth closed around one tight aching nipple, the sensation of his teeth scraping her making her hover for a moment in that sensual sphere located somewhere between intense pleasure and exquisite pain.

He left her breasts for a moment while he shucked himself out of his jeans, his shoes thudding to the floor, coming back over her with determined hands to deal with the rest of her clothes. She heard the sound of a seam tearing but was way beyond caring. His hands were on her naked flesh, hot and heavy, rough almost, unleashing yet another trickle of sensual delight right through her.

Feeling his naked skin on hers from chest to thigh was almost too much sensation for her to deal with at once. Her brain was splintering with the electrifying pulse of his body on hers, the probing, searching thickened length of him between her legs.

Suddenly he was there, the force of his entry arching her back as she welcomed him without restraint, her body so ready for him she had trouble keeping her head. She wanted to linger over the feel of him, draw in the scent of their combined arousal to store away for private reflection, but his pace was too hard and fast and she got carried along with the tidal wave of it. She felt the tightening of her intimate muscles, the swelling of her most sensitised point rising to meet each of his determined thrusts.

As if sensing she was close he backed off, withdrawing slightly, his mouth lightening its pressure on hers.

She dragged her mouth from under his and clutched at his head with both of her hands, her eyes searching his face. 'Don't stop now,' she begged in a harsh whisper. 'You can't possibly stop now!'

His mouth twisted into a rueful grimace and he sank into her warmth again, the tightly bunched muscles of his arms either side of her as he supported his weight indicating the struggle he was undergoing to keep some measure of control. 'I shouldn't even be doing this,' he said, his voice tight with tension. 'I'm not wearing a condom.'

'It's all right,' she gasped as he sank a little deeper, her hands going to his buttocks, digging in to hold him where she most wanted him.

'Are you on the pill?' he asked, stilling for a moment.

The pill? Oh, God, when was the last time she'd taken the pill? What was today…? Friday… Surely she had taken it some time this week? She had become a little careless… It wasn't as if Howard had ever…

'Are you on the pill?' he repeated.

'Yes,' she said, mentally crossing her fingers.

'I'll pull out just in case,' he said.

'No!' She grasped at him again, her eyes wild with need. 'You don't have to do that.'

He gave her a sexy smile. 'There are other ways of dealing with it, don't you remember?'

She did remember.

That was the whole trouble.

She remembered it all; the poignant intimacy of taking him in her mouth to relieve him whenever there hadn't been enough time to linger over the preliminaries.

His eyes burned into hers as he began his slow sensuous movements again, each surge and retreat pulling at her with exquisite bone-melting tenderness.

His mouth came back to hers and she sighed with relief,

her legs gripping him tightly, not giving him another chance to pull away.

She felt each and every deep thrust of his body, even felt him nudge her womb where his son had been implanted with his seed, and a great wave of overwhelming emotion coursed through her.

She loved this man.

He was her world. Her life had started the day she'd met him and the only reason it had continued after they'd broken up was because she had carried a part of him away with her.

They were forever joined by the bond of their child and no matter how much he hated being a father and was only offering to marry her out of a sense of duty, she still loved him and knew she would do so until the day she drew her very last breath...

Jake gritted his teeth as he tried to hold back his release. He closed his eyes and counted backwards, trying to think of something unpleasant to focus on instead, but it was no good. The pressure building in him was just too strong. He felt like a trigger-happy teenager with Ashleigh, instead of a thirty-three-year-old man who was always in control.

Always.

'Oh, God!' He felt himself tip over, the emission of pleasure sending shockwaves of shivering ecstasy right through him, great deep racking shudders of it, until he collapsed in the circle of Ashleigh's arms.

He waited for five or so heartbeats of silence.

'I'm sorry.' He eased himself up on his arms to look down at her. 'That was so selfish and crass of me.'

Ashleigh reached up and touched the line of his lean jaw where a tinge of red was already pooling.

'No...don't apologise.'

'I couldn't hold back,' he said, his breathing still a little choppy. 'You have this weird effect on me. I feel about sixteen when I'm near you. All out-of-control hormones, no finesse, no foreplay, just full-on selfish lust.'

'You're not selfish…' She traced her fingertip over the line of his top lip lingeringly.

He took her finger into his mouth and sucked on it, hard.

Her eyes glazed over with unrelieved need and he released her finger, pressing her hand back to the mattress beside her head.

She knew what that look in his eyes meant and her stomach folded over as he moved down her body.

'You don't have to…*oh!*'

He lifted his head for a moment and sent her a spine-loosening look. 'I do have to, baby. I owe you.'

'I…I…' She gave up when his tongue separated her, hot bursts of pleasure sending every thought out of her brain.

She was mindless under his touch, a touch her body remembered like a secret code. Her senses leapt in acute awareness, her pleasure centre tightening to snapping point, each sensitive nerve stretched beyond endurance until it was beyond her capacity to contain it. She felt the rising waves go over her head, crashing all around her, fragmenting her consciousness until she was a mindless, limbless melting pool of nothingness…

Ashleigh wasn't sure how long the silence continued.

She lay with her eyes closed, not sure she was quite ready to meet Jake's penetrating gaze. She knew she had let herself down terribly. Falling into his arms like a desperado was hardly going to give her the ground she needed to maintain her pride.

What a mess!

She gave a painful inward grimace. The irony of it all was gut-wrenching to say the very least. Four and a half years ago all she had wanted was a marriage proposal from him, a promise of security and a future family they could nurture together in the same wonderful way her parents had done for

her sisters and her. Instead, she had left him, pregnant, terrified and alone, knowing she had no future with him while she
carried his child.

Had he ever cared for her?

He had never said the words. Those three simple words
that had been uttered every day of her life in her family: I love
you.

No. Jake had never said he loved her. He told her he
desired her, he had overwhelmed her with the physical dem-
onstration of his need for her, but he had not once said he
loved her.

She felt the shift of the mattress as he got off the narrow
bed and opened her eyes, not all that surprised to encounter
the stiff line of his back turned towards her as he reached for
his clothes.

'How long do you think it will take to get this place clear
of all of this stuff?' he asked, zipping up his jeans and turning
to face her.

Ashleigh had to fight not to cover herself. Some remnant
of pride insisted she pretend she was totally unaffected by what
had just transpired. She crossed her ankles and, releasing her
hair from behind her neck, met his dark, unreadable eyes.

'I can get the house cleared within a few days,' she said.
'I haven't finished assessing it all, but that can be finalised
in Howard's showroom.'

'Good,' he said, reaching for his discarded T-shirt. 'I want
to get started on renovating so we can move in as soon as we
are married.'

She took immediate offence at his assumption that she was
simply going to fall in with his plans. 'Aren't you assuming
a little too much?' she asked. 'I don't remember agreeing to
marry you.'

His scooped up her clothes from the floor and tossed them
towards her, his eyes sending her a warning. 'Get dressed. I

want to meet with your family tonight to discuss the wedding arrangements.'

She flung herself off the bed and threw her clothes to one side, beyond caring that she was totally naked.

'You can take a running jump, Jake Marriott,' she snapped at him furiously. 'Do you think my parents are going to go along with your plans? I think I know them a little better than you do.' She folded her arms across her heaving breasts and added bitterly, 'Besides, I can't see my father giving his permission.'

'You're twenty-four years old, Ashleigh,' he pointed out neatly, his eyes flicking briefly to the upthrust of her breasts. 'I hardly think we need to have anyone's permission to get married.'

'I can't believe you want to go through with this. You've always been so against the institution of marriage. The fact that we share a child doesn't mean we have to get married.'

'No, but I have decided that I want to marry you and marry you I will.'

She sent him a caustic glare. 'Well, for one thing, your proposal certainly needs a little polish.'

'Yeah, well, I've never done it before so I'm sorry if it's a bit rough around the edges,' he said with an element of gruffness.

She turned away to step into her clothes, her fingers totally uncooperative under his silent watchful gaze. She bit back a curse as the zip on her skirt nicked the bare skin of her hip, the sudden smarting of tears in her eyes frustrating her. Why couldn't she be more in control around him? Why did he always reduce her to such a quivering emotional wreck?

She turned around at last, determined to have the last word, but he'd already gone. She stared at the wood panel of the door for endless moments, the scent of their recent lovemaking lingering in the air until she felt as if she was breathing the essence of him into her very soul...

CHAPTER TEN

ASHLEIGH drove away from Jake's house with a scowl of resentment distorting her features, her emotions in such disarray she could barely think.

She knew it was unreasonable of her, but a part of her felt intensely annoyed that Howard hadn't fought for her. She knew it was because of the sort of person he was, principled and self-sacrificing, the very qualities she'd been drawn to in her desperate quest for security. But he had caved in to Jake's demands without a single whimper of protest. And it totally infuriated her that Jake had borne witness to it; every time she recalled that self-satisfied smirk on his face her rage went up another notch.

She was far too angry to go home to face her family. She knew Ellie would hold on her promise to mind Lachlan for the evening, so instead of taking the turn to her parents' house, she drove on until she came to Balmoral Beach, a sheltered bay where she'd spent most of her childhood playing in the rock pools and swimming in the jetty enclosure.

She kicked off her shoes and walked along the sand until she came to Wyargine Reserve at the end of the beach, standing at the edge and looking out to sea, the evening breeze ruffling her hair.

After a while the breeze kicked up a pace and her bare

arms started to feel the slight nip in the evening air. She turned and went back the way she'd come, stepping over the rocky ground with care, her shoes still swinging from her hand.

Walking back along the Esplanade, she saw a slim figure jogging towards her and stopped as she recognised her sister Mia.

'Hey there, Ashleigh,' Mia chirped without a single puff. 'I thought you'd be home preparing for the celebrations tonight.'

Ashleigh frowned. 'Celebrations…celebrations for what?'

Mia gave her a rolling-eyed look. 'Your marriage, of course! Jake is around there now. He's brought French champagne. Loads of it. Mum and Dad are thrilled to bits.' She jogged up and down on the spot and continued. 'It was *so* romantic. Jake asked for a private meeting with Dad. How sweet is that? No one but no one asks a woman's father for her hand in marriage any more. Dad was really impressed. Mum was howling like an idiot, of course, and Lachlan has his chest out a mile wide.'

Ashleigh just stared at her, unable to think of a single thing to say. Her family had fallen in with Jake's plans without even consulting her to see if it was what she wanted.

'Is something wrong, Ash?' Mia stopped bouncing from foot to foot to peer at her. 'You do want to marry him, don't you? I mean Howard was all right, but he doesn't exactly ooze with sensuality the way Jake does.' She gave a chuckle of amusement, her grey-blue eyes sparkling cheekily. 'I could never quite imagine Howard dropping his trousers and going for it up against the kitchen bench. In fact, I can't imagine him doing it at all.'

'You are so incredibly shallow sometimes,' Ashleigh bit out and began to stalk back to her car.

'Hey!' Mia grabbed her arm and swung her around to face her. 'What's going on, Ash? Jake wants to marry you. *Hello?*'

She snapped her fingers in front of her older sister's face. 'Isn't that what you've always wanted, to be married to Jake and have a family?'

'He doesn't love me, Mia,' she said bitterly. 'He's only doing it because he found out about Lachlan.'

'I heard about Ellie's little clanger,' Mia said with an expressive little grimace. 'But, all things considered, he's taken it extremely well, don't you think? I mean, a lot of men would refuse to ever speak to you again and try and wriggle their way out of maintenance payments, not to mention insisting on a paternity test.'

'He did insist on one.'

'Oh…' Mia looked a little taken aback. 'Well…I guess that's understandable. I mean, you haven't seen him for years; Lachlan could easily have been someone else's kid.'

Ashleigh sent her a quelling look.

'I mean if you were any other sort of girl…which, of course, you're not,' Mia amended hastily.

They fell into step as they continued along the Esplanade and Mia tucked her arm through her sister's affectionately. 'You know something, Ashleigh, this is like a dream come true. Lachlan now has a father—his real father. I can already see how happy it has made him. Sure he's a little shy around Jake, but he keeps looking up at him with this big wide-eyed look of wonder and it just makes my heart go all mushy.'

Ashleigh kept walking, not trusting herself to respond.

'Jake even brought him a present,' Mia continued. 'It's one of those digging trucks. He said he could help him in the garden at Lindfield.'

He had it all planned, Ashleigh thought bitterly. She wasn't being considered in any part of this; even her family had succumbed to his plan to take over her life as if she had no mind of her own.

'Why are you frowning like that?' Mia asked. 'You love him, don't you, Ashleigh? You've always loved him.'

There didn't seem any reason to deny it.

'Yes, but that's not the point,' Ashleigh said, searching for her keys.

'Then what is the point?' Mia asked as they came to a halt beside Ashleigh's car.

Ashleigh shifted her gaze out to sea once more, a small sigh escaping before she could stop it. 'I have always loved Jake. From the moment I met him I felt as if there could never be anyone else who could make me feel that way. When we parted and I came back to Australia, I sort of drifted into a relationship with Howard, more out of a need for security than anything else. I thought if I settled down with some nice decent man I would eventually forget all about Jake.'

'Jake is not exactly the forgettable type,' Mia remarked wryly.

'Tell me something I don't already know.' Ashleigh gave her a twisted smile.

'Have you slept with him yet?'

Ashleigh felt her face start to burn and turned to unlock her car.

'*Ohmigod!*' Mia crowed delightedly. 'I knew it! You have! Look at your face—you're as red as anything!'

Ashleigh threw her a withering glance. 'One day, Mia, I swear to God I'm going to strangle you.'

Mia just laughed. 'I'll see you at home,' she said with her usual grin. 'I just want to run to the point and back again. Unlike you, my heart rate hasn't gone through the roof today.'

Ashleigh got into the car without another word.

Ashleigh had barely got in the door when Lachlan rushed towards her, his little face beaming.

'Look what Daddy gave me!' He held up the shiny truck for her to see.

She gave him an overly bright smile and bent down to kiss the top of his raven-dark head. 'I hope you said a big thank you,' she said.

'He did,' Jake said, stepping out into the hall from the lounge, his eyes instantly meshing with hers.

'I…I need to have a shower…' she said, making her way past him.

'Wait.' His hand fastened on her arm, halting her.

He turned to his son, who was watching them both with large eyes. 'Lachlan, give me five minutes with Mummy and I'll be up to read that story to you I promised earlier.'

Lachlan's face threatened to split into two with his smile. 'You mean just like a real daddy does?' he asked.

'You betcha.'

'And will you tuck me in and get me to blow the light out?'

Jake turned a quizzical glance Ashleigh's way.

'It's a little thing we do,' she answered softly so Lachlan couldn't hear. 'I put my hand on the light switch and as soon as he puffs a breath out I turn it off. It makes him think he's blown it out like a candle.'

'Cute.'

Jake turned back to the hovering child. 'Better get your lungs into gear, mate. That light might prove a bit difficult unless you start practising right now.'

Lachlan scampered off, the bounce in his step stirring Ashleigh deeply.

'He's a nice little kid,' Jake said into the sudden silence.

She raised her eyes to his, catching her bottom lip for a moment with her teeth.

'You left without saying goodbye,' he said. 'I was worried about you. Where have you been?'

'I needed some time alone. I went for walk on the beach.'

'I've told your family of our plans.'

'*Our* plans?' She sent him an arctic look. 'Don't you mean

your plans, meticulously engineered so that I have no way of extricating myself?'

'You know, Ashleigh, I don't quite see what all this fuss you're making is about. You were desperate for marriage all those years ago and now I'm offering it you want to throw it back in my face. What is it with you?'

'You're not marrying me for the right reasons.'

'What do you expect me to do?' he threw back. 'I come back to Australia to tie up my father's estate and suddenly find I have a nearly four-year-old son to a woman who is hell-bent on marrying a man she doesn't even feel a gram of attraction for.'

She blew out a breath of outrage, her hands fisting by her sides as she glared at him. 'What gives you the right to make those sorts of observations? You know nothing of my feelings for Howard.'

'Are you telling me you're in love with Howard Caule?'

'What difference would it make if I told you yes or no? You're still going to force me to marry you.'

'If he was truly in love with you he wouldn't have exchanged you for a houseful of useless antiques,' he said.

'He did not exchange me for the stupid consignment! He cares about me so, unlike you, he put his personal feelings aside so I could be free. It's called self-sacrifice, in case you aren't familiar with the term.'

Jake gave another one of his snorts of cynicism. 'It's called being a prick. If he was man enough he would have been round here by now knocking my teeth out.'

'But then Howard is not a violent man with no self-control,' she said with a pointed look.

She saw the flare of anger in his dark eyes and the sudden stiffening of his body.

'I have never laid a rough hand on you and you damn well know it,' he ground out.

'Yet,' she goaded him recklessly.

His mouth tightened into a harsh line of contempt. 'I see what you're trying to do. You're trying to push me into being the sort of man my father was. But you can't do it, Ashleigh. I am not going to do it. You can goad me all you like, throw whatever names and insults my way you want, but nothing will make me sink to that level. Nothing.'

'Er…' Ellie popped her head around the door, champagne bottle in hand, juggling two glasses in the other. 'Anyone for a drink?'

Jake gave Ashleigh one last blistering look and, excusing himself, informed Ellie he was going upstairs to put his son to bed.

Ashleigh stood rooted to the spot, her legs refusing to move.

'Trouble in paradise?' Ellie came to her, holding out a glass of champagne.

Ashleigh stared at the rising bubbles in the glass she took off her sister and, taking a deep breath, tipped back her head and downed the contents.

'Way to go, Ash!' Ellie grinned. 'God, he's gorgeous when he's angry. How in the world do you resist him?'

How indeed? Ashleigh thought. That was the whole damn trouble. She couldn't resist him. Her pathetic show of last-minute spirit was all an act. She had no intention of refusing to marry him, but her pride insisted she make him think otherwise.

'I'm going to have a shower,' she said, handing her sister her empty glass.

'Will I tell Jake to join you?' Ellie asked impishly.

'You can tell him to go to hell,' she muttered as she pushed past.

'Isn't that where *you've* been all these years?' Ellie said.

Ashleigh didn't answer. She didn't need to. Her baby sister knew her far too well.

* * *

Ashleigh took her time showering, trying to prolong the moment when she would join the rest of the family downstairs, champagne glasses in hand, wide smiles of congratulations on their lips.

She decided against dressing for the occasion and slipped into a pink sundress she'd had for years, not even caring that it was too tight around her bust. She dragged a brush through her still wet hair and, ignoring her make-up kit and perfume, left her room.

She was just about to go in and kiss Lachlan goodnight when she heard the murmur of voices in his room, Lachlan's higher pitched childish insertions once or twice, and the deep burr of Jake's as he finished the story he was reading. She stopped outside the open door, despising herself for eavesdropping but unable to stop herself.

'I love stories about dogs,' Lachlan was saying. 'I've always wanted a puppy but Granny has al…al…'

'Allergies?' Jake offered helpfully.

'Yes, I think that's what it's called. She sneezes all the time and has to have a puffer thing.'

'I had a dog once…a long time ago now,' Jake said. 'Her name was Patch.'

'That's a funny name.' Lachlan chuckled.

'Yeah…I guess…'

'What was she like?'

Ashleigh heard the sound of the mattress squeaking as Jake shifted his weight on the edge of the bed.

'She was the best friend I ever had.'

'Do you still miss her?'

'Sometimes…' Jake sighed and the mattress made another noise as he stood up. 'I should let you get some sleep.'

'Daddy?'

Ashleigh felt her breath lock in her throat and, before she could stop herself, she turned her head so she could see into the room to where Jake was standing looking down at his little son lying in the narrow bed.

'Yes?' Jake asked.

Lachlan's fingers began to fidget with the hem of his racing car sheet, his eyes not quite able to meet his father's.

'Have you changed your mind about wanting to be a daddy?'

It seemed a very long time before Jake answered, Ashleigh thought, her heart thumping heavily as she counted the seconds.

'I've changed my mind about a lot of things, Lachlan,' he said at last. 'Now go to sleep and we'll talk some more tomorrow.'

Jake took a couple of strides towards the door.

'Daddy?'

He turned to look at his son, something inside him shifting almost painfully when he saw the open adoration on the little guy's face.

'I love you, Daddy,' Lachlan said.

Jake swallowed the tight constriction in his throat but, no matter how hard he tried, he just couldn't locate his voice.

'I loved you even when I didn't know who you were,' Lachlan went on. 'You can ask Mummy, 'cause I told her. I've always wanted a daddy.'

Ashleigh hadn't been aware of making a sound but suddenly Lachlan saw her at the door and sent her a big smile.

'Mummy! Can I blow the light out now?' he asked.

'Not until I give you a big kiss goodnight,' she said and, moving past the silent figure of Jake, gathered her son in her arms and squeezed him soundly before kissing the tip of his nose, both his cheeks and each and every one of his little fingertips.

She straightened and went back to the door where the light switch was but as she put her hand out to it Jake's came over the top of hers and held it there.

'On the count of three, Lachlan,' Jake said, his voice sounding even deeper than usual. 'One…two…three!'

The light was extinguished on Lachlan's big puff of breath and he giggled delightedly as he burrowed back into his bedclothes.

Ashleigh slipped her hand out from under Jake's and met his eyes. She'd thought she had seen just about every emotion in those dark depths in the past but never until this moment had she seen the glitter of unshed tears.

'Jake?'

He reached around her to close Lachlan's door softly, his eyes moving away from hers.

'Come on, your parents are waiting to congratulate us,' he said and, without waiting for her, moved down the hall.

Ashleigh watched his tall figure stride away, the set of his broad shoulders so familiar and yet so foreign. She had shared his body that afternoon and yet he did not want to share his heart.

Did he even have one?

Or was it too late?

Had his father destroyed that, along with every other joy he should have experienced as a child?

'Darling!' Gwen Forrester swept her daughter into her arms as soon as she came into the lounge. 'Congratulations! We are so very thrilled for you and Jake.'

Her father came over and hugged her tightly and Ashleigh buried her head into his shoulder, wondering if he knew how confused she really was.

'Jake.' Gwen started bustling about with her usual motherly fuss. 'Come and sit down and have a drink. Mia? Get your brother-in-law-to-be some champagne, or would you prefer a beer?'

'Champagne is fine,' Jake said.

'When are you going to get married?' Ellie asked.

'In a month's time,' Jake answered. 'It takes that long to process the licence.'

'Wow! A month isn't very long,' Mia said. 'Can I be bridesmaid?'

'Me, too!' Ellie put in.

Ashleigh stretched her mouth into a smile but inside she felt her anger simmering just beneath the surface.

'Will you have a big wedding?' Gwen asked.

'No, I don't think—' Ashleigh began but Jake cut her off.

'No point getting married if you don't do it properly.' He sent her a smile. 'After all, Ashleigh has always wanted to be a bride, haven't you, darling?'

She gave him what she hoped looked like a blissful smile although her jaw ached with the effort.

'How did Howard take the news?' Ellie asked, twirling her champagne glass in one hand.

Jake didn't give Ashleigh the chance to respond. His smile encompassed everyone as he said, 'He was a true gentleman. He wanted what was best for Ashleigh and wished us both joy.'

Ashleigh was sure her dentist was going to retire on the work she'd need done after this. She ground her teeth behind her smile and downed the contents of her glass, her head spinning slightly as she set it back down on the nearest surface.

'How soon will you be able to move into the house at Lindfield?' Heath asked.

'It will take most of the month, I'm afraid. I'm starting work on it this weekend,' Jake answered. 'In fact, I was hoping Ashleigh and Lachlan would come with me. It will be our first weekend as a family.'

Ashleigh knew she would look a fool if she said she had other plans so stayed silent.

'Are you sure Lachlan won't be in the way?' Mia gave her sister a mischievous wink.

'I'd like to spend some time with him,' Jake said. 'I won't let him come to any harm. The workmen won't arrive till Monday to do the major renovations, so it will be quite safe.' He turned to Ellie. 'I was hoping to take Ashleigh out tonight to celebrate on our own. Is your offer to babysit still on?'

'Sure!' Ellie beamed. 'Go out and have a good time. In fact, why don't you take her to stay out all night at your hotel? Lachlan won't wake up till morning and it's Saturday tomorrow so there's no rush to get him to crèche or anything.'

'But I—'

'I wouldn't want to impose…' Jake said before Ashleigh could get her protest out.

'Rubbish!' Gwen joined in heartily. 'Go on, the two of you, have some time to yourselves. After all, four and a half years is a lot of time to catch up on.'

'Thank you,' he said and turned to face Ashleigh. 'How long will it take you to get ready, darling?'

How about another four and a half years? she felt like retorting.

'Five minutes,' she said and left the room.

'You're very quiet,' Jake commented once they were on their way to the city a short time later.

She swivelled in her seat to glare at him. 'How could you do that to me?'

'Do what?' He flashed a look of pure innocence her way.

'Act as if you're the devoted fiancé who can't wait to get me all alone.'

'But I can't wait to get you all alone.'

She sucked in a shaky breath as his words hit home, her stomach doing a crazy little somersault.

'That's beside the point…' She floundered for a moment.

'You had no right to pretend everything is perfectly normal, that we've patched things up as if the past didn't happen. Quite frankly I'm surprised my family couldn't see through it.'

'I had a long talk with your father before you came home,' he said. 'I told him I'd changed my mind about marriage and that I wanted to be a real and involved father to Lachlan. I also told him that I would look after you, provide for you and protect you.'

She folded her arms crossly and tossed her head to stare out of the passenger window. 'No doubt you threw in a whole bunch of lies about loving me, too, just for good measure.'

The swish of the tyres on the bitumen was the only sound in the long stretching silence.

Ashleigh silently cursed herself for revealing her vulnerability in such a way. What was she thinking? He hadn't even been able to utter the words to his three-year-old son. What hope did she have of ever hearing them directed at her?

'I saw no reason to lie to your father,' Jake said evenly.

She frowned, trying to decipher his statement, but before she had any success he spoke again.

'Your family want what is best for you, Ashleigh. They know that you haven't been happy for a long time, and to their credit they are prepared to put any past prejudices they may have held against me to one side in order to welcome me into the family.' He sent her a teasing little glance. 'Besides, both your sisters think I'm a much better deal than dear old Howard.'

'I wish you wouldn't speak of him in that way.'

'I still can't believe you were considering marrying him.'

'Yeah? Well, at least he had the decency to ask me,' she threw at him resentfully.

Jake's hands tightened on the wheel as her hard-bitten words hit their mark. He gritted his teeth against the surge of anger he felt. What did she expect? Some promise of blissful happy ever after, when all he could promise was to…*was to what?*

He dragged in a prickly breath and tried to concentrate on the line of traffic ahead, watching as each car edged closer and closer together, as if to nudge the red light signal into changing. His foot hovered on the accelerator, biding his time to go forward, his fingers drumming the steering wheel in increasing agitation.

All he could promise was to what?

CHAPTER ELEVEN

ASHLEIGH was so determined she wasn't going to say another word to Jake for the rest of the journey, if not the rest of the evening, that it took her a quite a while to realise that he hadn't directed a single word her way for several minutes. She cast him covert glances every now and again as he negotiated the city traffic, but his eyes didn't once turn her way and the stiff line of his mouth clearly indicated that he had no desire to engage in conversation with her.

OK, so he hadn't appreciated her little dig about his forceful proposal.

Fine.

She could handle his stonewalling. It would make for a long and tense evening, but why should she always be the one to smooth things over? Besides, he was the one who'd steamrollered her into committing to a marriage she knew he would never have been insisting on if it wasn't for Lachlan's existence.

How was that supposed to make her feel? He hadn't even tried to pretend to have any feelings for her, other than displaying his usual rampant desire which he no doubt felt for any woman between the ages of nineteen and forty.

Admittedly, he'd somehow convinced her family that things were now all rosy and romantic between them, but she knew that was probably because Howard had always seemed to them to be not quite the right partner for her. Her parents, of course, had known better than to say so out loud, but Mia and Ellie hadn't abided by any such polite boundaries. The open joy on their faces as they'd toasted her engagement to Jake that evening was testament to their relief that she had finally come to her senses. But exactly what was sensible about marrying a man who not only didn't love her but loathed the whole notion of marriage and family life?

The hotel valet parking attendant greeted Jake by name as he drove into the reception bay. Ashleigh stepped out of the car when one of the uniformed bell boys opened her door for her and stood waiting for Jake, who was exchanging pleasantries with another staff member.

'I'll have the young lady's luggage brought up to your room immediately,' the young man said as he took the keys from Jake.

Ashleigh gave an audible snort. Her small tote bag could hardly be described as luggage; she'd barely put a thing in it besides her cosmetics purse and her oldest, most unflattering, nightgown. If Jake thought he was in for a hot night of passion with her in his hotel bedroom he could think again.

'Will you require a reservation for dinner in the restaurant this evening or will you be ordering room service, Mr Marriott?' The concierge asked as they approached reception for Jake to collect his mail.

'Room service will be fine,' Jake answered without even consulting Ashleigh. 'Were there any messages left for me today?'

The concierge handed him two or three envelopes. 'That's all so far. Is there anything else we can do for you, Mr Marriott?'

'Yes.' Jake's mouth tilted into a smug sort of smile. 'Have the bar send up a bottle of your very best champagne and two glasses.'

'Right away, Mr Marriott.' The concierge's eyes went to Ashleigh, standing rigidly to one side. 'May I ask, are we celebrating something special this evening?'

'Yes. Ms Ashleigh Forrester and I are celebrating our engagement and forthcoming marriage,' Jake said and, tucking the envelopes in his back pocket, added, 'Oh… and could you also contact the press and make a formal announcement on my behalf?' He took one of the gold pens off the reception counter and, reaching for a hotel notepad, quickly wrote down what he wanted to appear in the following day's paper and handed it back to the concierge.

'Consider it done, Mr Marriott. And on behalf of the hotel management and staff may I offer you our most sincere congratulations.' He turned towards Ashleigh and gave her a polite smile. 'Nice to meet you, Ms Forrester.'

Ashleigh mumbled something in reply and stumbled after Jake as he led her by the elbow towards the bank of lifts.

Once they were out of earshot of the reception area she tugged herself out of his hold and dusted off her elbow as if to remove something particularly nasty from it before sending him a furious glare. 'You've got a dammed hide!'

Jake pressed the call button without answering and, folding his arms across his chest, leaned indolently against the wall.

Ashleigh felt like stamping her foot in frustration.

'You know what the staff are all thinking, don't you?' she hissed at him. 'They think we're going to hole ourselves up in your room for a night of raunchy sex, fortifying ourselves with champagne and bloody room service!'

Jake's eyes were still and dark as they met her flashing ones. 'Is that a problem for you?'

She let out a whooshing breath. 'Of course it's a problem for me! This time yesterday I was engaged to Howard Caule. What will everyone think when they see tomorrow's paper and hear that you are now my fiancé?'

The lift doors opened and Jake stood back to allow her to enter first. The door hissed shut behind them before he responded smoothly. 'They will think the best man won.'

She let out another infuriated breath. 'This is all a game to you, isn't it, Jake? All this talk about winning and losing, as if I'm some sort of prize that everyone's been bidding for.'

She caught her lip with her teeth and looked away from the glint of satire in his dark eyes. 'I don't want to even be here with you, much less sleep with you,' she said, privately hoping she had the strength of will to follow through on her rash words.

'You know you don't mean that, Ashleigh, so don't go making me get all fired up just so I have to prove it to you.'

She felt a flicker of betraying need between her thighs at his statement, the smouldering fire in his challenging gaze threatening to consume her on the spot.

The lift doors opened and she almost fell out in relief, her lungs dragging in air as if she'd been holding her breath for hours instead of a mere few seconds.

She suddenly felt faint, light-headed and disoriented, the carpeted floor rolling up towards her, the swirling colours getting all mixed up in a stomach-churning pattern that seemed to make the floor unstable beneath her feet…

'Are you all right?'

She heard Jake's voice as if he was speaking to her through a long tunnel, the words rising and falling like an echo, here one second, gone the next.

'I…I think I'm going to… She wobbled, one of her hands clutching at mid-air until she found something strong and immovable to keep her upright.

Jake held her tightly against him as he swiped his key card

to his room and, shouldering open the door, scooped her up and carried her inside, the door clicking shut behind him.

'I...I...I'm going to be sick...' Ashleigh gasped as she put a shaky hand up to her mouth.

'The bathroom is just through—'

Too late.

Ashleigh threw up the contents of her stomach all over his chest.

Jake managed to salvage the cream carpet by tugging his shirt out of his trousers to act as a sort of bib-cum-scoop as he led her to the bathroom. He set her down on the edge of the bath, one hand still holding the contents of his T-shirt as he frowned in concern at the pallor of her face.

'Oh, God...'

She swayed for a moment and then lunged for the toilet bowl. He winced as she threw up again, each harsh tortured expulsion of her throat reminding him of the weeks after she'd left him in London when a daily bottle of Jack Daniels had been his only comfort.

He gingerly removed himself from his T-shirt, leaving it in the bottom of the shower stall, and reaching for one of the hand towels, wet it under the cold tap before applying it to her shockingly pale face.

'Hasn't anyone ever told you never to drink champagne on an empty stomach?' he said, gently mopping her brow.

She gave him a withering glance and looked as if she was about to throw a stinging comment his way when her face suddenly drained of all colour once more and she lurched towards the toilet bowl again.

Jake waited until she was done before handing her the re-rinsed towel again.

Ashleigh buried her face in its cool, refreshing, cleansing folds, wondering if this was some sort of omen for the rest of their future together.

'When was the last time you ate?' Jake asked.

Ashleigh groaned into the towel. '*Please* don't talk about food!'

'How many glasses of champagne did you have at your parents' house?'

'I don't know…two…maybe three…'

'Too many, if you ask me.'

'I didn't ask you.'

'That reminds me,' Jake said, helping her to her feet, his hands on her upper arms gentle but firm. 'It has occurred to me that I haven't actually asked you to marry me.'

Ashleigh stared at him, her stomach still deciding on its next course of action, her throat raw and her eyes and nose streaming.

'You were right to be angry with me,' he continued. 'I didn't ask you, I just told you that we were going to get married. I didn't even give you a choice.'

She opened her mouth and just as rapidly closed it, not sure if words or something a little less socially appropriate was still intent on coming out.

'Ashleigh…' He cleared his throat, his eyes dark and steady on hers. 'Will you marry me?'

Jake stepped backwards as she lunged for the toilet bowl again and flinched as she gave another almighty heave.

She was right after all, he thought wryly as he rinsed out the hand towel yet again.

Maybe he *did* need a little polish on his proposal.

Ashleigh crawled into the shower a few minutes later, way beyond the point of caring that Jake was standing watching her shivering naked under the warm spray. She closed her eyes and let the water run over her, trying to concentrate on staying upright instead of sinking to the floor and disappearing down the drain, which her body seemed to think was a viable option.

'You don't look so good,' Jake said.

She opened one bloodshot eye. 'Thanks…just what a naked woman wants to hear.'

He smiled and reached for a big fluffy white bath sheet, holding it to one side as his other arm brushed past her breast to turn off the shower rose.

Ashleigh stepped into the soft towel he held out and didn't even try and take over the drying of her body herself. Instead she stood like a helpless child as he gently dried her, the softness of the towel and his soothing, caress-like touch making her throat threaten to close over with emotion.

'Do you want me to dry your hair for you?' he asked once he'd wrapped her sarong-wise in a fresh dry towel. 'There's a hairdryer on the wall next to the shaving outlet. I've never done a blow job before but who knows? Like someone else I know, I might prove to have a natural flair.'

She rolled her eyes at him and then wished she hadn't. 'I think I might just lie down for a while…my head hurts.'

He pulled back the bed covers and she climbed in, closing her eyes as soon as her head found the feather-light pillow.

Jake stood watching her for endless moments, wondering if he should have called a doctor or something. But then he remembered what a hopeless head for alcohol she'd had in the past. One drink and she was practically under the table.

His conscience gave him a sharp little prod of recollection which he wanted to push away but couldn't. She had held him off for two dates but on the third he had been so determined to have her that he hadn't thought much beyond getting her clothes off any way he could…

He gave a rough-edged sigh and, before he could stop himself, gently brushed the back of his hand across the velvet softness of her cheek, the feel of her skin under his work-roughened knuckles reminding him of the smooth cream of silk. She mumbled something he couldn't quite catch and, curling up into an even smaller ball, nestled her cheek further into the pillow.

He reached for the bedside chair and sat in it heavily, his head dropping to his hands, his fingers splaying over his forehead.

It was going to be a long night.

Ashleigh woke sometime during the night, her head feeling surprisingly clear but her stomach instantly clamouring for food.

'Did you say something?' Jake's voice came out of the darkness from the other side of the huge bed.

'No…that was my stomach,' she said, her insides giving another noisy rumble.

She felt the slight tilt of the mattress as he reached for the bedside lamp, her pupils shrinking a little when the soft light washed over her.

'What did it say?' he asked, his mouth curving into a small smile.

Don't look below his neck, she warned herself.

'It said it wants some food,' she said, fiddling with the edge of the sheet that only just covered her breasts.

'What sort of food?' Jake got up from the bed and stretched. 'Soup and toast or what about something greasy for a hangover cure?'

'I don't have a hangover,' she said a little tightly.

She sensed rather than saw his smile as he reached for the phone.

'Jake Marriott here, suite fourteen hundred,' he said. 'Can we have some bacon and eggs with a double side of fries?'

Ashleigh threw him a filthy look and he added, 'No, no champagne with that order. We haven't started on the other bottle yet.' He hung up the phone and gave another big stretch, his biceps bulging as he raised his arms above his head, his stomach muscles rippling like rods of steel under a tightly stretched satin sheet.

'Do you have to do that?' she said irritably.

'Do what?' He rolled his shoulders and dropped his arms, his look totally guileless.

She pursed her mouth and edged the sheet a little higher. 'You could at least put something on.'

'You've seen me naked before,' he pointed out. 'Besides, I fell asleep in the chair a little earlier and it made me a little stiff.'

Her eyes went to his pelvis, her cheeks instantly filling with heat. She wrenched her gaze away and fiddled with the sheet to distract herself from his tempting form.

'You know something? You never used to be such a little prude,' he commented. 'I hope Howard hasn't given you a whole lot of hang-ups about sex.'

'I don't have any hang-ups…' She chewed her bottom lip for a moment. 'It's just that…' She paused, not sure it was exactly wise to go on.

'Just what?' he asked.

She raised her eyes to his. 'It's just it's always been such a very physical thing…for you, I mean.'

'And it's not for you?' he asked, holding her gaze.

'Yes, yes, of course it is…but…' She lowered her eyes and began to tug at a loose thread on the sheet, wishing she hadn't drifted into such deep water.

'I don't like the sound of that "but",' he said after a short silence. 'What are you trying to say? That you're still in love with me after all this time?'

She stared at him for five heavy blood-clogging heart-beats.

'Ashleigh?'

There was a discreet tap at the door and their eyes locked for a moment.

'Room service,' a young male voice called out.

Jake reached for his jeans where he'd left them hanging over a chair, stepping into them, zipping them up and running a rough hand through his hair before he moved across to open the door.

Ashleigh hitched the sheet right up to her chin and watched as Jake tipped the young man who carried in the tray of food, waiting until he'd gone again before turning back to her.

'Come on, let's get some food into you, then we can continue that little discussion we were having on sex,' he said.

She propped herself up in the bed with pillows as he carried the tray over. He set it across her lap, giving her a little wink as he snitched a French fry and popped it in his mouth.

She gave him a guilt-stricken look as she suddenly recalled how the evening in his room had started. 'You must have missed dinner...I'm sorry.'

He gave her another one of his wry smiles. 'To be quite frank with you, sweetheart, I didn't feel all that much like food after your little bathroom routine.'

She grimaced and speared a chip with her fork. 'Don't remind me.' She gave a little shudder. '*Yeeuck.* I am never going to drink champagne again. *Ever.*'

He laughed and took another fry. 'You never could handle alcohol. One drink and you are anybody's.'

Her fork froze halfway to her mouth, her eyes slowly meeting his.

His smile faded. 'You know, I didn't actually mean that quite the way it sounded.'

'Yes, you did.' She pushed the food away in disgust.

'No!' He rescued the tilting tray and set it to one side before coming back to untie her hands from where she'd crossed them tightly over her breasts.

'Hey.' He gave her fists a little squeeze. 'I didn't mean to insult you. The truth is, I have never forgotten what it was like that first time…' His throat moved up and down in a swallow. 'I've tried to, believe me, but it just won't go away.'

She tossed her head to one side. 'You've probably had hundreds of lovers since then who have imprinted themselves indelibly on your sexual seismic register.'

'Maybe—' he gave a shrug of one shoulder '—but, as far as I recall, no four point fours.'

Her eyes came back to his, her look indignant. *'Four point four? Is that all I rated?'*

He tapped her on the end of her nose, the edges of his mouth tipping upwards sexily. 'Thought that would get a rise out of you.'

She reached past him for the tray of food and scooped up a rasher of bacon without the help of cutlery and stuffed it in her mouth, her blue eyes flashing sparks of fire as she chewed resolutely.

'You know something, Ashleigh,' he said, spearing a French fry with her abandoned fork. 'You're really something when you're all fired up.'

'Stop pinching my fries.' She slapped his hand away. 'I want them all to myself.'

He laid the fork down and, moving the tray just out of her reach, kissed her hard upon the mouth.

Ashleigh blinked up at him when he lifted his mouth off hers.

'What was that for?' she asked.

He picked up a French fry and held it near her tightly clamped lips. 'Open.'

She opened.

'That's good.' He smiled as she chewed and swallowed. 'Now we're getting somewhere.'

Ashleigh wasn't sure she wanted to know exactly what he meant. Besides, her stomach was still screaming out for food and he seemed perfectly happy to pass it to her, morsel by morsel. All she had to do was chew and swallow and avoid his probing gaze.

She opened her mouth on a forkful of easy-over egg and wickedly fattening bacon and closed her eyes.

Heaven.

CHAPTER TWELVE

ASHLEIGH woke the next morning to find Jake sitting fully dressed in one of the chairs near the bed, his dark gaze trained on her, his expression thoughtful.

'Hi,' he said, a small smile lifting the edges of his mouth.

'Hi.' She eased herself upright, securing the sheet around her naked breasts, wondering what was going on behind those unreadable eyes.

'I've been doing some thinking while you were sleeping,' he said after a little silence.

She gave him a wary look without responding.

He ran a hand through his hair and continued. 'I realised during the night that from the very first day I met you in London I fast-tracked you into a physical relationship. I did it to you again recently.' He held her gaze for a moment or two. 'I want to prove to you that I'm serious about making our marriage work by being patient, a quality you're not used to seeing in me.' He drew in a breath and added, 'In the next four weeks leading up to our wedding I promise not to kiss you, touch you or even look at you in a sexual way when we are alone.' He paused as if waiting for her reaction to his announcement but when she remained silent he shifted his gaze and, getting to his feet, walked over to the window and looked down at the street below, his back turned towards her. 'I want to get to know my son and start to build the sort of family structure I missed out on as a child.'

'I see…'

He turned back to face her, his expression giving nothing away. 'Four weeks isn't all that long when you consider we'll have the rest of our lives together, don't you agree?'

Ashleigh wasn't sure how to answer. She had spent four and a half miserable years missing him and now that he was back, four minutes without him touching her hurt like hell. How would she ever get through it?

'If that's what you want…' Her eyes fell away from the intensity of his.

He eased himself away from the window sill where he'd been leaning and reached for the room service menu. 'Let's have breakfast and get going. I want to spend the day with Lachlan. He's probably wondering where we both are.'

Ashleigh sat on the back step at Jake's house and watched as Lachlan helped his father complete the tree-house they'd been building in the elm tree.

Almost four weeks had passed and Jake had stuck to his promise; not once had he touched her while they were alone.

She gave a twisted little smile.

With all the rush of wedding preparations they'd had precious little time by themselves and she couldn't help wondering if he'd planned it that way to make it easier on himself. As for herself, she had ached for him relentlessly, her body tingling with awareness whenever his dark as night eyes rested on her.

Now, with a day to go before they were officially married, she could barely contain her nervous anticipation. Her legs felt weak and shaky whenever he smiled at her, the slightest brush of his hand against hers stirring her into a frenzy of clawing need.

'What do you think, Ashleigh?' Jake asked as he strode

towards her with Lachlan's small hand tucked in his. 'Do you think it'll do?'

She smiled at the pure joy on Lachlan's grubby face as he gazed up at his father. Her son had blossomed in a matter of days as he'd soaked up the presence of Jake. He had clung to him during every waking hour as if frightened he might suddenly disappear. It had made Ashleigh's heart swell to witness the sheer devotion on his little face and she knew that no matter what happened in her relationship with Jake in the future, Lachlan would always want to be in contact with his father and she would do nothing to come between them.

'It looks wonderful,' she said.

Jake helped her to her feet, his work-roughened palm sending a riot of sensations through her fingers to the centre of her being as his eyes meshed with hers.

'This time tomorrow,' he said on the tail-end of an expelled breath.

She didn't trust herself to answer without betraying herself.

Jake's eyes left hers to look at the house, his small sigh of approval speaking volumes. 'It looks like a real home now, doesn't it?'

Ashleigh followed the line of his gaze. The house had been painted inside and out, the threadbare blinds replaced with the soft drape of curtains and the floors polished, with new rugs laid out here and there for comfort and cosiness. The furniture was all modern and comfortable, all except for one small writing desk that Jake wanted to keep because it had been his mother's. The rest of the antiques had gone along with the outdated appliances in the kitchen; it was now newly appointed and the bathrooms beautifully refurbished as well.

The front and back gardens had been tidied, Jake doing a lot of the physical labour himself with Lachlan faithfully by his side.

'Yes,' she agreed. 'It looks like a real home.'

'Can I play with my cars now, Daddy?' Lachlan asked, tugging on Jake's hand.

'Sure,' Jake said, ruffling his hair. 'Thanks for helping me. I couldn't have done that last bit without you.'

Lachlan's proud grin threatened to split his face in two. 'I love you, Daddy.' He hugged the long legs in front of him. 'I love you *this* much!' He squeezed as hard as he could, the sound of his childish little grunt of exertion making tears spring to Ashleigh's eyes.

She blinked them back as she watched Jake bend down to his son's level, his voice gruff with emotion. 'I love you, too, mate. More than I can say.' His eyes shifted slightly to meet Ashleigh's over the top of their son's dark head. 'Sometimes words are just not enough.'

Lachlan scampered off but Ashleigh hardly noticed. She'd never heard Jake say those three little words to anyone before, not to her certainly, and not even to Lachlan until now, even though Lachlan had said it to him many times over the last four weeks.

She ran her tongue over her dry lips as Jake straightened to his full height, his body so close to hers that she could feel the heat of it against her too sensitive skin.

He gave her a small rueful smile. 'I promised myself a long time ago that I'd never say those words again.'

'Why?' Her voice came out soft as a whisper.

There was a small but intense silence as his eyes held hers.

'Remember I told you about my dog?'

She nodded.

'I really loved that dog,' he said after another little pause. 'But as soon as I said those words to her my father heard me and got rid of her.'

'Oh, Jake…' She bit her lip to stop it from trembling.

He took something out of his pocket and silently handed it to her.

She looked down at the decayed strip of red-coloured leather lying across her hand, the small silver buckle jangling against something metal attached to it. She turned the tiny name tag over to see the name Patch engraved there.

'He didn't send her to the country after all,' Jake said. 'He killed her and buried her in the garden. I found her body, or at least what was left of it, and her collar a few days ago.'

Ashleigh lifted her gaze to his, tears rolling down her cheeks as she saw the raw emotion etched on his face.

'Jake...'

'Shh.' He pressed a finger against her lips to stop her speaking. 'Let me get this out while I still can.' He took a deep breath and let the words tumble out at last. 'I love you. I guess I've wanted to tell you that from the first moment I met you but I was too cowardly to do so. Instead, I hurt you immeasurably, wrecking my own life in the process, robbing myself of the precious early years of my son's life. Can you ever forgive me for the pain I've caused you?'

She was openly blubbering by now but there was absolutely nothing she could do to stop it. 'There's nothing to forgive...I love you...I've loved you for so long...I...I...'

Jake crushed her to him, his face buried in the fragrant cloud of her hair. 'I don't deserve you...I don't deserve Lachlan either. You're both so incredibly beautiful...I feel like I'm going to somehow spoil your life now that I am in it again.'

'*No!*' Ashleigh grasped at him with both hands, holding his head so his eyes were locked on hers. 'Don't *ever* think that. I have spent four and a half of the unhappiest years of my life without you. I don't think I would survive another day if you were to leave me now. You are the most wonderful person. I know that. I know it in my heart. You are nothing like your father. Look at the way Lachlan loves you; how can you doubt yourself? I certainly don't. I *know* who you are, Jake. You might bear your father's name but you don't have anything else of him inside you. I just know it.'

His dark eyes were bright with moisture as he looked down at her. 'I didn't realise loving someone could be so painful,' he said. 'When I saw you at the bar that night I could barely breathe. I was so determined that I could handle seeing you again but one glimpse of you turned me inside out with longing.'

'Oh, Jake…' She looked up at him with shining eyes. 'What a silly pair of fools we were. I was feeling exactly the same way! I had to stop myself reaching out to touch you to make sure you were really back in my life after all that time. I loved you so much and was so scared you'd see it and make fun of me.'

His eyes grew very dark and his voice husky and deep with emotion. 'Promise me you'll keep telling me you love me, Ashleigh. I'm not sure if my mother ever told me because I was so young when she died, but you're the first person I can remember ever saying those three little words. You have no idea how wonderful they make me feel.'

'I promise.'

He brushed the crystal tears spilling from her eyes with a gentle finger. 'I love you.'

'I know…I can hardly believe it's true…'

'You'd better believe it because I'm going to say it about ten times a day to make up for all the times I should have said it in the past.'

'Only ten times a day?' She gave him a little teasing smile. 'What else are you going to do with your time?'

His eyes glittered as they held hers. 'You know all those kitchen benches that were recently fitted inside?'

She gave a little nod as her stomach flipped over itself in anticipation. 'I did wonder why you wanted such a lot of bench space. Have you suddenly developed an intense passion for cooking?'

He gave her a bone-melting look and brought her even closer. 'I'm not much of a cook but I'm sure between the two of us we'll think of something to do with all that space. Don't you agree?'

Ashleigh just smiled.

EPILOGUE

Eight months later...

ASHLEIGH was in one of her nesting moods again. Ever since she'd found out she was pregnant she'd been fussing about the house, rearranging things to suit her ever changing whims; now with only a month to go she was virtually unstoppable.

Jake smiled fondly as she instructed him to shift yet another piece of furniture, her swollen belly brushing against him as she moved past him.

He still found it hard to believe he was married with a son and a little daughter on the way. His life had changed in so many ways but each one was for the better. His bitterness about the past had gradually faded to a far off place which he rarely visited now. Ashleigh's love had healed him just as surely as his son's devotion, which still brought a clogging lump to his throat every time he looked into those dark eyes that so resembled his own.

'No...I think it looks better back over there,' Ashleigh said, turning around to look at him. 'What do you think, darling?'

His eyes ran over her, lingering for a moment of the full curve of her breasts before meshing with her blue gaze. 'If I told you what I was thinking right now you'd probably blush to the very roots of your hair.'

She smiled one of her cat-that-swallowed-the-canary smiles. 'What exactly are you thinking?'

He gently backed her up against the writing desk, his hand going to her belly, his open palm feeling for the movement of his child. 'That you are the sexiest mother I've ever seen and if it wasn't for Ellie and Mia bringing Lachlan back any minute now I would have my wicked way with you.'

Ashleigh felt her legs weaken and grasped at the writing desk behind her to steady herself. The fragile timber gave a sudden creak and part of the front panelling of the top drawer came away in her hand.

'Oh, no!'

'Did you hurt yourself?' Jake's tone was full of concern as he steadied her.

She shook her head, turning to look at the damage she'd done to his mother's desk.

'No, but—' She stopped as she stared at the small compartment that had been hidden behind the panelling she'd inadvertently removed. In the tiny thin space was an envelope.

She took it out, turning it over in her hands, her eyes briefly scanning the feminine writing and the name written there before she handed it to Jake.

'I think it's a letter of your mother's,' she said. 'It's addressed to someone in New Zealand. She mustn't have been able to post it before she died…'

Jake opened the envelope and read through the pages one by one, his dark eyes absorbing each and every word, the only sound in the room the soft rustle of paper that hadn't seen the light of day in close to thirty years.

'What does it say?' Ashleigh asked softly as she saw the sheen of tears begin to film over his eyes.

Jake drew in a deep breath and looked at her. 'You were right, Ashleigh. You knew it all along.'

'Kn-knew what?' Her voice wobbled along with Jake's chin as she watched him do his best to control his emotion. 'W-what did I know?'

'This is a letter to my father,' he said, wiping a hand across his eyes. 'My *real* father.'

'You mean…?'

'Harold Marriott was infertile.' He looked down at the words he'd just read as if to make sure they hadn't suddenly disappeared. 'He had testicular cancer as a young man and after the treatment was unable to father a child.'

'So you're not…' She couldn't get the words past the sudden lump in her throat.

'My mother was five months pregnant when she married him,' he said. 'She hadn't told my real father of my existence because he was already married, but when she knew she was dying she decided to write to him…but, probably due to her sudden decline in health, the letter was never sent.'

'Oh, Jake…'

Jake pulled her to him and hugged her tightly, his head buried into her neck. 'You were right, Ashleigh. You were right all along. I am *not* my father's son.'

Ashleigh looked up at him, her eyes brimming over. 'I would still love you even if you were his son. I'm happy for you that you're not but it makes absolutely no difference to me. I love you and I always will, no matter what.'

No matter what. Jake breathed the words deep into his soul, where Ashleigh's love had already worked a miracle of its own.

The World of Mills & Boon®

There's a Mills & Boon® series that's perfect for you. We publish ten series and, with new titles every month, you never have to wait long for your favourite to come along.

Blaze®

Scorching hot, sexy reads
4 new stories every month

By Request

Relive the romance with the best of the best
9 new stories every month

Cherish™

Romance to melt the heart every time
12 new stories every month

Desire™

Passionate and dramatic love stories
8 new stories every month